MUM'S
THE WORD

Other books by Dorothy Cannell

THE THIN WOMAN
DOWN THE GARDEN PATH
THE WIDOWS CLUB

Dorothy Cannell

MUM'S THE WORD

BANTAM BOOKS

NEW YORK · TORONTO · LONDON · SYDNEY · AUCKLAND

MUM'S THE WORD

A Bantam Book / March 1990

Library of Congress Cataloging-in-Publication Data
Cannell, Dorothy.
   Mum's the word / Dorothy Cannell.
      p.   cm.
   ISBN 0-553-05760-X
   I. Title.
PS3553.A499M8   1990
813'.54—dc20   89-29983
                                                  CIP

Published simultaneously in the United States and Canada

Bantam Books are published by Bantam Books, a division of Bantam Doubleday
Dell Publishing Group, Inc. Its trademark, consisting of the words "Bantam
Books" and the portrayal of a rooster, is Registered in U.S. Patent and Trade-
mark Office and in other countries. Marca Registrada. Bantam Books, 666 Fifth
Avenue, New York, New York 10103.

PRINTED IN THE UNITED STATES OF AMERICA

BG   10 9 8 7 6 5 4 3 2 1

To my sister Margaret,
for all the times she said,
"Put on the kettle and read me another chapter."

MUM'S THE WORD

1

I dream I am a child again, coming to Merlin's Court for the first time. No . . . that isn't quite the way it is. My grown-up self watches, off-stage, as ten-year-old Ellie is driven in that magical vehicle of childhood—a taxi—through the village of Chitterton Fells. The shops and houses, now steeped in twilight, are of classic Christmas card design. Look, there's the amputated Roman arch, and yes . . . the wavering moonbeam of coast road.

Child Ellie is wearing her blue-and-gold striped school blazer. The badge of her Panama hat heralds the motto of St. Roberta's: *Life Is Strife*. Her plaits are tied with bows the size of giant moths and her face is an all-over smile.

Does that make her sound an appealing little moppet? Sorry, the truth is that she is fat. Poor dear, she was born fat. And really there was no excuse. Her parents lived thin and productive lives. Aunts, uncles, and cousins were respectable in size. And the family tree revealed only one obese antecedent—Augustus Wentworth Grantham, 1784–1863, who was forced into exile after unlacing his stays at a regimental dinner. Not another blot on the record until I, Giselle Simons, weighed in. Giselle! I know my parents chose the name as a sort of magic talisman against the inevitable. My first word was chocolate.

Peering through the shadows of my dream, I remember all those years of shelling out blackmail money to my low-cal cousin Vanessa. Anything to retrieve damning photos of Child Ellie in varying poses of indecent exposure. Short sleeves, short socks . . . shorts. Destroying the evidence had become vital after I went on a diet at age twenty-seven and won. Days, weeks of complacency had followed wherein I was sure I had bumped off the Before version. But every once in a while Child Ellie would creep up behind me, tap me on the shoulder, and cry, "I'm still here!"

The taxi zigs around a bend in the road and Child Ellie winds down the window to sniff the scenery. Don't lean out too far, Child Ellie. The cliff sheers down like a bird shot from the sky. The taxi nears the top of the hill. Here stands St. Anselm's Church, walls the colour of pumice stone. The moon is its halo. A weary congregation of tombstones and trees that writhe as though wringing their hands at the wickedness of the world.

Child Ellie smiles. Anyone would think she had never smelled the sea before, never heard it break in white-foamed rushes against the cliffs, never savoured its Alka Seltzer taste, nor seen a gull cresting the wind. What blithe optimism! What wanton vulnerability! She lunges through the window, arms flung wide to embrace the moment. But all is well. She doesn't fall. The window is a tight fit.

The taxi glides through sagging iron gates onto a gravel drive riddled with weeds. Look . . . there is the old chestnut spreading its moon-dappled cloak upon the lawn . . . and there the lodge, a cobbled house with a brass plate on the door: Cliffside Cottage. The taxi slows, then moves on. Then suddenly the maternal ancestral home is in sight: Merlin's Court. Her breath catches. It's exactly as Mother had described it. Still, nothing could have prepared her for this Grimm's fairy tale castle complete with moat, ivied walls, turrets like witches' hats, and best of all, a portcullis.

A place of pure magic. Ah, but I know what Child Ellie

does not. A wicked wizard, Great Uncle Merlin, reigns within the castle walls. Picture him now, chomping on his toothless gums. Nightcap a-bobbing, he rubs fleshless hands together at the merry prospect of a child being left in his keeping. How touchingly naive of her parents to decide a holiday at the seaside will do her a world of good, while they sail off to America to prospect for fame and fortune.

The taxi rounds a final curve. While I am wondering how soon before I wake up, Child Ellie disembarks. Witness a flash of stout legs. Socks rolled into doughnuts at the ankles. I want to pull them up for her, straighten her bows, warn her. But she is headed for the moat bridge. Will it collapse under her thudding hopscotch? The immortal words of Aunt Astrid knell in my ears. "All cannot be blessed with beauty, grace, and charm, Ellie." Certainly not. After giving so generously of those blessings to Aunty's darling daughter Vanessa, God ran short. "But one can always strive to excel at something other than mediocrity, Ellie."

"Thank you, Aunty." Child Ellie might always be picked last for school games, but she would walk a tightrope across the Alps for a jelly bean.

Watch out! She almost goes over into the moat. A curtain twitches hopefully at one of the countless windows, then falls. Oh, no . . . Child Ellie has left her suitcase in the taxi, now vanishing into the blackness of time. But does her smile dim? Never! She discovers that the gargoyle beside the heavily studded castle door is a doorbell. A yank of the tongue, the mottled yellow-green eyes roll around in its head, and a deep ringing is heard.

Silence.

Child Ellie's chubby fists pound the door. "Uncle Merlin! It's me, Ellie! Mummy and Daddy said you and I would be good for each other. They don't believe you are bonkers. I am to be a little breath of fresh air, blowing away the cobwebs. Your life will gain new meaning when you help me grow gaunt and beautiful by not letting me have seconds . . . pardon me, thirds."

Silence.

"Standing here on the step like this, I can't help wondering if Mummy and Daddy decided I was old enough to travel on my own because they were scared."

Wind laughing among the trees.

"Surely, Uncle Merlin, you're not having a last minute charge round with the Hoover, are you? I've sworn on birthday and Christmas presents not to comment on the squalid state of the house. Believe me, I don't mind in the least if you do your washing up once a year rather than once a day."

Has she caught the attention of the silence?

"Uncle Merlin, you may be interested to know that I intend to be a house decorator when I grow up. Dried flowers need not look dead these days; and I know—from reading *The Wickedest Girl in the Class*—how to remove stubborn stains. Even blood."

Thicker silence.

Did the time draw near for me to wake up? But my eyes won't open.

"Uncle Merlin, perhaps I have come at an inconvenient time. Should I . . . ?"

With the appalling suddenness of an animal striking, the castle door flings inward. Legs moving pell-mell, Child Ellie is swept by an invisible force into the cavernous hall with its flagstone floor and peekaboo staircase. Cobwebs sway in tattered banners from the lofty ceiling. Moth-eaten fox heads grin from walls marbled with damp. Dead flowers, bunched into funeral urns, give off the odour of decay. In this house only the dirt is alive.

"Be nice, Uncle Merlin. Stop playing hard to find. I promise not to start screaming if you have come down with some hideous deformity since Mummy and Daddy last saw you. Cross my heart, I think werewolves are sweet. But if it makes you more comfortable, feel free to slip a bag over your head. Oh, crikey! Why there you are, naughty uncle!"

Child Ellie's brain is not overweight. She is addressing a rusty suit of armour, stationed against the banister wall. Not Uncle Merlin. Lifting the visor, she inquires within. No one home. But never say die. Our metal knight has an identical twin standing to attention a few yards away. Bother! He isn't hiding any fugitives either.

"Uncle Merlin, I'm warning you—I'm going off you in a hurry." She digs into her blazer pocket for the friend that never fails—a bar of chocolate. Restored, she blunders about some more. She pokes her nose through the banisters, she checks a mound of formless debris, she opens doors that go nowhere.

Time is running out. I try to enter the dream.

"*Pssst!*"

"Listen to me, Ellie," I try. "You don't need to find Uncle Merlin. I can tell you how it really was on that holiday. No electricity. Cold baths. Everything mildewed—including the food. And always that sense of something refusing to let the house rest. But I did come to realize that Uncle Merlin was not the monster of your exuberant imagination."

Is the child paying any attention as she walks in circles, making snuffling noises? Not so brave now.

"Look, I'm sorry, but there's no point in crying for Mother." I stop, unable to say that Mother is dead from a fall down a flight of railway stairs when I was seventeen. "Uncle Merlin was a lonely old man—locked up, emotionally speaking, in a cupboard that rattled with skeletons. His greatest enjoyment was terrifying the family out of its wits for fear he would leave his fortune to a cat home."

Talk about wasting my breath. Talk about talking to myself. Child Ellie is gone. Hiding. "Would you get back here!" I huff. "Am I supposed to lie in bed all day trying to talk sense into you? I have a life to lead. And, if you don't mind my saying so, I am rather disappointed that you haven't bothered to ask how things turned out. Believe it or not, Merlin's Court is now my home and at the risk of sounding boastful, I have used my considerable talent as an interior designer to restore it to former glory. Uncle Merlin, you see, did *not* leave everything to a cat home. The house and a considerable sum of money was willed to me jointly with a gentleman by name Bentley T. Haskell, who, I am proud to inform you, became my husband."

Do I hear Child Ellie's ears prick up? "Surprised, aren't you? Never thought I would land a husband, did you? And believe me, Ben isn't your common or garden husband— the kind cousin Vanessa would try on for size, then donate to the Salvation Army. Ben is a Three-D Man: Dashing, Debonair, and Devoted. And he's employed, too. Presently he's asleep after an arduous day at Abigail's, his restaurant in the village. Otherwise I would introduce you."

Silence.

Those fox heads grin from the walls, but I don't see another face.

"Would you please look at me!" My voice fills up the hall, the house . . . the night. "Take a good look. Can't you see what a success I have made of myself? And, if you don't mind my saying so, with very little help from you. I'm thin. Radiantly thin. Ben happens to be one of the greatest chefs in the world—Paris trained. Which makes it a miracle that he was the one who brought out the new me. My darling seduced and reduced me. I now spurn chocolate. The word cream is obscene. Raw vegetables and clear broth excite me."

I begin to feel a bit of a fool, but I won't be intimidated by a pair of gawking suits of armour.

"Child Ellie, are you there? Answer me!" All this shouting is making me dizzy. The rooms in Merlin's Court, past and present, merge into a whirlwhip of faded colour.

"Why won't you answer?" My voice is far away. "How can you be so selfish? Do you think I would have come all this way back to find you, if there were anyone else for me to turn to? Don't you see, you are the only one who can show me . . . remind me . . . what it is like to be a child."

And I need to know. I am going to have a baby.

2

I, Mrs. Bentley T. Haskell of Merlin's Court, Chitterton Fells, retired interior designer, proud owner of a gifted cat named Tobias, experience no sense of impending doom. On that Saturday morning in June, I lie amidst the burgundy and silver-grey ambience of the matrimonial bedroom. Sunshine turns the latticed windows to harlequin dazzle, highlighting the dark glow of mahogany furniture.

Idly I pick up the hand mirror from the bedside table. Ugh! Keep up this brutal honesty and out the window you go! Do I need reminding that I have foam rubber cheek bones? Or that I failed to heed Aunt Astrid's dictum that crying over trifles washes all colour from the eyes? Fortunately I have long hair. I arrange it artfully over my face. The pheasants on the wallpaper have never heard the word migration. They aren't the only ones who will be utterly unprepared for what lies ahead.

"Ben, darling . . ."

"What is it, sweetheart?" responds my dark, handsome, and devoted spouse.

"I had such a strange dream last night. I was a child again, visiting here for the first time. Little did I know then that years later Uncle Merlin would come up with the bizarre idea of hosting a family reunion, resulting in my inspired idea of renting you for the weekend from Eligibility Escorts. Doesn't it seem like only yesterday that, for a modest fee, you agreed to pose as my besotted fiancé?"

"And here we are, my treasure!" He sat down on the edge of the bed, stroking my cheek with those slim, elegant fingers which can arouse such passion from a simple sponge cake. His touch was incredibly gentle, his voice incredibly absentminded. "Speaking of dreams, Ellie, I received by this morning's post a letter which I read before bringing up your breakfast tray, and believe me—the news is a dream come true!" Blue-green eyes sparkling enticingly, he patted the pocket of his black silk, man-about-the-bedroom dressing gown.

Smiling wanly from my pillow edged with Nottingham lace, I ached to tell him how desperately I loved the way his dark hair curled against his neck. But I wasn't up to the exertion. I had discovered that morning sickness was something for which I had natural flair.

"Exciting news, darling? Has the Electricity Board written to say it will adjust our bill?" I fingered his manly chest where the black silk gapped away. "I was afraid they wouldn't believe me concerning the heated towel rail's habit of turning itself on at will, but possibly my assertion that Dorcas and Jonas have also noticed did the trick."

Dorcas, let me explain in a swift aside, came to Merlin's Court as housekeeper, shortly after Ben and I took up residence. An avid sports woman, she is happier with a hockey stick in her hands than a mop. And that's fine with me. Dorcas is one of life's creature comforts. The older sister I never had. During the last few weeks, she had done some straight talking about this being the time for her to move from the main house to Cliffside, the cottage at the gates. She claimed to relish the idea of being several hundred yards closer to her new job as gym teacher at the village school. Huh! Had I believed she really wanted a place of her own I would have understood, but I know Dorcas. Nobility is her besetting sin. She had this bee in her red head that Ben and I should be on our own. As if there weren't more than enough room in this huge house for us all to wallow in privacy. If Dorcas were off the premises, she might miss the baby's first smile . . . first step. I'd had to put my foot down and tell her in no uncertain terms that in my condition I was not up to turning her bedroom at Merlin's Court into a shrine. Embroidering a plaque to place above her bed—*Gone But Not Forgotten*—would take forever.

Now for Jonas. He also lives in, while maintaining a separate suite of rooms over the stables to which he retreats whenever any of my relations brave his displeasure and show up for afternoon tea. Tobias, who is supposed to be my cat, sneaks off with him. Later I find the two of them seated in the rocking chair reading *Of Mice and Men*. Brindled moustaches dampened with Ovaltine. Good cheer restored from plotting the murders of Aunt Astrid, Aunt Lulu, and Uncle Maurice, and the rest. When it comes to flowers, Jonas is second to none. His dahlias are the size of tea plates and he produces colours not yet invented. I tell myself (and sometimes him) that he is entitled to his quirks and crotchets. Well past seventy, to outsiders he is the gardener who has been a fixture since the late Mr. Merlin Grantham was a lad. To we who love him, he is someone else entirely.

Ben shifted on the bed. The breakfast tray which he had set across my middle tipped and tilted like a ship in a storm. "Ellie, I am not talking about the electric bill or the towel rail which hates you. I am trying to talk about a letter sent to me from America."

My eyelids weighed as heavy as piano lids. But Chapter One of *The Pregnant Pause* stresses not playing the invalid. "From whom in America did this letter come?" Why did he keep bringing me breakfast in bed? I had begged him to stop. That poached egg was staring at me. A gargantuan eye. Filmed with cataract. The few sips of tea I had swallowed sloshed up and down in the hull. Marmalade? I couldn't face the stuff. Ah, but what was this cannily concealed under the pot? An envelope. Reaching for it, I perked up. A letter from my friend Primrose Tramwell was always a treat. She and her sister Hyacinth have confirmed my faith that the years of discretion—or mature indiscretion—can be life's great adventure. The sisters, both of them over sixty, owned Flowers Detection agency.

"Sorry Ben, I didn't quite catch . . ."

His black brows merged. "Am I losing my voice or is the baby pressing on an auditory nerve?"

"I'm not yet three months."

"Once more with feeling, then, my correspondent is the Secretary of the Mangé Society."

Instantly I was all sympathy. "Oh, not one of those crackpot organizations that promise to trace your family tree for a nominal fee of a thousand pounds? Drop it in the waste paper basket, darling!" I shifted the pillow under my head.

"Ellie—"

"Do listen to this. Primrose writes, 'Dearest Ellie, Hyacinth and I send our best love to you and Bentley. Life is tranquil here at Cloisters. We are sadly underworked in our chosen profession. Butler, speaking with authority—having, as you know, acquired his start in life as a burglar—asserts that crime doesn't pay what it once did.' "

"As well no one has poisoned the old girls' smelling salts." Ben, pacing at the foot of the bed, did not sound pleased.

"Must you use the word old?" I reproved.

"Why not? It's a status most of us wish to achieve. We want time to fulfill our dreams, one of mine having always been—"

"Darling," I said, "you will be so touched by this. Primrose encloses an old family remedy, ideal for someone in my delicate condition. She says it has been favoured by members of the Royal Family in times of stress. It uses only natural ingredients."

Ben dredged up a smile. "Sweetheart, you have mag-
nanimously led this conversation back to the Mangé Society. It does not dig up family trees, but is a custodian of
history in the ultimate sense." He withdrew his letter from
its envelope and crackled the stiff parchment. "The Mangés
are a secret organization of chefs, dedicated to the noble
cause of tracking down long lost recipes of cultural importance."

"My word!"

"Ellie, we are not talking about Aunt Maddie's mislaid
variation of jam tarts."

"I should think not!" I laid Primrose's letter down on
my paperback copy of *Pregnancy for Beginners*. Tobias Cat
strolled out from behind the wardrobe and I tried not to
meet his eyes.

Ben made himself comfortable on the bed and my feet.
"None but the Crème de la Crème are admitted to membership and those fortunates only after arduous admission
proceedings."

"Such as?"

"My dear, all that is kept exceedingly hush-hush. The
members take a vow of silence. As for those who don't
make the grade, blabbing would be professional suicide."

"Heavens!" If that poached eye did not stop gawking
at me, I might be driven to take a poke at it with my fork.
Maybe not. My mind dodged the dreadful vision of yellow
goo running out. "In other words, these Mangés are sort of
like Masons with cooking spoons? Given to secret hand-
shakes and coded eye twitchings?"

Ben caressed my layman's brow.

"These are the people who one year ago announced to
the world—the thinking world, Ellie—that they had singlehandedly tracked down a recipe for a minestrone dried
soup mix, created by none other than . . ." The maroon
velvet curtains stopped rippling in the breeze from the
open window. Tobias Cat, who been stalking his tail, sat
frozen. ". . . By none other than Leonardo Da Vinci."

"Gracious! And history has written him off as an artist

who dabbled in aviation, anatomy, et cetera, et cetera."
Must quell the urge to ask if the soup would be marketed
under the label Momma Mona. My beloved was clearly
infatuated with this gourmet sect.

"Why have the Mangés written to you?"

Ben stood up. The bed heaved, threatening to keel
over. I hugged the rim and the room settled back into
shape. My spouse was standing before the dressing table
mirror, taking a good hard look at himself. His eyes danced
with emerald sparks.

"Ellie, I hold here in these hands" (staring as though
they had sneaked up and attached to his arms while he
wasn't looking) "I hold here an invitation from the Society
to present myself for consideration as a Potential Member."

I strove to look dazzled.

"Speechless, aren't you? The question I keep asking is,
Why me?" He was pacing in front of the marble fireplace,
every fourth step hitting the board that squeaked.

I adore this man. He is my knight in shining armour.
He who saved me from a fate worse than death—Aunt
Astrid's scorn, thinly veiled as pity: poor Ellie, single by
default! But there are times when his masculine smugness,
poorly disguised as self-deprecation, irritates me just a
smudge.

He stopped pacing and tossed me a wry smile. "Hard
to credit isn't it? Me! Son of a humble greengrocer!"

His father is as humble as the ruler of an oil well
kingdom. Poppa considers himself a fruit and veggie
magnate.

"And think how proud your mother will be," I enthused. Confidentially, Magdalene is opposed to any organization not run on strict Roman Catholic lines. And surely
it was too much to hope that all Mangé members were of
the faith.

"Ellie, I wonder what made the Mangés pull my name
out of the hat? Abigail's is doing well but not on an interna-
tional scale, and *The Edwardian Lady's Cookery Book* has yet to
make me a household name."

"You're far too modest." I was background music.

Ben leaned forward to touch my hair. Missing by inches he paced on. That dratted board still squeaked with every fourth step.

"My entire life hanging in the balance and I did not know it. Do you think the society may have sent one of its members to dine at Abigail's undercover?"

"A point to ponder."

Gripping the letter with both hands he strove to unravel its secret code. "Sweetheart, I told you about the suspicious-looking chap with the ginger wig and the eye patch."

"I remember being quite frightened."

"Oh, my God, Ellie, wasn't that the Thursday when Freddy let the salads reach room temperature?"

Freddy, for the record, is my cousin. Supposedly he is Ben's right hand man at Abigail's. We felt we owed him something because on the whole he was pretty decent about our inheriting Merlin's Court. He may have thrown things in private, but he never tried to throw Ben or me out a window.

"Why couldn't the Mangés have sent their spies on a Tuesday? Nothing, if I do say it myself, compares with my escallop of escargot—the sauce gentle, almost shy . . ."

Once, believe it or not, I had found the way Ben talked about food one of his most sensuous qualities. Now I resorted to an antacid tablet. He smoothed out the letter, kissed it, and returned it to his pocket.

"Darling," I said, remembering it would soon be time for me to take my nap and I hadn't yet got up, "where will your meeting with the Mangés take place?"

He tightened his dressing gown belt, eyes fixed on my face. "Ellie, the society's headquarters are in the States. Where else would we meet?"

"I . . ."

"Ellie, it's not the *moon*. Jonas and Dorcas thoroughly enjoyed their stay in Chicago."

"So they did." I sank back against my pillow. The thought of his being gone from home was a bit of a shock.

A sigh escaped me. How desperately I would miss him. What wife of less than a year would not repine? But surely he wouldn't be gone more than a week or a fortnight at most? Unbidden came a rush of euphoria. Scant weeks ago my definition of bliss was being in bed with Ben. Now I must strive not to betray—by sparkling eyes—that I might adjust to being alone. Especially at night.

What ecstasy not to have the bed plunge and plummet every time my beloved turned over in sleep or roused up on an elbow to inquire how I was faring. Oh, that I might in the early hours of morning crawl into the bathroom and drape myself over the blessed chill of porcelain without that dear male voice explaining through a crack in the doorway that we were moving hour by hour ever closer to the end of this disagreeable, but stock, manifestation.

Euphoria ebbed. Guilt flowed in. I do guilt awfully well. Wasn't I the woman who only two years ago at the declining age of twenty-seven would have bartered thirty years of life for thirty minutes with a man? Wasn't I the one who had put in an official request for a baby? I had taken up the rosary, given to me by my mother-in-law, ostensibly as a souvenir from Rome, and I had prayed for the rabbit to die, the test tube to stop fizzing, the word Yes! to appear on the litmus paper.

My fertile hero! After having to be persuaded by all the wiles and negligees in my repertoire that fatherhood was for him, he had committed himself to the parenting project with zeal. From day one he had insisted that we eat right, exercise, and think Lamaze. He had set aside quality time to be spent with the embryo. My darling knew to the second when we would be talking fetus. He was heavily into such involvement as reading to our child—*now*. Thus ensuring genius level or above. Daddy Dearest believed in singing to the baby. He had no conception of the horror I endured, having my abdomen serenaded, while my insides heaved like a tempest and the bathroom was a thousand-mile trek across burning desert sands. He had no idea because I hadn't told him.

I didn't want to hurt him. I was ashamed of the botch I

was making of this joyous experience. Women today are giving birth on their lunch breaks or while standing at the Xerox machine; the race is on to see whether the copies of Mr. Brown's memo or the baby will be delivered first. Every photo of an *enceinte* female shows her garbed in moonbeam white, holding a rose to her parted lips, while waves froth over her polished toenails. What happened to me? Less than three months along and I already felt as though the timekeeper's watch had stopped. I didn't have the energy to look dewy and radiant. Most mornings I didn't have the energy to get up and start counting the minutes until my nap. I lived in constant fear that my mother-in-law would arrive unexpectedly and demand a count of the woolies I had knitted for the layette.

One of these days I would have to drag myself down to Rock-A-Bye Baby in the village, buy a couple of lacy coats, unpick the labels, unravel the necks, and stick knitting pins through them. What I needed, yearned for, was an intermission, only a short one, so I could gird myself to continue with the next six months. That being an impossibility, I would settle for Ben's going to America. I would sleep until his return. Dorcas would fend off cobwebs with an occasional charge of the mop. Jonas could be guaranteed to be rude to unwelcome visitors.

"Are you asleep?" Ben loomed over me.

"Just doing my eyelid exercises, darling! Close, push up and hold; close . . ." Dorcas stressed the importance of prenatal Physical Education.

"Ellie, we'd better see about booking our tickets. Not much time if we are to leave in a month."

"Did you say . . . *we*?" My eyes were opened. The air stretched tight as a drum.

"Darling, would I go without you?" He reclined with rakish elegance against the mahogany wardrobe. "The society urges that you accompany me. You are banned, of course, from meetings in the Inner Sanctum. But you are part of the package. Spousal support is considered crucial. Think of it, Ellie. If I am admitted to membership, there exists an excellent chance you will be invited to join the auxiliary."

Oh, cripes! As if I didn't have enough to do feeling rotten.

Inching to the edge of the bed, I sat looking into those marvelous eyes of his, flashing now with opal fire. "Ben, darling! You Odysseus. Me Penelope."

"Meaning?"

"You go, I stay."

Tobias yawned his boredom and disappeared back behind the wardrobe.

"Surely you jest!" Eyes dark and brooding, Ben slumped into the fireside chair. "You can't send me off alone. I might do something both of us would regret."

"Have an extramarital fling?"

"Use foul language—convenience foods, for instance."

"Darling, I'm sorry. Even at the best of times the words Selection Committee make me want to stick pins in animate objects." True enough. I was the fat child who never made it into the inner circle of schoolgirl secret societies.

If Ben wanted to be a Mangé, let him. He was his own grown-up person and thus entitled to be childish when he chose. He might need deprogramming when I got him back, but I could think up ways to make that fun.

Lying back down, I said, "My personal prejudices aside, the trip wouldn't be good for the baby. All the books stress stability at this period of a child's life."

He scraped his chair back with enough force to make ruts in the floor. "Rubbish. I read in an American newspaper only last week that prenatal travel is crucial to the development of inquiring minds."

I toyed with the idea of luring him down on the bed, twisting my hair into a rope, and wrapping it around his throat. "Ben, what if I should want to eat while over there? Dorcas says the Americans do unspeakable things to baked beans instead of serving them as God and Heinz intended: straight out of the tin. And they serve jelly—named Jello—on the same plate as meat and gravy. Physically I'm not up to all that."

"Baked beans and Jello"—he spoon fed me the words—"are on the Mangés' list of outlawed foods."

The room reeled. Tobias had landed on my stomach. "Ben, I'd be a burden. Whenever you attended one of your meetings and had to leave me alone for hours—maybe days on end—you'd be worried to death about me."

"I would not."

"You wouldn't worry"—my voice went all stringy, like chewing gum—"that I, who have the worst sense of direction in living memory, might head out on the wrong bus to Iglooville, Alaska?"

"Ellie!" He thumped a fist against his forehead and the whole room shook. Incredible to think that only fifteen minutes ago this had been a happy marriage.

I stroked Tobias' ears. "Ben, please understand! I've had a grudge against America ever since my parents left me with Uncle Merlin while they went job hunting over there. But if I have to set aside a pet phobia, I would wish to travel light in every sense of the word. As it is, I will only be pregnant enough to look *fat*. And haunted as I am by my fat past, that would be demoralizing."

What I didn't tell him was that I was gaining weight at a frightening rate. When next visiting Dr. Melrose, I would forego makeup and pop the fillings out of my teeth. Unfair! My food, when I could eat, mostly didn't stay down long enough to do good or harm.

Ben dropped down on the bed, sending the pheasants on the wallpaper into eddying flight. "Sweetheart, treat yourself to some maternity clothes."

"I'd feel presumptuous at this stage."

Gripping his head, he fell back on the bed.

I closed in for the kill. "And what about Abigail's? Agreed, Freddy is improving. He no longer tells customers that the desserts are chock-full of cholesterol. But can he be left with no one to restrain him? I know how his beady mind works. He'll introduce a Leftovers Special before you can say jet lag."

Ben sat up. "I believe my reputation can withstand

Freddy. And he has earned the right to fail or succeed under his own steam."

Sometimes the man was diabolical. Appealing to my sense of fair play like that! He was gaining on me to the point where I was reduced to wondering how the weather would be in the States at this time of the year.

"Whereabouts in America are we talking?"

A smile slithered on and off his face. "Where would you like it to be?"

"Boston." A fifty-to-one chance that I was in the wrong state. I hoped to see his eyes cloud with disappointment, but he was looking down, fiddling with his dressing gown belt.

"Amazing!" he said.

"You don't mean . . . ?"

"Well, not in the *heart* of Boston."

I breathed easy again.

"Some miles outside."

Tobias got off the bed. Smart cat. I was ready to throw something at Ben—if only I'd felt up to it.

"I don't want to go on a plane." Definitely scraping the bottom of the barrel here.

"You're not afraid of flying."

"I'm afraid of turbulence and those horrid little paper bags and the horrid waits outside those horrid little toilets."

Scowling, he kicked the side of the bed. "Ellie, I want to be a Mangé. I know you're feeling frayed around the edges, but remember, Chapter Two of *The Waiting Game* stresses that's a positive. I'm not asking you to go mountaineering."

Smoothing my hair off my brow, I fought to look fragile. "Ben, we've been married nearly a year now. We don't have to keep proving ourselves. Love doesn't mean driving oneself to the brink of nobility." I patted his cheek. "Be selfish, my love, and Godspeed."

"Such is your final answer?" Rising, he spoke in the voice of one who is going down with his ship. "Foolish of me to be surprised."

"Why?" I asked.

"I'd rather not say." Putting his best profile forward.

"As you wish, dear." Already I was planning my days without him. Bed until noon. Could I possibly be eligible for Meals on Wheels?

"Then again, if you insist on dragging it out of me, Mum did once voice concern that you might be something of a . . . well-intentioned wet blanket."

"Your mother said what?" About to hurl myself off the bed, I was saved by a surge of dizziness and the reappearance of Ben's slippery grin. Almost taken in by the oldest trick in the world!

Trembling fingers pressed to my eyes, I quavered, "And I suppose your father agreed! How sharper than a serpent's tooth it is to have ungrateful in-laws, and here I am carrying their grandchild."

While Ben strove to disentangle his tongue, I reflected that he did not mean to be an insensitive clod. He had simply bought into the hype that everything about pregnancy was nature at its awesome, exhilarating best, exclusive of morning sickness. Oh, to have lived in the good old days when being with child meant keeping to the boudoir. A dish of bonbons at the ready to tempt one's flagging appetite. A novel—with its unsullied heroine—always within reach. And mustn't forget that most indispensable of old world conveniences—the maid, tiptoeing in to stoke the fire. Stop. Quench that fantasy! With my luck I would have been the perennially pregnant maid. I sighed. Life in this day and age might have its pluses. Could it be that gallivanting to America was not as barbarian as it sounded?

A brave smile touched my lips. "Ben, may I have a small respite before letting you have my R.S.V.P.?"

He knelt at the bedside, picked up my trailing hand, and crushed it to his lips.

It was one of those scenes sculpted by Venus, the two of us alone, as one! But as happens when the door springs open and a third party intrudes, we ended up looking a prize pair of twerps. To give her credit, Dorcas did knock; her omission was in waiting for "Entre!"

"Frightfully sorry barging in like this!" Red hair bristling out from its confining barrettes, she tugged at the whistle around her neck. Fortunately she didn't blast it, as was her habit when someone (herself included) needed to be galvanized into action. Her hazel eyes zeroed in on Ben, who was still on his knees. "Caught you bang in the middle of morning exercises, have I? Oh, I say . . . didn't mean . . ." Middle age had not cured Dorcas of blushing fierily when the occasion arose. I rescued her.

"Ben was playing peekaboo with Tobias."

Man and beast, who don't much care for each other, each curled a lip.

Dorcas strode forward. "Jolly ho! But what isn't quite so jolly is that you have visitors."

"Anyone we know or might want to know?" Ben stood up.

"Not," I said aghast, "one of my relations?" Frankly the last thing I needed in my expectant state was to take a good hard look at my genes. Best of the bunch Freddy had put it in a nutshell when saying that were he to murder his mother, his father's response would be, "Damn it all, boy, I trust you're going to cough up for the funeral, springing it on me like this!"

"Not one of them," said Dorcas. "It's the Misses Tramwell."

"But that's marvelous! I wonder if Primrose mentioned in her letter—which I never did get to finish—that they would pay us a visit?" My happy anticipation did not bounce back at me off Ben's face. He likes the Tramwells but he likes getting to Abigail's by 10 A.M. on Saturday mornings better.

I dabbed a toe out of bed to test the *mal de mer*, so to speak. "No need, my Lord Faint Heart, to cut out by way of the window. Hyacinth and Primrose wouldn't dream of subjecting you to girl talk." I broke off, startled by the expression on Dorcas' face. Make that her nose, which twitches when she is agitated.

"Hate to cast a rub, Ellie, but the ladies aren't feeling girlish. Said they had come on a matter of life or death."

"Oh, Ben!" My hands gripped the bedpost. "We should have guessed! They would never have come this early in the day unless something were wrong."

His arms encircled me. "A matter of life or death! What a cliché!"

"Only where strangers are involved," I whispered against his manly chest.

"Dearest Ellie," the sisters rose from the drawing room sofa as one. "Oh, how dreadfully frail and drawn you look."

My spirits lifted. The potpourri of fading summer wafted in through the open windows. What pleasure to be fussed over! Taking one of my arms apiece, they lowered me onto the ivory brocade sofa as though I were eminently rare and imminently breakable. I had forgotten how fond I was of them. Primrose with her silvery curls, crumpled flower face, and limpid blue eyes; Hyacinth, taller and sallow, with her black cone of hair and hooded eyes. Surely the likeliest reason for their presence, and for the message relayed through Dorcas, was that they wished to discuss an urgent case with me. Not long ago I had assisted Flowers Detection when a local women's group had taken the law into their white-gloved hands and made murder a community project. Another reason I was against organizations. Who knew what the Mangé Society got up to in its spare time? As my Uncle Maurice is wont to say, "Causes breed fanatics."

"Sweet child, I trust you did not come downstairs by yourself." Primrose arranged a pillow behind my head before fetching the familiar smelling salts bottle from her handbag.

The primly tailored effect of her wool suit was canceled out by its Donald Duck buttons, which went very nicely, however, with her oversized Mickey Mouse watch. As for the satin bows tucked among her curls, they seemed a bit much until one took a good look at her sister. Hyacinth was attired in harem trousers and a baggy-sleeved scarlet blouse. Brass birdcage earrings hung against her neck. Whenever she moved, the tiny canaries inside warbled.

Involuntarily my eyes veered to the portrait of Abigail, Uncle Merlin's mother, which hangs in pride of place above our mantel. Her plain, forthright face and kind eyes would have made the room home even had it not contained a stick of furniture. Did I detect a suggestion of a wink as she smiled down at me now?

"Really, you mustn't fuss over me," I scolded the sisters. They sat down on either side of me, each clasping one of my hands. "Ben is preparing to go to the restaurant but will pop in to say hello before leaving. He wouldn't miss seeing you for the world. And Dorcas promised to bring in coffee after we've had time for a chat."

"Ben continues to attend his place of business?" Hyacinth's brow creased. "One would think he could find someone to take over so as to allow him to be with you during these trying days."

"Men!" I spread my hands.

Hyacinth repeated the epithet—getting even more mileage out of it. "I am proud to say our paternal parent never indulged in employment during those times when our mother was expecting."

"He never did so when she was not." Primrose set the smelling salts down. "The demands made by his club were extremely onerous, and when we were young, it was not the accepted practice for either parent to work unless vulgarly pressed." She clasped my hand. "I believe your father maintains some of those old values."

"Certainly. He resides still in a grass hut on the tropical island of Kiwikki, living on mulled coconut milk and organizing the local beauty pageant—Miss Blue Lagoon."

Primrose murmured, "Tut-tut," but I noticed a gleam in her pansy eyes. Did she harbour a heart-shaped fantasy of my father—decked out as a combination of Errol Flynn and Tarzan—swinging in through the open window on a rope some day when she might happen to be visiting?

"Remember, Hyacinth, when Father moved the family into a tent on the lawn for a fortnight in order that we learn how the masses live? Oh, the chagrin of the servants at fetching meals back and forth!"

"Very true." Hyacinth inclined her head and the canaries in the birdcage earrings began to trill. "But let us not fritter away the hour in reminiscing. We must explain our visit."

Primrose, nervously crocheting her fingers, twittered an interruption. "Yes, yes, so we must, but perhaps it would be best to wait until the estimable Dorcas fetches in the coffee. Dear Father used to say that there were no dry topics, just dry throats. Admittedly he was deploring the absense of port . . ." She plucked at her pearls. "Ellie, my dear, is that tapestry footstool new? Such a dear, sweet room this is! We have been pondering the possibility of a similar ivory silk wall covering for the Novice's Suite, sometimes known as the Bridal Bedchamber, at Cloisters."

Hyacinth frowned. "Primrose, these stalling tactics serve only to make our mission more painful." She gripped my hands, her painted fingernails glowing like hot coals. "Dear friend, we have intruded at this unseemly hour, unannounced, because we have grave concerns for your well-being."

I had been feeling a little faint but her words brought me round like a dash of cold water. What could the sisters believe threatened my halcyon existence? Light dawned! Pregnancy, even at its most normal, was assuredly a matter of life or death to the Misses Tramwell. Sitting vigorously upright, I bit back a smile at the thought of their coming post haste to insist that I stay in bed the full nine months.

"Please, you mustn't worry about me. Other than the mandatory morning sickness, I am fine, truly!"

Hyacinth *tutted*. "Do understand, Ellie, that Prim and I are not averse to your having this child. Indeed, we received the news of the anticipated joyous event with pleasure. We are both singularly fond of babies."

"And only the tiniest degree afraid of them," contributed Primrose with her pastel smile.

Hyacinth's brow darkened. "Doubtless, Ellie, a child will add much to the felicity of your life with Bentley—once you emerge from the early travails of broken nights, broken bones, and broken romances. We did telephone our local midwife—the sage Nurse Krumpet—who assured us that childbirth need no longer be the primitive ordeal of the past. Antiquated as I am, nothing will convince me that birth is fit television entertainment or that the labouring mother's smiles are not dubbed in, however." She drew breath.

"My dear Hy"—Primrose fussed with the bows in her hair—"are you not taking the scenic route in getting to the point?"

Hyacinth nodded. "I, trust, my dear, you are a believer in the Psychic Force?"

"I'm sort of agnostic on the subject."

Her black eyes held me, and the canaries ceased tweeting in the birdcage earrings. "Yesterday Primrose and I were at the breakfast table in the morning parlour. I was showing her the matinee coat I am knitting for a certain baby when Chantal entered with the toast rack."

"Our maid," Primrose chimed in. "A superior girl of gypsy extraction."

Hyacinth quelled her with a look. "During Chantal's hours off she is progressing toward an advanced university degree. The employment conditions at Cloisters being ideal in that her subject is monastic herbalism. That nerve remedy Primrose sent you was one Chantal came across while cleaning out a cupboard which hadn't been touched in several hundred years."

Primrose tapped on her Mickey Mouse watch. "Indeed, yes, and we do trust, Ellie, you will find it as salutary as did Anne Boleyn and dear Sir Walter Raleigh in their hour of need."

Hyacinth closed her eyes. "To proceed apace—as fate willed, I dislodged my ball of white three ply and Chantal retrieved it from the floor."

"Always so willing," fluted Primrose.

"Chantal is a gifted clairvoyant," said Hyacinth.

"Dear child," said Primrose, "you may accuse us of reading too many romantic novels, but Hy and I both witnessed Chantal freeze in the act of handing back that ball of wool. Her eyes became black ponds, pardon me, pools of horror. Her dark hair formed a mantle about her blanched cheeks. Her fingers crushed the wool. And when at last she spoke, her voice did seem to emanate from every crevice in the room, save her struggling lips. Chantal's words, dear Ellie, were these." To cushion the blow, Primrose rearranged the one behind my head.

" 'I see a house with many turrets, surrounded by water.' "

"The moat at Merlin's Court! What could be clearer!" Hyacinth supplied.

Her sister's papery hands clutched at the pearls around her neck until they chattered like teeth. Her voice became ghostlike. " 'I am now inside the house of turrets. The walls are red. And red means anger. The air I breathe is thick with jealousy and fear. An explosion is building, throbbing until—*poof!* A huge cloud masses in turgid blackness above the rooftop. It threatens to destroy the hopes and dreams of all who dwell within. Beware the black cloud!' "

Primrose fell silent. Tobias Cat entered the room like a walking bad omen then turned tail. In the gapped doorway stood Ben. Hand clapped to his brow, he effected a palsied stagger. I was doing a palsied slither off the sofa. Hyacinth repositioned me. Her satin blouse glistened blood red. Did either of these delightful women realize what they were doing to me? My hands moved protectively over the baby.

Primrose was off again. "Poor Chantal's breath now fluttered like the wings of a tired bird. 'That house is built

of fire and brimstone and swathed in shadow . . . Trouble
in the North Tower . . . No place out but up . . . Writing
not on the wall . . . Pen nastier than the sword . . . Mrs.
Haskell must find the truth within herself.' "

Primrose passed the smelling salts under my nose as
well as her own. "My dear Ellie, Chantal's voice faded to a
shiver which had Hyacinth and myself reaching for our
shawls. Well may you look shocked. Administering Flowers
Detection as we do, we are known for our nerves of steel."

My head felt like a gun about to go off. "Merlin's Court
is a house with a past, but it certainly does not seethe with
unrest these days." I raised my voice. "Sometimes Ben and
Jonas annoy me, but men will be boys. As for Dorcas, she
doesn't have a jealous bone in her body."

The shrill sound of a distant teakettle was in fact Dorcas nervously blowing her whistle. She and Jonas had joined
Ben in peeking through the doorway.

Tobias Cat wasn't helping my nerves either by circling
the sofa.

"I am sure, my dear," Primrose consoled, "that no one
presently in residence could be the primal source of danger.
One day I suspect there will come a knock at the door . . ."

My left leg jumped convulsively and down came my
foot on Tobias' tail. He leaped three feet in the air and
hailed me with meowing curses. "Did Chantal say anything
else?" I whispered.

Hyacinth shook her head, sending the canaries into
chirruping spins. "To have taxed her further would have
accomplished nothing other than to have resulted in her
being in no condition to top and tail the Lavender Bedroom. Prim and I pondered all yesterday as to what was
best to do. We retired early to bed still sorely tried in spirit,
but arose this morning serene. We drove here in our trusty
hearse, at reckless speed, to urge you to fly these portals
before Destruction strikes."

I would have swooned, had I felt up to it.

"Leave here! What a positively ripping suggestion!"
Ben stepped out of the doorway with the startling effect of
a portrait come to life. Crossing to the sofa, he seemed to be

treading on my mind. The door was now wide open and Jonas and Dorcas were gone. Were they upstairs packing?

Under the pretext of kissing the top of my head Ben whispered, "The curse of the gypsy woman—eyes like dank pools! Sleazy black clouds! It's enough to make me eager to try my hand at writing trashy novels again." Straightening, he walked around the front of the sofa to shake hands with the sisters. "How splendid to see you both!" He availed himself of one of the Queen Anne chairs, eyes sparkling like stolen jewels. "Forgive my eavesdropping, but talk about being held spellbound! I was unable to move a muscle."

The Misses Tramwell had been reared in an age when forgiving male misdeeds was a fact of life. Primrose blushed to match her rose pink blouse. Hyacinth touched a gleaming red fingernail to her cone of hair and said, "Your gentlemanly apology is accepted, Bentley. I trust you do not believe Primrose and I are making too much of Chantal's dark vision."

Re-angling his chair, Ben's face planed to geometric shadow, he avowed, "On the contrary, I fear you may if anything be understating the seriousness of the situation. Ellie and I owe you an immense debt. The moment you uttered the words jealousy, anger, and fear, I knew what form danger would take. We are in for a visit from the relations."

He meant my family of course, an insult which I embraced like a life jacket. Uncle Maurice would be on the run from his creditors, Aunt Lulu would be needing a respite from the daily grind of shoplifting. I gave the baby a reassuring pat. I was flooded with joy. God wasn't about to punish me for forgetting my iron tablets twice last week.

"What say you, sweetheart?" Ben spoke with degenerate suavity. "Where can we flee that is sufficiently far from the Black Cloud?" Pressing a finger to his forehead, he closed his eyes. "How about America?"

"I think that might be a bit close, darling." Happiness tends to effect me like champagne. "Wouldn't Australia be safer? Just think of the exciting gourmet things you might do with kangaroos. Quite tasty, I would imagine, and so easy to stuff."

Hyacinth's painted black brows converged. "Australia! Are you sure? One cannot but feel that a country which has its seasons the wrong way around isn't quite civilized."

Ben placed his hands behind his head, crossed his ankles and bestowed upon me his sultan smile.

"My dear Ellie," said Primrose, "I do feel America would be preferable. On the admittedly remote chance that Chantal's dire predictions do not come to pass, Hyacinth and I would be mortified at having put you to the expense of travelling to the under world. Then too, we do wish to please Bentley, don't we?"

"Not obsessively."

Primrose hastened on. "We have a sister, Violet, living in Detroit. Quite one of the garden spots of the country, so she has given us to understand. Her married name is Wilkinson and her husband and sons are in the undertaking business. Never the least need to worry that dear Vi won't be well taken care of when the time comes. Pray do look her up if you have the time and tell her how well you find Hy and myself." She tweaked one of the bows in her hair. "And, if you would be so good, reassure her that our doctor thinks we look remarkably young."

"I think we can promise a phone call, don't you, sweetheart?" said the louse . . . I mean *spouse*.

Ben can read me like a kindergarten book. He knew that I would travel to the ends of the earth given the least chance that the Black Cloud was my cousin Vanessa arriving for an extended visit. Over the phone the other day she had purred, "Darling, I'm sure you'll look *lovely* pregnant. Being heavy was always so . . . *you!*" Nothing would give her greater pleasure than to flaunt her elastic-band-sized waist in front of me and Ben, not that *he* would take the least bit of notice.

I heard a wink in his voice when he assured the Tramwells we would send them postcards from America.

Why fight on? Once fate has you by the collar, struggling is useless. Besides, I was late for my nap and Ben was late for Abigail's. Let the Mangés but send us the secret password and we would be on our way. A sideways glance at the bookcase stiffened my resolve. Those scrapbooks Dorcas and Jonas had kept during their sojourn to America seemed to have mated and bred to the point where they had taken over the shelves at an alarming rate. Better to see the New World for myself than through weekly *National Geographic* sessions with a pair of former explorers.

Ben's voice addressing the Tramwells brought me back. "Ah, here comes Dorcas with the coffee. And I believe you've met Jonas."

"They've had that pleasure." Jonas gave the braces holding up his baggy trousers a twang. Dreadful man! He hadn't removed his gardening boots. His hoary moustache twitched wickedly as he held out a plate of teacakes to Primrose.

Dorcas held her whistle at the ready (Ben having taken over pouring the coffee in order to speed up the job and make his get-away to Abigail's) but Jonas was irrepressible. Gripping the teacake plate, as if for courage, he growled, "I do be risking the sack putting meself forward so, Miss Primrose, but I be born and bred a liar if you don't look like one of them film stars sitting there."

Such charming rusticity caused Primrose to slop her tea.

Hyacinth's expression turned frosty. "One feels so glad, Prim, that one leant you one's blouse. As you will recall, I have on several occasions been compared to the famed Theola Faith in her kittenish heyday. Which does remind me"—taking her sister by the elbow, she propelled her upright—"we must be on our way."

"So soon?" Ben downed both cups of coffee he was holding.

Hyacinth gathered up her bag. "I fear so. On our way back to Cloisters we will attend a rally of the Warwickshire branch Theola Faith fan club. Her daughter—an absolute nobody in her own right, no one even knew there was a daughter—has penned one of those abysmal mud-slinging books about her. We intend to picket the library."

The name Theola Faith scratched at an old memory. Theola Faith had been the sex goddess of her generation, adored by millions. My mother, when I was about nine or ten, performed a small dancing role in one of her films, *Melancholy Mansion*. But this wasn't the time to brag. Turning my thoughts forward, I wondered if there were any female Mangés. Not that it mattered—a tall white chef's hat does absolutely nothing for even the most divinely inspired female.

I have none of Chantal's psychic powers. So often I don't see what's under my nose, such as Tobias circling the sofa, ready to take a flying leap at Hyacinth's birdcage earrings. Had the room chosen to darken and develop an arctic chill I would not have taken the hint that in fleeing the Black Cloud Ben and I were destined to run toward it.

We were going to America.

The morning of departure day I awoke knowing something was wrong. I felt well. Every part of me was alive—
waiting to experience all the wonders of marathon waits at
the airport. The joy of shouldering sideways down the aisle
of the airplane, my carry-on bag balanced on my head! I
could have been the happiest woman on board but for
Ben's claustrophobia.

"No, darling." I squeezed his hand as the plane took
off. "Better not open your window." I'm ashamed to say I
hadn't looked at *Pregnancy for Beginners* since the day we
received the Mangés' invitation. Now, watching Ben listen
with petrified attention to the captain's weather bulletin, I
was tempted to climb over my companion on the aisle seat
and retrieve the book from the overhead compartment. But
Ben wouldn't let go of my hand. The drink trolley was
rattling its way down the aisle, and I did have something
else up my sleeve, or rather in my handbag, which might
have a calming effect upon us both.

"Ben, dear." I turned his face toward me and looked

deep into his eyes. "A letter arrived this morning from your mother. Would you like me to read it to you?"

"That would be nice."

Like Jane Eyre ministering to Mr. Rochester after the fire, I drew out my mother-in-law's letter, written in response to one of mine. Ben, like so many of his sex, would no more handle family correspondence than wear lace underwear.

" 'Dear Ben, please give our best to Ellie. Also thanks for her last of two days since. Poppa says it is kind of her to write often, but what with postage getting so dear, letters do become an extravagance. Have a good trip, both of you. Never mind that Poppa and I can't sleep nights for worrying how you'll go on. Haven't we always said we knew what was in store when we signed on as parents? We raised you, son, to have a life of your own. Not a word from Poppa or me when you went to work for Eligibility Escorts.' "

Exactly true; they simply stopped speaking to him.

" 'My prayers are answered if you don't let our peace of mind stand in the way of your happiness. Mrs. Badger, next door but one, tells such dreadful stories about her niece Rosemary who lives in New York. Seems every other week the poor girl nearly gets murdered and has to write home for money, so's she can move to a safer place.' "

"What a blessing we are going to Boston!" I said brightly.

Ben had grown paler. "Not the city proper. You do remember my explaining we have to travel some distance from there to meet with the Mangés?"

"Yes, dear, and you promised to rent us a nice car." I watched him swig down his medicine—whisky over ice. Raising my voice so that my aisle companion—an oriental gentleman in a T-shirt inscribed Made In Japan—need not struggle to eavesdrop, I continued.

" 'I must say, son, I'm not much taken with the sound of these Mangé people. Are you sure you've got the name right? Mrs. Wardle round the corner says it puts her in mind of that disease dogs get. Then she went and stuck the fear in my head that you're being lured over there by the white slavers or something worse. Poppa says he sent you that write-up in the newspaper about some nasty religious group that believes you can't get to heaven unless you stop eating. A quick way to go, Poppa says. Diethelogians they call themselves. They think of chefs the way we Catholics think of Henry VIII. Poppa, as you might guess, says I'm getting worked up for the wrong reason. He thinks these Mangés want you over there to sell you something. A plot in some cemetary just for chefs is his guess. Mrs. Wardle says this world is going downhill faster than a runaway pram. Doesn't come out and say it, but I know she's thinking as how those who live in houses with posh-sounding names like Merlin's Court are asking to be taken for a ride by all sorts of riff-raff.' "

"Mother speaks wise words." The oriental gentleman bowed his head over steepled fingers. "Very many bad people in this world." Face impassive, I bowed back, then smoothed Ben's damp curls off his brow. Have to read on at a rush. Lunch only few seats away.

" 'I trust, son, that Ellie isn't having the difficult pregnancy I went through with you. Every day a heaving, shoreless sea. I'd get one hour of feeling good, just so's to remember what it felt like. But the great blessing, as they say, is that after the baby comes you forget!' "

"Veal marsala or peppered beef?" inquired the blonde flight attendant with the hundred-watt smile.

Some things science can't explain. Ben emerged from his claustrophobia when his little white tray was placed in front of him. Artificially flavoured meat? Reconstituted lettuce? Thinking up rude names to call his meal promised to keep him occupied—if not for the rest of the trip, at least while I went to the loo.

I staggered down the aisle toward the lavatory. A woman waiting ahead of me suggested that a priest might be hearing confessions. She'd been waiting, she informed me sourly, for ten minutes to get inside.

Out came a brazen hussy, Gucci makeup bag tucked under her arm, hands clutching a hardcover book, a corner of which almost got me in the eye. But the person who can hold fifty-some people hostage while she lolls in the loo is unlikely to be the sensitive type.

"So sorry," she fibbed through lips as violently red as the blood enlivening the glossy black jacket of *Monster Mommy*. "I'm afraid I was swept away by one riveting scene after another and completely lost track of time." Snap-snap of her fingers at the steward. "Drinks for everyone aboard. No, nothing for me. I have an extremely taxing cocktail party to attend immediately after we land and I'll be as déclassé as dry roasted peanuts if I can't quote chapter and page. *People* magazine said, 'This book will find its way onto every coffee table in America, even the vinyl coated ones. It will burn its way into your heart, brand the letter M on your soul.' " Snap-snap of her fingers at a man who looked as though he hadn't taken his daily Milk of Magnesia, her husband seemingly because he swept her away by her ear. To add insult to injury for us cross-legged sufferers, a stewardess was sleepwalking her way down the gangway reading what looked like the same book. What were the airways coming to?

When I finally did enter the standing-room-only convenience, my usual panic set in. We'd be landing before I figured out how to engage the lock in accordance with instructions in three languages—none of them English. Instant darkness when I pushed a button. Afraid to touch anything else, lest it hurtle us into a forced landing, I kept a restraining elbow on the door and succeeded in dropping my bag. Down on my knees, retrieving the bits and bobs, my panic elbowed off in new directions. Had I left home responsibly? The last few days had tumbled over one another. Had I stocked up on enough Ovaltine for Jonas? Had I reminded Dorcas enough times to give Tobias his vitamins? What if all my relations *did* materialize on the doorstep, empty suitcases in hand, ready for a raid? Dorcas is cursed with a kind heart. So too, is Mr. Jonas Scrooge, however hard he fights the demon. Yes, I had taken the precaution of hiding the few pieces of jewelry left to me by my mother under the loose floorboard in my bedroom, but Aunt Lulu has the nose of a search-and-seize police dog.

Squeezing back into my seat, I whispered in Ben's ear (so as not to alarm the oriental gentleman), "I've ordered our flight captain to turn back."

He gave me a seasoned traveller's smile. "Ellie, you must rid yourself of the idea that we've abandoned Dorcas and Jonas to a fate worse than death. I don't believe in Chantal's psychic powers."

"The Tramwells think the world of her."

"They'd think the same if she were a vampire. So long as she served a decent cup of tea."

"Darling, you're so right!" Suddenly I wasn't merely happy, I was bursting with the conviction that together Ben and I were invincible. No matter that I wasn't the woman of my mother-in-law's dreams, I was a consort fit for a Mangé! Who better to know the fat content of an orange? Shifting in my confined seat, I wrapped my arms around my husband's neck and kissed that marvelous, seductive mouth of his. I breathed in his aftershave, felt his sensitive knowing hands moving to my shoulders . . .

"Blue skies are here again," said the oriental gentleman.

"He means we are about to land," Ben whispered.

Boston's airport provided an immediate sense of the proverbial vastness, the fabled brashness of the United States. The ebb and flow of humanity, galvanized by foghorn blasts of loudspeakers, banished any fleeting thoughts of curling up on the luggage merry-go-round for a siesta. The customs man was nice. He accepted my assurances that I did not have Swiss watches or antique jewelry stuffed in the toes of my shoes, and I invited him to come and stay next time he was in England.

There I was, seriously considering having a good time— until I saw our luggage closing in around our ankles like a pack of stray dogs. The small bags were the puppies.

"Want to give them to good homes?" I asked. But as far as Ben was concerned I might have been another blast of the loudspeaker. He was off in search of a cart, his progress closely observed by several stray females. A dire thought occurred. Could they be Mangés sent to welcome him with open arms?

"Absolutely not." He strained to grow more arms to stack the cases. "We are to make our way to headquarters on our own. The organization doesn't want any tenderfoots."

"Good thinking!" I certainly preferred not having Mangés underfoot while we enjoyed the few days sightseeing Ben had promised, indeed, insisted upon.

"Are you feeling all right?" Buttoning my rain-or-shine jacket I strung the strap of my bag over my shoulder. Ben did look like a sickly Lord Byron, ebony curls dampened to his pallid brow.

He managed a tubercular laugh. "Just wondering, sweetheart, whether you've given me your morning sickness."

So he had noticed that I was feeling better. Probably afraid to say anything in case it was a false alarm.

My face pressed against his tweedy shoulder, he said, "I'm fighting fit. Let's to the car rental place."

His eyes roved the LuxaLease showroom for a full one-and-a-half seconds before lighting on a voluptuous convertible, all bosom and no rear end. The agent, with his clown's nose and yellow bow tie, put me in mind of a game show host surrounded by prizes. He assured us that our choice would cruise comfortably at one hundred miles per hour.

"Starts like a dream, sir! Get your foot within an inch of the gas pedal and she's gone—with or without you!"

"Like it, Ellie?" Ben fondled the bonnet.

"Love it. Black is so slimming."

"You are slim, sweetheart."

He should start wearing his glasses more often. I had gained three pounds in three days. Goodness knows where they had come from. Could some evil force be polluting the Chitterton Fells water supply with calories?

Ben was circling the car, eyeing it with the look that should have been reserved for me alone. "In your expert opinion, sir, is this the vehicle for the expectant mother? The right suspension, the right brake linings?"

"Darling," I cringed, "can't we go native with buses

and taxis? There's so much to see and do in the city, we may not have time to go far afield."

I couldn't get him to look at me, let alone convince him the Mangés might consider his pioneer spirit was not being sufficiently tested.

But fifteen minutes later, when we were tooling down the wide open streets with the top down under a canopied blue sky, I experienced an exuberant urge to shake my hair loose from its knot and let the breeze take it. Whatever the meteorologists might say, that big orange sun was not the same one that rises daily in our English skies. For the first time in my life I felt properly aired out, and not the least tired—even though it was four P.M. here, which translated into nine P.M. at home.

"Happy?" Ben squeezed my hand.

"Blissful."

"And we are not going to allow any small disappointments or twists of plan spoil the trip?"

Had the car agent slipped him some bad news about our hotel? Were the rooms opulently vulgar? Did a live orchestra play under each rotating bed? Or worse—considering our entourage of luggage—were the lifts out of commission?

Happily, my fears were in vain. The Mulberry Inn was everything I could have hoped. The plank floors in the reception hall shone the colour of maple syrup, the walls were fresh cream, and the doors patriot blue. A Mayflower matron, middle-parted hair, and a voice flavoured with a teaspoon of Irish, looked up reluctantly from her open book and greeted us from behind a handhewn desk, centered on the sort of rug that grandma would hook on long winter evenings. Made from strips of rag, some from Uncle Franklin's long johns.

Only minor disappointments. Instead of a jigger of rum, our hostess promised cheese and wine to be served in the Pewter Parlour between five and six P.M. And the book she had been glued to was not *Puritan Fashions for the Mature Figure*, but a modern tome with a black and red cover. It was the same nail-biter as had caused that woman to hole up in the plane loo.

She laughed defensively, and her plump hands covered the title as though it were a bare bosom and Ben and I church elders. "I never read this sort of thing." An old world blush. "I'm not interested in film stars and the nonsense they get up to, but everyone's bleating about this book—the huge advance, the paperback deal, the movie rights. And the clientele we get in here expects a certain, ah, sophistication."

A glance at the bill she nudged toward us indicated that the rates were certainly sophisticated. Ben was looking displeased, but wifely intuition told me he was regretting the difficulty of writing a cookery book shocking enough to attract any wild clamouring of public opinion. Perhaps his sequel to *The Edwardian Lady's Cookery Book* could be a little less restrained in its language and less sensitive in its treatment of such subjects as killing little lobsters. . . .

"Books of this sort"—he tapped the glossy black cover—"are very much like wine. I understand that in this country the only requirement for joining most country clubs these days is drinking white zinfandel."

The Mayflower Missus agreed pleasantly that zin was in and tucked the book beneath her arm.

"Mr. and Mrs. Haskell, you have yourselves a grand stay." Having presented our key, she escorted us past the long case clock to an elfin-sized arched doorway leading both to a sun lounge and a twisting witchy staircase. Best not to ask about a lift in case they were deemed papist inventions.

A soldierly septuagenarian, wearing a uniform dating back to the War of Independence, took charge of the two suitcases Ben had brought in from the car. Cheeks going like bellows, he chugged ahead to the third floor to deposit us in a clove-scented sprig muslin room. If ever people need parents, it's the elderly! No mother worth the name would allow him to work like this! I gave him a tip he could retire on. And he departed with that lovely blessing—"Have a nice day."

Enraptured, I sank down on the brass bed. An electric kettle nestled against the forget-me-not blue dish of teabags on the coffee table under the narrow paned windows hung with angel wing curtains.

Side-stepping the luggage, Ben joined me on the bed and unwound my hair.

"Shouldn't we unpack?" I asked virtuously.

"Later!" He drew me down upon the cross-stitched quilt.

"Are you sure you're up to . . . taking a nap?" I turned my lips to his, but held them tantalizingly at bay.

"What?"

The glints of sunlight gold in his eyes turned me weak and at the same time all-powerful. "You seemed a bit off colour back at the airport. Remember?"

"You're right." He slid my jacket off my shoulders, twirled it on one finger and sent it into a free spinning arc, to land on the petticoat shade of the bedside lamp. "Time for some physical therapy."

"Let's not overdo things," I warned. "Must have you in tip-top shape for the Mangés."

He was undoing the buttons of my blouse. "To hell with the Mangés."

Instantly the room darkened. There came a rasping sound as of the wind gathering for a storm. My eyes were closed and he was breathing hard.

Sometimes I had trouble believing I was the woman who had been wearing a marked down sticker when Ben took her off the shelf and dusted her off. He was so incredible! Everything about him impeccably groomed, down to his long lashes. At that moment I would have promised him anything short of agreeing to name the baby Esau. Turning my head on the pillow I hoped my hair would spill about my shoulders in the manner of the heroine of *Love's Last Lament*. But, true to form, the rubber band confining my torrid locks refused to snap. And my legs didn't writhe between satin sheets because the Mulberry Inn didn't go in for anything so vulgar. I had to make do with kicking off my shoes and rubbing a foot against Ben's.

The scent of cloves receded; the feather mattress embraced our bodies. For some weeks I had not been myself matrimonially speaking, but now the spice of his aftershave, the rasp of his manly chin, the lingering dexterity of his hands upon every button of my blouse brought back the sublime ecstasy of knowing I was loved for something other than my mind.

My lips toyed with his.

"You drive me insane with desire," he whispered.

"Likewise," I murmured.

Yes, it was all very lovely, but afterward . . . well, I would have been failing as a tourist had I continued lying there, the holiday ticking away, while I gazed into his eyes.

Semi-respectably dressed in my aqua and sea foam lace negligee (purchased as a last fling before giving myself over to maternity bras and smocks with bumble bees on the pockets), I suggested we get our first taste of American culture.

"You want to go out and tour the U.S.S. *Constitution?*"

"No." I readjusted a loose end of the Laura Ashley sheet he wore with such fetching machismo. "I want to watch television."

"Very well, but remember you only get three wishes." He waved his remote control wand. Amazing! The dry sink in the corner turned into a television set. The picture slid around as though greased. The words *Melancholy Mansion* had leaped upon the screen.

"Looks like your cup of hemlock, Ellie."

"My mother had a part in this film."

"You never told me." He touched my hair.

"I've never seen it." I pressed a hand over his mouth. "She gave me a choice of this or *Bambi.*"

A surge of surflike music holding undercurrents of tidal terror. A swirl of mist, momentarily twitched away—in the manner of a magician's hanky—to reveal a full moon, hovering above a house of finest Gothic Horror design, rising up out of a body of water—a river or perhaps a lake. A crashing of cymbals, the scarred front door lunges inward, and the viewer is swept into a wainscotted hall of magnificent gloom. All in glorious black and white.

My breath caught when the imperious butler, complete with patent leather hair and penciled moustache, descended the stairs, a candle held aloft.

"Ladies and Gentlemen," he intoned, his voice dripping with gore, "I regret to be the bearer of inclement tidings." His lips crept into a travesty of a smile, emphasizing his unearthly pallor. "The master is dead of unnatural causes, and the will is as full of holes as cheese."

A shifty-eyed hush from the recipients of this news—a matriarch, who is clearly a man with eyes sharp as hatpins; a stout bespectacled schoolboy; and a bubble-head blonde fan dancer in working clothes, doing a half-hearted bump-and-grind while tearing a small piece of paper into confetti.

"That's your mother?" Ben whistled.

I shushed him. "No. Hers was just a non-speaking bit part in the chorus line scene. Don't let's miss . . ."

Too late. *Melancholy Mansion* faded out, to be replaced by a close-up of a greyhaired, broad-shouldered man with TV interviewer regulation features.

"Good evening. I'm Harvard Smith and this is *Talk Time*. What you just saw was a scene from one of actress Theola Faith's most popular films. We have in the studio with us this evening her daughter Mary Faith, author of the newly released, bestseller, *Monster Mommy*, an exposé of the chilling childhood she experienced at the hands of the woman known to millions as Kitten Face, the sexy comedienne who during the fifties and sixties paid the rent of movie houses across the country."

The cameras shifted across the table, past two glasses and a water jug, to the woman who had readers turning pages on land and in the air, a woman with a rubber stamp smile and cookie-cutter features. Hair tailored into a French twist, she sported wing-tipped glasses. Her age was forty and fibbing.

"Thank you, Harvard." Her woolly voice complemented the double-breasted trouser suit and bow tie. Picking up a pencil, she put it down. "As your guest this evening, I take the opportunity to reassure any of my mother's fans who may be listening that I feel pain for their disillusionment. Please believe me"—her face softened with the quivering of her mouth—"I did not write *Monster Mommy* to pay Theola Faith back for the years of neglect—the cocktail parties in the bathtub, Father Christmas coming down the chimney wearing only soot."

"The chicken noodle soup game shocked me, Mr. Unshockable." Interviewer Harvard solicitously handed her a glass of water.

Mary Faith set it down. "Through my book, which was sheer migraine to write, I am reaching out to the woman who for years denied my existence, passing me off as her maid's daughter, keeping me a virtual prisoner in a plush Hollywood mansion. To her, I say, Mommy, it is not too late. You can change. You can become a human being. If—*when*—you do, I'll be waiting, arms outstretched. I won't ask my father's name, I won't ask why you had me dressed as a boy until I was six and put my best doll down the garbage disposal. All I ask is three little words—'I'm sorry, baby.' "

Interviewer Harv stretched a smile. "Mary, you're sure one courageous woman. During the break you mentioned your mother sent you a death threat for your birthday."

"Yes, Harvard! But knowing I had pursued truth took much of the sting out of her words."

"You don't take her threats seriously?"

Oops! Mary Faith had knocked over her glass. The camera closed in on her fixed smile. "Harvard, murder takes a certain strength of character that Theola Faith lacks. Coming out of the closet is the nicest thing I've done for myself in years, and I would like to make one thing perfectly clear. Behind every successful writer is a whale of a good agent and an inspired and inspiring editor. So, if I may, I wish to say thank you and God bless to Sadie Fishman and Monica Mary O'Bryan."

Whipping the control out of Ben's hand I blinked off the TV.

"Ellie!"

"I'm sorry," I folded down on the bed. "Suddenly I remembered the baby might have its ear pressed to the belly button keyhole. And I don't want him or her getting any ideas."

"Darling, you won't be a Monster Mommy," avowed the man in the Laura Ashley toga, as he switched on a bedside lamp.

"Ben, I've no credentials for the job. No prior experience. Tell me, if you were the baby would you be happy?"

His face and torso were air-brushed with the rosy glow from the lamp. Lying down beside me he soothed a hand down my arm. "Tell me more about your mother."

Turning away from him, I twisted my hair into a knot. "I have only wonderful memories of her. She was beautiful, clever, and breathtakingly *thin*. She was like a Christmas sparkler bursting into the air in a shower of silver light. My father adored her. When she died, he escaped into his midlife amusement park and has never jumped off the merry-go-round."

"You've got me," Ben murmured against my neck.

"Do you come with a free coupon for dinner?"

"I was wondering about room service," he said, undoing the toga and drawing me inside.

'Twas the middle of the night and I awoke to sweating, heartpounding terror. Where was I? The room was a black box with threads of light breaking in through the cracks. As for the person in bed beside me, I reached out and felt blindly over his face until slowly the familiar feel of him warmed my hands and I was able to settle back against the pillows. My breathing slowed. This had happened before on trips away from home ever since Child Ellie paid that first fateful visit to Merlin's Court. And this time the change in time zones didn't help when it came to dozing off again. At home this would be mid-morning.

Hugging my pillow, I remembered I'd forgotten my evening prayers. "Please God, I don't mind whether the baby is a boy or a girl, so long as it's thin. And while we are having this little talk, please don't ever get the idea that I want to be famous."

I was sinking back down into the glorious welter of sleep when Ben tapped me on the shoulder with a finger that felt like a mallet. "Wakey! Wakey!"

The ensuing scene was from a speeded-up horror movie. I was thrust into a steaming shower, spun around, towel-dried, hurtled into my clothes. Still raking a comb through my hair, I ran out the door, raced down the stairs, skidded across the lobby and out onto the street where I was assaulted by brutal Boston sunlight.

What a ghastly mistake I'd made wearing the salmon pink silk shift. My face would clash with it in minutes. The sky was bleached almost white, and though we were walking fast, my shoes kept sticking to the pavement like hot irons on nylon undies.

"What's the obscene rush?" I asked the mad dog of an Englishman who had brought us out in the 8:00 A.M. sun. His looking as though he'd just been lifted from the tissue paper of an Austin Reed box made me no less cross.

"Sweetheart, do we want to waste the day?" His eyes shifted away from mine. Naively, I thought he was making sure we didn't get nailed by one of several cars, all trying to beat the amber light, as we dashed across the brick street, heavy on charm and hard on the feet. For one bulgy-eyed moment I feared I'd have to vault the bonnet of the last car between me and the pavement, or—as was my habit when faced with leaping the Wooden Horse at school—crawl underneath. All by way of explaining that I still didn't twig that Ben was keeping something from me when he guided me toward the Golden Arches and into McDonalds.

On home soil he would only have entered such a place feet first. But surely the possibility had occurred to him that here in Boston Mangés' spies might be anywhere! To be fair, he sounded edgy when ordering for us and sought out a table screened by plastic leaves entwined around the brass rail room divider. But he had almost finished his Egg McMuffin before he even broached the possibility of danger.

"Ellie, this is great! I may find myself fighting an irresistible urge to return."

"Good heavens! I don't know which I dread more—
your having a fling with a fast woman or fast food!"

Ben insisted we go back for seconds. Big mistake. The
red-headed man ahead of us was telling the sweet young
thing who was trying to take his order about the book he
was reading.

"First time in my life I didn't just read the jacket notes."
Voice deep with pride.

"Say, you talking about *Monster Mommy*?" This came
from the wisp of a woman behind us.

Without a do-you-mind, a burly man in a hard hat
elbowed me sideways. "Anyone here hate the part about
the Sunday outings to *that place* as much as I did? Dang
me, if I wasn't afraid to sleep with the light out and me born
and bred in the Bronx. That poor Mary kid! A mother like
that, who needs enemies? My dad always had the hots for the
Sex Kitten and now Mom's laughing fit to bust a zipper."

I could feel varicose veins popping up in my legs as I stood
there. And we English are always yabbering on about the pace
of life in the States being too fast! Still, my discomfort wasn't
only physical. I was beginning to feel pursued by those words:
Monster Mommy. I wanted to swat them away, pluck them
out of my hair. Wouldn't you know that when we got back to
our table we found droppings on it—cigarette ash and a
copy of *People* magazine, with the Monster Theola Faith's
face blazing up at me from the cover. A hasty thumb through,
while Ben devoured his milkshake, brought me to a three-
page spread: "Is Motherhood Becoming a Questionable Activity?" A profile shot of Mary Faith, all nose and headscarf,
followed by a lengthy comment from the Monster Mum on
her daughter's sizzling bestseller. "Why wouldn't darling
Mary's book be a smash! I'm sure she stuck to words she
can spell—the four-letter ones."

"What's up, sweetheart? A ghost walk over your grave?"
Ben asked.

"Two. The Tramwells." How it all came back, the dire
warnings about the Black Cloud, followed almost in the
same breath by their mention of Theola Faith, a person

linked to my mother's one and only trip to America. The fates would certainly seem to be up to something fishy . . . Time to leave. Time to pull myself together. Happily, my unease soon melted, along with the ice cube I dropped inside the front of my dress before braving the scorching heat again.

Ben advocated that we leave the black sports car in the Mulberry Inn's parking lot while we took buses or walked. If I hadn't been afraid of breaking his pioneering spirit, I would have asked if we'd rented the vroom-vroom so we could go out and pet it once in a while. A woman's patience is never done. Best turn my energy to embracing the opportunities for self-enrichment Boston offered.

My education in history had been hampered by teachers who classified anything after 1750 as current events. I would be newly educated knowing that Paul Revere charged travelling expenses incurred in stabling his horse to the Massachusetts Bay Colony when we British were coming. The great patriot's first wife (so sayeth our bus driver guide) departed this vale of tears after bearing him numerous offspring. And Wife Number Two, we learned, did in the goodness of time shoulder her yoke in the cause. Previously, I had not pondered why Mr. Revere was out roaming about on his horse, come night time, in the vicinity of the Old North Church. Now all was made plain. Hubby had been booted from the bedchamber and the house.

Trailing after my husband, down endless pale green museum halls, peering into glass cabinets at sets of mangled spurs and rusted water flasks, I sensed that history may well have hinged on one woman—a good woman clutching the bedsheets to her beleaguered breast and snarling, "Husband, enough! Am I not prithee already stretchmarked from head to toe?"

Some things can only be understood by members of the oldest club in the world.

Back on the outdoor trail we peered over an iron fence— the sort that looks like a row of spears held in the hands of the unseen enemy—into a heroes' graveyard. Rain fell in gentle teardrops as we continued to explore. We also serve who only stand and stare at doorway plaques. So-and-so dwelt, served, and plotted in these narrow houses with the white paintwork and scrub-worn steps. The so-and-so's all being men. Their women being too busy raising little patriots to do anything meaningful. Thank God for this modern age, when being female doesn't mean being kept in the dark.

Brushing aside cobwebs of rain, Ben aimed his Nikon at the Old North Church. "All this fresh air has done you the world of good, sweetheart. Your cheeks glow like pomegranates." The camera went back into his pocket and he took my hand. "Think my blue tie with the red and gold stripes would be suitable for my first Mangé Meeting?"

"Splendid," I said. A pair of lovers passed us, entwined like a Rodin sculpture. Someone kicked an empty Coke bottle toward a litter bin, where it reeled drunkenly. "May one ask where you are to make contact?"

Ben squinted like a Siamese cat. Meaning he didn't look at me. "Good question, Ellie. I think we should start making tracks immediately after lunch."

"So soon!" How had I latched on to the idea we were to be blessed with two or three days to ourselves? Feeling rotten, I must have done some hearing without listening. Said reflections kept me from noticing that Ben had sidestepped my question, the way we were stepping around the banjo player seated cross-legged on the pavement. Whither my love went I would go, but I was no wiser where.

Taking hold of my hand he galloped us along. "Sweetheart, I don't want to rush you."

"What, and spoil a lovely, leisurely day?"

"Has it been . . . nice?" Maybe an insect got him in the eye; maybe he didn't twitch, but I got the peculiar idea that he hoped Boston failed to meet my expectations. Of course. *Yes, We Deliver* does say pregnancy effects men in strange ways.

During lunch in a restaurant whose marble slab and stainless steel decor suggested a converted fish morgue,

Ben confessed that he hadn't been impressed with the harbour.

"What did you expect, boats shaped like teapots?"

And, later, when we were organizing our luggage in the boot of the black convertible, he claimed the proprietress of the Mulberry Inn had looked suspicious when he paid in cash.

"Well, darling, that *was* quite a wad you flashed her. I did wonder myself if you had nipped out to rob the corner bank while I was in the bathroom."

"I wanted to use up the cash Dorcas gave us before starting on the traveller's cheques."

"Sensible. When she offered us the remains of her U.S. money, I thought she was talking about loose change. Maybe Dorcas robbed a bank?"

Three women with spray net hair, about to enter the car parked next to us, clutched their handbags. All had the initials D.A.R. monogrammed on their knit suits. Was it my little jest about Dorcas that had shocked them or our British accents? Would one of them lift up her skirt, whip out a musket from her garter, and cry, "Charge!"?

"Come along, Doris."

"Yes, Dillis Ann."

"You going in the back, Deborah?"

Away they went with an engine blast that rocked my socks. Ben, tossing in the last of the bags, closed the boot and narrowly missed losing a hand. "You do have the traveller's cheques?"

"Gave them to me yourself, didn't you, sir?" I patted my shoulder bag. "Said I'd be mincemeat for Christmas if anything untoward happened to them. And while we're on the subject, I've never fully grasped what you have against credit cards."

"A foible which dates back to my days with Eligibility Escorts." He was nursing a finger of his left hand. "Some insensitive clod of a woman, having hired me to be her date at a grouse shoot, wanted to put me on one of her charge cards."

"What?" I cried, aghast.

"Ellie, please!" His black brows slashed together. "I've never made a secret of my past."

"You never told me you put on woolly britches to kill wee animals."

"If it makes you happier," he said as he came around the side of the car, "I missed every shot. Miss God's-Gift-to-Herself thought I was a complete incompetent and refused to pay me at all." He held the car door open for me. "Why are you wearing that face?"

"Why am I sitting in the driver's seat?"

Stepping backward, he almost got deveined by a motorcyclist zooming into the parking lot. "Because I want you to drive."

"Never! Dr. Melrose said I must not put my foot to the pedal on foreign soil."

One of those much vaunted earth-stopping silences.

"Sweetheart, there's nothing to driving over here. And I can't find my glasses."

"You put them in the glove compartment."

"True enough. I didn't want to worry you but . . ." Wincing, he held out his hand and averted his eyes. "You remember the time I poisoned my finger and nearly died?"

"Rings a bell."

"I caught it with the boot lid just now."

"Ben, it's not the same finger."

"Isn't it?" Brow furrowed, he prodded the nail. "Well, do you concede it's the same hand and that Dr. Melrose warned me to be exceedingly careful of post trauma? Ellie, I can't take any risks. Not now. If you drive for an hour or so and I give my hand complete lap rest—"

I shook the wheel, hoping it would come off and end this madness. "I can't learn to do two new things at once. Pregnancy is enough. Driving on the wrong side of the road is too much."

He slid in beside my gibbering self, drew a pen from his breast pocket and triumphantly scrawled an *R* on my right hand.

In the first flush of marriage I had thought I owed Ben

my life. But not my life's blood. A thousand curses on his head! May his anti-perspirant fail in the middle of a Mangé Meeting!

Shaking like a paint pot in the grip of one of those mixing machines, I turned the key in the ignition. *Vroooommmm.* The car shot backward, snapping my neck like a dandelion stalk. Into a sickening skid before hurtling toward the parking lot exit. My foot had yet to touch the accelerator. The car rental man had spoken true when saying the car would take off with or without driver intervention. We were about to enter traffic in a single bound over four jam-packed lanes. Would we land on a car? Or something taller—providing a better view of the city?

No time to hit the brake. I swung the wheel left—or do I mean right? Brilliant instinctive ploy. The sweat dried on my brow. Perhaps if I kept up not actually hitting anything . . .

"Feeling better?" Ben rubbed my shoulder. "Told you there was nothing to it."

I couldn't bite his good hand without taking my eyes off the road. The street was postively littered with traffic lights.

"Sweetheart, I'm doing this for you. What would you do if something should happen to me?"

"Marry a chauffeur," I snarled.

Traffic lights charged at us. And, making misery perfect, rain started down in slow, heavy plops. Barely enough to dampen a pile of ironing, but a little goes a long way in a convertible. Ben hates to drive in cars with the lids down because of his claustrophobia.

"Want me to close . . . ?" He pointed a magnanimous finger upwards; heavens, it was the injured one! Gently he restored his hand to his lap as if it were a sickly and dearly loved puppy.

"No." When we were sitting waist-deep in water, the man might realize what a prize—idiot—I was.

Endeavouring to milk every ounce of fun, I pretended I was playing one of those driver safety games on a small

screen. The kind where you can get killed more than once
with no side effects. Vehicles, pedestrians, buildings whizzed
by.

"How far to our destination?"

"Sweetheart, follow the signs to the motorway." Ben
sounded a bit choked up. Was he also catching pneumonia?
Never mind that. Was I ever going to get a straight answer?
"Somewhere outside Boston," he had said when persuading
me to answer the Mangé call with him. Truth finally reared
its ugly head. I was about to spend the next several days
one hundred miles from here in a suburb of a suburb.

No time to extort a confession. Lots of honking from
outside the car. Was that woman in the Volvo waving hello
to a friend? Or shaking her fist at me? Feeling unwelcome
in my lane, I switched and managed a nip-and-tuck retreat.
Ben was pretending to be asleep. All was coming back to
me now—the way he turned green at the airport when I
mentioned being met by the Mangés, the way our sightseeing had been accomplished with the speed of a fast-forwarded
video cassette.

Poor baby's finger, my foot! He had insisted I drive
because he didn't want my hands free when the truth sank
in! Even his lovemaking of last night now attained sinister
connotations.

Wiping my face free of rain, the better to glare at him,
my heart turned traitor. He looked so innocent with his hair
damp and rumpled. Hadn't I brought this on myself by
being so difficult about this trip? Upon my admitting I
wouldn't mind seeing Boston, he must have been elated
that the Mangé meeting place was in the general vicinity.

Abstraction had turned me into a regular will-o'-the-
wisp driving one handed; now a truck dive-bombed in front
of me. Inadvertently I risked changing lanes again. Strange!
The car immediately in front of me had a little white flag
waving from its bonnet. So too, did the car in front of him.
Time for a rear view mirror inspection. The car behind me
had a flag. I was being pursued by a line of flags. My
clammy hands slid off the wheel. I was remembering an

American film I had watched recently. Opening scene—a
funeral. These cars were headed for the cemetery, and I
was among the mourners, without a wreath in my hand.
Faces pressed against the back window of the car in front
of us. The traffic in the other lane hooked together for
a mile.

"Ben!" I whimpered.

"What?" He bolted upright.

"Nothing." Rain teemed down, bawling in sympathy.
A huge green and white sign flashed before my eyes.

Interstate.

Ben wrenched a piece of paper from his pocket. "Ellie,
this is where we get off . . . I mean on."

"Thanks for the advance warning." Drying my face on
my sleeve, I gripped the wheel, sucked in my breath and
plunged sideways.

Heading onto the ramp. The wipers being unable to
keep up with the down-put, I can't tell whether I'm supposed to be going thirty-five or fifty-five miles per hour.
Merge! screams the sign now hurtling toward me. Somebody's idea of a joke? To my left flows a river of trucks,
each one taller than the average house, each one rocking in the wind. My hands keep sliding off the wheel.
My ramp is dwindling to keyhole size. My feet cramp and
go dead.

"Merge!" Ben shouts.

I close my eyes and do as I am told.

Peace descended on my soul. The road unwound before me like black oil cloth, and the rain stopped as though
God had snapped his fingers. Boston gave way to hills and
fields, all sliding by like a giant mural. Surely that was a
rainbow overhead? I was beginning to like the Colonies.
Turning on the radio to a melodious hum, I flexed my
fingers and smiled at Ben.

"Where to, Mr. Haskell, sir?"

His hair was washed Brutus-style over his forehead.
And Brutus was an honourable man. "Sweetheart"—he
made a valiant effort to muster his charm—"I may have
misrepresented or should I say . . ."

"Lied?"

"That's the word."

I patted him on the shoulder. "I'm not angry, really. Every place has some charm." My hands fell off the wheel. Had I blindly, ungratefully misunderstood the quality of his silence? Had he planned a wonderful surprise for me all along?

I began steering again. "Is it that sort of place? Somewhere small and out of the way? Steeped in witchcraft, with a treasure trove of antique shops and a little white church on the hill?"

A death rattle sigh. "Sweetheart, I'm sure the folks of Mud Creek, Illinois think it is all that and more."

Had Christopher Columbus reached Illinois he would have realized he was wrong about the world being round. Here was a land flatter than the ocean on a stone calm day. The road sliced broad and straight through cornfields stretching from here to eternity. Even the trees had been set down courtesy of the Tourist Board, the way people put those miniature ornamental ones on Christmas cakes. Any moment now, Mr. and Mrs. Bentley T. Haskell, in their LuxaLease convertible, would reach the Dead End sign and plummet into infinity.

I had forgiven Ben his wicked deceit. I even understood why he hadn't booked flights from Boston to Mud Creek. Who wants to land on a runway that gets rolled up at night? And to be fair to him, the man was completely incapable of translating the vastness of America into English terms. England is a country of day trippers. Dorcas and Jonas had quite thought when they went to Chicago that they would be able to motor off to the Grand Canyon, spend the night, and be back the next evening. Ben was a little more realistic. He appreciated that Mud Creek, Illinois, was a goodly distance from Boston, but he had figured it would be on a par with driving from Scotland to Devon, not from London to Warsaw.

I hadn't even complained when we stayed at the Happy Hang Out Hotel, in Plainsville, Ohio, last night. We had been lost for hours when we thought we were right, and right for miles when we thought we were lost. All I had asked then was to lie back upon pillows the thickness of sliced bread. And enjoy my migraine. What I couldn't forgive was this merciless heat. Ben's idolatrous obsession with the Mangés was the cause. Who could blame God for turning the heavens into an inferno?

"Water?" I whispered through parched lips.

Ben squeezed my shoulder. His finger had made a miraculous recovery. "Sweetheart, I offered to put the top up."

"Mustn't spoil the view."

"I'll stop at the next exit."

The sun was the yolk of a fried egg surrounded by a white of cloud. My frock clung damply to my body. Voluptuously appealing perhaps in someone with a model figure, but between breakfast and lunch I had added several more pounds to my misery.

"Ben, look at those birds."

He followed the angle of my finger. "What about them? They're just flapping along minding their own business."

"They've been following us for an hour."

"Ellie," he adjusted those same glasses he claimed to have lost when insisting I drive, "those are a few harmless crows."

"Wrong. They're vultures waiting to pick our bones clean the minute we admit that this cruel land has won."

"You said you liked Chicago—"

"Loved it. I *would* have liked to stop and buy a post card." The moment the words were out I regretted I hadn't snapped at him sooner. Clear the air and start anew. Knowing marriage is oft times a bed of nettles makes the roses smell sweeter.

Entering the parking lot of the Log Cabin Diner, he

asked in a voice fraught with tenderness whether I had the traveller's cheques handy, because he was down to a couple of dollars of Dorcas' money.

"Right here, darling!" I jiggled my bag strap as we drew into a space along side the doorway. Optimism fired my soul. Our marriage was stronger for having been tested. "Won't be a second."

Ben watched me drag out my huge key ring, my packet of tissues, my mother-in-law's letter . . . "Ellie," he said in wry amusement, "you cart around stuff that's useless as an umbrella in the desert."

I shoved my hair out of my eyes. "Good news! I've found my comb. It's in two pieces but who's counting?"

"This place could be closing any minute."

"Silly," I soothed, "it's only six o'clock and nothing ever closes in this land of convenience." I spilled the contents of my makeup bag over my lap. "Maybe I put them in the side pocket." My hands stopped rummaging and started trembling.

The love light faded from his eyes. "Don't tell me you've lost them."

I never could understand Henry VIII's wives laying their heads down on the block, all nice and neat, waiting for the blow to fall. Now, fighting for my life, I realized that Ben was bigger than I remembered. "Those cheques are here. Just give me an hour or so to keep looking."

Ben was furious in that intensely masculine way of his. A growl tore from his lips, backing me against the door.

"Say it!" I counterattacked. "Say you should never have trusted them to me! Say the holiday is ruined. Say I've dished your chances of becoming a Mangé."

A lion's roar of thunder, coming out of the blue, drowned whatever it was he did say. Seconds later the sky darkened, I felt the first plop of rain, and remembered the Black Cloud. Chapter Three of *Growing Babies From Seeds* stressed that odd fancies are common.

Bunging everything back in my bag, I flared, "Kindly remember, darling, who drove me to a state of nerves where I'm turned inside out and back to front."

He feigned patience. "Nothing gained in turning this into a merry-go-round of blame. Could you have put them in another bag or a pocket?"

"No."

"When was the last time you saw them?"

"Don't talk to me in that tone. I am not a suspect in a robbery."

"I gave them to you at the airport."

"So you did." Rain descended at quite a clip now, blurring his face and the whole miserable business, until . . . Memory struck like a blade between the ribs. Me—reading my mother-in-law's letter, with all its dire warnings, to Ben on the plane. And the charming oriental gentleman saying, Very many bad people in this world. Oh, surely he couldn't have been a gloating pickpocket? But think of Aunt Lulu! Looks like a middle-aged Shirley Temple and would steal the gold teeth out of a corpse.

"Oh, hell!" Ben slumped back against his seat. "What's the point! They're gone. Too much to hope, I suppose, that you purchased American Expr—"

"The bank was having a promotion on another brand, one apostle teaspoon for every five hundred pounds."

"Pity," he remarked. "But thank God we have the receipts. We do have receipts, don't we, Ellie?"

I knotted my fingers into a cat's cradle.

"You left them in the folder with the cheques?" He doubled in bulk like the bread dough he is forever making. "I believe, Ellie, that is a federal offence over here."

People were emerging from the Log Cabin Diner looking well-fed and happy. Dreadful to think two dollars stood between us and starvation. Could we go in and pretend we had forgotten our doggie bag?

Shame! Food should be meaningless when the life of a loved one hangs in tatters. Ben did not have to explain to me—although he did so—repeatedly, that he was due at the Mangés' Mud Creek headquarters at seven-thirty that evening, meaning there was no time for us to go and throw ourselves on the mercy of the nearest police station.

When everything had been said that could be said to

make matters worse, Ben jammed in the ignition key and the car purred back onto the motorway. Not a companionable silence this. He had done the decent thing and purchased me a small carton of milk. While I sipped, he ostentatiously tightened his seat belt.

The road unwound like paper towel being blown on the wind. The trees whizzing passed us were beaten into fans and my hair kept escaping from its knot and flapping in my eyes. . . . I came to with a start to find that Ben had pulled over to the side of the road and was turning off the engine.

"Time for a Thermos break?" My voice polluted the air with sarcasm. "After all your talk about time being scarcer than a good woman." He was slumped over the wheel. He'd had a heart attack . . . he was dead! How could he do this to me—leave me a widow out here in the middle of nowhere? I grabbed his shoulders and pried up his head.

"Ellie, we're out of gas."

This was worse than death. If I hadn't lost the traveller's cheques, he would have bought petrol at the Log Cabin pumps. Now even if we could cut through this jungle of corn and reach life-giving fuel, what were the chances that we would be allowed to write an I.O.U.? I tried to reassure Ben that the Mangés would be understanding, that having assembled to meet him they wouldn't turn tail and go home just because he was five minutes—or five hours—late. But my voice was blown away on the wind and I wasn't sure whether that was rain or tears on my face when his hand closed over mine.

"You mustn't blame yourself, sweetheart." His voice was a quiet blend of fatigue and heroism. "I'm beginning to believe in Chantal's Black Cloud."

Being wet and scared was bad enough, but doomed? I wasn't physically up to that. Opening my bag, I rummaged around for a tissue and drew out the envelope containing my mother-in-law's letter. Funny, it felt bulkier than I remembered. And no wonder! Inside the envelope were the traveller's cheques.

"Ben, I see it all now! I must have stuffed them in with

the letter when I dropped my bag in the airplane loo and got in such a panic. When I think of how I blamed that innocent oriental gentleman . . ."

My love wasn't listening. He was standing on his seat. Arms waving wildly, he shouted, "Saved! Saved!" Miraculously the wind had died, the rain stopped and the sun burst in blazing splendour through the clouds. And a car was easing to a stop behind us. The couple inside thought Ben was shouting "Help! Help!" What ambassadors of goodwill. Dr. Bernie Wetchler and his wife Jorie from Peoria. They produced a petrol tin, did the honours and waving aside our thanks, sped on their way.

"Awfully decent of them to come braking to the rescue. I must say, darling, it quite restores my faith in human nature; from this moment forward I am done with all superstitious folly. What's the matter, do you have something in your eye?"

"No, sweetheart." A grin got the better of him. "I hate to burst your bubble but they pulled over because they had reached a madly exciting part in the book the wife was reading aloud."

"Don't tell me . . . not *Monster Mommy*! Ben, that horrible book is *following* us!"

He drew me to him. "Hush! A while back it was vultures. You're exhausted, and I'm a thoughtless devil to put you through such a journey in your condition. Let's shake the dust of this place off our feet. Not another cross word the entire holiday, I swear!"

My darling was right. We must focus on the road ahead.

We were back in the mainstream of life. If Ben gave the car its head he might make his Mangé Meeting on time.

Mud Creek, population four hundred and thirty-six. Its charm lay in the convenience factor. Getting lost here would be difficult. Main Street was backed by fields and faced the muddy Illinois River. Driving past Nelga's Fashions, with its One Size Fits All print frock in the window, I reflected that this might be the ideal hideout for the compulsive shopper. We drove past The Scissor Cut Hair Salon, the

Lucky Strike Bowling Alley, and a corner cafe with a cardboard menu in the window. Approaching a set of traffic lights strung on sagging wire and now level with Jimmy's Bar, a corrugated brick building with Old West saloon doors. Would a spurred boot kick them open, sending a couple of bodies somersaulting onto the dusty pavement? Would a gun-twirling, tobacco-chewing Bad Guy saunter into the middle of the street and, with the sun as his backdrop, order us to get the hell back to Dodge?

"Ben, you never told me why the Mangés chose Mud Creek."

"Who would suspect them of holding meetings here?"

"Clever."

Time for me to start worrying about the impression I was about to make. Peering in my compact mirror I saw the sun had done a job on my nose, but I didn't have time to repine. A series of jolting bumps and Ben swung the car into a curve. Were we here? Was this the place? No, unless the Mangé meeting place was a petrol station with antique pumps. Parking beside the rusted fizzy drink machine, Ben announced he would check his directions and, if necessary, ask assistance.

"Isn't the house on Main Street?"

Ben unfolded the Mangé communique and cupped it with his hands. "Sorry, sweetheart! You realize I would be breaking faith if I let you see even the signature."

"Am I to be taken there blindfolded?"

"The house is Mendenhall, named for the first owner. No harm telling you Josiah Mendenhall was a whisky baron who made his fortune from distilled corn. That's bourbon," he added kindly.

"And I thought the smell of the river was what I was imbibing," I informed Ben's back. He had leaped out of the saddle—I mean over the side of the car—and made for the glass door of the garage. Soon he was joined by another head and I could see hands pointing.

Gosh, I was tired. What heaven an hour's soak in a hot scented bath! Easing back against my seat, eyes half closed, I studied the warehouse style building across the street.

Was it the distillery? Had old Josiah used the river for transportation? Through a gap between the garage and a putty-coloured frame house with sagging veranda, I could see a stretch of water and what might be a lighthouse, rising up from a tiny island.

Aunt Astrid's warning—that no good comes of superfluous thought—came back to haunt me. I was shaken out of my revery with sufficient violence to throw me against the dashboard. Fast on the heels of fright came the crystal clear realization that I had been rear-ended.

That our car had been parked minding its own business and that I had not done the parking did not prevent me from blaming my lack of U. S. driving experience for the accident. A driver was coming around the side of my car. He was a hulk of a man. His seersucker jacket flapped open, his yellowish white locks lifted in the air with the force of his stride. Wildly, I looked toward the glass door for Ben. But the heads had disappeared.

Nothing to do but assume an assertive smile and remember I was a British subject.

The man was holding a leaflet. A do-it-yourself summons? "Don't you go worrying yourself, young lady, not a lick of damage on yours and no more than a scratch on my old jalopy."

"That's nice." If only Ben would hurry up! There was something about this man I didn't like: he had failed to comment on my charming English accent. Other than that he was too genial. His smile took up the entire bottom half of his face, revealing higgledy-piggledy teeth of the same yellow as his hair. Mesmerized, I let out a screech when a woman's face peered over his shoulder. A washed out face with faded auburn hair. She stood two paces behind him, twisting the front of her colourless sweater into a knot.

"A blessed evening this!" The man lifted his face to the sky, and radiance overtook his features, spoiled, alas, by those teeth.

"Perfect," I said.

The woman risked a smile, then took it back.

"Try as sinful man may, he cannot destroy all that is good! Is that not so, ma'am?"

"Very true."

"Young lady, I worry that you drive a high-priced car. But I don't judge you. My hope is you are numbered among those who are mightily concerned about the wickedness that is overtaking the American family." Lifting a hand to smooth back his hair, he continued to hold it aloft to keep sin at bay.

"Not really." I backed away from his smile. "Everyone I have met since coming to this country has been most frightfully kind."

"The devil has his sidekicks. Don't we know that, Laverne?"

"That's so, yes it is, Enoch," the woman said.

"I really do have to be going," I stammered.

His face burrowed through the window as I slid over to the driver's seat. "Young lady, I must ask the question. Are you saved?"

Was I morally obliged to tell this Pharisee that I attended service regularly at St. Anselm's and was working on bringing Jonas back to the fold by insisting he take the altar flowers over himself? "Saved? I felt perfectly safe until you crashed into me."

"The workings of Providence." Enoch bent his head for a moment of silent prayer, before thrusting at me the leaflet he had been clutching. "We pass through this life but once, and in the infinite wisdom of His ways it may be written that we do not meet again. Read and all will be made plain. Young lady, this very evening you go on our regular prayer list. For a donation in that there envelope you can be added to our Blessed Brethren portfolio."

When Ben emerged one minute later, the old jalopy was a rumble in the distance and I had voted unanimously not to mention the collision if he did not. I didn't think I would go to hell for keeping quiet. I looked at the pamphlet, *One Hundred and One Deadly Sins*, and was aghast to discover that it was the work of the Diethelogians, the very group my mother-in-law had warned about so eloquently in her letter. The Food Haters. Those fanatics who earned extra stars in their halos if they fought the good fight with the archfiends—chefs. Ben must not be allowed to fall prey to the Diethelogians. As eccentrics went, the Mangés might not be so bad.

"Sweetheart?" Ben loomed over me much as Enoch had done. "I didn't mean to startle you."

"You didn't; I squealed to clear my lungs."

"Ellie, I was gone so long because I discovered I needed more than directions to the Mangé meeting place."

"Really?" Oh, how I did love his teeth, but why didn't he get back in the car, instead of standing, hands behind his back like the Duke of Edinburgh? Why that haunted look in his eyes, that desperate note in his voice?

"Ellie, Mendenhall is located on an island in the middle of the river."

"Darling, what a kick in . . . the knee!" A glance at my watch showed twenty minutes past seven. Ten minutes to get to his Mangé Meeting. No wonder he was in a tizz! But surely the Mangés would not refuse to conduct the interviews because he was a trifle late. We must not let panic drag us by the coattails. I offered to drive if he would relay instructions on how to get to the ferry.

Ben's face was pale. "There isn't one."

"Can we rent a boat?"

He opened the car door. "We are wasting precious time! I purchased a boat."

"A what?" My mind became a slide show of yachts, motor boats, sail boats, tankers. "You mean you bought a boat sight unseen from the garage attendant?"

"He was a decent chap, though not at all forthcoming about who owns Mendenhall—the Mangés are apparently borrowing it for the weekend and he had some foolish misgivings about the organization."

"Where is this boat docked?"

"Right here." Bringing his hands out into the open, he held out an orange package, not much bigger than a plastic raincoat in a zipper bag, along with a pair of over-sized

wooden salad stirrers. "Just what you always wanted, Ellie!
An inflatable rowing boat."

"Didn't it come in other colours?" I asked.

Time being of the essence, Ben began blowing up the
Nell Gwynn as I drove toward the dock. Thank God for a
convertible. The boat grew with frightening speed to un-
wieldy orange proportions. Ben could control it only by
kneeling on his seat, face to the rear. Even so, the thing
was like a whale, whapping back and forth. As I swerved
close to a shack on the mud track leading to the river, it
almost got away. I could picture it soaring out over the
water, then with a mighty hiccup plummeting like a gunned-
down bird into the briny depths.

"Will it hold our luggage?" Parking under a scroungy
weeping willow, I made a futile grab at the nether end of
Nellie.

Cheeks blown out like baseballs, Ben nodded. Moments later we carried our skiff over a scuffle of pebbles to a
stretch of mud the consistency of underdone toffee and
reached the river's edge.

"Here, let me—before you blow yourself up." Grabbing the nozzle from him I let out almost as much air as I let
in, but the feeling was terrific. At last! Here I was on an
even footing with all those other mums-to-be. The ones
who prop themselves against their executive desks, dab
white-out on the shadows under their eyes, and tirelessly
tackle the latest merger . . . or mop and glow the home
front with assorted infants under the age of four clinging to
their legs.

"Hurry!" Ben yelled, causing me to nearly swallow the
cap.

We rushed around in a blur of speed. Suitcases got
tossed aboard, and it was time to splash off.

"Come on, Ellie!" Clambering aboard, Ben held out
his hand.

The time had come for truth. "I can't! I've lied to you
about how much weight I've gained. My feet will go through

the bottom. Ouch!" He landed me like a fish. Crossing to my section was like walking in a net. One of my legs kept getting longer than the other.

He tossed me a grin along with the oars. "The island is straight ahead. Mind doing the honours, while I wipe the mud off my shoes, darling? Can't arrive looking thoroughly disreputable, can I?"

"Heaven forbid!" Strange to tell I was quite the oarswoman. A sport where I got to sit down could not fail to appeal. Meet Ellie Haskell, captain of the St. Roberta's team. Fondly known as the Skullduggeries. Plunging my salad spoons into the bronze water, I felt good. The air smelled liked sun-baked algae and my love looked rakishly wonderful. His hair expensively disheveled, his tan a twenty-four hour success story. Mendenhall was still too far away for me to make out its features clearly.

"Deuced jolly, being bumped along in a sofa without springs, right, sweetheart?" Ben took the oars.

"Still worried about being late?"

"Not frightfully." His elegant stroking revealed all was in the wrist. "Blowing up this vessel helped clear my head." A flick of the oar sent a spray of fishy water my way. "The Mangés' letter talked tough about no commitment being made, but the petrol chap mentioned several out-of-town cars coming through today, and it hit me. The Society wouldn't congregate in a place like this—where you couldn't get fresh figs if your life depended on it—unless they need me."

"How did the Mangés get to the house?"

My informant grudgingly admitted the owner keeps a power boat; he imagined that would be sent out to meet those who arrived at the designated time . . . Ben's lips kept moving but the audio part of his statement was lost. Out of the watery wasteland there arose a geyser of spray, and rip-roaring through it came a motor vessel manned by two nauticals, spiffed out in white peaked caps.

Curling my lip, I trailed a hand overboard. "Aren't these Americans a bit much with their hobbies, darling? Have to wear the outfit!"

Ben was not amused . . . and rightly so. Why did

I never think before I sneered? This could well be our host boat.

"Ellie!" his howl penetrated the tempest, "It's the Coast Guard!"

"Oh, cripes!" If I prayed fast, would God grant us a puncture? Captains Glower and Grimace were zooming around us in a tidal wave, their scowls every bit as natty as their uniforms. Would they demand we produce our passports? Would they order us deported?

"Evening, sirs!" Attempting a salute, Ben almost knocked out his eye with an oar. "Just taking the little lady for a spin."

"May we suggest you take her somewhere less hazardous to her safety and that of other traffic." They spoke in unison in the monotone of a prerecorded message. "You be out of this channel within two minutes, or we'll have you towed in!"

"Aye, aye!" I said as they blasted off.

Grabbing up the oars, Ben smacked them in and out of the water, muttering, "Damned humiliating."

"With some people a little uniform goes a long way," I consoled, my eyes burning holes in the backs of the two nosy parkers. "Don't worry, darling, I'm sure the Mangés are too busy waiting for you to be gawking out of windows."

No answer but the rhythmic displacement of water.

The island appeared no bigger than a large rock even when the house moved into view. What an incredible monument to bad taste. Picture Josiah Mendenhall, whisky baron, thumping his fist on the table while demanding the best of everything. And everything was what he had got. The roof sprouted four onion domes plus one shaped like a bell. The grimy red brick was embellished with ironwork and lattice galore, and mustn't miss the moldy green shingles like fish scales, on the bow frontage. Some of the windows were stained glass, some were beveled; and the whole shebang was set down on a giant tea tray of a veranda. "Ben, Mendenhall is an absolute . . . gothic horror!"

The words came accompanied by a dizziness such as I had not experienced since my days of morning sickness.

Cleaving to the sides of the boat, I clung also to the hope that I was acting peculiar due to my condition. Anything was preferable to the recognizing that fate had made total fools of us.

"Ben!" Struggling to my knees, I grabbed his arm. "Don't you remember? Chantal spoke of the house being surrounded by water? We assumed she meant Merlin's Court because of the moat, and we didn't take the bit about fire and brimstone literally—but look at those sooty red bricks."

His yell of alarm was all I could have wished.

"Sit down!"

And so I did—with such a thump that an oar flew out of his hand. He made to grab for it, lunged too far, the boat did a spin, and before you could say bobbing for apples, we were both in the drink.

"Forgive me, darling," I spluttered. "I know this isn't how you pictured meeting the Mangés."

Belly-flopping back into the boat, my love said conversationally, "You do realize you've ruined my life?"

I didn't reply. Now was not the time to break the news that the house was Melancholy Mansion.

6

"There, darling! You look as good as new!" Not by a quiver of the voice would I reveal the smiting of unwifely jealousy when he poked fingers through his hair and the curl bounced right back. What did it matter if anyone thought I had joined Jonah in the belly of the whale? "Ben, if I spray you with this air freshener, we'll get rid of that last whiff of *eau de river*. Then you won't have to shy away whenever a Mangé gets close."

The boat house had proved a port in a storm. We had dragged in the deflated *Nell Gwynn*, the remaining oar, and our luggage. And by the time we had dragged on dry clothes, this place was home. Overlaying the rowing boats, canoes, lawn furniture, and coiled cobras of rope, was the safe, dry, stored-away smell of varnish. I never wanted to leave here. But two hearts can't always beat as one.

Ben wouldn't stand still for me to spray him. He kept hopping around, trying to put on two socks at once. His attempt at perching on a rowboat had resulted in his falling in. Poor darling! Boats had that effect on him one way or t'other.

"Ellie, put that stuff away. It's fly spray."

"Dear me!" Returning the tin to the shelf, I stuffed *Nell* into her little orange bag. "Darling, why don't you sit on that marble garden seat across from the canoes?"

"You think I've got time for a recess?" Backing up as he spoke, he sat down involuntarily on the seat in question, which skidded out from under, landing him on his rear. The awaited masonry crash was not forthcoming. A pity Ben did not keep equally quiet. But perhaps this wasn't the time to admonish with, Not in front of the baby. Tossing *Nell Gwynn* on the floor, I rushed to the rescue.

"You call yourself an interior decorator, Ellie? Your marble bench is as light as a melon shell."

"Hollow is right." Uprighting the object, I tapped knowledgeably. "Man-made Melolite, circa 1956. Convincing sand cast finish. Wouldn't you think it weighed a stone?"

"Would you mind foregoing the museum appraisal so we can get out of here before we're had up for vandalism? We'll come back for the luggage later."

"Brilliant," I agreed. Silly to mind that he hadn't complimented me on my looks. Did he think this navy frock with its sailor collar in poor taste? Usually he liked my hair looped into a plait on my neck, but working with only a compact mirror is never ideal.

Hurrying after him across the island my thoughts were herky jerky. Lamps flickered with glow worm brightness among the trees. A Lilliputian kingdom this. Not much more than three acres. A limestone realm, with stunted trees, an untidy lawn, and gloomy flower beds.

But was it Melancholy Mansion? Could this really be the gothic house featured in the film my mother had made with Theola Faith? Back at the boat house I'd decided I was the dupe of my imagination. Too much *Monster Mommy*. And seeing that televised clip in Boston had dredged up forgotten guilt stemming from not having gone to see my mother in the film. But what I should bear in mind was that she would never have set foot here, even if the house were used for the set. Her part in the chorus had been shot at a nightclub in Chicago. Mounting the rugged steps behind

Ben to the front door I wasn't sure of anything except that this could well be the devil's summer residence. Mud Creek would be hell for some people.

"Wonder what they do for electricity?" I watched Ben reach for the knocker, which was in the shape of a clenched fist.

"Imagine they have a generator."

The door was framed by panels of stained glass. Roman ladies eating grapes. Was that the clump-clump of approaching feet or the echo of the knocker? Wrong on both counts. The culprit was a loose drainpipe smacking against the wall overhead.

Did the island possess a well or must the inhabitants boil and strain river water? What was that? Another false alarm? No! The door was creaking open. Immediately I was ten years old again—sent all alone to visit Great Uncle Merlin.

"Yes?" A flickering light, emanating from a candle, haloed the speaker. He was tall, despite being stooped, and bald as a light bulb. His face was wrinkled, his hands trembled with the palsy, but his ice blue eyes never wavered from our faces. "Your names please?"

"Bentley Haskell." Why had I never noticed Ben had the smile of a salesman with six starving children and a dying mother at home? "And this my lovely wife Giselle."

"Late, ain't you!" reproved the Greeter.

Yanking on his tie, Ben almost put himself out of his misery. "My heartwrung apologies! A series of unforeseen, unfortunate occurrences—"

"No excuses!" The candle shook with ire, dripping wax on my hand. "I am the Keeper of the Door. And your instructions was specific. Time of arrival—seven thirty." Cupping a hand to his ear, the Greeter harkened to a clock chiming five times somewhere in the cavernous house. "You hear that? Twenty minutes past eight. Ain't none gets to thumb their noses at the Mangé mandate. Out! I say, out the both of you."

"What do you mean, out?" I glared him. "We're not even in!" Blame the hormones, but if this taxidermist's exhibit had been younger, I would have dropped my overnight bag on his foot. "Some ambassador you are! Here we are uprooted from our native soil, weary from crossing the burning plains, to say nothing of braving raging storms and foaming rapids! And all so you can evict us." Shoving my bag into the breach, I cried, "Take me to your leader!"

"Someone take my name in vain?" The scuffed gravel voice came accompanied by the stomping of feet. "What's all this row? Ain't I never to get five minutes' peace?"

My overnight bag dropped from my hand, the door was yanked wide open again and behold—an extremely short woman with a hand puppet face appeared, her brownish grey curls bunching out from under a frilled cap. She glared up at us.

"Good evening, I'm Bentley Haskell, and this my lovely wife Giselle."

"Know yer lines, I'll say that for yer." Elbowing her cohost aside, she backed up with a sort of gnome hop. "Get yourselves in here, the both of you. Ain't gonna have it said you didn't get to use the bathroom before I threw you out."

She was no taller than a leprechaun. I could have picked her up and put her in my pocket. But I was afraid she would bite.

"What you wanting?" She rounded on her fellow servitor, who had nerved to touch her arm.

"The young woman was very difficult." Voice turning tremulous as his candle, he aged before my eyes. A victim of geriatric abuse. "I'm all done in; have to go sit down with the newspaper and chew on some melon seeds."

Eyes tender, our tiny hostess reached up a mile to pat his boney shoulder. "You do that and I'll see you fired."

Taking my bag, Ben whispered, "I think they're beginning to take to us."

"Can't say I am," the woman gave her crisp white apron a twitch, "but I am taking you to the meeting room. Was only joshing about booting you out. Ain't my place or old Baldy's to do the honours."

Ben's sigh of relief could surely be heard all over the

midwest. I was afraid he would kneel down and kiss her feet.

"The name's Jeffries," she informed us, "and this here's Peeps."

"Spelled P-E-P-Y-S," boasted the sour-faced owner.

"A descendent of the great diarist?" Ben enthused. "How I enjoyed being forced to read his stuff as a schoolboy!"

Jeffries smacked her flabby lips. "We don't hold with them spill-yer-guts books here. We like nice stories about people sitting down to breakfast eating their eggs benedict and making plans for lunch and dinner."

Ben and I opened our mouths; but Jeffries turned on Pepys and blew out his candle. "You and that damn thing! Carrying it around like a hot water bottle. Give here and stack their cases with the others by the stairs."

At funeral speed we processed through the depressingly cavernous hall, under the varnished beams of a ceiling laid out as if for multiple games of naughts and crosses. Ben, every minute going against him, must have been dying to break into a run. A three-ball chandelier, reminiscent of a pawnbroker's sign, hung unlit from a second story rotunda, but Pepys' candle must indeed have been for show because gas lamps mounted on the mahogany walls bathed the staircase in mystery and cast gloomy shadows on dark oil paintings and the maroon and cream diamond tile.

I pictured a butler descending the stairs, candle held aloft. *"Ladies and Gentlemen, the master is dead of unnatural causes and . . . the will is as full of holes as cheese."*

"Seen som'at worth stealing?" Pausing beside a door, Jeffries' face split into a troll grimace.

"I . . . I was just admiring that painting." My finger wavered toward an oil portrait. Background was the greenish black of motor oil. Subject: a starch-and-vinegar woman wearing voluminous black, relieved only by her white cap, which was tied under her chin with a venomous bow. But could be there was life in the old girl? A finger of her right hand was raised.

Pepys' cracked voice leaped up behind me. "The lady

is pointing heavenward, as was the fashion in them times when a picture was painted in memorium."

"And if you're keen on that sort of thing," added Jeffries, "you'll love the portrait of the Cat Cadaver over the fireplace." And on that ghastly note, the door yawned open.

Ben would see a roomful of Mangés and experience the urge to prostrate himself, crying, "Mercy, mighty masters!" I saw only the room with its carved oak paneling and red flock wallpaper, the table covers with bobbled fringe, the ruby lamps with their dingle-dangle shades. Blood-red velvet curtains swirled back from windows, aping the entrance to a fortune-teller's crystal ball domain. The air was stale with dust. What vibes would the gypsy Chantal pick up in this horrible room? Were evil forces at work here? Other than those of bad taste?

Upon the mantelpiece reposed a bronze urn. Did it hold paper clips and string or the ashes of Josiah Mendenhall? I fought to keep from looking, but there it was—the famed portrait of the Cat Cadaver. Oh, my darling Tobias, how you would hate to be remembered in such a state of rigor mortis!

I heard Jeffries loudly announce us. Time for me to wish I were twenty pounds thinner, not pregnant and five thousand miles away. Critical eyes studied us.

"Good evening, I'm Bentley Haskell and this my lovely wife Giselle—"

"*Enchante, mon ami!* I am Solange and next to me *mon mari* Vincent." The voice was creamy rich as French chocolate, its owner a tall woman with gleaming upswept hair, and the aristocratic air of having just stepped off the tumbril. Her greeting had broken the spell. The mass of formless humanity began to shift and separate into living, breathing entities, some male, some female.

Ben gripped my hand. Face flushed, eyes lowered (as befitted a believer in the divine right of Chef Kings) he approached the closest chair. A chair occupied by a woman in a pumpkin trouser suit. "To be permitted into the presence of the great Mangés is so immense a privilege, I am rendered speechless, except to say thank you for counting me worthy of your time."

I braced myself for the grand piano in the library corner to break into "This is my moment! My moment sublime!"

"You are sadly erroneous, *mon frére*," announced Vincent, husband of Solange. "We are all candidates, same as you. Only deeference is we answer the call a leetle more prompt."

"My Lord!" Dropping my hand, Ben would have sunk onto a maroon brocade chair, had it been vacant. "This can't be! I thought I was the only candidate—"

"Jeez! Reminds me of a joke." The speaker was a stout boy of about eleven. He wore an Hawaiian shirt, wire-rimmed glasses and a smirk.

"Eez eet suitable for adult company?" Vincent had dyed black hair and a complexion *vin rouge*.

"Bingo, honey, is it rude?" This from the stocky woman who could have passed for Friar Tuck but for her pumpkin-coloured trouser suit.

"Mom, please!" The kid pressed his hands down on his plump knees. "This man dies and thinks he's the only one who made it to heaven. There are no other guys around, see. Then St. Peter comes knocking on the door and says 'You're in hell, and worse—you got solitary!' Get it?"

A forced sputter of laughter; followed by silence emanating most strongly from the four people seated on the scroll-backed sofa. A grey-haired matron wearing a corsage, a grey-haired man with a worry-worn face, a spindly man with a Charlie Chaplin moustache, and beside him, a youngish female with flowing hair, a bloodless complexion and so thin that if you held her up to the light you'd see right through her.

"Don't you think it's funny?" the kid demanded.

Ben was rigid as the Cat Cadaver. What a time he must be having dealing with the presence of a child here in the sacred womb of the Mangés!

"I theenk, *mon petit choux*"—the Frenchwoman addressed the boy—"we are none of us much for laughter while we wait for the Mangés to arrive. How say you we all introduce ourselves *encore* for the benefit of Mr. and Mrs. Haskell?"

Bingo's mater produced a grim smile. "I'm Ernestine Hoffman, homemaker . . ." Pause for applause, which did not come. "My hobbies are gardening, mug collecting and decorating with doilies. I've been married twenty-one years to my lovely husband Frank, who can't be with us due to the pressure of business." She picked at her pumpkin collar. "And last but also first—proud mother of the wonderful young man to my right."

Understandably, Ben was dazed. The woman had failed to mention the field of expertise that had brought her the Mangés' attention. To say nothing of why she had toted her rotund son along.

"Meet the great one!" Lolling back in his chair, the pudgy kid pushed back his hair from his middle-aged executive brow and placed his hands over the dome of his blinding Hawaiian shirt. "Don't everyone get intimidated at once. And feel free to blame Mom. She dragged me to this fun fest. It's not easy, you know, being Bingo Hoffman, Child Prodigy. Here's the bio: I began reciting recipes at age seven months. I was flipping crêpes at age two; at age five I had accumulated the scientific data to finally answer the question, Should an omelet be beaten clockwise? At six I had my own newspaper column . . ."

A yawn blew across the room. A guilty look crossed the Frenchman's face. Bingo's mom glared.

". . . have lectured and performed all over the States." Bingo blew out his already balloon cheeks, then deflated them with a weary sigh. "And when I get back to Cleveland I start my own TV show."

"Wonderful, hon!" came the pleasant voice of the grey-haired woman wearing the corsage. "But don't you go overdoing. You're still a boy. Find time for a little fun."

"No one pushes Bingo but himself," bristled Bingo's Mom.

Jerking forward on his seat as though responding to an electrical shock, Ben said, "I thought Mangé members had to be chefs in the orthodox sense of the word."

I could feel myself turning as red as the room. This use of burgundy and crimson was suffocating, especially with that mahogany ceiling bearing down on us like a coffin lid.

"Times change, *mon garçon.*" The Frenchman rose to his feet. He was dressed in a conventional dark suit. Nevertheless, I could picture him in top hat, swirling cape, and white gloves. "The Mangés must be out for zee fresh blood. I myself come from one of the noblest families in all of France. But that does not put lobster on the table." Lifting a silver snuff box from a whatnot table, he enclosed it with the long white fingers of his left hand. "I am zee magician Comte Vincent!" He opened his right hand and there was the snuff box. "In my night club act I toss zee eggs, flour, chocolate in a skeelet, I move my hands—*une, deux, trois!* A burst of flame, a loud bang! I lift my hat, so! to take my bow and voila, *Un Gâteau Magnifique!*"

Applause from the pleasant woman with the corsage, echoed faintly by the rest.

I could see the imaginary billow of Comte Vincent's cloak as he replaced the snuff box and picked up a long-handled shoe horn which he proceeded to twirl à la baton. "*Ma chère* Comtesse Solange is always my assistant." The lady inclined her head. Her flawless bluish hair and discreet black taffeta gown seemed belied by her heavy rouge and the impish beauty mark above her lip.

"Makes me into one hell of an ordinary chap," grumbled the skinny man with the Charlie Chaplin moustache. "Name's Jim Grogg, caterer for a major airline, and I make no bones about enjoying the challenge—make that the thrill—of being a Prepackaged Gourmet. The cherries on our puddings are never off center."

The memory of our transatlantic flight was too recent for Ben. His face turned bloodless as the skinny woman with flowing hair, whom Mr. Grogg was introducing pridefully as Divonne, his live-in lover. Tension mounted.

Ben wasn't entirely to blame. The words *When will the Mangés put in an appearance?* seemed strung in a blazing banner across the infernal room. Bingo kept aiming bits of paper at his mother's pumpkin trouser legs and her smile stretched thin. The pleasant faced woman repinned her corsage. Mr. Grogg put his arm around the wafer-thin Divonne. The comte was juggling pencils, faster and faster . . .

"My name's Ellie Haskell." I addressed myself particularly to the woman with the corsage, seated beside the gentleman with misery lines carved deep in his handsome face.

"Pleased to meet you. I'm Lois Brown and this here's my husband Henderson." She smoothed the draped frontage of her floral silk frock. Her laugh was pleasant. "Feel done up for a prom. The kids picked this out for me and bought me the corsage. We've got seven of them. All good decent kids. Sometimes I wish they weren't so happy at home. Henderson and me keep rattling the nest; but bless their hearts, they refuse to fly out or fall out." She turned an affectionate glance on said husband, whose gloom increased. "Like Ernestine, I'm a housewife. Don't mind the work but hate the hours! When it came to cooking I never thought whether I enjoyed it or not. Feeding those ever open beaks sure was a challenge. Took a few ribbons at the county fair for my pies, but never thought I was any different from any other Josephine Blow. Then a couple of months ago I sent in my recipe for Applesauce Ice Cream to the Fruit Growers of America Bakers Benefit and won the grand prize: a ferry trip, two nights on Nantucket, and fifty dollars. And I see you're expecting a little one, my dear."

"God help you," snapped Ernestine Hoffman, Bingo's mom. "I sure hope your delivery is easier than mine was." She cast a mildly reproving eye at the Child Prodigy, who was stuffing his pockets with the dusty-looking contents of a candy dish. "The doctor, of course, had never seen anything like it—not even in medical school, not even in the six years he aided Third World Natives—"

The hollow-eyed Divonne studied my burgeoning middle with a nasty expression on her pallid face.

Lois Brown laughed cheerfully. "Perhaps you'll be as fortunate as I was, honey." My spirits rose. Perhaps motherhood would not be all pain and anguish. "Why, each and every one of my seven darlings popped out in less than five minutes. Easy as cherry beehive pie. I even invited the neighbors in for my last two deliveries. And they all stayed afterward for the nice little buffet I served them—"

Someone groaned. I think it was me.

Hand over his eyes, Ben didn't see the door open. Everyone else slid to the edge of their seats except for the comte who was still juggling. Misjudging a pencil, he got hit on the ear. Would the Mangés all wear white hats and black handlebar moustaches? Even the women?

The answer was not immediately forthcoming. Entering the room, by themselves, were Jeffries and Pepys. She carried a tray of edibles. He carried another loaded with bottles, glasses, and china that made his boney knees buckle and his bald head gleam with sweat.

With relief, the gourmet gang gathered around a table at the library end of the room. Everyone that is, except the bloodless Divonne and my spouse Ben, who would have to be pried up from his gloomy sulk with a spatula.

He groped for my hand. "Ellie, I can't believe it. I'm competing with a magician, a caterer of disposable food, a child, and worst of all, an ordinary housewife."

"Be a man, my lad!"

Rising from his chair, his eyes turned black as his hair. "Ellie, you don't understand this *attack* on my manhood."

"Oh, for heaven's sake, Ben! Are you afraid Mrs. Lois Brown will come after you with the nutcrackers?"

He didn't answer because Jeffries had appeared beside us. Frilled cap down low on her forehead, she had the sort of face my cousin Freddy would insist had been turned inside out. Especially when she smiled.

"Want to fight or want to eat?" She proffered a tray of perfectly executed stuffed mushrooms and bacon-wrapped shrimp. Ben's appraisal was a mixture of admiration and envy.

To cover his silence I loaded up my plate. "Is it *Mrs.* Jeffries?"

"That's my business." Her curls bounced. "Ain't much else a woman in my position can call her own. Independently poor, that was my folks." That said, she was off, to present her tray to Bingo. I could hear him theorizing on the oregano content of the mushrooms, cheeks bulging as he munched. Poor kid. He reminded me of myself as a child.

Turning to Ben, I found him making painstaking conversation with Mr. Henderson Brown, husband of the nice woman with the corsage.

"Hot today, wasn't it?"

Mr. B reacted as if asked to name ten major cities in Yugoslavia. "Sorry, I'm no judge of the weather. Always feel cold myself."

"These mushrooms are tops," I contributed.

"Yes, but are they good for us?" Perhaps it was the greyish-brown hair, but Mr. Brown put me strongly in mind of Eeyore. "So often we're taken in by the pleasure of the moment," he gloomed. "Will my wife's success be good for her? For me? She was always so plain down-home sensible but this could change her into one of those women on *Dynasty*. What if she starts wanting to jazz herself up wearing hats and see-through nighties. I'm not the man for that sort of thing, you know." The lines on his face were permanent press. Pity. He would have been quite handsome if the weight on his shoulders hadn't shortened him by several inches and bowed his back.

"How did you get over to the island?" Ben asked him.

"Motorboat. It was waiting for us when we reached the river at seven o'clock." He waved his hand to include the group milling about the room. "We all came over together."

An unhappy reminder that we had arrived late. Caught up in the horror of discovering he was not the lone candidate, Ben may well have forgotten he was in violation of the punctuality rule.

For occupational therapy, I sent him to fetch me a tonic water. Mr. Brown offered to walk over to the drinks table with him. He himself did not indulge—something to do with his stomach or intestines. The comtesse tapped me on the arm.

" 'Allo! I intrude to ask—how far along are you expectant?"

"Four months!" I waved Ben and the drink away. After all it had been decades since I conversed with a woman.

"What, so leetle far along!" She waved her hands in disbelief. Her cerise nails were longer than my fingers. "You are *très grande* for four months." Patting my abdomen, she raised her voice. "Leesten up everyone, is she not *huge* for only four months *enceinte*?"

No one looked our way. As well, because my smile did not extend to my lips.

She pinched my cheek, eyes shiny bright as onyx. "You must not be embarrassed. Have a happiness splurge! Call me Solange!"

"Do you have children?"

"Vincent and I have six. All with sweet brown eyes and the curly hair."

"How lovely!"

"They're poodles."

When Divonne, Mr. Grogg's vampiric love, had drifted past, I asked Solange if she knew who now owned Mendenhall.

"You do not know?" Surprise stretched the rouged skin tight over her cheekbones. "Why, *ma chérie*, this house belong to the great actress Theola Faith."

Pepys toddled up and tried to take my plate, but I needed something to hold onto. Of course if the walls closed in completely, they would support me. Were one to look coincidence straight in the eye, stripped of silly superstition . . .

"Frog legs," Solange said.

I thought she was offering me something to eat. I shuddered.

"The butler, he walks like zee frog." Solange watched Pepys cross the room. "I wonder, was he here when Mendhenhall was given to the beauteous Theola Faith by one of her lovers. The one who directs the film made here—where she eez a burlesque queen married to the eighty-year-old *homme horrible*, what eez stabbed through the ear with one of the feathers from her fan dance."

"Then this *is* Melancholy Mansion."

The room fell abruptly silent, as though someone had made a pronouncement on the stock market. But the group wasn't staring at me. Bingo was standing off by himself, holding up a hardcover book. The title leaped off the red and black cover: *Monster Mommy.*

"Read any good books lately?" When boy genius speaks, people listen. You could have heard a paper plate drop, before his mother crossed the room in a rush of pumpkin polyester.

"Bingo, hon! You don't open that trash!"

No child of mine would ever learn to read.

"Shush!" The word swept through the ranks. The door was opening. Was this Theola Faith, right on cue?

My cousin Vanessa entered the room. Or so I thought for a jelly-kneed moment. Thank God my eyes deceived me. The lithesome lovely with the tawny hair, sherry-coloured eyes and glorious complexion was not my cousinly nemesis. Merely as close to being her double as made no difference. I couldn't move. I couldn't even fall into Ben's arms because he was somewhere behind me, way out of catching distance.

"Ladies and gentlemen, please excuse my having kept you waiting." The Vanessa clone crossed the room with fluid grace, her black knit dress moulded to her faultless figure. Her smile as much a celebration of self as a greeting.

A chorus of inaudible response. Pepys showed an unwillingness to exit. Jeffries, skirt bunching out like a feather duster, stood on tiptoe, grabbed him by the ear and marched him out the door.

Taking pride of place under the portrait of the Cat Cadaver, the newcomer continued in her throaty voice. "I am the Mangé member assigned to conduct the Interrogatory Proceedings that will determine which of you candidates is to be honoured with an invitation to join the Mangé Society."

I could see Ernestine Hoffman fussing with son Bingo's hair and witnessed his accompanying scowl. Jim Grogg, fiddling with his Charlie Chaplin moustache, had already shrunk two sizes. His lady was playing dead on the sofa. The comte absently plucked silver coins from his wife's hair. I could feel Ben's shadow. I recognized his breathing.

"I am Valicia X." The lady Mangé fingered the pearls at her pearly throat. "Sorry, no last name supplied. You will understand the necessity to keep such information top secret. And I trust even my first name will not go beyond this room."

Valicia! The similarity to my dread cousin's name was frightening.

"A special welcome to spouses, and"—a glossy lipped smile for Ernestine Hoffman—"mothers. Am I neglecting anyone?"

The vampiric Divonne opened her eyes. "I'm his insignificant other," she said, pointing a languid finger at Jim Grogg.

Valicia X smiled without straining her lips. She could have been posing for a fashion layout, using the fireplace and Cat Cadaver portrait as a whimsical background. Had I been wearing maternity clothes I could have made the fashion statement that I was pregnant. Solange had recognized that I was dressing for two, but Vanessa . . . Valicia X would never consider pregnancy a viable excuse for gaining weight. She was detailing the program for the next three days. No formal meals, except for one outdoor evening barbecue, the day after tomorrow on the Fourth of July, and a farewell dinner to be prepared by the candidates, after which the name of the chosen candidate would be announced. Otherwise, Jeffries or Pepys would set out buffet meals. Times to be posted outside the dining room. Mangé candidates were precluded from participating in any activity associated with cooking other than when specifically instructed. Neither were they permitted to leave the island. Anyone else might do so, whenever Pepys was available to man the motor boat.

"And so, Mangé candidates"—gaslight rippled through the masses of her hair and stroked the perfect cheekbones—"we now adjourn for our first session."

In the ensuing flurry I caught sight of Ben's sleeve. Later I would attempt to pry from him his opinion of Valicia X, although his opinion wouldn't be worth much considering he would be looking at her as a Mangé, not a woman. I was turning to him, ready to wrap my love—if not my arms—around him and whisper words of good luck when Pepys came in, his hands atremble. The face of death warmed up with righteous fire.

"Ms. Valicia, ain't no joy to me, but I know my duty. I must bring to your attention a Fearful Violation!"

Someone gasped. Oh, no! Here it came—the revelation of Ben's late arrival. Now I couldn't look at my love. All my fault in losing those blasted traveller's cheques.

She turned her serenely beautiful face toward the skeletal butler. Bingo lunged toward the plate of hors d'ouvres and shoved three in his mouth.

"What is it, Pepys?" Valicia inquired.

He stretched panic to breaking point before answering. "I was taking luggage upstairs when this fell out of somebody's bag." A packet of white powder dangled from his fingertips like a rat by its tail.

A gasp rocked the room.

What were we talking here? Heroin? Cocaine?

Gliding forward, Valicia X removed the plastic Baggie from her henchman's gleeful clutches, dipped in an elegant finger, dabbed it to her glossy lips, and made her pronouncement. "As I suspected. Baking powder."

Silence most aghast.

Snap snap of her fingers. "Whose bag, Pepys?"

"Mine." Jim Grogg stepped forward. "Hell, I knew it was against the rules to bring in any illegal substances, but I figures what chance do I, an airline caterer, have against a pack of cookery celebs. So I decide to up my odds. Guess this means I'm out on my can, right?"

Valicia X dropped the packet into Pepys' skeletal hand, then signalled him to leave. Upon the closing of the door, she said, "Mr. Grogg, every candidate in this room was selected because he or she does not fit into the Jello mold. You would have started out even. As it is, you may remain the night and avail yourself of the buffet breakfast before getting the hell out of here."

"Lady, if I had a Popsicle on me I'd ram it up your . . . nose." Hair wafting around her face, as if blown by a fan, Divonne wafted over to Mr. Grogg and pressed his head to her *non existent bosome.* "Come here, Babykums. You wouldn't have liked being a dumb old Mangé anyway." The sound of his sobs was heartrending. This was no time to rejoice that the axe had not fallen on someone nearer and dearer.

Finally I faced Ben. His eyes were stunned, dazzled. He was gawking at Valicia as if she were some incredible apparition. Mr. Grogg's plight was swept from my mind. With a wife's sure and certain instinct I knew Ben had been standing thus since she had entered the room. Even more horrible, Valicia X chanced, at that moment, to look toward the man I thought of as my husband. His bedazzlement was reflected in her eyes. Her breath hung in the air . . . her heartbeat was the pounding in my ears. And realization knifed through me.

Oh, God, how I remembered the feeling. The certainty that I was standing knee deep in clouds, the day I met the man from Eligibility Escorts. Somehow, someway I would get him back. Tomorrow be damned, I'd do it tonight.

7

Homewrecker Valicia X and the Mangé candidates departed for the secret meeting room. Ben, Bingo, Lois Brown and the comte went off in eager, humble silence, clearly awed to be undertaking the first step in the Mangé competition. As for poor Jim Grogg, he was shuffled offstage by Divonne, a woman proved to be made of flesh and blood. I hoped with all my broken heart she would bite him on the neck, or whatever it took, to turn their bedroom into a haven. My misery did not demand that others suffer. Indeed, I was already beginning to question whether I might have been overdoing the woman scorned bit. Insecurity had brought Mr. Grogg down, and there was no denying I was prone to the condition.

Ellie, this is your ego speaking. Do you really wish Ben to be the sort of man whose blood fails to turn red hot when a woman turns on the burner? Yes! He can look but he can't gawk. Oh, hell, I know the credo! When the going gets tough, the tough woman stays put.

Hitching up my smile, I smoothed my sailor collar and

declined the dish of cashews Solange offered. Not another gained ounce until I could get into maternity clothes.

"Anyone for bridge?" Ernestine Hoffman clashed horribly with the ruby lamp standing next to her. But I liked her bellbottoms and the way her pudding basin hair gave fashion the go by. Here was a woman who wouldn't consider it a social requirement to flirt with the handsomest man in the room.

"Zat is fine wizz me, but what of you, *ma petite?*" Solange tapped me on the cheek with a cerise nail.

"I only play a little, by ear."

"And how thinks you, *monsieur*, who sit so quiet under the tall lamp with shade like a *grandmère's chapeau?*" She crossed toward Henderson Brown. But not as a predator. Her black and white chic was not dependent on wearing her sensuality as a silk scarf around the neck.

Not that Mr. Brown would have noticed had she thrown herself across his lap and begun undoing his waistcoat buttons. Was it my imagination or had he grown greyer since I first met him?

"Forgive me." He gripped his knees gloomily. "I don't play any card games." His eyes strayed to a wall clock, with wooden leaves garlanding the birdhouse face; he flinched as if pecked when out popped a cuckoo, who proceeded to sound off ten times. I found myself remembering Hyacinth's birdcage earrings, swaying against her neck as she recounted the dire sayings of Chantal: *writing not on the walls . . . in the book.*

Ernestine had picked up the copy of *Monster Mommy* and was leafing through it, her expression grimly rapt.

Mr. Brown kneaded his brow. "What is going on at that meeting?"

The urge to put him in the corner was strong. His worries were popcorn compared to some. The comtesse patted his arm. "Relax, my turtle! The *bonne femme* talks about zee placing of the cherry on the *gâteau*. She does not place one in a man's navel when dancing zee seven veils."

He pried himself out of his chair. "My Lois was always a good woman, a regular churchgoer. She never went to

Tupperware parties. Why has this madness seized her? I haven't looked at another woman since the day I walked into Smart Mart to buy an engagement ring for another girl. Lois was the salesgirl. She smiled and that was it. We married six years later."

"You old romantic you!" Ernestine continued to leaf through *Monster Mommy*.

"Gave her everything including seven kids."

"*Très bon!*" Solange moved to the piano, then back.

Standing under the portrait of the Cat Cadaver, Mr. Brown appeared also to suffer from rigor mortis. "Always tried to appreciate her. When she'd clean out the linen closet, I'd go take a look at it. Always told her she was the best cook in town. Why wasn't that enough? Why must she go join some damn, pardon my French"—there was a pardoning smile from Solange—"secret society?" He thumped a fist into the palm of his hand. "That Valicia X female—I wouldn't trust her any further than I could kick an elephant."

On second thought, I liked this man. "Women have needs," I said sadly. "That doesn't mean we get the urge once a week to run naked through a department store chewing on a piece of red meat, but we can't always find ourselves in the linen closet."

But my words of solace were wasted on the stuffy air.

"I don't know how Lois can be taken in by all this." Throwing out an arm he caused a candlestick to do a jig on the mantel shelf.

Ernestine looked up, marking her place in the book with her finger. "My Bingo said when we came in, 'Mom, the room looks like it's waiting to murder someone.' "

"*Mais oui*, was that not so for zee evil butler in *Melancholy Mansion*? Was he not found stabbed through the heart on that very window *embrasure*?" Black eyes flashing, the comtesse pointed toward the red velvet curtains.

A gurgle of alarm from Ernestine. Her plump cheeks ballooned out in a sudden unbecoming likeness to son Bingo. But let it not be said our conversation was the cause. "Merciful God, this dreadful book!" She suffered through several more pages of *Monster Mommy* read at a flip. "As a child Mary Faith suffered the 'torment of the damned'—her very own words—being raised by that depraved woman. She tells here how for years she thought Begita the maid was her mother. She had to address Theola Faith as Miss Faith until her eleventh birthday, when, for her present, she was allowed to call her Theola."

"Did they spend much of their lives here?" Interested, Solange perched on the sofa arm, black skirt brushing her ankles.

Rustle of pages. Ernestine crossed her pumpkin legs and took a breath which popped a button off her jacket. " 'My mother attested that Mendenhall was a gift to her from Richard Greenburgh, who had purchased it for the filming of *Melancholy Mansion*. On her rare excursions to the house she always refused to let me accompany her. Her reason? She was afraid I would get sick from having a good time! Her spaniel, Vanilla, got to go in my place, dressed up in my clothes. My tears and pleas moved her not at all. I still see her throwing back her silver-blonde head and laughing that manic laugh.' "

"*Mon Dieu!*" Solange clenched her hands against her forehead. "A devil woman! If theese Theola Faith were in the house now, I would murder her with these naked hands."

Henderson Brown shot up from five foot eleven to six foot six. "Lois does not belong in this evil place. I'm going to phone the kids and get their input."

"Not from here you're not." Ernestine stopped his rush to the door. "When I wanted to call Frank, I was told by that Jeffries person there isn't a phone."

"Damn!" Without a word of apology Mr. Brown stormed from the room. You may be too late, John Wayne, I thought. Undoubtedly you tried your best to bring your wife up to be a credit to you. But somewhere down the years you accidentally left the front door open. Was I guilty of shackling Ben's ankle? Was our marriage destined to become a three-legged shuffle? Would the baby's arrival improve, or make worse, the situation? These and other earth-shaking questions must wait. As Aunt Lulu is wont to say, We do not live in a vacuum cleaner.

"Poor leetle Monsieur Brown!" Solange consoled herself with a cashew.

"Poor little Mary!" Hair sticking out in tufts, two more buttons gone from her pumpkin jacket, Ernestine was halfway through *Monster Mommy*. "My Frank would kill me if I let Bingo get his hands on this! So what, if I don't let him away from the stove until he's done his practice! So what, if I tell him baseball's for kid's who don't know their *pâté de foies de volaille* from their *chou farci*! Being a genius is an opportunity not given to most. Did Mozart's mother let Wolfgang goof off?"

A sigh wrenched from the maternal bosom. "My Bingo, he's never gone to school unless I've driven him. This poor tyke"—sound of pages frantically turned—"she's sent God knows how many miles to stay with some nutso grand dame in the backwoods of nowhere. Listen: 'At the tender age of nine or ten I was sent to stay with Guinevere DeVour at Tottery Towers. Her connection to my mother remains a mystery to this day. All I knew then was that Theola Faith wanted me out of the apartment because she had an orgy planned for over fifty people and was beside herself deciding what not to wear.' "

"*Tres* witty!" Solange moved toward the velvet curtains. "Permit that I open a window. I am all over stuffy." Her rouge did stand out on her cheeks like pox marks and I too was wilting. Kicking off my shoes, I eased my swollen feet onto the brocade-covered sofa.

"Read on, Ernestine."

" 'Begita, the maid, wept and pled for me. She swore to keep me out of the way in a cupboard, but Theola would have none of it. She was terrified I would catch the eye of some Hollywood hotshot. She was phobic on the possibility that I might be offered the part of Little Lucy Lamplight in her current film, *While the Mouse is Away*. I was shoved onto a bus late at night, Guinevere DeVour's address clenched in my timid hand, and told not to return under two weeks— unless I wished my parakeet to sleep on a bed of wild rice. Theola threatened me with other terrors, if I talked to anyone on the bus, even to ask directions.

" 'Twenty-four hours later I was a frightened child on the steps of Tottery Towers. No answer to my frantic knocking! Was I totally abandoned? In desperation I tried the door, discovered it unlocked and found myself in a nightmarish hall. What I took for unwashed curtains were giant cobwebs. Animal heads grinned a welcome from the walls. I was fighting down panic when Guinevere DeVour materialized on the stairs, wearing a shroud nightgown and emitting a piercing scream.' "

"*Mon Dieu!*" Solange sank down on the window seat. "You make me hear that pig squeal."

Ernestine let *Monster Mommy* fall in her lap. "Frank always does say I read well."

"I think that was a real scream," I interrupted. "Coming from upstairs."

"Zee tragic Monsieur Brown. We are criminals to let him go off alone, up to his nose with worry. He may have leapfrogged out zee window. No, *ma chérie*," Solange pressed me back down. "You stay. Madame Hoffman and I go see."

And poof! There I was alone in that devilish red room. Surely nothing too dreadful had happened or there would have been a scurry of congregating feet out in the hall. Even were the Mangé candidates and their luscious leader out of earshot, Pepys and Jeffries would not fail to pounce on any unorthodoxy. Perhaps Mr. Brown had stepped on a mouse.

Crossing to the drinks table, I poured myself a gargle of red wine, brought it to my lips, then came to my senses. I had not touched a drop of anything stronger than tea since the baby. And I would not let this house turn me into a health hazard.

A bell rope hung on the wall to my left; I gave it an authoritative yank. Minutes passed. The cuckoo shot out of the clock and counted to eleven; the tiny door clapped shut. I myself was ready for darkness and shut-eye.

"You rang." Jeffries bundled into the room, frilly cap down on her eyebrows, nose down on her chin. Best not to mention the scream in case she took it as criticism of her housekeeping.

"Hello!" I gushed.

"What you want?"

"Only a glass of water, but if it's any trouble . . ."

"Might be and might not. My psychiatrist tells me not to make hasty decisions. Which tells you why Pepys is still alive. That man's three-quarters crazy and one-fourth mad. He hates that woman."

A man who did not fall under the spell of Valicia X was a man after my own heart.

"Last night he hid an escargot in her bed."

"Good for him!" Warming as we were toward civility, I decided to stick out my nose. "Jeffries, does Theola Faith come often to Mendenhall?"

Her face squeezed shut. I had crossed the line drawn by her psychiatrist. "I'll go think about that glass of water."

Alone again, I suffocated in the room's silence. The mahogany, the red flock wallpaper and the bobbled velour were oppressive. I don't like rooms that play games and this one was still pretending to be a movie set. Sinking down on the only comfortable looking chair, I immediately felt trapped in a quicksand of cushions. Worse, my back was to the door.

Time fell away like a stripper's clothes. I was Child Ellie again on that first fateful visit to Merlin's Court. Aunt Sybil had left me alone with instructions to sit and not move a muscle, an easy enough task, until I heard the drawing room door pounce open behind me. My stout legs had begun thrashing in a vain attempt at reaching the floor, as the rest of me sank deeper, deeper into the bottomless pit where the springs should have been.

Back in the here-and-now I reclaimed my courage with the silent admonition that I was frightening the baby.

"Ahoy there!" Rasping whisper.

The door hadn't opened. My ears being all atwang, I would have heard.

"Anyone there, m'hearties?"

I stopped breathing. The voice came from the window— which the comtesse had left in open invitation to the arm and knee now putting in an appearance.

"First bloomin' bit of luck all day."

Relief poured over me. Whoever this was, it wasn't the enemy. That voice was British.

By the time I had fought my way to my feet, a stout, white-haired woman with a St. Bernard dog face, wearing a flower seller hat and—of all improbabilities—my dressing gown, was sitting on the window seat.

"Foiled!" Face sagging, she lumbered over to the sofa. "Knew I was crackers to hope, but that's the way Marjorie Rumpson was reared. Neither a bawler nor a loser be. Entering the house unnoticed was asking for miracles. Ah, woe! The world won't be the poorer if I don't get to be a Mangé."

"You're a candidate?" Coming up close to her I caught the unmistakable whiff of *eau de river*.

The black hat nodded; a tear coursed down Marjorie Rumpson's cheek.

"So is my husband. Did you make a mistake about the time?"

"Never! The day, the hour are tattooed on my heart. But this morning my dear old mum took one of her queer turns and I couldn't bring myself to leave her until the doctor came and said it was just a matter of prune juice. The old sly puss had been pouring it into the plant pot beside her bed."

"Your mother must be getting up there."

"Ninety-seven."

"Remarkable. No wonder you seem so fit."

"Couldn't have reached here otherwise, my love. Borrowed a friend's plane to fly down from Canada (lived there, have Mum and me for the last thirty years), landed at Chicago, hitchhiked from there—ever such a nice motorcycle chappie. Then when I got to Mud Creek—"

"You found a boat to bring you over?" I found I was sitting beside her, holding her hand.

"Wasted an hour knocking on doors, before taking the only course open to me. Stripped down, put some undies and a cotton frock in a plastic Baggie; stowed my luggage under a tree, and paddled out to the deep water."

"You mean you swam out here?"

"Nothing to it."

"Naked?"

"No, m'hearty—not in the rude! Wouldn't want to put the fishies off their supper. Wore m'all-in-one girdie, Baggie tied to brassiere strap."

I squeezed her hand. "You might have drowned or . . ." I almost said "worse," "been spotted by the Coast Guard."

"Midchannel caught sight of an official-looking boat, so took the precaution of swimming a stretch under water. Afraid I'm not in shape I was when practicing crossing the English Chan with my cousin George. Have lived near water all my life. Bournemouth when we were in England."

"Thank God you made it across." I perked up the flattened ribbon on her hat while not looking at my velour dressing gown, which she filled out so nicely.

"No scare there! One calamity only—lost the Baggie en route. You can guess I was tickled pink to come aboard that boat house and its suitcases of old clothes. Salvation Army's loss is my gain. None of the frocks or shirts made it half way around me, but this"—she smoothed velour over her queen-size knees—"does beat arriving like Neptune roused from the deep in my all in one."

"Absolutely!" Choking cough. "And those rubber thongs do complete the ensemble. May I ask why you entered by the window?"

Marjorie's St. Bernard cheeks quivered. "Bloomin' stupid, I know! But thought if I could get into the house unobserved I might be able to weasel out of being late. Never flattered myself I was the one and only candidate. So got this notion in my silly old noggin of a welcoming cocktail bash under way. Everyone in too much of a duster to count heads. A little bit o' luck and I'd slip into the house unnoticed and pretend to have been present all along. Too bashful to put meself forward." Pulling a tissue from the box I had placed on the arm of the sofa, she blew. "There isn't a party, is there?"

This was worse than telling a child there isn't a Father Christmas. Over the lump in my throat I explained about the meeting in progress, in some undisclosed room, under the direction of one Valicia X. Impossible to hold back that the number of candidates was insufficient to justify any hope of confusion. My turn to reach for a tissue.

"Sorry! I am a little emotional these days." For emphasis I jolted off the sofa when the door opened. I had forgotten Jeffries and my request for water. But, as it perchanced this was the return of the wanderers. Ernestine Hoffman and the Comtesse Solange had been gone so long I should perhaps have reintroduced myself, but settled instead for doing the honours for my new friend.

"This is Ms. . . ."

"Miss Marjorie Rumpson." Squaring her jaw, straightening her hat, she stood up.

"Another candidate?" Ernestine did not look thrilled.

"Forgive us not being here to greet you," Solange extended a bejeweled hand, "*mais* Madame Hoffman and I had went in search of the screamer."

Miss Rumpson looked confused.

"We find nothing disordinary and were making the return when we became separated."

"I went to the bathroom and got locked in!" Ernestine's heightened colour clashed horribly with her pumpkin outfit and I, remembering the terror of the plane, assured her I suffered from the same syndrome.

The comtesse's streamlined courtliness showed to great advantage alongside Miss Rumpson's unorthodox attire. "*Mes amis*, I have my intuition about scream. I theenk *Monsieur* Grogg and *Mademoiselle* Divonne make the *grand amour* so they forget this foolishness of the baking powder!"

Miss Rumpson looked even more confused so I hastened to explain her plight to the others. The results were mixed. Ernestine did not exactly bubble over with sympathy. What a pity, she said, but the lady would appear to have missed the boat on all counts. Solange, however, began circling Miss Rumpson, flouncing the bodice of the dressing gown out above the cord, assigning the collar a twitch and administering a pat on the shoulder.

"I say this *bonne femme* who brave the river should lie her way into zee house and out of zee problem. Thees is the story she tells: She arrives on time—goes knock-knock on the door, but no one comes. She lets herself in—heart making boom-boom and make ready for to say 'Here I am!' Where is everyone? She finds the convenience, decides to jollie herself up and is locked in."

Miss Rumpson trembled from head to thongs with emotion.

"Sounds sufficiently unreasonable to work," I enthused.

Ernestine picked *Monster Mommy* off the floor where it must have fallen from the sofa and set it on a table. "Believe me, I don't like coming across as hardhearted Hannah, but I surely have a responsibility to think of my Bingo first. A mother's first task is to fan the flame of her offspring's genius. With Mr. Gross and now Miss Rumpson out of the running, his chances of being selected look better all the time."

"Will you squeal to Jeffries or Pepys?" I asked.

"Shush! I hear the pitpat of foots." Solange gathered us into a huddle.

"Quick! Hide Marge behind the curtains!" Ernestine looked as surprised as the rest of us that she had thrown in her lot with the conspirators.

It was Jeffries who entered with my glass of water. Did something about the hang of the red velvet curtains arouse her suspicions? Would she be as slow taking her leave as she had been putting in an appearance? She stood, hands on her hips, until it dawned on me she was waiting for me to drink my water. Taking a sip, I half expected my throat to swell closed, my eyes to pop out of their sockets as the poison took me.

"Excellent!" I managed.

"Natural carbonation. Comes from a well in town. We have our supply delivered mornings."

"May I have a glass?" asked trooper Ernestine.

Mission accomplished. As soon as Jeffries scowled her way from the room, Miss Rumpson came out of hiding; we hastened to explain that it would have been folly to trust her fate to one who had helped bring down another candidate.

"So you think, m'hearties, the wisest course is for me to throw myself directly on the mercy of this Valicia X?"

Fighting off the shudder that name evoked, I nodded. "As long as you remember your lies—lines."

Amazing what French chic Solange had tweaked out of my dressing gown. How well Ernestine's pumpkin jacket worked in bringing out the bloom in Miss Rumpson's cheeks.

"Flushed with bloomin' terror!"

"Nonsense," I said. Finding the secret room without the help of Pepys or Jeffries would not be a piece of cake, but I sometimes have a sixth sense where houses are concerned. It was therefore agreed that I sally forth with Miss Rumpson while the other two held the fort.

Onward and outward into the hall.

"What a handsome painting!" Marjorie dallied before the portrait of the old dame, peering out sans mercy through layers of dark varnish to give the finger to posterity.

"You wouldn't want to meet her on a dark staircase." Propelling my new friend forward, I crossed the shadowy floor as though this were Leicester Square at rush hour and any moment we would get clobbered by a bus driven by Pepys. Was the secret meeting room somewhere in the great beyond above that rollercoaster sweep of staircase? My head said maybe, but my legs—having begun to appreciate the lateness of the hour—voted to check this floor first. Several darkened corridors elbowed off the hall. Any one of them might provide the privacy demanded by the Mangé Manifesto. The trick would be not landing in the kitchen. And the soup.

Pinned beside a door was a bulletin board containing a schedule of meals and a listing of rooms to be occupied by the candidates and Insignificant Others—to quote the vampiric Divonne. Should I turn the knob, open this door? If so, then what? In the first flush of heroics I hadn't faced up to this moment. What if I not only brought rejection on Miss Rumpson, but ignomy on Ben? Would he be held accountable for my violation of the sacred Mangé codes? Then again, could I tell the woman who had been prepared to sacrifice all for her aged mother that we had come on a wild goose chase? Life, I decided sadly, is strewn with ifs, ands, and buts. Ben would simply have to say, Am I my wife's keeper?

An empty dining room came groggily to life in the light from the hall when I opened that door. Did America go in for king-sized tables as well as beds? This oak slab was ideal for your average estranged family. A town crier's horn would be needed to request the salt. Those weren't chairs, they were thrones, and the iron chandelier sounded a gallows creak in addition to casting dismembered shadows on the wall. Out of the gloom, six huge knives gleamed menacingly in their place of honor on the wall. Surely that couldn't be dried blood which limned the razor-sharp edge of the largest one? I could have lingered soaking up the charm of the swashbuckler knives, but Marjorie Rumpson was taking panting breaths and her brown eyes reminded me more than ever of a St. Bernard.

We headed up one corridor and down the next, opening up one fruitless door after another. At one point I thought I heard a third pair of footsteps, but the mind plays tricks. I'm sure, too, that the scent of fried banana was only a product of my imagination.

I was about to suggest to Marjorie that we proceed to the upper floor, when I noticed a door cut into the paneling of the staircase wall. Easy to miss because there wasn't a knob, only a finger groove.

"Lead on, Macduff." Miss Rumpson was panting in my ear as I slid back the panel and fumbled for a light switch. "Don't bust your stays, all is not lost!" She crossed the hall, surprisingly light on her feet, the gaslight and her flower seller hat making of her a music hall figure. She had spotted Pepys' candle left on the marble topped table. She returned with it lit and a packet of matches.

Stepping onto the enclosed staircase, I was sure I had

lost my mind, never to be found again. Miss Rumpson slid the door shut and we began our descent. The railing was a slackened rope strung between posts standing top and bottom. The steps were so narrow I didn't look beyond the one immediately below until suddenly I was in a subterranean room.

"Great balls of fire," Miss Rumpson said.

My sentiments exactly. The place was a combination of the Old Curiosity Shop and Alice's Wonderland. As far as the candle could see were hand-painted leather trunks and marble columns and statues and clocks and silk screens and stone garden seats and feather fans . . .

But no Mangé Meeting.

"Well, m'dear, if that doesn't beat all!" Miss Rumpson's voice bounced off gilded mirrors, over stenciled chests, and under japanned tables. "There's a coffin down here."

Had I not gained so much weight I would have leaped into her arms. "Wh . . . Where?" No sooner were the words out than I could have kicked myself for my gullibility. She had to be pulling my leg.

Wrong. Following the trail of her finger I saw a coffin, snuggled into a space between a Victorian love seat and a tallboy.

The bow on Miss Rumpson's hat was all of a tremble but she avowed stoutly that we owed it to the health department to investigate.

"Certainly!" I matched my teeny weeny steps to hers. Had I been right about Divonne? Did she never travel without her coffin? Had six phantom horses dragged this piece of furniture across the river, or had she sat inside and rowed? Surely I wasn't putting Our Baby in supreme jeopardy by investigating? "Want to do the honours?" I whispered to Miss Rumpson.

"Not on your Nellie, m'dear." Ducking behind me, she re-thought cowardice. "Shall we make it a team effort?"

Certainly not one of my favourite ways to end a day. But musn't show cowardice while the little one was in its formative months. Setting the candle down on a table, I said, "On our marks, get set, lift!"

I didn't expect any body to be inside, truly. It had come to me in a flash that the collecto-maniac responsible for loading up this room must have bought the coffin from an undertaker having a going-out-of-business sale. The lid groaned—or was it Miss Rumpson? We would surely find the space used for storage of a different kind. Sheets was my guess. Those won't-wear-out ones that have to be ironed.

Wrong! I couldn't breathe—partly because Miss Rumpson was clutching my throat. Someone lay against the white satin pillow. Someone I recognized.

Miss Rumpson screamed loud enough to waken the dead, and the corpse sat up. Whereupon the woman who had braved the skies and waters of the deep to keep her date with destiny dropped her hands from my throat. Picking up the candle, I mustered my voice.

"Ms. Mary Faith, as you live and breathe!"

Silence, giving me pause. Was this the woman I had seen on *Talk Time* with Harvard Smith? Same brown hair beehived in front and folded into a French twist at back. Same wing-tipped glasses. Up close, observation was less kind than the camera. Her complexion looked as though it had been vaccinated and her mouth owed more to lipstick than nature. The woman had an unfortunate fondness for makeup. But how does one ask, without appearing vulgarly curious, what she was doing in a coffin?

"Oh, my life, I can't take this!" Hand pressed to her brow, the shoulders of her mouse-coloured angora sweater shaking. "Why me? What sins did I commit other than to be born? Is there to be no peace in my own home, no lid that can ever be closed without reporters hounding me!"

Her spiraling voice caused the candle flame to waver. The furniture and objects d'art shifted, as if creeping up close to listen; the rest of the room remained cloaked in darkness. We could only see what was under our noses. And strong as the smell of concrete and dust was the smell of time put on hold.

"We're not news scavengers! We're part of the Mangé contingent," I floundered.

"Heaven forbid we intrude!" Miss Rumpson, having seemed to shrink, once more filled out my dressing gown and Ernestine's jacket to the fullest. "No one is a greater believer in the right to die than Marjorie Rumpson!" Her cheeks were going like bellows. "The moment my dear old Mum tells me she's ready to snuff it, out will come my packets of Mrs. Belcher's Old Fashioned Sleeping Powders. I'll stir some in her hot milk, sprinkle the rest on her cinnamon toast and tuck the sweet love in for a last good night!"

"You fiend!" Mary Faith sat rigid, hands gripping the coffin sides as though they were the rails of a junior bed, her glasses flashing. "You . . . you parent abuser!"

No longer did Miss Rumpson look like Nanny, the dear old doggie who took care of the children in *Peter Pan*. Her cheeks shook as she spoke. "If I were a man, I would call you out, madam."

"And I'll have you know this is not a suicide attempt!" Ms. Faith crushed the satin pillow to her chest and burst into great, wrenching sobs. "I was attempting to lay some ghosts. Mother kept a coffin at every one of her homes. She always said there was nowhere better to make love. When I was little and did something—breathing was enough—to send her into a tornado fit she would lock me in a cupboard. But one time, when she was suffering delusions of royalty and insisting I curtsy every time I came into her presence, I tripped and she shoved me inside the coffin and put a chest on top of the lid, and didn't let me out until I turned blue."

"Awful!" Nothing like this was touched upon in *Raising Babies From Seeds*. Could any woman turn into a Monster

Mommy if the ground were fertile? "Poor Ms. Faith!" I, who carry diffidence to the point of knocking on my own wardrobe door before opening it, knelt on the stone floor and touched her hair. Thickly coated with spray it felt like nylon. I was afraid I might have left a dent as in an underdone cake.

"My husband Ben would empathize with you. He suffers from claustrophobia. Your mother might have killed you."

Ms. Faith let the pillow fall. Her tormented eyes, so like those of her beautiful mother, rested on mine. "I kept imagining I heard her footsteps. I started counting them to stay awake and finally she came. This coffin and the other junk"—she gestured with a ringless hand—"was used in the filming of *Melancholy Mansion*. Afterward the director Richard Greenburgh indulged Theola's whim by leaving all the props here. He had purchased this awful house for pennies."

"And after the film, he presented it to your mother?" Swept along by the tawdry romance of it all, Miss Rumpson seemed to have forgotten her difference of opinion with Mary Faith.

"You think the great Richie tied a red bow around Mendenhall and gave it to her as a token of their undying lust?" Mary's voice emerged in such a shriek I jumped up from the floor. My knees had been killing me anyway. "That's what Theola claimed! But more of her lies! He intended the house for me, as a birthday present. Begita said so. Now at long last I have accumulated the courage to shake off the ropes of my mother's domination and claim my heritage. Last week I walked in and took up residence at Mendenhall."

"Good for you, m'hearty!" cried Marjorie Rumpson.

I was remembering my assumption that Jeffries was speaking of Valicia X, when she had said, "Pepys hates that woman." Maybe the hated woman was Mary Faith.

"About the Mangés," Marjorie prodded.

"An odd group." Mary stood up in the coffin as gingerly as I had stepped into the orange boat. "I'd met an editor who specialized in cookery books and talked with her about writing a sequel to *Monster Mommy: Foods Your Mother Made You Eat.*" She held out a hand for me to help her aground, in the manner of Queen Elizabeth stepping off the *Britannia.*

"The editor was a Mangé?" I could feel Marjorie's concern that the meeting would be over before we found the secret room.

"I don't know, but shortly afterward I was contacted by the Society—taking me up on my offer to allow the use of Mendenhall for one of the Candidate Investigatures. What cinched the matter was their mention of Pepys and Jeffries."

"You mean . . . ?" I faltered.

"Mangés, the both. They had always hated me as a child, but, what the heck! I decided to begin anew. Years of servitude to my mother might have brought them to their senses, although they hardly ever see her. They clean up each of her homes before a visit and move on to the next pad. I prayed we could make peace! I have spent the last several weeks trying to learn their language!"

Mary's features threatened to break through the heavy pancake makeup. "I *tried*! By heaven, I *tried* to bury the past! Those two helped keep me a prisoner when I was a child. Theola only had to say jump and they hopped like rabbits." Bang went the coffin lid! Her shoulder blades poked through the mouse-coloured sweater. Her glasses slid down her nose and got rammed back into place. "I know!" Mary Faith's chin lifted and her eyes glinted with fury. "I shall write a book about them!"

"Excellent!" At Marjorie's nudging, I explained her plight and asked Mary if she knew in which room the Mangé Meeting was being held.

"Here is a woman"—I rested my hand on my friend's shoulder—"who put her mother ahead of her own wants and needs. Heroes don't come one a penny anymore. We can't allow them to be downtrodden by mediocrity."

Humble yet worthy stood Marjorie Rumpson, candidate for Mangéhood.

Mary looked at her, conflicting expressions waging war on her face. "Your mother must be a real human being."

"She's the best." Marjorie stood taller, enclosed in an aura of candlelight. But had she removed herself beyond the range of Ms. Faith's understanding?

A pause which threatened to run the duration of my pregnancy. The coffin began to look rather inviting, but finally she said, "I'll help you."

Her uplifted hand silenced our thanks and picked up the candle. "Come!" Mary wended her way through the byways of furniture and other artifacts, her voice flowing over us as we mounted the shadowy stairs. "I'm a person who makes up her mind very quickly. And I've decided you two—Ellie and Marjorie, is that right?—were led to the coffin . . . to this house."

I really should repay her kindness by trying to like her. Pity is no basis for any relationship, as I knew well from my fat past.

Blowing out the flame she stepped into the darkened hall. In silence, we traversed the maroon-and-cream tiles. No creak of doors opening. No one watching other than Dame Gloom from her portrait. Mary sped up the stairs, Marjorie Rumpson and myself trailing after her, as I had trailed after Ben down museum corridors in Boston. "I don't know what it is about you both—a feeling of *sympatique* perhaps, but I want you to be my friends. Close friends. You'll stay on after the others leave and we'll do things together. Go sightseeing in Peoria, or just scruff around Mud Creek. Do either of you bowl?" She didn't wait for an answer. "All my life I've ached to belong and now it's all coming true. You don't just like me because of the book, do you?"

"Oh, no!" I cried. Marjorie could only pant.

"You do see how terribly important it is that I am liked for myself, not for printed words on a page? I resent the reality of being fawned over because I've written not only a bestseller, but *the* mega major bestseller. *Monster Mommy* speaks to what I am, but is not who I am—if you understand me."

I was a panting echo of Marjorie. My legs raced on ahead of me—the real me, as I kept my eyes glued to Mary's head. The red carpeted floor, encircling the staircase well like a race track, had more doors than I had breaths.

"A reviewer for *Panhandle Postscripts* wrote of the book that it 'lifts the veil of human frailty and offers up new insights into the spectrum of elitist depravity, while slicing to the core of . . .' "

I lost the next word because my shoe came off. Marjorie tripped on it, I got it back on—backwards—while hopping in pursuit of Mary Faith's offers of friendship.

"The *Daily Dispatch* declared it a serious book on a serious subject."

Crossing my toes, I said I hadn't been able to put the book down. True enough considering I hadn't picked it up; I broke into a lathering sweat for fear of being asked to quote chapter and verse.

Happily, my panic was put on hold when Mary opened a door standing in plain view. Could this be the secret meeting room? Would Ben be endearingly cross at my barging in on the holy of holies without respect for password or privacy?

But it was a bathroom—possessed of enough dark oak to have destroyed a forest, a W.C. requiring you stand on the seat to pull the chain, and a bath enclosed like a bed for the dying. Did the Mangé candidates and their luscious leader lurk behind its white sheet? Or were they squeezed into the cupboard under the basin with its brass taps? Hold those horses! Mary Faith was opening the medicine cabinet. Oh, come on now!

Beckoning Marjorie and me to gather close, she emptied the glass shelves of a bottle of antacid tablets, a gooky tube of toothpaste and assorted deodorants, then pressed a tiny button not much bigger than a screw above the middle shelf. Presto, the back of the cabinet changed from smoked glass to clear; the shelves creating a Venetian blind effect.

"These modern advances!" Marjorie said.

Mary shook her beehive head. "Installed for the filming of *Melancholy Mansion*."

We were looking into a windowless room lined with bookshelves. Furniture was limited to a cart, holding a jumbo coffee pot and paper cups, and a table, around which sat the Mangé party. Ben was facing us. His hair was rumpled, his tie over to one side and a pencil dangled cigarette style from his lips. Foolishly I lifted a hand and mouthed "I love you." Next to him sat Bingo Hoffman, spectacles sliding down his snub eleven-year-old nose, expression one of unmitigated smugness, his Hawaiian shirt a hodgepodge of colour in this room that resembled the inside of a cardboard box. Her back to us, Lois Brown sat, the set of her broad shoulders, her weekly wash-and-set hair marking her as the salt of the earth. A woman who would be baking brownies for the fourth grade, even when she hadn't had a child in school for years. Next to her was Comte Vincent LeTrompe; there went his hands stacking paper cups and covering them with his serviette.

"Behold the competition!" I put an arm round Marjorie.

"What about Pepys and Jeffries?" she said.

"They told me they weren't going to sit in on all meetings," informed Mary. "The woman at the head of the table is the Mangé in charge."

No longer could I squint the other way every time Valicia X turned her face our way. Studying her with complete detachment, I conceded her profile was perfection, her figure stunning and her hair marvelous. A pity the woman lacked flaws.

Rising, she distributed sheets of paper. Ben glanced up only briefly on being handed his. Splendid! Whatever her initial lure, it was over, burned out in the seasoned tenure of misplaced hopes. Was that a line from *Monster Mommy*, read aloud by Ernestine? Surprising how much I missed her and the Comtesse Solange, after so short an acquaintance.

Thought screeched to a halt. Mary pressed a second tiny button in the medicine chest and suddenly we could hear what was being said within the inner sanctum. My heart pounded like fists on a door.

Ben was speaking. "Ms. X, don't you consider this rule—forbidding any cooking until preparation of the final

meal—cruel and unusual punishment?" Elbow on the back
of his chair, he raised an inquiring eyebrow.

Poor darling, the sophisticated Ms. X was bound to be
repelled by his ingratiating manner. If only I could break
the glass barrier, protect him from himself . . .

"Mr. Haskell," she began. Her voice was like lemonade
—a little tart, but refreshing. "I assure you I intend to make
all as painless for you as possible."

The comte's hands whipped the serviette away from
the paper cups and they were gone. Lois Brown asked a
question about a pop quiz.

"My genius has to be nurtured," Bingo growled. "I
therefore move that we order a king-sized pizza with everything on it. And immediately following I want my mommy
to tuck me up in bed and read me a story about Vitamin E."

The childish innocence of his words returned me to my
senses. "Ms. Faith," I said, pushing back a wayward strand
of hair. "Should we be eavesdropping like this?"

"Wise words, m'dear!" Marjorie strove to make the
edges of her pumpkin jacket meet across her Dunlop pillow
bosom. "What say I get in there before Madam Mangé calls
it a night. Oh, woe! The longer I wait, the more I don't
believe my excuses for being late." The ribbon on her hat
was a trusty weathervane of her motions. Better get her out
of here before she camped on the privy, begging Calgon to
take her away from here.

"Come on, ladies." Mary's thin lips broke into a smile.
"Remember my immortal words in Chapter Seven?"

I struggled not to look blank. "Ms. Faith, I won't pre-
sume to paraphrase."

Mary would seem to have inadvertently inherited some
of her mother's famed flair for theatrics. Crossing her hands
on her angora chest, she lifted her face heavenward and
proclaimed, "Truth is an enemy to be embraced."

"Well said!" Marjorie dabbed at her eyes.

Turning off the medicine cabinet, Mary restored it to
the natural order and suddenly embraced Marjorie and me.
"How good it is to have you both as my dear, dearest

friends! As a child, the only arms ever wrapped around me were my own. Now I believe I will never be alone again!"

The responsibility was awesome. Would I be morally obliged upon leaving here to pack her in a suitcase and take her home? Certainly we had room for her at Merlin's Court. Under the gruff influence of Dorcas and Jonas she might even blossom into a woman who no longer felt the need to stab with the pen. Who could doubt she was already a woman of courage? She was offering to escort Marjorie to the meeting room and inform Ms. X that should Marjorie Rumpson not be permitted to attend the sessions as a viable candidate, the investigature would have to continue elsewhere.

The three of us trooped back down the main thorough-fare of the second floor and entered a bedchamber. The floor-to-ceiling four poster with tapestried hangings and the cast iron fireplace pronounced this a room designed for deaths and difficult confinements.

"My mother's room, mine now." Mary sucked in a breath and fondled a stiff-necked standard lamp, before leading the way toward a heavily carved wardrobe capable of housing a family of four. She opened the door, pushed aside a wall of clothes including several fur coats and a velvet cloak, to reveal an inner door, leading—you've guessed it, into the secret meeting room. Another Melancholy Mansion attraction.

This was as far as I went. We had come to a parting of the ways. Time to wish Marjorie all the best, make one small adjustment to her hat and administer the requisite small push. Good-bye and many thanks, Ms. Faith.

Alone at last. Leaning against the closed wardrobe, my mind picked away at a country-and-western dirge. I'm so all alone, so far away from home, shadows on the wall, say don't go down the hall . . . Oh, I was clever, no mistake, at frightening myself silly.

What was that . . . fluttering noise outside the door—the one to the bedroom, not the wardrobe? I contemplated going under the bed; but when push comes to shove I'd rather be caught standing up than lying down. Smoothing

back my hair I sallied from the room to . . . be met by a
pigeon. A real life bird of the species capable of singlehandedly
bringing hats back into vogue. Being taller than he (or she) I
didn't feel at too much of a disadvantage and was about to
ask for some form of identification, when Solange and Ernestine came up the stairs.

They had been in the hall below, looking for some sign
that Marjorie and I had survived our mission, when Pigeon
scooted past and they had been sufficiently intrigued to
follow. Unfortunately not being a parrot, he refused to provide
information as to age, sex, political persuasion or position
in household. And the moment I began to account for my
recent whereabouts, Pigeon cocked its pearl grey head,
fixed me with a bored, beady eye and did a flit down the
hall.

"Tell on," Solange prompted eagerly. "After you meet
Mademoiselle Mary, what next?"

Knee deep in my monologue it did occur to me I might
be making a mistake in revealing that I had been where
wives of Mangé candidates had never trod—had seen things,
heard things that stretched the boundaries of credibility.
But these were my trusty associates, weren't they? And
believe me, when you have been the fattest girl in the
fourth form, you tend to butter your relationships. Put jam
on when necessary. Besides, both crossed their hearts and
hoped to die, should they squeal to their respective candidates.

Ernestine's eye might twitch a bit, but which of us
wasn't tired? Solange looked *splendide*. She claimed fatigue
suited her and I could only hope it would not be equally
kind to Ms. X—doing marvelous shadowy things to her
eyes while putting hollows under her cheek bones.

The comtesse pinched my cheek and called me little
wilted cabbage.

"*Ma chérie*, the *bonne* Ernestine and I took Jeffries to our
hearts when she brings our glasses of water. I tell her we
should warm our hands on her smile, that she eez *enchante*
and I am blue with envy. At that she hots up to say, she eez
invited to be a mannequin in a parade of fashion tomorrow
at Jimmy's Bar, but she eez too busy."

"Sure she is, if she's working overtime as a Mangé! Come on gals, let's not knock her! She and Pepys are out there doing a job that has to be done, if we're to see the advances in food preparation the nation demands." Ernestine sounded revved up, but her face looked as though it hadn't been slept on for a week. I was about to call it a night when I remembered something.

"All the time I was with Miss Rumpson I never asked what her area of culinary expertise is."

Ernestine snickered. "You sure don't read *Tattle Tale*, the magazine for people who want the pooper scoop! Shucks. Between these four walls, I'll admit to a free read at the checkout now and then. A couple of weeks back there was a full page spread on Marjorie Rumpson. The woman makes a living off that old saying about the way to a man's heart. Say there's some guy you want to reel in, but who keeps wriggling off the hook, you send Miss Rumpson his astrological sign, place of birth, favourite colour, names of both parents, you know how it goes, and she'll send you— for a fee—recipes assembled with you in mind. That'll bring his erotic juices to boiling point, and make him yours for life. And if you believe such crap I'm Miss America."

Marjorie Rumpson—maker of spells! And to think I had complained about being dragged away from Massachusetts without having seen Salem.

"We burn Jeanne d'Arc." Solange sighed. "Time for bed I theenk, and hope that my familiar soon comes. Ellie, your room eez 3L, third from left at top of stairs. *Bonne nuit.*"

My response was a little absentminded. It had occurred to me that I had not seen Mary Faith since she disappeared into the wardrobe with Marjorie. Considering all the talk of top-level secrecy, I doubted she would be encouraged to stay after making her appeal for Marjorie. Was it possible she had exited this floor by way of another staircase?

This house cried out to be explored in all its bizarre entirety. But it was the need to retrieve my handbag from the Red Room that sent me downstairs. As I passed the dining room I found the door open. I paused to contemplate the knives displayed on the wall. Surely there had been six. Now only four glittered in the harsh light. I pictured Pepys and Jeffries skulking in the shadows, blades at the ready to fillet any who dishonored the Mangé name. Odd, what fancies pregnant women have! I vowed my child would not have her mother's overblown imagination and hurried upstairs.

Entering the bedroom I was to share with my one-and-only I uttered a four letter word. Poky. And I had thought everything was bigger and better in America! Our assigned room was the size of a pantry and had more angles than a geometry lesson. The walls were papered in silver lurex accented with burgundy thread. The lampshade reminded me of a rag-and-bone woman's hat and the curtains could have been someone's underwear, hung up to dry. Curses! In attempting to reach the bed I became trapped between the plastic walnut dressing table and a nightstand with laminated carving. Was this what eclectic really meant?

Kicking off one of my shoes, I scored a goal between the bed posts and a rebound on my overnight bag. All criticism of Pepys aside, it was kind of him to carry it up for me. Knowing my toothbrush and nightdress were close at hand made me feel somehow less alone. Time to prepare myself for bed and the return of Candidate Haskell. My jealousy of Valicia X seemed a lifetime away. Ben wouldn't have all his male hormones if he hadn't done a double take on meeting her. Poor woman, she was—to put it crudely—gorgeous. Something society rather frowns upon these days. Brushing out my hair, I thought, lucky me, not having to face the mirror each day, wondering what on earth I could do to make myself look worse in order to be taken seriously. I picked up a pair of tweezers and sympathy for Ms. X went out like a light. Think she ever plucked an eyebrow in her life?

My hair down, sporting the white lawn nightdress Ben's mother sent for my last birthday, I looked like a well-fed ghost. A mirror had never been my best friend. Hunching an offended shoulder I sidestepped my way to the bed and lay down on the spread that pretended to be a field of poppies. The temptation to get between the sheets was strong, but I recalled Aunt Astrid's words: A wife should always be ready to do her duty. Probably accounted for the late Uncle Horace always having those dark shadows under

his eyes. Tossing and turning, I tried to find a really un-
comfortable position. No good. Sleep hovered ready to
pounce the moment I closed my eyes. Why not fetch *Pregnancy for Beginners* from my bag and look up the illustra-
tions showing the baby's prescribed appearance at this stage?
Better not. I preferred my own version of what the wee elf
looked like. Silken curls, a button nose, dimpled knees, and
dressed in a smocked white frock and bonnet. Stretching, I
almost knocked the bottle of water off the bedside table.
Deciding a glass might revive me, I toyed with a swig,
trying to determine the vintage and deeming it a fine natural spring water with excellent clarity and spirited carbonation . . . when I realized sleep was impairing my vision. A
copy of *Monster Mommy* lay beside the table lamp.

Usually I prefer bodice rippers to soul barers, but Mary
Faith had been so pleasant in her peculiar way, I felt obliged
to open up, sink back on my pillows, and try to enjoy being
depressed. Chapter One.

> *Hello Mother, this is your daughter speaking. Are you
> out there listening? It matters terribly to me that you under-
> stand this book is written out of love. I offer you the opportu-
> nity to grow—to change. I want you to know that I don't
> hate you for what you did to me—starting with the day you
> brought me into the world. I should have been born on
> November 23rd, but you had to go mountain climbing and so
> gave birth to me in an old hut on November 15th. Small
> wonder that all my life I've felt I'm being ripped in two.
> Inside I'm Sagittarius, but on the charts I'm a Scorpio.*

My heart bled—for me. I was in the wrong profession.
I had no more business becoming a mother than a doctor
performing sex change operations. I had never changed a
nappy, never said more than two words to a baby—if goo-
goo counts as two words. How would I know if it were
getting enough to eat? Or too much? Do cats really suck the
breath out of babies? Should I have a talk with Tobias the
moment I got home and explain the time had come for him
to make a life for himself outside?

Monster Mommy had flopped open, and it was impossible not to be wearily interested in it.

But after a page and a half of the sexually active suit of armour, I, Ellie Haskell, cried "Tommy Rot!" as I tossed down the book in disgust. "Unfair!" cried the ghost of childhood past. Mary might be viewing the world through the distorted lens of prepuberty, but her terror was real. Theola Faith was a brute. Drawing the sheets up to my chin I fought down a panic I couldn't explain, but which had the clammy chill of familiarity and absolutely nothing to do with the fact that the door was opening.

"Ellie!" Crossing the room in half a stride, Ben flung himself down on the bed and crushed me in his arms. "The meeting went on so long I was afraid you would have me declared legally dead. Come to me, my angel." He ran his fingers through my hair and kissed my eyes, my nose, my lips. "Did I never spill the beans that you are my sanity, my strength, my very reason for being?"

"Have you been drinking?" I raised him up by his hair to look deep in his eyes. He didn't have boozy breath, but I wouldn't have put it past the Mangés to invent a drink that was kiss-proof as well as eighty-proof.

He stuck a finger into the knot of his tie. "Darling, you know better than to ask questions about what went on in the secret meeting room. But I can tell you that nothing intoxicates like you . . ."

"Hmmmm." This did not bode well for Valicia X. I took over undoing his tie and told him to get his shoes off the designer poppy spread. "Would it be a breach of Mangé morality to tell me what you thought of the other candidates?"

"Meaning as fellow members of the human race?" He sat up and dropped his shoes on the floor. "Ellie, had I been expecting other candidates, these would still have floored me. Vincent LeTrompe, magician! A child prodigy named Bingo! Lois Brown, housewife. And Margaret Rumpson, latter-day witch."

"Marjorie," I corrected.

He didn't ask how I knew. He was unbuttoning his

shirt. A faraway look turned his eyes the colour of the sea on a cloudy day.

"Ben." Kneeling on the bed, I massaged his shoulders. "One does wonder why you are the only traditional chef in the bunch."

"Darling"—he reached back for my hand—"my lips are sealed."

"Because you don't know? Or because you're afraid this room is bugged?"

His laugh was no answer. But I still hoped that were I to stroke his hair just right and nibble his ears just so, he might become putty in my hands. If it can happen to case-hardened spies like James Bond, why not a woman's own husband? I certainly deserved some reward for not mentioning Valicia X. An inner voice whispered coward, but I didn't bite.

Time to work my way in by the back door. "I really liked Solange LeTrompe and Ernestine Hoffman." I rubbed his shoulders.

"Great."

"Mr. Henderson Brown certainly adores his wife." Nibble, nibble on his neck. "Darling, I know you will respect my confidence as I will yours. He's fearful of Lois's involvement with the wacky world of cookery. Afraid she might start tippling the cooking sherry perhaps."

This time I got a reaction. Ben abandoned my hands and started to pace—although, space being limited, he appeared to be treading water. "Lois Brown is a gem. Kind, decent, always thinking the best of others. Damn her! Why did she have to be on the team! I have absolutely no compunction about beating out the chaps—and that includes Miss Rumpson. She can take it on the chin; but when it comes to Mrs. Brown . . ."

"You're afraid of Lois Brown, hubby mine!"

"Hell, Ellie"—he kicked a shoe toward the door—"must you see through me, to the venal core? My feelings aren't those of chivalry. She's the one to be knocked off the horse. I can compete with a man who pulls cooked rabbits out of a hat. I'm not afraid of some snotty-nosed child star who asks several times during the evening "to be excused." I can surpass Dame Lovecharm. But a woman who puts three meals on the table for a family of eight, day after day, year after year—never once being sued for botulism poisoning—*she* has me worried."

"Darling, you'll fight a fair fight," I soothed. Should I mention Valicia's likeness to Vanessa so he could explain away the rude way he had stared? Too late! The peace of our boudoir away from home was shattered by a piercing scream.

"Don't worry," I reassured my hero as he grabbed for me. "Old houses always manufacture these strange noises. Our group heard such a scream earlier. But no bodies turned up. We concluded that Jim Grogg and his lady Divonne must be having a moon howl."

"What, Mr. Baking Powder? That weedy chap?" Ben smiled at my gullibility. "Not so! *That* was a scream that bears investigating. Sweetheart, hide under the bed if you feel the least bit insecure. Remember your delicate condition." And with that he was gone.

Was this to be the story of my stay at Mendenhall? Bedtime always an unrealized hope? Stop, cried a voice inside my head. Must you forever carp? Ben didn't leave you to rush out on a date. He . . . Footsteps beyond my door, voices congregating in the hallway . . . My stomach began to churn. I was afraid to venture into the hall to discover what dread misfortune had occurred, but I couldn't stay here. Peering around for my dressing gown, I remembered it now belonged to Miss Rumpson. Never mind. When without, go like Scarlett O'Hara. Dragging up the poppy field spread, I wrapped it around me. That lump in my throat must be my heart!

As far as my eye could see, the hall was empty. Then the bathroom door opened and out came Bingo Hoffman. A towel rolled up under his arm, he wore a bright red dressing gown which made him look like an apprentice Father Christmas.

"Get a load of you!" He thumbed his specs back on his nose. "What you supposed to be, an American Indian?"

Refusing to explain my attire, I solicited information on the scream.

"Oh, that!" His scowl filled out his already full cheeks. "I told the posse it wasn't me, but when in doubt—blame a kid. I was on my way along to Mum's room to tell her something, when I glanced over the railing and saw the ghost of Mendenhall. She was dressed up in a freaky long dress and a black bonnet with a ruffle of white round the face. And this is the fun part . . ." Bingo smacked his lips ". . . she was sticking up her finger."

"Dame Gloom," I whispered.

"What?"

"The woman in the portrait downstairs." Gingerly—I tend to approach children as if they are stray dogs—I touched his shoulder. "You poor old thing; someone's idea of a joke, which gave you a real scare."

He hugged the towel tighter. "So! I yelled. More of a gasp really. Sure didn't scream like I was in a Stephen King movie. My guess is it was Ms. Faith, waking up from a nightmare."

"You are a genius!" Convinced Bingo was anxious to see the back of me, I excused myself and entered the bathroom. Leaning against the door I took a couple of restorative breaths—one of which went down the wrong way. What was that scratching sound behind the bath curtain? Would a knife plunge through the fabric if I moved a muscle? I had my hand on the doorknob, when there came a whirring sound—rather like an electric blender. Sometimes I think I spend my life in a blender. The curtain moved and . . . that damn pigeon plopped onto the exposed portion of bath ledge.

"You!" Drawing back the curtain to ascertain he was alone, I saw scrawled on the tile behind the bath in big green letters: THIS HOUSE IS GOING TO GET YOU. Ah ha, was that why Bingo was carrying a towel? Somewhere to hide his markers. Was the prodigy a mean-spirited kid at heart? For a moment Pigeon and I looked at each other, before I turned pointedly away and opened up the medicine cabinet. If ever a night called out for an antacid tablet this was it! And I remembered seeing a bottle when Mary Faith showed Marjorie Rumpson and me the added dimensions of the cupboard.

I don't know what made me do it. A chance to show off for the pigeon? Removing the deodorants and such like, I pressed the miniscule button above the third shelf. Abracadabra! I was a magician equal to the comte. I could see right into the secret meeting room. I could see the stand with the coffee pot and paper cups. I could see the table . . . and I could see the demoralizingly beautiful Valicia X talking to Ben!

My heart squeezed closed, but I managed to press the button to my left; his voice was so close he could have been talking to me. "The moment you walked into the room I knew," he said.

"Did you?" Her Titian hair rippled back from her ivory brow. "And have you been counting the minutes until we could talk alone?" Her laughter was an avalanche burying me in cold. "Do tell, Ben, does your wife suspect?"

9

There being nowhere else for me to turn, I went home that night to St. John's Wood where I grew up. I had always thought the house rather like my Uncle Maurice— double-breasted, glassy eyed, a little shabby under the new coat of paint, but none the less thinking itself a cut above the neighbours. We lived in the top floor flat, a makeshift renovation of what had been servants' quarters—Dad's little joke being that one day we would move down to something better.

The dream wasn't fuzzy around the edges. No sensation of looking through the tattered film of sleep. I was there, climbing the sheer rock face of stairs, the naked boards worn slick as ice. I could feel my skirt grazing my legs, I could smell damp newspapers, and brass polish and fish. The banister was hard and real under my hand. Up, up, past Flat No. Five where old Mrs. Bundy lived. Terrible woman, forever thumping on the ceiling with her stick. But given to kindly lapses. I remember she let me stroke her cat Angela on my seventh birthday. And another time she slipped a tube of fruit gums into my school satchel, accompanied by a wheezy, "Not a word to Father." She meant Mr. Bundy, not my father.

The air grew thin. Out of condition, I was forced to use the banister as a tow rope. Dad took pleasure in proclaiming that we lived up in the Gods. Theatrical expressions fell lightly from his lips. He had trod the boards in his youth. Bit parts. Soldiers or policemen, that sort of thing. "Paid to be seen and not heard," was the way he put it. A severe test of the spirit for someone who believed Shakespeare wrote with him in mind. Once when playing a corpse in a graverobbing scene he burst into fiery rhetoric, failing to shut up until run through by the leading man's sword. He and my mother, a dancer, met while performing in the *Mikado*.

Always a performer, my mother. Was the role of parent any more real to her than Giselle, for whom she named me? Would she be home? My hand weighed heavy when I knocked on No. Six. The door barely visible under the collage of theatrical posters. And suddenly, I was terrified that I had made a mistake in coming. There was nothing for me here. Mother had been dead for years and Dad was God alone knew where. Neither had met Ben or, for that matter, Mrs. Bentley Haskell.

Too late. The door had slowly blown open, and a dreamy voice called out, "Come in, Ellie darling."

The sitting room was exactly the same as the day we moved in. Cosily, crazily crowded, with furniture set down in most peculiar places. The grandmother clock stood in the middle of the bare floor. And a desk was edged in front of the fireplace as if waiting to be moved into proper position. Christmas ornaments from years back dangled from the candelabra. A rug was rolled into a bolster, while linen curtains lay folded up on the window ledge waiting to go up. When there was time. My parents never had enough time to do everything they wanted to do. Case in point— Mother had been racing down a flight of steps—not the death-defying ones I had just mounted, but ones leading to a railway station, when she fell and died.

For a ghost, she looked awfully good. No more altered

than the room. One of the few advantages of dying young. Strange to think that one day, before too long, I would be older than she had ever been. But then some people have a talent for being young. At age six I was the one reminding her to wear a scarf out in the smog. I'd even threatened to sew her gloves on elastic strings inside her coat, if she lost another pair.

"Come and give me a hug, darling!" She was attired in several transparencies of muslin draped into a sort of Grecian tutu. Naturally she was as at the barre. Dad had installed the ballet barre and, true to form, it didn't run true. I blew her a kiss. She was in the arabesque position and a trifle unsteady en pointe.

"Ages since I heard from you." She wobbled slightly as she went into a deep knee bend.

"You're not easy to reach." I sat on a chair stacked with papers. "Mother, we have to talk."

"Any time, my little girl." She was doing a floaty motion with her right arm. "So lovely of you to come. Your father's always too busy being alive to keep in touch. And people have this silly idea that I've grown deadly dull since I passed over."

"Mother!"

"In all due vanity, I'm more alive dead than many people I know . . ."

"Oh, please!" I pressed my hands to my temples. "You never change! Always adrift in your own private sea."

Mother stopped standing on one leg, removed her hand from the barre and pressed it to her elegantly boney breast. "My darling, are you and that gorgeous husband having problems?"

I fought the snuffle in my voice. "Our relationship is in shreds and, Mother, I am here to assign blame. Had you but raised me to be beautiful, charming, and witty, Ben would never have turned to another woman."

She raised her left eyebrow and right leg simultaneously, but I didn't give her a chance to open her mouth. "How can you justify bringing a child into the world who would weigh more at age eight than you did at thirty? Where was your sense of responsibility when saddling me with a father who believes everything one owns should pack into one suitcase? You say he doesn't have time for you, well, what about me? I'm supposed to be *alive*."

"Ellie, dearest." She kept going at the barre. "All this resentment! Was I too busy to notice?"

"Too busy to be a mother. I wrapped my own Christmas presents."

"Was that wrong? Daddy and I wanted you to experience every facet of the excitement."

"I hosted my own birthday parties from age six."

"We wanted you to be self-reliant."

"Thank you. That explains your sending me alone by train and taxi to Merlin's Court to stay with an ancient great uncle whom I had never met? Let me tell you, Mother, that experience scarred me for life. The breakup of my marriage is the result. And don't tell me that I would never have met Ben but for Uncle Merlin. This is no time for relevancies. You never even noticed I'm going to have a baby, did you? Did you?"

"Ellie," Mother was standing still, only her tutu astir. "You could write a book about my sins."

"Why not!" I stood up and rigorously smoothed down the sleeves of my blouse. "Other people do it. How else is a divorced expectant mother to support herself?"

"My poor darling." Her voice was a whisper against my face, but I couldn't see her any more.

What a relief to wake up and realize that sleep had not impaired my memory. I could recall every anguished breath of last night's betrayal. Thank God for pride. When Valicia X referred to me as the unsuspecting wife, I had switched off the medicine cabinet and fled back to the bedroom. And when Ben returned some five or ten minutes later, I pretended to be dead. Oh, the horror of that Judas kiss upon my neck, the treachery of his hands smoothing back my hair, the anguish of hearing him murmur, "Sleep well, my love."

Sunlight knifed through the window and spattered the walls. Nine A.M. by the travel clock. Turning over, I found Ben's side of the bed empty. He must have heard me talking in my sleep and realized his life was in danger. Life loomed before me, insurmountable as a mountain of clothes to be washed. No one to bring me flowers; no one to tell me I looked great when I felt like hell; no one to do the ironing. The beast! Why couldn't he have made life unbearable so it would be easy to leave him?

Were there no depths to which he would not sink? Over by the window was our luggage, rescued from the boat house. How did I know he, and not Pepys, was responsible? Easy. The traitor had left me a note on the dressing table. I read it quickly, then ripped it into confetti. He hoped I had a happy day! And signed off with kisses. Ha! Did he already suspect that his fling with that woman would soon burn out in a blaze of passion? Was I to be kept around like a hot water bottle in case the central heating went out? The man must be made to pay.

Looking out the window at the water surrounding the island, I toyed with the idea of dying—from some rare river fungus, exacerbated by marital neglect. Let him put that kind of remorse in his pipe and smoke it. No! I mustn't indulge in these fantasies. Nothing must disrupt the even tenor of my misery. I had my child to consider. And truth be told, I felt wretchedly fit. Which left me no choice but to have a bath and get myself dressed in preparation for a flagrant affair with the first man to cross my path. My hopes weren't high because my skirt wouldn't button and I had taken no more than a couple of steps when I heard a rip. Oh, well! The sexy slit from knee to thigh went with my new image. I had stopped tearing my hair out and let it hang loose.

Fate handed Mr. Brown to me at the head of the staircase. His handsome face was a thoroughfare of emotions. None of them happy.

"Good morning," I said, batting my eyes at him.

"Yes, but *is* it a good morning?" Shoulders slumped, he made a half-hearted attempt at pulling my name out of the hat.

"Ellie Haskell," I helped out. "Also married to a candidate."

"Right—you're not the French one, or the one in orange trousers, but the pregnant one. Tell me, aren't you up to here"—he thumped a fist under his chin—"with this un-American, godless bunch of mumbo-jumbos?"

I reached up through my own misery to assuage his. "Mr. Brown, The Mangé Society is not a religious cult."

"We don't know what it is, do we? The Frenchwoman told me when I was downstairs trying to force down some breakfast as how the latest candidate is a witch."

Et tu, Solange?

"Mrs. Haskell, have you no fear? Don't you wonder what your husband will be turned into behind closed doors? Will you even know him when you get him back? Think of your child!" Mr. Brown's voice petered out. Accidentally, or on purpose, he had brought my face into focus, causing his to pucker in revulsion. He was looking at the slit up my skirt and my wanton hair as though I were a disease his Lois might catch. I wanted to shout, You're unhappy because your wife is in love with the idea of being a Mangé! Big deal! My husband is in love with a Mangé. And you, sir, have blown your chances! I'd sooner take a fast-acting depressant than have an affair with you!

I scraped up a smile. "If you'll excuse me . . ."

"Don't expect to see your husband downstairs," he said glumly. "Today's meetings are already in progress."

Perfect. I would rather walk the plank than descend those stairs to collide with Ben . . . and his Valicia. I wasn't ready to see anyone or to rub shoulders with them in the dining room. I needed time. Time for a face lift, time to learn to play the piano, time to acquire fluency in six languages. A witty, charming, accomplished woman can smile in the face of betrayal.

I abandoned Mr. Henderson Brown. Two doors down from the bathroom, tucked into an alcove, I found . . . a lift. Well, why not pamper yourself, Ellie dear? After all, you're pregnant. Opening the narrow wooden door I found another door—the brass accordion type, which separated me from a wooden platform suspended in the dark shaft. Careful. Sometimes the morning sickness had included a dash of vertigo. Ellie, you don't have to do this. Take the stairs for exercise! Nonsense! This was an adventure! Entering the elevator cage with its six-foot-high, iron mesh sides, I refused to believe I was about to become a prisoner of my own making. A light came on. The floor buttons were conveniently at hand. An electrical hum glided up my arm, a groan of ropes being churned over a rusty caster. Three, two, one: rocket descent. My insides lurched up as the floor dropped down. I gripped the sides of the cage, then dragged my hands inside; the walls of the shaft pressed closer with every downward jolt.

A half century later I reached the main hall. Amazing how all was the same as last night—the oppressive opulence of mahogany, the pawnbroker candelabra, the breathless air. Melancholy Mansion. Home of the Black Cloud. Might anything have been different if I had visited the Tramwells and spoken with Chantal? What was it she had said about my having to find the answer within myself?

"*Bonjour*, Ellee! You travel in style." Solange might have been clipped from the glossy page of a fashion magazine, circa 1789. She glided toward me, the cape collar of her cloak gown falling to her elbows; a wide black belt cinched in her waist. She wore bold black earrings and her hair was plaited into a knot low on her neck. "Why, what hurts you, *ma cherie*?" She touched a flame-coloured nail to my cheek. "You look fit to cry."

I very nearly threw my arms around her neck and sobbed out the whole dreary tale. Saved by the fear that my skirt would split further up my leg, also that, being French, Solange might think it not only acceptable, but *tres bien* for a man to have a mistress. The last thing I needed was to be called a spoil sport.

"These shadows under your eyes, you too find sleep hard to catch after the big scream. But I theenk we not have to be jolted up in our beds again. Mr. Grogg and Mademoiselle Divonne are gone. Never the word of good-bye. Never the word of good-bye, unless . . ." She figeted my collar straight. ". . . I count what I find on my pillow last night as the bon voyage."

"Escargot?" I asked.

"*Non!* That would be the good party favour. Someone take my Vincent's prize recipe for *La Potage Grandmère* and stab to zee pillow. My Victor is afraid to say 'boo!' because he think it some Mangé exam of will."

"Oh, dear." For no good reason I was remembering Ben's mentioning that Bingo had asked "to be excused" several times during the evening.

"We went into the dining room together. Having thought I never wanted to eat again, I discovered I was not immune to the enticing aroma drifting up from the sideboard buffet. "Did Pepys take the Groggs over to Mud Creek in a boat?" I asked Solange.

"What? Allow in my boat those who smuggled baking powder into this house! Over their dead bodies!" Laughter crackled. Sunlight was less kind to Pepys than the comtesse. Ice blue eyes peeped through lids resembling button holes frayed at the edges. His wrinkled face and bald head could have been a rubber mask—a couple of sizes too big. The rest of him was a sackful of loose bones shaken into a dark suit.

"How did Jim Grogg and Divonne leave?" I asked. I hadn't imagined the missing knives. Only four now hung in the elaborate display on the wall. Two brackets were empty.

"Don't know, neither care a tin nickel!" Pepys' eyes rolled upward until I could see only their sallow whites. "Have enough on my plate wondering what my sterling new employer, Miss Mary *Faith*, is doing in her room all day."

"Making of you the immortal?" Solange poured herself coffee.

Pepys shuddered. "Her mother now, what a difference! Never a moment's sitdown when Miss Theola's in residence! Through the house like a tornado, tripping on her feathery fripperies. Knocking ornaments off the piano. Shouting for Jeffries and me to join her in a sing song." His calloused hands adjusted some grapes on a platter of smoked salmon. "Enough! You ladies will excuse me if I shuffle off." Fists clenched, arms bent at the elbows, he did a slow jog out the door.

"Worry not." The comtesse set down her coffee cup, lips curving into a three-quarter smile. "We have not seen the last of him. My Vincent tells me Pepys is instructed by

Valicia X to take any who wish to the mainland. No skin off his knees. He has to collect Mees Rumpson's luggage anyway. I go now to put on a new face. Mrs. Hoffman comes with; so you also, Ellee, please!"

I promised and she left. Well, why not? Mud Creek did number among its attraction the black rental car. The keys were in my bag along with the infamous traveller's cheques. Wouldn't it be best for everyone concerned if I slid behind the wheel and drove off into the sunset?

"Nobility does not become you, Ellie!" Aunt Astrid was so fond of saying. My mother had put it a different way: "Darling, with your nose up in the air you can't see where you're going." A tear dribbled down that nose and plopped onto my lips. Curses! My eyelashes would shrink to nothing. What was that about starve a fever, feed a broken heart?

I was hovering indecisively between two chafing dishes set out on the black oak sideboard, when in came Jeffries. Luckily the room was shadowy. Jeffries wouldn't notice I had been crying.

"What you blubbering about?"

"I'm allergic to dust," I flared back.

She was the spitting image of Crosspatch the fairy. Her maid's uniform did as much for her as my tutu had done for me when I was eight years old and about her height—in both directions. Those horsehair curls and a face like a doorknocker! She was to be congratulated for not taking one look in the mirror and going to bed for life. Without flexing a bicep she had driven me back from the sideboard and was standing guard over the assembly line of silver chafing dishes and domed platters. Did I need a ticket to be served? Oh, crumbs! She lifted the lid and the most marvelous aroma of tomato and herbs, fortified with bacon, steamed forth. She stirred with a massive spoon and moved on to raise another lid. This time the aroma caramelized on my tongue. Brandied fruit baked into a sticky sponge.

My stomach rumbled.

"You say som'at?" Jeffries wielded a spoon that had to be taller than she in a pan of scrambled eggs, rich with cheese and cream and chives. "Someone standing on your tongue?"

"I'll take a lit—make that a *lot* of everything."

Fixing me with her walnut eyes, she jabbed a finger at the three plates I held out. "Collecting for your bottom drawer?"

"Eggs is eggs and tomato is tomato and never the twain shall meet."

"Ain't you the oddball!" Surprisingly, she made it sound like a compliment. "And I don't suppose you go for paper plates either."

"No, I don't."

She spooned eggs onto one of my plates, white china with a blue rim. "I tell Pepys that paper plates has done more to bring down the good old U.S.A. than anything else. Back in the days when I was a dresser to Theola Faith and His Nuttyness was doorman at the Palace Theatre, people *knew* how to party."

I handed over another plate. "What is she like—Miss Faith? I got the impression from something someone said" (best not to mention Mary) "that you don't see a lot of her."

In the manner of a revolving door, Jeffries went back the other way—into unpleasantness. "She's a boss—that's what she's like! Any more I won't say. Not while that woman who calls herself a *daughter* is in this house. Here the walls don't just have ears, they got mouths too!" Her vehemence had me backing away from her. "We're in that book of hers you know, me and Pepys. Calls us by different names—to protect the innocent. Don't that beat all? Think I wouldn't know myself anywhere? Bouncing curls and a pixie smile. You tell me you ain't looking at it?"

Quick! Grab for a change of topic. "This must be a busy time for you, but at least you are down two with the Groggs gone. Who took them to Mud Creek?"

"Wasn't me. So what's your guess?"

"I . . ." Backing away from her serving spoon.

"And don't hold your breath for any of the candidates to own up that they stuck their oar in the river. You heard the rules about none of them being allowed to leave the island. All you auxilliary folk have played dumb, so the only one left would be *her*."

"Valica X?"

"Not likely! She's afraid of water."

"I see . . . Mary . . ." Dragging out one of the throne chairs, I sat in solitary splendour at the table. Some habits are hard to break. I was worrying about Ben. Would he have been so rash as to row the Groggs to freedom had he spotted them standing forlorn on the shore when he went down to the boathouse for our luggage? Acts of derring do appeal to him.

"Food not good enough for you?" Jeffries was at my shoulder with the coffee pot.

"Delicious!"

"Always stare at the wall, do you?"

"No." I removed my elbow from something soggy. "Last night I happened to glance in here and there were six swashbuckler knives on that wall. Now there are only three."

A bloodcurdling scream ripped from Jeffries' lips. I caught the coffee pot just in time. She was hopping from foot to foot, face twisted into the rage of a gnome who comes home to find all his spells stolen. "First someone tampering with the rules and now this! Those knives were used in *Melancholy Mansion!*"

"Really!" I gripped the seat of my chair. "Do you mind my asking if you often give that scream?"

"Primal yell. Psychiatrist's orders. Sometimes I can go days without giving vent but I was overcome twice by the healthy impulse last night and—"

Her next words were lost. The room did not possess an electric ceiling fan, but suddenly it was as though one were turned on full blast. Two of my plates leaped in the air and the coffee pot went into another skid. We had been invaded by the ubiquitous pigeon. Our feathered friend must have been hiding behind the curtains, eavesdropping on our conversation. But what was this . . . ? I was seeing double! There were two of them. Around they went in a power play, beating me into the submission position, arms over my head.

Jeffries to the rescue! "Cool it, Derby! And you too, Joan! Or I swear I'll break your legs."

Tamely the two birds perched on the curtain rod, fixing their beady eyes upon us, as if to say: "What fools these mortals be."

Behind us, I heard a door close.

Collecting my shoulder bag from my room, I had second thoughts about the excursion to Mud Creek. Two's company, three's a crowd when one of the trio is down in the dumps. Ernestine and Solange would be all buddy-buddy with good cheer, whispering middle-age secrets, and giggling at the latest divorce jokes. I would laugh dutifully in the wrong places. And they would nudge each other. Perhaps tap their foreheads. Honestly, did I need this? A woman can only take so much abandonment. All by way of saying that my reason for going along to Mary Faith's room and knocking on her door was not altruistic. I needed the solace of her wounded smile, the uplift of her plaintive voice.

"Come in."

The invitation was every bit as unenthusiastic as I could have wished, and the room exactly as I remembered from last night. A place reserved for layings-out and lyings-in. The massive wardrobe was the gateway to the secret room. The dun-coloured curtains were drawn back against the wall—doubtless a job for two strong men. The dark furniture would seem to have been bought for weight, like coal, at so much a ton. The inert form in the middle of the Henry VIII four-poster bed surely had to be Mary. Pepys and Jeffries couldn't keep disrupting their busy schedules to slip something vile under their employer's sheets.

When a hand edged back the bed-hanging cordoned by gold rope, I suppressed a whimper.

"Put my tea on the table and stay out until I ring again. You're dealing with the woman who has been reviewed in *The New York Times* and twice invited on *Good Evening, U.S.A.* I'm no longer the child who can be threatened with the dryer."

None but Mary. As she sat up, I nearly screamed.

The sun zeroed in cruelly upon her mashed beehive and face slathered in masklike cream. She had no mouth and dark holes where her glasses should have been. They lay next to the phone upon a nightstand on the side of the bed furthest from the door. Obviously she took me for Pepys or Jeffries even though squinting my way. And, true to form, I felt guilty—as though I had crept in upon her under false pretenses. Poor Mary. I could hear my cousin Vanessa or Valicia X remarking admiringly, "No one is born that plain, they have to really work at it." The long-sleeved nightdress Mary wore was demure to the point of being hopeful.

"It's me, Ellie Haskell!" I tiptoed forward, my bag slapping against my side. "Sorry to barge in like this, but I wondered if you would care to go into Mud Creek. Several of us—"

"What, me!" She flinched back against the headboard. "Do you really mean me?" She reached for a tissue but did not burst into tears. Instead she set to scrubbing the white muck off her face. Kicking off the saffron sheets and tapestried spread in a coltish flurry, she stood up. "Theola always drilled into me that I didn't have what it takes to make friends; but I knew last night you and I were soulmates. You have that same downtrodden air that I have."

"Thank you." I tried to look gratified.

"On you it looks good." Mary tossed aside the tissue. "Hand me my bathrobe, will you, sweetie. Oh, this is so merry—like the morning after a slumber party! Lunch will be my treat."

"Oh, no!" I protested.

"You're right. Best friends always go Dutch. Will we have the other two tagging along with us all day?"

Bother. I couldn't spot the dressing gown among the clothes tumbled on chairs and spilling over the window ledge, and I was beginning to suspect that Mary was developing a schoolgirl crush on me. A fine time for my mother's words to come back to haunt me: Ellie darling, if you really want to be popular become a recluse. That way you are a name on a thousand tongues, you get invited to parties no one expects you to attend, the merest glimpse of you causes a stir, and you never have to deal with people.

Trailing across a grizzly bear rug to the black marble fireplace and back, I almost tripped over the dressing gown's dangling cord. I attempted to hand it to her but she was putting on her glasses. And the phone rang. We both stared at it as though unable to believe our ears.

"Jeffries said there wasn't one," I sounded accusatory.

Brrrrrr! Brrrrrrr!

Mary, the grease turning her face sallow as melted butter, sidestepped toward the nightstand, reached out a hand and . . . stood rubbing it. "A phone, you mean!" Her eyes fixed on it, she took one step forward, two back. "Mangés speak with forked tongue! Valicia X didn't want any of the candidates to know there was one lest someone cheat and contact outside sources for help."

The phone continued to bleat. "Would you like me to get that?" I offered. "I imagine you have been besieged by reporters."

"Yes, that must be who it is! Or someone from my publisher . . ." Her expression eased, but she lifted the receiver as though it were a dead rat. "Hello?" Before my eyes she shrank, incredible as it sounds, to child-size. Suddenly I could picture her with pigtails, wearing a panama hat like I had worn to St. Roberta's. I hovered forward with her bathrobe as she slithered down onto the edge of the bed.

"Theola!" She gripped the phone with both hands, her knuckles turning blue. Oh, dear! I didn't like the sound of her breathing! I wished I had a tank of oxygen handy or at least Primrose Tramwell's smelling salts. I also wished I hadn't cracked my shin on the knight's chest at the bottom of the bed. But never mind that! Mary was sitting up straighter. Her mouth had firmed up and there was a gutsy sparkle to her glasses.

"Enough with that cute stuff, Theola, where the hell are you?" Her voice shot up shrilly. "Guess? Why should I? I won't be drawn into your devilish game . . . All right—Florida! What do you mean stone cold? Miami is never . . . damn it, you've done it to me again, made me the butt end of one of your stupid jokes! But to show there's no hard feelings"

—her laugh came out in a rush like a shaken up fizzy drink—"why don't you let me buy you a nice little place in the country, a mausoleum in Happy Meadows Cemetery? I can afford it. The millions I'm making from *Monster Mommy* are almost as obscene as your fling with the Tarzooki boys— father, son and grandpa. What do you mean I should shut up while there's still time? How do you plan to make me shut up—put my toys down the garbage disposal? No, I will not recant." Mary's voice now came in jerks. "You did too ruin my sixth birthday insisting that my hair be dyed to match yours and we dress alike so we could pretend to be sisters. Everyone thought I was your little old *grandma*." Mary's laboured breathing could surely be heard all the way to Mud Creek. "You listen to me, Theola—or would you like it in writing in the sequel? Either you treat me as an adult, entitled to form my own opinions—one being that you have a heart of stone and a brain of silicone—or there is no hope what-so-ever of our ever being able to relate. . . . What's that? You are going to sue me for every penny I've made on *Monster Mommy*? Don't make me laugh!" A laugh heavily laced with hysteria. "Your days as a comedienne are over, *Theola Faith*."

"Maybe I should leave," I ventured.

"No, please!" Mary pressed a hand over the receiver. Her face was greasy pale.

Aware I must keep up my strength, I sat down in a chair with lion's head knobs.

"So it's threats now is it!" Mary wrenched to her feet, her chest heaving under the maidenly nightgown; somehow she had managed to wrap herself in the telephone cord. "Come again . . . you'd like to do *what* to me? Hold on one minute! Why don't you repeat that for a witness— the bit about tucking me up for the night in the trunk of your car and sending me rock-a-bye-bye over the edge of a cliff." Hands shaking, Mary held out the receiver to me, nearly strangling herself in the attempt.

Scrambling up, I was uncertain whether I would be helping or hindering by lending an ear, but Mary's cry— "Ellie, listen to her. She means what she's saying!" broke through my British reserve.

"Too late! She hung up." Mary's eyes took on a blank stare. The receiver dropped from her hand and she fell against me. Awkwardly I patted her shoulder. "There, there!" I said over her heaving sobs.

"If only I could have pried out of her where she is staying. The more states between us, the safer I feel." The face that lifted to meet mine looked truly terrified. "You don't know what she can be like! I must get away from here at once." She dodged over to the wardrobe, opened the door, and let it hang.

"No!" She pressed fingers to her temples, shifting the wing-tipped glasses upward. "The new Mary Faith—the darling of the literary circuit—does not turn tail and run. Ellie, I am as safe on this island as anywhere. And one thing I can put a stop to." She trod firmly over to the nightstand. "You won't be calling back, Monster *Mommy!*" On the last word, she savagely yanked the telephone cord out of the wall.

She'd certainly made a truth teller out of Jeffries. There now was no telephone at Mendenhall.

"Ellie, do you mind if I don't join you in going into Mud Creek?"

Mary lay back down on the tapestry spread, eyes closed, completely rigid, causing, I am ashamed to say, the words of a music hall style ditty to creep up on me . . . "Oh, she do make a love-rly corpse, she do, her face the sweetest shade of blue . . ."

Drawing the dun-coloured curtains against the false heartiness of the sun, I thought it was pity that someone didn't murder Theola Faith.

The ride across to Mud Creek in the cabin cruiser brought out all Pepys' charm. His ebony suit bathed in greenish light, his narrowed lids revealing slivers of white, he was a drowned soul risen from the watery depths. Conversation was desultory among the passengers, who included in addition to Solange, Ernestine, and myself, Henderson Brown. Perhaps it was his gloomy face under the white linen hat which strengthened the mood of a ghost ship, never destined to reach shore.

The sun fired up the sky, and before we had covered half the distance, my back threatened to crack from the heat and my eyebrows had been singed off. A flicker of wind faded quickly. Spray roused by the boat stung my face, but did not cool it. The river was as smooth as brown bottle glass, except for the occasional *pop-plop* of a wave.

I tried to focus on the scenery—the limestone cliffs to the rear, bristling with trees on top, like a Mohawk haircut. Easy to imagine Indians scouting up there when Mud Creek was only a settlement. Ah, here came the shore, rushing toward us like an unwanted destiny. Through gaps in the buildings I could see cornfields beyond . . . and part of a red barn. Away to the right was a white clapboard church. Same puritan tranquility as I had spotted on the drive from Boston. Now I could see the mud track where we had parked the car. The trees were pretty. But you can only stretch appreciation so far. The petrol station wasn't cute, the Lucky Strike bowling alley wasn't quaint, and Jimmy's Bar looked like a warehouse. Suddenly Henderson Brown was treading on my heels in his haste to leave the boat.

Clustered with my fellow voyagers on the dock, I heard the motor burst back into life and watched Pepys head the boat back to Mendenhall. He'd said something about returning for us, but I'd missed the details. I felt lifeless. A piece of driftwood washed upon the shore. And when next I looked, there I was on the corner of Main Street and an alley, inhabited by rubbish bins, being investigated by a cat. The resemblance to Tobias was no stronger than two ears, four legs and a good set of whiskers. But I felt the urge to kidnap him and . . . I was back in my body—such as it was, with a morning to kill and a husband . . .

The others were agreeing to split up and regroup at Jimmy's Bar at one o'clock. Fighting down the childish urge to beg Ernestine to let me tag along while she went shopping for sunscreen, I swung my bag over my shoulder. Really, Ellie! You should be wearing one of those unaccompanied minor tags the airlines provide for children travelling alone.

Yesterday I'd experienced the feeling that Mud Creek was shut down, awaiting a gun fight. Now I wondered if its good citizens were down for their midmorning naps. Ernestine, the comtesse, and Henderson Brown were gone. Was the one traffic light permanently stuck on red? No, a pickup truck cruised around a corner, driven by a youth wearing a baseball cap. A giant of a man in work overalls came out of nowhere to go bulldozing up the broken-down steps of the diner with its cardboard menu in the window. The spring door banged behind him. Did a teeming shadow life exist behind all these dusty windows?

My brains were frying along with the rest of me, but I was to be sent a sign. It swung above the door of a sagging grey house that had been turned into a shop. Nelga's Fashions, with the One Size Fits All frock in the window. An inspection of my split skirt convinced me I needed this place almost as much as it needed me.

A blunt-faced woman with cropped hair sat on a kitchen chair with her back to a rack of print and check garments.

"You looking for anything in particular?" She uncrossed her legs but didn't stand up.

"Something in maternity." I hovered by the counter, cluttered with toy animals. "Perhaps I'm jumping the gun somewhat, I'm only four months. What do you think?"

"Go right ahead and look." From the sound of her she disapproved of people buying anything, but—the world being what it is—nothing's gonna stop the offenders; so might as well make it legal. "Find something that suits, ten percent off the sticker price."

"Thank you."

"Don't mind my saying, love the way you talk."

"Thank you."

She recrossed her legs. "My grandmother used to talk that broken English. Came over as a girl from Li-ces-ter-shire, I think it was. You know anyone named Wright?"

"I'm sorry . . ." There went my discount.

"You passing through, or did you come with that Mangé group?" She made them sound as if they came in a packet with instructions for French onion dip on the back.

Shifty-eyed, as though confessing to membership in Jesse James's gang, I admitted the association.

"Tell me"—she reached over to a dish of mints—"what sort of goings-on is there . . . over to Devil's Island?"

"I really can't say."

She juggled the mints in her hand. "Dice you into egg noodles, would they—if you squeal?"

"Nothing like that." I was rifling through the rack of skirts with elastic fronts. "Society regulations demand absolute secrecy."

"What?" She tilted her chair around on one leg to face me. "Passwords and contracts signed in blood—that sort of screwy business?"

I had nothing against her curiosity. It was, after all, perfectly natural. A healthy interest aroused by the possibility of unhealthy practices. Such attitudes abound. They explain the enormous success of books such as *Monster Mommy*. But all this talk of the Mangés was reminding me of that most covert of all operations—the . . . *don't think 'undercover'* . . . secret doings between Valicia X and my husband. On the verge of crying all over a candy-striped dress with a huge pink bow, I scooped it up along with several skirts and smocks and told Nelga Fashions that the Mangés might sign in gravy, but not blood.

One o'clock was still an hour out of reach; so on returning to the pavement I did a daring thing. I walked into the Scissor Cut, took deep breaths of hairspray and decided I was in luck.

My mission in the Scissor Cut was to be transformed from Before into After. I did not have Valicia X's flawless face and figure. My hair lacked amber highlights. But it was longer than Valicia's, and in a blaze of insight I knew that my marriage was salvageable. I was not compelled to tie Ben up with a red ribbon and hand him over to that woman. All I needed to do was get rid of my split ends.

Only one of the hairdryers was occupied and there were no heads in any of the three basins. The receptionist, who wore a T-shirt with "World's Best Great Grandma" on it, ran a finger down the book resting on the glass cabinet and said Barbara could take me.

Coming over, Barbara administered a quick smile without looking at me. Usually the kiss of death from a hairdresser. But maybe she was embarrassed. Her eyes were a little red, and she spoke as though she had a cold. I followed her past the client under the hairdryer, an elderly lady sleeping as soundly as the terrier on her lap.

I was soon sitting on a black vinyl chair, neck arched back over the rim of the sink. Not the most comfortable of positions; the same I suppose could be said of childbirth.

The water was soothing. Barbara asked if I wanted conditioner and I gurgled a response. Hairdressers and dentists! Her massaging hands were relaxing. I was sinking into a warm well of comfort. Mendenhall brought in its drinking water, but there must be a well somewhere on the island. I wondered about the missing knives. Surely a Mangé competitor had not armed his or herself for the upcoming trials? I knew competition was fierce, but surely no one would carry things that far?

Suddenly water was splashing all over my face, gushing into my mouth, filling up my nose. I couldn't breathe, my neck was breaking and those hands, Barbara's hands, the hands of a woman who hadn't known I existed three minutes before, were pushing me down into a world of darkness where ghosts are the living. Strange, my last thoughts weren't of Ben, but of Rowland Foxworth, dear handsome vicar of St. Anselm's. How awfully sad if the economics of returning me to British soil cheated him out of performing last offices.

10

"There, there cookie, you'll be fine. You've had a shock, is all. Here, take a couple of my nerve pills."

A second voice—mentioning hot tea. Not too appealing considering it would be served the American way. Without milk. And none of my business, seeing I wasn't recipient of all this kindness. Great Grandmother Receptionist and Roxanne, hair stylist, were seated on a vinyl bench, arms draped around Barbara as she sobbed into a fluffy towel. I wore a similiar one, which Grannie had absently dropped on my head, rather as though I were a parrot in a cage, whose squawks must be silenced before everyone developed screaming headaches.

"I'm so sorry!" Barbara lifted a face raw with tears. "I must have gone mad. You look like that little slut who stole my Dave. She bet Dave a *Bud Light* at the Catfish Fry she could eat him under the table. That's how it started. And I know I'll never get him back—not while she works at the bank!"

"Hush up, sweetie!" Roxanne rocked Barbara like a baby.

"If I don't let him see her Thursday nights, she could

foreclose on the house. All week I've been thinking what if she comes in for a wash and blow dry. And just now it all got mixed up. That was Darlene's head over the basin . . ." The flood gates reopened.

"You cracked, is all!" Great Gran pressed a Styrofoam cup to the trembling lips, while Roxanne stroked the red hair.

"I'll lose my license. Then what happens to me and the kids? And *she'll* sue me for millions." Her finger pointed at me. "Nothing else for it, I'll have to kill myself for insurance." Barbara's voice rose, shrill as a whistling kettle.

Finally, the three of them were looking at me—not as a bona fide participator in this human drama, but as a witness who must be made to see reason.

Great Gran aimed a smile at me, guaranteed to warm the cockles of my heart, if not my soaked torso. "You do see, hon, how things are! Barb's been through one real hard time."

Before I could answer, however, Roxanne grabbed my towel and began massaging my hair. "That red mark on your throat comes from wearing the neck of your dress too tight. Now how's about I give you a blow dry on the house and all the coffee you can drink?"

Gently but firmly I removed the towel and wadded it up into a ball. "Please, all of you, don't give my involvement another thought. I'm fine . . ."

"Are you sure?" Tears still splashed down Barbara's face.

"Yes." Standing up, I patted her on the shoulder. Remembering Mary, I realized I'd been doing a lot of that today. "This has been a positive experience for me. When I came in my life didn't look too good—for reasons similar to yours, but I have been reminded that however bleak life is, it still beats the alternative."

"Then you won't say a word?" Barbara said, still eyeing me suspiciously.

"Promise." A wistful smile brushed my lips as I followed her to the loo to change. The Mangés had their secrets and so did I.

When I walked into Jimmy's Bar, I wasn't surprised that none of my fellow auxiliaries rushed up to me with cries of welcome. I was a changed woman. Roxanne had decided a blow dry was insufficient compensation. She had wound my hair on fat pink rollers, sprayed it with Stif-Set, and popped me under the dryer to bake until golden brown. And thus a country-and-western songstress was born. As for my clothes—I had expected the switch over from regular wear to maternity to be an occasion worthy of a champagne toast, but it had happened in the loo at the Scissor Cut, without any beating of drums.

Jimmy's Bar might do great business, but I wasn't smitten with the red rubber floor or Styrofoam ceiling.

A good-looking chap in ultra-tight jeans wouldn't move fore or aft to let me pass. "Miss . . ." He was so close I could count his eyelashes.

"I'm trying to meet some people." Scanning a tunnel between heads I saw Ernestine, from the neck up, over by the back wall.

"Miss, you are standing on my foot."

"Sorry!" Men today are such frail creatures.

"'You're also wearing a price sticker."

Shucky darn! I climbed over three people to reach Ernestine and found her at a table with Solange and Henderson Brown, who was hiding out under his white sun hat. His gloom did not lift when the waitress headed our way. Probably disapproved of her substantial bosom refusing to be confined within the ruffled edge of her blouse. And from the looks of her Roman nose and iron jaw, she wasn't all that tickled with being decked out like Heidi on her way to Grandfather's chalet. Licking her thumb, she flipped over a page in her order book. "What's your pleasure, people."

Henderson fought for the courage to speak out. "We need separate checks."

"Ain't no extra charge." Heidi had her pencil poised. "What you all want to drink?"

Solange and Ernestine ordered white zinfandel.

Henderson forced a thin smile. "I'm a chronic abstainer. Water please, if it's fresh."

"Won't find better anywhere, with or without the French labels." Heidi had a deep voice. "Natural spring water, crisp and clean as a spring day."

For the first time post–Valicia X, I had to swallow a laugh. She sounded like a television advert. Flashback to the Mulberry Inn. Ben and I watching the excerpt from *Melancholy Mansion* and Theola Faith's interview with Harvard Smith. Now sitting there in Jimmy's Bar, the realization swamped me that I was a puppet in the hand of fate, pranced and danced across thousands of miles to this place.

What can't be changed can be improved by a good lunch. "Hamburger, double fries, and a Coke, please."

"Rest of you want to order?" Heidi cocked an eye at the big round clock above the bar. "Fashion show's due to start in ten minutes."

Ernestine reminded us that Jeffries had turned down the chance to be a model. Henderson said he would have the vegetable beef soup, then changed his mind. Lois, he informed us sourly, made the best soup in the world. Trust Ernestine to hotly disagree. Her Bingo, at age three, could produce a *potage de légumes* that had your mouth watering a mile away. The comtesse, her heavy rouge darkening, stared into the crowd. Poor Eeyore—I mean Henderson! Mouth set in mutinous lines, he joined the rest of us in ordering a hamburger.

Before Heidi could escape, Ernestine asked if the man behind the bar was Jimmy.

"Him—grey-haired guy with chipmunk cheeks? That's our good old boy Sheriff Tom Dougherty. Comes in every day along of this time to check if there's any fight needs breaking up."

"This town has its own sheriff?" Henderson would be writing his congressman to protest abuse of taxpayers' money.

Heidi looked him smack in the eye. "Believe it or not, sir, Mud Creek used to be the county seat. That's Jimmy up next to Sheriff Tom."

"Jimmy's a *she*?" Henderson couldn't keep on at this pace, shocked one moment, aghast the next.

"You're looking at her! Name's Jemima on her birth certificate. But don't never let on I told." Tucking the pencil behind her ear, Heidi was off with a rolling gait toward the door marked Private.

The crowd had shifted away from the bar providing us with a good view of the big-boned woman with hair that was stained, rather than dyed, a metallic red. She wore a satiny garment which could have been a negligee; a faded rose was stuck into her cleavage. Her face was caked with enough paint to do up a semidetached inside and out, and she had a voice guaranteed to stop rabble-rousers dead. "Dad-blamed fly!" she roared, hand whapping down on the counter.

The conversation at our table flowed like water up hill. "Should always wear your hair like that, Ellie," Ernestine said. "Makes your face look thinner."

"You are an authority on fashion?" Solange surveyed the other woman's Friar Tuck coiffure, mustard dress and frog green beads. Did I detect a growing coolness between these two?

"Honey, I don't claim to be a glamour girl. Never could go out in the sun without turning into a hot dog. But that's all right with me because my family is what's important. Frank's and my money is spent on our child. But being childless, you can't know what real self-denial is. My Bingo's happiness, his . . ."

"His being a Mangé, *n'est pas*? *Mais oui*, you don't like so much when I tell you—before Monsieur and Ellee come—that my Vincent will not hand in his dreams to please you. He has tricks up his sleeve you don't dream!" Solange had changed from a photograph into a woman of fire. The cape collar of her black dress brushed the table as she snapped her flame-tipped fingers in Ernestine's outraged face. "I give this much for your Bingo. My poodles are the children of my heart. Angelique, Fleur, and the rest, how can they be content when their *papa* is sad? My Vincent is near to fifty and I am running close behind. He is bored of putting me in the oven on stage—making the big bang explosion before he brings out the burned chicken. My wish is for

Vincent once in his life to find a dream that does not ask for me to be sliced in two."

What had fueled such animosity? We had seemed harmonious enough friends last night, when conducting Operation Marjorie Rumpson.

Ernestine's hair stuck to her red face. She looked ready to speak volumes, but fortunately our drinks and food arrived and I was able to move smoothly into praise of the crispy golden fries, the artful way the onion and tomato slices were nestled on the hamburgers.

"Yes, but is the beef Grade A?" fretted Henderson.

Heidi shouldered off and a voice bellowed through the hubbub. "Hush up, all you big time yackers, this is Jimmy speaking." The ogress in satin with the rose growing out of her bosom tapped cigar ash in a glass and leaned forward, elbows on the bar. "We've had some problems raising money for repairs to the kiddy playground, but a challenge is what the Hope Church women likes best. So sit yourselves down, hold up the walls or whatever suits, and listen up while our very own Sheriff Tom Dougherty gives you the run down on our Fashion Fantasia!"

Applause.

"Shucks, folks." The sheriff smoothed a hand over a thatch of hair which was at once grey and boyish. A hoist of the gun belt slung low on hips. Just like the movies. "Howdy do, friends, neighbours, and tourists!" His eyes picked out our table as though committing each of us to a file marked vagrants. "Don't anyone go expecting me to come off sounding like some spokesman for Dior." A suggestion of dimples in his chubby cheeks as he smiled. "But I tell you we've got some down-home goodlooking gals for your viewing pleasure. And, remember, the voluntary contribution isn't voluntary, not unless you want to be charged with leaving the scene of a good cause."

The jukebox began playing drifty, dreamy music. The sheriff pulled out a notebook. "A big welcome if you please for Mud Creek's favourite twins, Terese and Teresa Brinharter!"

Through the door marked Private, down the rectangle of space between the people lining the bar and the tables lining the window wall, came two young females. Hair: Swedish blonde. Tans: California's best. Their skimpy outfits could have served as wrist bands for sporty males. Their giggles floated among the outcry of admiration. "Clothes made by the gals' mother Irene, God bless her." I vowed every scrap of clothing worn by my child would be lovingly stitched by hand.

Next a fresh-faced young woman in a barn dance outfit, a check blouse and blue skirt flounced out by a white frilled petticoat. Almost as much applause for her as the twins. Now came a sweet little girl about four. She wore pink and carried a basket of posies with all the aplomb of a grownup.

My interest didn't fade. *I* began to fade. So little sleep last night. The figures coming down the ramp began to blur one into another . . . I hoped I wouldn't slide off my chair or worse, start talking in my sleep. I heard a click, as of a door opening, and Ben strolled nonchalantly into my mind.

"Ellie, I love you."

"No, you don't."

"Sweetheart, you can't believe everything you see and hear."

He had swept me up in his arms, I was floating . . . in circles. *"Well, I suppose if you care enough to lie . . ."*

I snapped awake when the music changed pace to a bump and grind. Why all the gasps from the audience? Had the Brinharter twins been called back for an encore? Even Henderson Brown was straining forward in his seat.

"Friends, darlings, country people! Lend me your ears!" The voice was spun sugar. The woman drifting down the ramp wore white silk edged with ermine, and swirled two gigantic feather fans before her. She was thirty—perhaps forty—years older than the twins, nowhere near as beautiful, but a hundred times more fascinating. Hers was a gamine face framed by bobbed silver hair. She had panda bear eyes and a vivid mouth stretched into a "gee whiz" smile.

Theola Faith.

"Theola Faith!" Ernestine clutched my arm, her expression repeated on forty some other faces. Only Henderson

Brown looked aghast, as the woman in white pointed a dainty silver toe out from her skirt, arched her neck and swiveled her slender hips. "I do not come to bury my daughter under the kind of abuse she has shoveled on me. The quality of mercy is not strained, it is mightiest in the mother." Two quick steps forward. Waggling one of the fans, Theola Faith tickled Henderson on the nose. He sneezed. Not another sound anywhere in the bar. She stood centre stage, the fans trailing to the floor. "I could have resisted the urge to return to the heartland, had not my darling daughter Mary usurped my house, my servants, and my pigeons."

"What you want, Theola?" The sheriff tucked his notebook in his belt.

"Revenge."

"Hey, we don't want trouble." Unidentified male voice.

The clown bright smile didn't dim. "And you lot call yourselves the Welcome Wagon! As well Jimmy remembers, she owes me for all those nights I paid the rent on this joint, sitting on the bar singing 'Love Me or Leave Me.' Jimmy's paying up by putting her penthouse at my disposal." A flourishing sweep of the ceiling with one of the fans punctuated this avowal. "Any of you guys got a better offer?"

A woman near our table shoved a hand over her male companion's open mouth.

"Theola," the sheriff said, his face, under the grey thatch, as bashful as a boy's. "You won't find *Monster Mommy* on the book mobile when it comes through. Our Jane Spence, of Citizens For Decency, wrote over to the library and told them we wouldn't have it."

"What! None of you has read the sweet things my darling Mary wrote about me?" The panda eyes grew big. The crimson smile broadened. "Don't you home-grown tomatoes keep up with what's in in sin? Or do you only believe your eyes?"

Executing a slow turn, Theola Faith brought the fans up over her eyes, slowly lowered them and purred, "Hit it, maestro, please!" The jukebox was silent, but she swayed to an inner rhythm. The silver hair curved against her cheeks; her ageless face was spread with a smile, coy as a bared ankle.

Theola Faith sang in a bouncy, music hall voice

"Oh, Ma whatever have you done
Say you didn't kill the lodgers just for fun!
It simply can't be true
Mr. Jones hung in the loo . . ."

Hard to tell the reaction to the ditty because the cat-calls, and now Henderson sliding under the table, could have resulted from Theola Faith having tossed first one of her long white gloves then the other into the crowd. Oh, no! Everyone close their eyes! Holding both fans in one hand, she was unzipping the side of her white silk gown.

"Mr. Green bumped off a treat.
Mr. Smith laid out so neat!"

Thank goodness Sheriff Dougherty was present to uphold the moral code of Mud Creek. Whipping his guns from their holsters he shouted "Freeze!" Scattered cries of "Shut up, Tom!" The effect on Theola Faith was minimal. She was sliding the sleeve of her shimmering dress off her shoulder. How far she would have gone to shock the homespun citizens of Mud Creek was not destined to become a matter of public record. Debate on the issue would continue well into the next century.

The entrance door slammed inward, as if kicked by a spurred boot. A voice rang out, powerful enough to jiggle the bottles behind the bar and sway the plastic stained glass light fixture. The crowd fell back.

"Hell fire and damnation! Wicked are the ways of woman! The serpent has taken her to its bosom and the Beezlebub put his thumb upon her brow. She takes up drunkards and pleasure seekers in the house of the grape!"

The eyes of the speaker would burn holes in the carpet. His white hair flowed back from a domed forehead; he carried a black book and was dressed to match. And I recognized him. He was the fanatic who had crashed into me at the petrol station—the Reverend Enoch, Diethelogian minister. That wasn't the Bible he was carrying, it was the *Book of Salvation Through Starvation*. "Retribution shall seek out the vixen, she shall be thrust to her knees, and the sound of her wailing . . ."

Returning his gun to its holster, Sheriff Dougherty stood scratching his head. Jimmy lit up a cigar and Theola Faith rested a hand on her hip, the feather fans trailing alongside her still unzipped silk skirt; her smile bright as lipstick could make it.

"You talking to me, sweet darling?"

The face of vengeance darkened to hell-fire red. But the minister had taken no more than two steps forward before we had another disruption. A woman in a beige raincoat broke through the crowd by the jukebox and burst upon centre stage. Laverne of the faded auburn hair and washed-out face, wife of Enoch. The same woman . . . but different. She was tearing at her raincoat belt, eyes on Theola Faith, as she screamed—"Better the company of sinners, than life with you, Enoch! I won't live another day standing to heel like a dog. I won't pretend anymore as how I don't see the looks in people's eyes when you rant at them about punishment and starvation and the glory of misery!"

Theola Faith held her silken arms out toward Laverne. The Reverend dropped to his knees, wringing his hands and thanking the Lord for bringing him to this den of iniquity where he might suffer the torment ("praise His name") in order that the brand should be snatched from the flames.

"Where's the hope? Where's the love?" yelled his doubting wife, who now stood on the ramp with Theola Faith. "God didn't appoint you second in command! I shouldn't have left that note saying I was coming here for to get drunk." She was unbuttoning her raincoat. "I should have written I was casting off the shackles by coming here to strip naked before the whole town."

An "Ooooh!" rose from the mob.

Laverne flung the raincoat toward the bar. Neat catch by the sheriff. Having shifted the neckline of her own dress back into place and zipped up her side, Theola Faith studied the competition. Everyone else seemed in shock. Certainly no one at my table moved a muscle.

"I haven't a daughter to write a bestseller about how often I change my underwear"—Laverne had half the buttons of her blouse undone—"but seems to me if I do a real good job of letting it all hang out, I could make one of the smut sheets. Who knows—even the one for people with perspiring minds!" The blouse went sailing into the crowd. The Reverend Enoch's rantings reached a crescendo. Theola Faith seemed to be trying to shield Laverne with a fan. Jealousy? Finally Sheriff Dougherty took action.

He strode over to Laverne as she got busy with her slip, and clapped a hand on her shoulder. "Why not sit awhile, Mrs. Gibbons. Take things easy. Mebbe go upstairs with Jimmy and talk things out."

The crowd went wild. Theola Faith and the unhappy Laverne disappeared from view.

I stared down at the table, amazed to discover I had finished my hamburger, all the fries, and half a pickle.

"So big a tragedy!" Solange said.

Ernestine shuddered. "That horrible man!"

"He's affiliated with the Diethelogians," I contributed. "A group which is opposed to eating."

Henderson gripped the arms of his chair.

"Wrong, Ellie!" Ernestine responded smugly. "They are not opposed to eating *per se*. Bingo wrote an article, "The Danger of Dietheology," for the magazine *Dining Out at Home*. What they oppose is eating for pleasure. You may eat as much as you like of anything you dislike."

"Same old basic diet," I said.

"My Lois should never have gotten involved!"

"Monsieur Brown, you are a royal pain in the donkey! You are as bad as that man, seeing the evil everywhere!" Solange gathered up her bags. *"Pardonez moi!* I wish to visit the *toilette."*

Ernestine and I immediately jumped up to join her.

"Women!" Henderson curled his lip. "If a man says he's going to the gentlemen's room, his companions don't leap to their feet with 'I'll come too!' "

Did the poor man suspect us of holding a private party in the ladies room? There wasn't the time, Solange reminded me, when Ernestine vanished into the one stall. We were due to meet Pepys at the dock in ten minutes. In a whisper, she said, jerking a thumb towards Ernestine's feet, "I saw her."

"Saw her what?" I mouthed back.

"Coming out of your room thees morning when you was at breakfast."

No time for more. Ernestine came out tugging at her skirt, her froggy beads askew. How could I suspect this woman of being up to tricks? The rivalry which had sprung up between her and Solange had twisted the Frenchwoman's thinking. Besides, who was I to criticize anyone for snooping, especially after my encounter with the medicine chest? We found Henderson waiting as though we women were children who had defied parental curfew. Jimmy, back behind the bar, fed us a fly catcher smile and we walked out the door . . . bang into Mary Faith. Her complexion matched her prison grey dress and her Richard III bob didn't go with the wing-tipped glasses.

"Hello, dear ones!" Her enthusiasm was touching. She held onto my hand as though it were a prized toy and whispered "I pulled myself together and decided a public figure must stay public. I had Pepys bring me over; he was coming for you anyway. Usually I don't go to Jimmy's. Too many people. I prefer the Mexican place a few doors down— Martin's Mexican Café. Marvelous food. So hot, you'd think your mouth's on fire. But they close between lunch and dinner. And all I want is a Coke."

How to stop her from going in there? The other three stood like statues. "I'm so pleased to see you!" I gabbled. "Nosy of me, but I didn't get to ask you earlier if you took Jim Grogg and Divonne off the island this morning. No one else seems to know when or how they left."

"A mystery! How intriguing!" She still held my hand,

but her smile included the others. "No, I was not their pilot, although I am quite a whizz with boats! Mustn't put Pepys' nose out of joint! Now you don't all have to rush off, do you? I so much hope we can all be dearest friends. Yes, that sort of thing takes time, but you'll come back into Jimmy's with me. We'll sit down and all pour out our hearts."

"Honey"—Ernestine met her eyes unflinchingly— "There's no easy way to say this. Your mother's there. Inside."

"No!" Mary fell back. "Even Theola cannot be so great a monster as to deny me this one small corner of the earth!" Clutching her middle, mouth sagging, she looked the way I had felt in the throes of morning sickness.

I had to get her out of there, away from the mother whose acclaimed antics now made her daughter the darling of the talk show circuit and the *Publishers Weekly* bestseller list. Taking charge of our little group, I led them back to Pepys and the boat.

When we reached Mendenhall, we were met by the news that Bingo was missing.

11

The entire household, inclusive of my husband and the infamous Valicia X, was gathered in the great hall. But no one gasped at the sight of Mary's wan face or rushed forward with a stretcher. Ernestine was the one who finally offered her a seat.

Mary was obviously looking forward to being laid out on the sofa, damp cloth pressed to her brow. A servile scurry of footsteps would answer the frantic pulling of the bellrope. An order would go forth for a double brandy, on the double! The mistress of the house had suffered a frightful shock. Monster Mommy was in town. And none could tell what evil would befall.

Ms. X stood under the pawnbroker chandelier, a stunning authority figure in spotless cream linen. Ben maintained a discreet distance—about three feet—from her. I ground his smile underfoot. His companion in slime was informing Ernestine there was absolutely no reason for alarm. None whatsoever. Bingo had participated in the morning session, had eaten lunch with his fellow candidates and had departed the dining room, but had failed to reappear for the afternoon session.

"I was all for scratching his name and proceeding without him, but Mr. Haskell"—Ms. X shone her golden smile on Ben—"made an eloquent plea on young Mr. Hoffman's behalf. I therefore requested that Jeffries try and locate the boy. Her efforts coming up shorthanded, I have decided the Mangé Society will be best served by everyone present assisting in a search of the house and grounds."

Ben was still trying to catch my eye. But this seemed neither the time nor place to ask for a divorce.

Hair spiking, eyes blank, Ernestine turned helplessly toward the Mangé candidacy. "Late for a meeting! That's not in my Bingo's nature. An A for punctuality on every one of his report cards since he entered kindergarten at eighteen months of age. I tell you he'd never do anything to jeopardize becoming a Mangé. No! Someone has it in for my boy. Someone who's afraid to compete fair and square with genius. A cowardly grown-up picking on a poor little boy—"

"Madame"—the comte juggled plastic fruit without missing a beat—"your son is a damned—pardon my English—pain in the bottom. But there *is* honour among chefs!"

Lois Brown, a comfy figure in beige silk, rustled over to put her arms round Ernestine. "Hush now, your Bingo is somewhere safe and sound. Perhaps shut in the bathroom. Didn't you get stuck there last night?"

Ernestine's face turned the sickly yellow of her frock. She shook the other woman off. "A mother has a seventh sense! I knew someone was trying to frighten Bingo off last night." Her voice broke down into splutters. "Someone playing at ghosts."

Miss Rumpson, wearing a black hat with a multi-coloured fish on the brim, looked vastly worried. Henderson stood by, mute. On the sofa, Mary moaned. The sherry-coloured eyes of Ms. X, so like those of my cousin Vanessa, missed nothing. I pictured her mind as a score pad. Points added or discounted according to the candidate's performance during this break in official procedure. Suddenly everyone was putting in their twopenny worth, while Jeffries jockeyed from group to group, her white cap low on her forehead, face scrunched up like a thirsty sponge. Where, by the way, was Pepys?

"How long are we going to stand here?" Ben inquired. "The boy isn't lost on some mountain. He's in this house. Or on the grounds. He's not in the bathroom, Jeffries checked. But could he be locked in a cupboard or a shed?"

Whatever our differences, I mentally applauded my husband for not mentioning the river. Was Ernestine already battling the fear that Bingo might have taken out one of the rowing boats? My heart began thumping wildly. Surely if he were trapped somewhere close we would have heard him. Remembering the coffin, my blood chilled. What if Bingo had indulged a whim to play Dracula and the lid had jammed?

The hall was emptying. The comte and Solange volunteered to search the grounds. Henderson and Lois said they would take the lift up to the attics. Were the husbands unwilling to have their wives go unaccompanied?

Someone gripped my arm and I jumped. Mary! Rouge glared like welts on her pasty cheeks. "I know you are concerned about the coffin," she whispered. "I'm going to check it out. But I don't think . . ." On a trail of unspoken words she was gone.

"Listen up, real good!" Ernestine was saying to those of us remaining. "If one hair of Bingo's head is hurt, the person responsible will have to answer to my husband Frank." Her anger reassured me, at least on her account. She wasn't cursed with my overactive imagination. She wasn't fearing the worst. Jeffries marched her away, and now it was just the three of us, Ben, Valicia X and me. My spouse was smiling at me in a perplexed sort of way. Was he having trouble placing my face? She was talking to him in the for-your-ears-only manner. Cutting a wide swath around them, I headed for the Red Room where we had congregated last night.

"Mrs. Haskell," the throaty voice said, laced with con-

cern, "I was saying to your husband that this sort of com-
motion can't be what the doctor ordered. Why don't you go
upstairs and rest?"

Was Ben to be kept from my clutches lest I make the
ignoble attempt to get him back? Fat chance! Wrong word
choice. Never had I been more certain that pregnancy was
no excuse for gaining weight.

"Sweetheart"—Ben broke from her and reached my
side— "Ms. X is right. You should go up and rest."

"No! I won't be sent to bed like a naughty child." Oh,
how I hated everything about myself. My plaid smock with
the bumble bee pockets. My country-and-western hair which
was regrowing split ends even as I pouted. The glance Ben
sent his Valicia spoke louder than words. *Remember her
condition, my sweet! We have to pander to her.* Should I bite the
bullet and give them my blessing?

"Whatever you say, sweetheart." Ben touched my face
as if I were a mare to be gentled. "We'll look for Bingo
together."

Pulling away from him, I said, "Thank you, but we will
find him three times quicker if we go our three separate
ways."

"You're right there." Valicia glided up the stairs.

Arm around me, Ben walked me in a circle, ridding the
mare of colic, "Ellie, Valicia was doing her damndest to
show concern and you were ungracious."

"Thank you, I work at it."

"This isn't like you. You know that woman means the
world to me. Professionally speaking."

"When she smiles, you haven't noticed the signs of
early gum disease?"

"My God, you don't sound well." He was rooting
around in his pockets for a copy of *Parenting for Pleasure and
Profit.* "As a matter of fact, I haven't been feeling so great
myself. No joke, I think I may have caught your morning
sickness. I'm queasy. My head is fuzzy. And my limbs feel
all of a jumble."

Please, no! The man was telling me he was lovesick.

Rage flared within me. "Nice knowing you." His blank stare imprinted on my back, I dashed toward the Red Room.

The sweltering atmosphere was not conducive to lifting my spirits. The Victorian bric-a-brac, the bobbled velour, the sandbag sofa, and especially the Cat Cadaver portrait over the mantel provided a stage readied for Machiavellian melodrama. Never the bravest of the brave, the sudden spatter of rain on the windows unnerved me. Silly of me even to bother in here. There were few places for Bingo to hide, and why would he pull such a stunt? I lifted the curtains at the library end of the room. What if he had become despondent during the Mangé morning session. Even an adult might crack under questions such as, What were the cakes Alfred The Great burnt? Were they Eccles cakes, rock buns, butterfly cakes, or an assortment of the above? Poor Bingo. Failure may require no particular skill, but it is never easy to learn. Especially for a prodigy.

Wending my way between two maroon armchairs and several potted plants ready to bite the hand that tried to water them, I noticed a carpet stain next to one of the pots in the shape of Australia. A spill that had turned rusty.

Keep moving, Ellie! Don't listen for Ben's footsteps. Don't fume over his tame—nay, cowardly—acceptance of your demand to be left alone.

The red velvet curtains at the north end of the room were closed, to block out the glare from the sun I supposed, but now, with the rain coming down I drew them back without any real suspicion that Bingo might be hiding on the broad ledge.

Pepys lay there in his shirt sleeves—a smile branded on his waxen face, feet together, hands folded below the red stain surrounding the massive knife handle which protruded from his breast pocket.

The room swayed like a hammock. Hanging onto the curtain with one hand, I bit down on the other to stop from screaming. Ghastly! If only I could take back all my unkind thoughts of this unpleasant man! A sob went down the wrong way when he sat up. Knife still in place, he

swung his bandy legs over the sill and screeched, "April
Fool!"

I could have cracked his bald head like an egg. "Cor-
rection," I fumed. "This is the third of July."

"At my age," he rolled his eyes until only the whites
showed, "time ain't of the essence."

"And the knife?" Arms folded, I tapped a foot.

He touched it fondly, as if it were a rose pinned to his
lapel by the woman of his dreams. "One of the props left
behind when *Melancholy Mansion* was done finished being
filmed. That boy disappearing went and reminded me."
The ice blue eyes looked directly into mine, but I got the
shivery feeling no one was currently living behind that
wrinkled face. "Ever see the film?"

"Only an excerpt."

"People kept disappearing. First old Lady Farouche,
then Herbaceous, the butler, found just as you found me."
Pepys tenderly smoothed out the wrinkles I had put into
the curtain. "Getting worried, ain't you?"

"Life up to a bit of plagiarism, you mean?" I managed
a laugh which didn't ring true. That stain by the plant
stand—was it still damp? "You're trying to frighten me.
Small wonder the Groggs decided to slip away unnoticed
after being publicly humiliated over something as silly as
baking powder!"

Pepys, plainly delighted at having goaded me into indiscretion, sat swinging his legs like a child on a wall at the
seaside. Remembering one of the few pieces of advice my
mother gave me—do good to those who hate you, nothing
infuriates them more—I smiled at him. "Do you often play
practical jokes? Last night for instance, did you write, This
house is going to get you! on the bath or prowl the hall
dressed up as Dame Gloom?"

"Wasn't me." Smirk.

"I'm sure Bingo Hoffman has been found by now."

"Here's hoping you're right, kid, and that Mr. Grogg
and his lady are alive and well." Again he fondled the knife
handle. "That scene when Herbaceous the butler was found,

Theola Faith cried buckets all over him. She was fond of him even though he'd been blackmailing her since he found out Lady Farouche was really her father—the mobster King Fido, and the night club act—a front for tuna smuggling. But all ended happy because Malcolm Morrow who played Herbaceous also played Sir Roderick, the heir returned from the dead." Pepys lay back down, feet together, hands folded as I had found him. "I remember Herbaceous' last scene with her," he mused. " 'Ain't none to touch you, Bubbles. That merry kitten smile of yours. The way you talk wicked and still sound like an angel. My whole day shines just from opening the door for you. Ain't nobody going to hurt you ever. I'm none so young as I once was and the armour's kinda rusty, but surely and forever I'm your knight.' "

"So *Melancholy Mansion* had a happy ending?"

"Sailed off into the sunset did Sir Roderick and his Bubbles, and the boat blows up."

Guilt dogged my footsteps as I returned to the hall. How could I have wasted precious Bingo-finding time? My nerves were as jumpy as Mexican jumping beans. I leaped three feet in the air when Mary caught up with me by the stairs to tell me she had checked the coffin and found it empty.

"Any news of Bingo?"

"Not as far as I know." Her cookie cutter features were softened by the warmth of her brown eyes. "You ask me, he's hiding out from his mother. All that pressure put on the kid! He's liable to flip out and she'll be wringing her hands looking to put the blame anywhere but four square on her own two shoulders." Abruptly her voice changed to a rasping whine, as though she had used up her stock of sympathy for others. "My own situation was the opposite. Never any pressure put on me to be anything, do anything— except stay the hell out of the way. When the great Theola Faith said, 'Go out, sweetie, and play in traffic,' she meant it." It was an eerily accurate impersonation of her mother's voice.

"Awful!" I gripped the banister. Was I really ready for motherhood?

"I was misplaced on several occasions as a child, only to be told afterward that I wasn't lost if *I* knew where I was." Mary mounted the stairs ahead of me. In her grey dress and sensible shoes she looked more like the housekeeper than the lady of the manor. And a daughter less like her mother would be hard to find, even though height and build were similiar and the shape of face was the same. Would my—*did* my baby look like me?

"I'll take the rooms on the left of the stairs, if you'll tackle the right," Mary suggested when we reached the second floor. We could well be retracing ground covered by other members of the group, but to dither was to do nothing.

As it happened the first room I checked belonged to Bingo. The Hawaiian shirt he had worn the previous night was laid over a chair and several other articles of boyish apparel lay folded on a case next to the massive wardrobe. Everything was extremely neat. And I had thought all children had a gift for muddle. The blue toothbrush lay straight across the travel soap dish sitting squarely in the middle of the glass tray on the dressing table.

Purely as a formality I peeked under the bed. Finding nothing, not even dust, I trod gingerly across to the wardrobe. The thought of Bingo, talented and obese, huddled there loomed very real. A floorboard creaked, turning my fingers to thumbs. The wardrobe was empty.

Fear took on the bitter aftertaste of disappointment. Wearily, I leaned against the coolness of the window. Rain slithered down. Branches of a dead tree, bleached white as antlers, grazed the pane.

A moment's blackness, perhaps I closed my eyes. The sound of the rain turned into the patter of voices inside my head—the Tramwell sisters repeating the words of Chantal. ". . . *Trouble in the North Tower.*" If I had my bearings right, this room was directly under that tower, the one with the overgrown onion dome. As a child I would have found the temptation to explore such a hideaway irresistible. And surely a boy still lurked in the heart and mind of Bingo Hoffman, prodigy. Hope pried me away from the window. Could there be a door in this room leading to the tower?

Found! In the nook between wardrobe and wall. Stepping onto a twist of stairs, the door banged shut behind me. I was inside a drum, one being battered by rain. On a recent visit to Merlin's Court my mother-in-law had slept in our North Tower. She said she enjoyed the privacy and the view. She had even grown to like me . . . I think. The closer I came to the top of the stairs, the more furious the rain grew. Hard to believe such violence was impersonal. I had reached a landing and was confronted by an arched doorway.

"Help! Save me!"

The words stabbed into me. But immediately, I wondered whether to blame them on my imagination, egged on by the storm. The huge iron handle turned slowly. The oak door must be a foot thick—in keeping with ye goode olde days when smothering one's overnight guests was a national pasttime. A nervous groan as the door inched open. Or had I cleared my throat? The round room was lit by a bulb swinging skull-like overhead, which had to mean something, even if only that the room had already been searched by someone who had forgotten to turn off the light.

"Bingo?" A giant bed covered with ancient green velvet was mounted on a dais, centre stage. I pressed the door shut as gently as possible, so as not to frighten anyone, myself included. The floor boards creaked with each tiptoed step forward.

Whose laboured breathing was that? Mine. Stupid of me, but my skin prickled at the thought that I might be about to meet the ghost of Dame Gloom. Might she have spirited Bingo away because he had blabbed about seeing her last night? My eyes were drawn irresistibly to the narrow aperture enclosing the strip of window. A place only to be entered sideways, and even then with a shoehorn. A marvelous hiding place for a ghost . . . or a boy playing Ivanhoe.

"Bingo?"

Answering sobs.

Before you could say Rescue!, I was whispering words of comfort to the boy huddled on the round floor, which wasn't much bigger than a tea tray. Removing my nose, in case it got stuck, I asked the prizewinning idiocy question of all time, "Can't you get out?"

I had done him the world of good. He puffed to his feet, knocking an elbow against the wall in the process. His pudgy face was red and sticky. His glasses were so fogged up he couldn't possibly see. "Do you have to work at being stupid? I'm not in here meditating!"

"Of course not."

Polishing his glasses with the front of his shirt, Bingo pushed them back on his nose. "Oh, it's you." His lip curled. "The other fat member of the group."

"Now wait a minute . . ." I was saved by the memory of myself at his age. Equally portly, almost as cranky when anyone pushed the wrong buttons. "Shall we pass on the hostilities until we get you out of there? Your mother's worried about you."

"Then she's happy." Folding his arms he stuck out his chins. "Mom enjoys suffering for my art. The woman needs to do something meaningful with her own life."

The Do's and Don'ts of Discipline is vehemently opposed to the raised voice, so I said through my teeth, "After I pull you out, you can tell me how such a smart lad got into such a tight squeeze."

"Oh, all right." He shoved a pudgy hand my way. "But I don't think all your yanking will do more than get me wedged."

He was right. After much huffing and puffing, I felt like Rabbit and all his friends and relations put together, trying to get Winnie the Pooh unstuck.

"I'll go and get your mother."

"You do that," Bingo growled. "You fetch anyone and I swear I'll jump out the window." An idle threat considering he couldn't have got a letter through it, let alone the rolls of fat around his middle, but his desperation reached me. "I don't mind you so much"—his cheeks were chapped by the dry sheen of tears—"because you seem to understand about looking ridiculous."

I rubbed my hands, trying to get the circulation going to the brain. "Bingo, why did you come up here?"

He stopped tugging on his shirt, and it rode up—revealing a strip of porky tum. "Swear on your life not to tell! If you do, I'll ruin that husband of yours. I'll see he never works again. I have the contacts, you know. There are guys who'd kill for my pigeon liver *pâté*. Hey! Where are you going?"

I turned back to face him. "I'm sorry for you, Bingo, but I've better ways to spend the rest of my pregnancy than letting you vent your stupid temper on me."

His face crumpled. "Okay. My troubles are due to that dumb Mangé rule, the one that brought down Jim Grogg. When I saw what happened to him over the baking powder, I got the jitters."

"You smuggled baking powder in, too?"

"Don't be dumb. I can make a cake rise to dizzy heights by blowing on it. What I brought in was my secret supply of . . ." He gnawed his plump lower lip.

"What?"

"Junk food." He glared at me. "I don't know why I am baring my soul to you. Do you think we have met in a former life? Perhaps you're a skullery maid I was kind to. Never mind. I'm addicted to Ding Dongs, Ho Ho's and Twinkies. Last night I ate down part of my hoard and decided to find a safer place for the rest."

"So that's what you were up to last night!"

"May I get on with my story?" His fat face filled the aperture. "I had found a temporary place, but all this morning at the meeting, I pictured Pepys as a bloodhound. Sniffing. And then I remembered opening my window this morning and seeing the bird's nest at the top of the dead tree."

"Ideal."

"Unfortunately I am not a tree climber. After lunch I went outside and discovered that the nest was in line with this window. After making certain architectural computations I returned to my room, located the door to the tower. Once up here I squeezed through here, without scraping off more than a few layers of skin, but . . ."

"Yes?"

The prodigy frowned. "I hadn't counted on the window being narrower than a pencil. I thought it only looked that way because I was seeing it from the ground. Must need new glasses." He tapped them. "All that stair climbing had made me ravenous, so I decided to stash the stuff where it couldn't be found." He emptied his pocket of wrappers.

"You ate everything?"

"What if I did? A few mouthfuls can't make the difference between my getting out of here or being kept prisoner." Expression sullen, he thumped concrete. "These walls are defective. They're swelling."

"Bingo dear," I said. "You have to let me summon help. We can tell an abridged version of the truth. We'll say you came up here to admire the view."

His cheeks blew out in fury and his glasses bounced on his pug nose. "I thought you might be different, but you're no brighter than any other adult! The Mangés won't excuse my missing a session because I'm a scenery buff. I trusted you with the truth because I thought you might be able to help me think up a convincing, heroic reason for my being here. One which would remove the stigma of my ridiculous incarceration."

I did not reply. The tower door groaned open.

"Ellie?"

"My husband!" I warned Bingo, as though the former love of my life were a moustachioed villain come to hurl us both off the battlements. Too late to hide. Too late to think. I was caught and crushed in Ben's arms. His fingers stroked my hair, his lips found mine and my heart lurched in that irresponsible way it has.

"Sweetheart, did I tell you I like the maternity outfit?"

The medieval bed on the royal dais mocked us with the promise of a fairy tale idyll made for two. Saved by a watching child.

I found the strength to pull away and study Ben's face with detachment, while he explained how he had gone into Bingo's room and found the tower door. He had aged in the last day. Those tiny lines around his eyes came from wanton living. And it struck me that his dark hair and blue green eyes were a little gaudy. Thank God, getting over him was going to be a breeze.

"Ellie, I've been worried. You seemed different somehow in the hall. And call me the overprotective husband if you wish, but I didn't relish the idea of your racing all over the house looking for the boy. You shouldn't be climbing all these stairs."

All my pregnancy I had yearned to be treated like a fragile flower . . .

"But, sweetheart . . ." Eyes avoiding mine, he touched my hair. "There is something I feel compelled to mention . . ."

"Don't either of you mind me." Bingo to the rescue.

"Why, hello old chap," said Ben, with less enthusiasm than the situation merited.

"Please refrain from staring. I am not in a zoo."

"Sorry." Ben approached the aperture. "Am I to understand that you are not receiving guests?"

I expected a sullen outburst from the boy, but he actually grinned. "I was about to say"—my voice came out in an earsplitting blast, as though someone had turned up the volume on the TV—"Bingo has suffered a bizarre and brutal experience." Deep breath. "He was having a browse around after lunch and heard this strange fluttering behind the door closing off the tower stairs. Being the conscientious person he is, he checked to see what was what and there was this pigeon. I myself had met one last night, once on the second floor and . . ."

"Is this a shaggy bird story?" Elbow on the wall, Ben smiled.

"Don't interrupt," snapped Bingo. "I want to know, er, *relive* what happened."

I stuck my hands in my bumble bee pockets. "The idiot bird balked at being rescued. It flew back up the stairs and kept banging into the door at the top until Bingo opened it. Once in this room it dive-bombed through the aperture. And would you believe the poor thing went smack against the window and dropped to lay for dead until our hero here—"

"That's right!" Bingo's smirk was as expansive as his shirt front. "With no thought for my own safety, I squeezed in after it, ready to provide artificial respiration, but . . ."

I retook control of the story, anxious to end it lest Bingo get stuck in his own yarn. The first sweet rapture of paying back Ben lie for lie had faded. My mouth held a bitter aftertaste. "Pigeon came back to life. It belongs to Theola Faith, so it's not too surprising it has histrionic tendencies and was only playing dead. Whatever, it left the aperture and flew down the stairs, leaving Bingo trapped."

"You'd left both doors open?" Ben addressed the boy.

"Naturally," I said, "otherwise Pigeon would have had to open them with his little feet. I closed the one leading to the stairs and this one when I came up."

"Ah!" Ben's face was set in tight lines. Was he angry with Bingo for upsetting the precious Mangé schedule, to say nothing of Valicia X, or was he having trouble repressing a grin? "An incredible adventure." Ben walked around me and stood eyeing Bingo through the aperture. "Also frustrating. I know the feeling. I once got wedged between the refrigerator and a stack of packing cases at my father's greengrocery."

Now who was telling unvarnished lies? Ben could suck his abdomen against his spinal cord and crawl in and out of a letter box if necessary.

"So far I haven't been too impressed with you, Mr. Haskell." Bingo wiped off his glasses which had fogged up again. "However, if you can get me out of here, I am prepared to give you the answer to that embarrassingly easy question on Trojan cookery that stumped you this morning."

"Thanks a lot, old son, but I can't take advantage of your generosity. Your predicament is the same as when trying to remove a ring that's grown a little snug. The more you push and pull, the more the ring won't come off. Because the finger gets puffier."

"That's so!" I agreed. How hard it was not to think of

this husband as my hero. "Bingo's shoulders definitely look swollen to me. Are you suggesting . . . ?"

"Precisely! We soap him up and he slides right out. And afterward, Ellie," he said, gently touching my hair, "when the search is called off, there is something I must tell you."

12

Bingo was returned to his mother and Valicia X declared the event cause for celebration. The afternoon session was postponed to the evening, which had originally been designated for free time. Pepys with a snarl on his lips and Jeffries with a flounce to her skirts went in search of champagne. The rest of us (except Mary, who had gone upstairs when Bingo came down) herded into the Red Room. Ben and I had yet to have our moment alone. And I was not sorry when the comte requested a moment's conversation with my husband. Something to do with truffles. I donned my best smile and wished them *bon gossip*.

My thoughts as I milled among the group were not totally engrossed with my marital problems. I found respite in thinking about the fable I had told on Bingo's behalf. Better to blame a bird than a ghost for luring him to the tower, especially when Bingo may have invented or imagined his encounter with Dame Gloom, but I did hope the lie would not unravel.

My eyes found Ben over at the library end of the room, still in conversation with the comte. Why couldn't I have yesterday back again?

"Hey, there, m'hearty!" Marjorie Rumpson touched my arm. She still sported the hat with felt fish on the brim, and the expression on her baggy face remained as worried as when Bingo was missing. "See here, m'girl, Aunty Marge owes you a favour. Several of them, in return for last night. And I know just the jobbie."

"Really?" She was comforting as a big stuffed animal, the kind children take to bed at night.

"Plain as the nose on your face, and the tears in your eyes! You're afraid your husband doesn't love you any more. Not to worry! Help is just outside the kitchen door, in the herb garden. I can give you a recipe, tell you what plants to pull and how long to steep the brew."

"You mean to be kind," I lowered my voice because the Browns and Solange had moved close, "but I don't believe in love potions."

"M'dear, *mine* work."

"That's not what I meant." I cast a furtive glance around to make sure Valicia X wasn't listening. "If Ben only loved me because he was under the influence, it wouldn't be the same."

Miss Rumpson didn't answer because we—meaning the entire room—were galvanized into silence by the sudden arrival of Jeffries and Pepys. Both carried silver trays. She had wine glasses on hers. His held several bottles of champagne and . . . one pigeon. Could Salome have felt any more ashamed when beholding John the Baptist's head . . . ?

"Is that the one?" Marjorie nudged me.

"I'm not sure. All pigeons look alike to me."

Ben's mirthful mocking gaze burned my skin. He knew I had lied, because he had made it his devilish business to really know me during our marriage. I smiled brightly at Bingo, looking well-scrubbed in a fresh shirt and jeans, he stood next to his mother.

The pigeon slithered and slid, while retaining a toe hold on its dignity as Pepys set down the tray on the liquor table.

"He's one of a pair," Lois Brown said to her husband.

"Completely devoted to each other I understand. They are carrier birds, presented to Miss Theola Faith by a doting fan." Pigeon, having hopped onto a chair, permitted her to stroke him, while ogling Valicia X with its beady eyes.

"Careful, Lois!" Henderson raised his worry-worn face from the paperback he'd been pretending to read. "Pigeons breed disease."

Valicia X laughed musically. "I think he's sweet!" She extended a finger. The bird turned his beak away. He must have just eaten.

"He's a she." Pepys didn't add the word "dummy!" But it was there in his voice. Not much deference for his fellow Mangé as far as I could see.

As for Jeffries, I was sure she feared neither man nor bird. "Back up all of you!" She shooed back the crowd with a champagne bottle. "This ain't no petting zoo."

"Did someone say her name is Joan?" I asked. Anything to keep my mind off Ben, heading my way with a glass in each hand.

Pepys kept splashing out the bubbly. "Has her mate Derby henpecked something wicked."

"What I call wicked . . ." Ernestine was decidedly hot under the collar of her mustard frock. "What I call outrageous is allowing that fistful of feathers into this room after all my Bingo has been through."

Sullen glare from her pride and joy. "Oh, Mom! I do not have pigeon phobia."

She rounded on him. "Don't you Oh, Mom! me. You may be smarter than your dad and me put together, but when it comes to knowing what's best for you, I'm the one!" Her fist thumped her chest. Her frog green beads bounced once . . . twice. I didn't like the ugly light in her eyes. For some reason, I thought of the mysteriously departed Mr. Grogg and his *Divonne*.

"Think I don't know what's going on here! When I saw the awful room they put you in." She clamped Bingo to her side. "You're a threat to the other candidates. They've reached the top of their ladders and there's no place for them to go but down. Maybe things would be different if you had a phoney baloney title or were the winner of a rinky-dink cookery contest, or better yet were tall, dark and handsome."

Ben's breathing was ambiguous. He could have been furious or battling a laugh.

"Mrs. Hoffman," Valicia said, her face as silky smooth as the scarf at her throat, "I must caution you that should you continue to comment on Mangé business, your son will suffer. The Society encourages spousal and parental involvement as the best means of ascertaining drawbacks." Behind her back Jeffries had produced a notebook and was scribbling grimly away. This celebration was going downhill fast.

"See, Mother, see what you've done?" Arms folded, Bingo stood over Ernestine as she sank into a chair.

"Phony titles!" Very much the comtesse, Solange headed toward them with a slash-slash of taffeta. "Madame will translate, *s'il vous plaît.*"

A shattering silence, followed by a thunder clap as Henderson tossed his book on a table. In a mental aside I noticed the title: *The Captive Bride.* His expression wrenched from gloom to anger. "Rinky-dink cooking contests! I tell you every time my wife puts my meal on the table, she wins the one that rates."

From across the room I could see the shine of Lois Brown's tears. "Henny, hon!"

Whatever else might have been said wasn't. The pigeon chose that moment to light on Valicia's golden head. For one evil moment I hoped it would make a public statement. But it was not to be. Before Ben could brace for the rescue, she calmly reached up and chucked it under the chin. That woman had everything—my husband and *savoir faire.* Curses! The bird actually suited her. The chug-a-lug of voices could not drown out the words going around inside my head . . . *Ellie, I have something to tell you . . . tell you . . .*

Without disrupting the give and take of ill will, Pepys and Jeffries proceeded on their merry way with the champagne. The comtesse declined, but Miss Rumpson availed herself of a glass. In the manner of a doggy mum rounding up her pups, she barked a toast. "To Sportsmanship, m'hearties."

A shriek of laughter from Jeffries—more startling than one of her primal screams. Several people slopped their drinks. Picking up his, Ben twirled the stem. "With respect to Ms. X," he said, "I believe allowances should be made for Mrs. Hoffman. She has been through a rough time this afternoon, and as an expectant father, I . . ."

He was drowned out by the pigeon taking to the air again, but all on its own my hand reached to touch his. I was reaching toward hope. Then Ms. X smiled at him and his generosity of spirit turned to dust. What did I care if he won Mr. Congeniality! The comte, who must have felt his Mangé chances slipping away, offered to pluck a trick or two from his repertoire in hopes that a little entertainment would restore good cheer.

"I don't see why not." Valicia sat on the sofa arm, short skirt riding above her lovely knees. "No food involvement, please."

"Madame X"—the comte brushed a hand over his Grecian Formula hair and swept her a bow—"I do desire use of zee pigeon, but I swear on the honour of France I will not turn him into *pâté*."

"I should hope not!" Bingo scowled. "That's my specialty."

The comte puffed up his cravat and flourished a hand toward his wife. "Solange, *ma chérie*! If you love me with half a heart, respond with zee assistance!"

"*Non, non! Mon angel!*" She crossed to his side, more courtesan than wife, the beauty spots and décolletage much in evidence. "I am not in the costume, also I am rusted through."

"Hush, *ma fleur*! Get the damn bird!" The comte whipped a black handkerchief and a large penknife from his pocket and borrowed a lacquer box from the mantel. "Perceive! Nothing hides away inside." Flapping open the lid, he flashed the box as the group closed in for the fun and games to begin.

I sat down on the closest chair.

The pigeon, certainly a quick study, preened upon Solange's wrist like a royal falcon, while the comte with the requisite hoopla explained that he would put Madame Joan in the box, cover it with the black handkerchief and make the slice in two.

"I don't like this one bit, I don't," Pepys quavered. His face was grey.

"For once I agree with the old gizzard!" Jeffries banged down her tray. "That bird is the property of Miss Theola Faith. Harm one feather on its head and we'll all be *pâté*."

Serenely, Valicia X waved her down. "I take full responsibility."

The pigeon was duly in the box, the box was covered in black and the penknife clove the air. I closed my eyes. Bingo grumbled that this was kid stuff.

"Voila! I remove the shroud, hand it to my trusty assistant, the lid it rises slowly . . . slowly . . ." The suspense was too much. I cracked open an eye, in time to see triumph fade from the comte's face to be replaced by perplexity as he stared down at the lacquer box. *"Mon Dieu!"* he whispered. "What have I done? What went wrong?"

Ben sat on the arm of my chair and pressed my face to his shoulder. "My pregnant wife must not see carnage."

"You mistake the seriousness!" The voice of Solange. "The bird it is in one piece, but so still! A petite matter of being dead of the fright."

Mandatory primal scream from Jeffries.

Valicia stood up. "I suggest we stay calm!"

Lois Brown began to cry. Ernestine was trying unsuccessfully to cover Bingo's eyes.

Pepys' voice, along with his legs, turned tottery. "Derby and his Joan! They were everything to each other. One of the great love matches of all time." A tear trickled down one of the cracks in his face. "Who will break it to her?"

Sound of door opening. And Mary Faith entered. "Break what? Who will break what to me?"

A silence almost as unpleasant as the moment of death. The copy of *Monster Mommy* on the coffee table suddenly dominated the room.

"Madame"—The comte hid the lacquer box behind his back—"I throw myself on your mercy."

Mary stood, back hugging the door, her narrow mouth uncertain whether to smile or frown. "Has something been broken?"

"Yes, in a manner of speaking." Valicia X, her beauty undeniably ennobled by tragedy, led her to a chair. "No need for you to demand that Comte Vincent be dropped from the Mangé interrogatories. He is in violation of Code 3936, Section M. And is thus . . ."

Mary resisted being eased into the chair.

Jeffries stood like a feather duster with a talking head. "Ain't no nice way to slice—sorry—say it, Ms. Faith. Pigeon Joan is dead."

So many expressions chased across Mary's face, her features blurred. The communal voice elaborated on the tragedy, culminating in Bingo's ghastly *faux pas:* "Do I get to make *pâté?*"

"Honey!" admonished Ernestine.

"If he were my kid . . ." Ben's outburst was silenced by Mary—lashing out with hands and voice.

Somehow Mary seemed the wilder because every hair was in place and she was defined by her wing-tipped glasses and prison grey dress as a woman of some restraint. "Oh, why in mercy's name did I let you in my house? You are monsters, all of you! Feeding on the helpless. This is how it was at my mother's orgies. No perversion too vile!"

"Madame, please." Handing the lacquer box to Solange, the comte knelt at Mary's feet, clutching her ankles. "I would give my life, even my wife, to bring back the bird. I have tried the artificial respiration, the kiss of life! Ah, if I could but hear those words—she is not dead but sleeps!"

"Get him out of here!" Mary's voice ripped the air. Wrenching her skirt from the comte's clutching hands, she backed into Henderson Brown.

"Your servant, ma'am." Pepys shuffled forward like some blood hungry henchman of the Tudors, ready to grab the comte by the hair and hurl him out the window. But so oft the hopes and dreams of man are foiled! A sound was heard from the lacquer box, a rustle, followed by an inquiring grunt. The comte's prayers had been answered.

"A miracle!" went up the communal cry. Ben was prying Pepys off the comte. I thought I had made good my escape. In the ensuing confusion I slipped from the room. I was within reach of the stairs when I heard the dreaded sound of footsteps.

"Are you all right, hon?" Lois Brown asked.

"Just a little tired," I confessed.

"Sure that's all?"

Her face was so comfy, her grey hair so pretty and sensible. Remembering last night's dream visit to the flat in St. John's Wood, I surged with ill usage. This woman looked like a mother. She would not be into deep-knee bends and arabesques. When she hugged her children, she would smell of gingerbread and crayons and fresh air. Why couldn't I have had a mother like that? Why couldn't Mary?

"Know something, hon?" she said. "I sure do envy you."

"You do?"

"Your first baby!" Her smile turned wistful. "And young enough to dream dreams and still believe in them. Henny wasn't always a meat-and-potatoes husband. But time came when fixing the refrigerator pushed ahead of what was broke between the two of us. He's a good man. But for romance, I read books."

I picked at the bumble bees on my pockets, not knowing what to say.

"That's a mighty handsome husband you've got," Lois said. "How I remember when I was having my first. I couldn't believe Henny wasn't after every thin woman who came within a block of our house." Still talking she put her hands on my shoulders and prodded me toward the stairs. "You go have your rest, hon."

"Your husband worships the ground you tread!" My feet dragged on the stairs. About halfway up, I heard a door open . . . and again footsteps. I peered through the bars in fearful hope that it was Ben . . . about to come racing two stairs at a time to sweep me into his arms and carry me off to our bedroom, to the tune of broken murmurings. He had made a consummate fool of himself. And frankly my dear, he no longer gave a damn for Valicia X.

But Ben wasn't one of the three people in the hall. Jeffries and Pepys stood cosying up to Mary Faith. A touching scene of devoted servants consoling the lady of the house after her ordeal, but those two had made plain to me they disliked her. My skin prickled a warning that I was glimpsing something sinister. But blame that on my emotional state. I slipped past them to the sanctuary of our room.

Someone had been in my bedroom. Oh, I don't mean that it had been ransacked—only that the bed had been made. In my haste that morning I had left it in a heap. And, looking around, I saw other signs of an intrusion. My overnight bag was now zipped and I was sure it hadn't been. And had my copy of *Pregnancy for Beginners* been on the bedside table? Perhaps Pepys or Jeffries had come and done the room—or was Solange correct in her suspicions? Was Ernestine guilty of snooping? Was her belligerence today explained by her having made discoveries about Ben— and perhaps other of the candidates—which had invoked maternal fear as to Bingo's chances? Or was I growing paranoid? *Parenting for Pleasure* didn't conceal anything but words of wisdom and Primrose Tramwell's letter. I have this habit of tucking correspondence in books . . .

Time to lie down; never mind that I felt a trespasser in this caved-in cardboard box of a room. The silver lurex wallpaper hurt my eyes and an inadvertent glance in the mirror hurt more. My worst fears confirmed. Those were stretch marks on my face. No wonder Lois Brown had been so sympathetic. If only Mary had not disconnected the only phone in this house of horrors. Pouring out my tale of betrayal and deceit to Dorcas and Jonas would work wonders. If, that is, they believed me. Those two had been sadly taken in by Bentley T. Haskell, alias Mr. Letch. They thought him honourable, lovable, and only slightly cracked on the subject of haute cuisine.

"Thinking about me, sweetheart?" He crept up on me and gently turned my face to his.

"Yes." I stretched out on our bed as Pepys had done on the window seat.

"Nice thoughts?" He sat beside me and traced a finger from my brow to my chin.

I addressed his nose. "When we were in the North Tower with Bingo you said that you had something important to tell me."

"Ellie, this isn't going to be easy." So spoke the stranger—this insidiously handsome man, his afternoon shadow of beard intensifying his ravaged appeal.

"Just say it!" I huddled deep in the mattress.

"Very well." His eyes met mine without flinching. "I hate your hair this new way."

A few moments of numbness, before I managed, "You can't blame your love affair with Ms. X on my hair!"

He managed to look stunned. "Are you out of your mind?"

"Don't deny it!" I slapped away his hand. "I heard you last night in cooing cahoots with that woman." A laugh which chilled me, if not him. "Mary Faith showed me a viewing screen and listening device to the secret meeting room hidden in the medicine chest in the bathroom. I turned it on when looking for an antacid tablet. Just playing around with a gadget. I never expected anyone to be there at that time of night."

Ben stood, arms folded, looking coldly down at me. "Ellie, you should be ashamed."

"Me?" I squeaked. "You are the one who left our bed promising to return—presumably in the monogamous state you left it."

He sucked in a breath. "Hard as it may be for you to believe, I was not pleased when Ms. X collared me and insisted on a quick word. But I could not refuse on the grounds of the scream; she did explain that Jeffries . . ."

"Yes, I know all about the primal yell. What I don't wish to hear are your excuses. I saw the way you looked at Ms. X from the start. Eyes burning with passion."

"You're joking!" He did a commendable job of looking revolted. "Ellie, you sound like a character from that sleazy novel I was writing when we first met. I feel absolutely no passion for Valicia X. Through no fault of her own she reminds me of your cousin Vanessa. She's hardly my type." He glared at me ferociously. "And even if she were God's gift to men, what would I need with her when I have you?"

The room turned into one of those glass-domed ornaments. The kind that turn snowy when you shake them. "But, Ben"—I lay still—"I heard you. My ear was to the medicine chest when you said that the moment you saw her you *knew*. And Valicia X said—*asked* if your wife suspected."

He paced the few inches the room allowed. "The wages of eavesdropping," he said, sounding like the Reverend Enoch, "are misery! And now I am placed in the invidious position of breaking a Mangé confidence." Hand on the bedpost, he said, "You asked me when I paid the Mulberry Inn bill in cash, why I dislike credit cards. And I revealed how during my days and nights—at Eligibility Escorts I was hired to accompany a young woman to a grouse shoot."

"You don't mean . . . ?" I was on the edge of my bed.

"Valicia X, as we will continue to call her, was in her rebel phase. She was thumbing her nose at the parents for dragging her over to Europe when she wanted to demonstrate her social consciousness by living in squalour. Refusing to accept Daddy's choice of male companion for the grouse shoot, she hired me."

"Spirited." What else could I say—having done much the same thing myself?

"As things worked out, the other chap showed up. A case of love at first sight and Valicia bunked off with him without paying me."

I gripped my hands to stop them from applauding. "How embarrassing for her meeting up with you again here! I can understand her hoping I didn't know! Are she and the other man married?"

"Separated. We didn't dwell on her personal life. The encounter had been a shock to both of us and I was anxious to get back to you. She did tell me—and again I violate the bonds of secrecy—that each candidate was selected because of his unorthodoxy. I—on the grounds of having worked for Eligibility while attempting to write a novel. Ms. X had seen my file but it didn't ring a bell. She had forgotten both my name and that of the agency."

"Felt guilty about Mummy and Daddy," I suggested, "so she blotted out the experience?"

"Whatever. Such is the great impression I made on her."

Ah, but would the mature woman take a more lingering second look? Ben thumped the bedpost. "Ellie, your suspicions have wounded me deeply. Nipping out for . . . a quick one with Ms. X, as though I were going down to the local for a pint."

"Does sound rather vulgar, I admit."

Another thump of the post. "I thought you loved me."

Gnawing a finger, I tried to come up with a defence.

"And don't give me some such idiocy as she's so beautiful. I like the way you look much better. Or I did before you had your hair all stretched out of shape."

How could I tell him I had entered the Scissor Cut that noon in hopes of being remodeled into a Valicia X lookalike? But as it happened, our time for talking was up.

A boom shuddered the room.

Ben thumped a fist to his brow. "There goes the damn gong. Ms. X instructed Pepys to sound the alert when the next session was due to begin. Jeffries is to bring the candidates' dinner to the meeting room. You will be sure and get something from the buffet?"

"Promise." My heart was heavy as I trailed after him to the door. *What have I done?* I cried silently. His farewell kiss was absentminded. Rather as if my face had got in the way of his.

The moment I was alone I rounded on my reflection in the mirror and screamed, "Idiot!" This is all your fault, I thought. And don't start blaming your mother or Fat Child Ellie! Flinging down on the bed, I burrowed under the poppy field spread. For comfort, not warmth. The horrid little bedroom was perspiring heavily. Willing myself toward the oblivion of sleep, I vowed that things would be better when I woke. Our love would be stronger for being tested. *Please God, let Ben be the chosen candidate. I feel bad about Miss Rumpson and Lois Brown and being asked to play favourites can't be easy for you. Bingo says he doesn't want the honour, but he could have been talking tough. And you don't have to worry about the poor comte. He's out of the running . . .* I fell asleep to dream of a swashbuckler knife being lifted from the dining room wall by an unseen hand. Where there had been five there now only two . . .

I came awake with a horrible abruptness as if something had touched me on the shoulder and whispered, "It's time!" The dark summons, however, was internal—not external. I was alone in the room, feeling exceedingly peculiar, in the grip of sensations astonishingly new, whilst unnervingly familiar. My travel clock said seven o'clock. The Mangés must still be in session behind closed doors, making up for the lost afternoon. Otherwise, Ben would have come for me. I wasn't sorry. Feelings that have been rubbed raw need time to heal. Platitudes. To be honest, all thought of my husband slipped away like sand swept away by an incoming tide of emotions—ones I had thought dead forever.

"Stop playing the ascetic, Ellie!" the demon whispered. "You're not fooling anyone. Get up, get dressed and get thee gone from this barren room. You know what you want. And who's to be hurt? Remember how late last night's meeting went on? Cinderella, you have until midnight."

A dictionary could not provide enough adjectives for the craving—desperate, urgent, insatiable, voracious. I was like the headmistress of the girls' finishing school who discovers she is a werewolf. Inching up on my elbow, a chill prickled my flesh.

I fought the need, truly I did. Pulling the bedclothes up to my hairline, I ordered myself back to the safety of sleep. I might not feel weak or woozy, but this was a sickness. These last few days I had felt well. But not like this! For the first time post-pregnancy I surged with vitality.

My hand tossed back the spread. Why fight the inevitable? There was a place in Mud Creek that offered all the spice I craved. I would sit in a dark booth, heavily disguised! The fantasy played on; but even as I got out of bed and began assembling clothes, I told myself I could back out at any time. The square eye of the window turned accusing. And my conscience turned to sandpaper. The risk of being spotted as I crossed the island to the boathouse was considerable. But I couldn't worry about that now.

Donning the sack-style dress I had purchased that morning at Nelga's, I voted it as slinky as maternity in Mud Creek was likely to get. Oh, but surely that moon-coloured person in the mirror wasn't me. How could I go anywhere with a face like that? As for my hips, they looked detachable. Would Mud Creek believe a new fashion fad—on the wave of shoulder pads?

Small wonder cosmetics found favour with the masses after the advent of electricity. Candlelight gilds the lily. As does emolient rich moisture balm, liquid-pearl foundation, blush, perfume, and lip gloss. My hands played over the bottles and plastic compacts like a concert pianist. Subtlety. That was the key word. No thornbush of back-combed hair. No beauty marks such as distinguished the comtesse. One should always look like a lady, especially when one doesn't intend to behave like one. So says Aunt Astrid.

Seven minutes later I was presentable, if not reincarnated. Britain's Ellie Haskell looking darling, darlings! I had left my hair loose, handy to duck under should anyone look at me boss-eyed. Picking up my bag, I watched my fingers do a slow walk toward a pencil lying on the bedside table. What word could I leave for Ben—on the off-chance that the Mangé Meeting ended before my return? That a woman has needs? A faint hint of Mr. Right aftershave lingered in the air. I wondered if I could go through with this. My hand was trembling as I wrote: *Gone into Mud Creek. Expect me when you see me.*

Making a face at the watchful window, I switched off the light and, vowing this would be a quickie, slid out into the hallway, which was heavy with silence. Did the film

Melancholy Mansion silently . . . endlessly . . . replay itself within these walls? Was death forever crouched at the crook of the stairs waiting for the murder victims? Would I, unknowingly, rub shoulders with any of the ghost characters— the blonde, the butler, or the schoolboy or . . . even my mother? That her part had been played in a nightclub didn't alter the fact that she was part of the history of this house. Suddenly, remembering her fatal fall down a flight of railway steps, I could not face the stairs.

Heading toward the lift, my footsteps echoed after me. I opened the outer door and viewed the hanging cage with a jaundiced eye. Only the craving got me aboard. What if it stalled? What if knives came slashing through the grid iron sides? Silence, craven adventuress! Grabbing the elasticated brass gate, I rammed it shut. With courage that astounded, I pressed First. An electrical hum glided up my arm as my insides lurched down. So far so good. No dead body dropping as a free gift into my arms. Downward and Onward. All clear on the hall front. Out into the sultry air.

Instantly I felt better. Mendenhall was a breeding ground for the fungus of imagination. Hurrying down the herringbone path, I skirted the rockery. Poor old Josiah! He should have chosen either a smaller house or a bigger island, if he didn't want his home to look too big for its britches. In half a dozen strides I was level with the herb garden wherein grew, according to Miss Rumpson, all the ingredients to enable me to hold onto Ben's love. We have an herb garden at Merlin's Court. Jonas is a great believer in the power of mint sauce with his roast lamb.

I had reached the boat house. Ah, yes! Here was the *Nell Gwynn*. A neatly wrapped orange square on the right hand shelf. Unfortunately, I had not enough puff in me to get it inflated this side of Christmas. Dropping my bag on the Melolite garden bench, I assured myself that borrowing a rowing boat without first acquiring permission was not contrary to any house guest rules I had ever read.

Urgency gave me the speed and strength of . . . one pregnant woman. Once launched I became again the pride of St. Roberta's rowing team. My oars moved with the steel rhythm of connecting rods on a steam engine. I inhaled deep breaths of river smell. Water the colour of stewed tea slopped and surged against the sides of the boat. I was free, I was racing to meet my destiny. No time to cry, Halt, who goes there, as a motor boat roared into view, sending up a geyser of spray. Pepys in pursuit or worse yet—the Coast Guard? Neither, thank goodness! Just some snooty river rats who wouldn't give the wave to a nameless rowing boat. Off in the distance a couple of white sails hung like pillow slips out to dry, but otherwise it was just me and the river.

By the time I tied the boat to a scrubby tree at the water's edge, I'd had enough of the nautical life and was ready to give anyone who looked at me sideways the back of my oar. But upon reaching Main Street, the fever that had driven me to these shores was back full force. No traffic moved. I saw no pedestrians. Again I seriously wondered if this was a town existing only in the imagination of the stranger passing through. Silly! The bearlike dog fenced in alongside the B. & W. Hardward Store was too real for comfort. Jaws slathering, he ripped chunks out of the night. Should I turn tail and flee back to Mendenhall?

Impossible! I sped past Jimmy's Bar. My footsteps echoing the thump-thump of my heart, I crossed at the traffic light and came with a rush of ecstasy and longing to the place.

But what was this? Confronting a Closed sign on a locked door, I could have wept with frustration. Martin's Mexican Café. The restaurant was exactly as I had imagined when Mary had mentioned it outside Jimmy's Bar—a flat-faced building with peeling boards and a straggle of plants clawing at the inside of the window. I smelled the spices, felt them seeping into my pores, tasted their burn on my tongue. When the craving had first taken hold, it had been for curry. But this wasn't England and I am adaptable. I clawed at the door. Tacos, enchiladas, tamales! All begging to be devoured one slow nibble at a time.

I sagged against the wall. Where was it written that I should suffer like this? All the pregnancy How-To books stressed the importance of giving in to this most basic of urges. Easy for the books to say. Easy for those women not haunted by a fat past. For me had come denial, followed by that terrifying exhilaration. The urge has come upon me! cried this Lady of Shalott. I had been so pure since marriage: no food orgies. I had come to believe that passion for food had been sublimated by nobler desires. I had determined not to use my pregnancy as an excuse to backslide. And how easy to walk the straight and narrow during those days of morning sickness. Now, true to form, the sin without the satisfaction.

Drearily, I stopped using my hair as a face cloth and dragged myself into a walk which ended abruptly after half a dozen steps. I was at the door of the Lucky Strike Bowling Alley. Taped to this door was a sign that read:

Enjoy Life In The Fast Lane
Annual Bowling Banquet, Six To Nine, July 3
Buffet—$5.00 per person
Anyone interested in joining Wednesday or Thursday night leagues
is welcome.

I moistened my lips. What sort of a buffet? Was I putting one and one together and making four? Martin's Mexican might be closed for any number of reasons. Admit defeat! Return to your boat and head back to Mendenhall. As Child Ellie you may have been known as the Midnight Marauder for your successful nocturnal raids on the school pantry. But the woman you've become isn't brazen enough to walk in there only to have your legs mistaken for skittles. Remember, you have the Mangé name to uphold. You have your marriage to consider. Ben is already unhappy at being blamed for an affair he did not commit. You're going to fight this thing and win.

Ellie, come back! Don't do this! Don't gate crash the Mud Creek Bowling Banquet!

13

A sport where you are meant to drop the ball had always appealed to me, but I had never been in a bowling alley before. And, to my untutored eye, the Lucky Strike resembled a bomb shelter down to its last candle. Overhead fans moved whirligigs of shadow over the empty lanes. Did the dim lighting indicate a desire for ambience or were they conserving on electricity? Immaterial, my dear Ellie! Cloaked in shadow I scooted unchallenged past the pay desk and ball racks.

The bar was mobbed. Did the entire population of Mud Creek leap at every chance to party? Cigarette smoke breezed my way. Voices flowed past me, gentle as the river I had so recently rowed. "As I said to her . . . after she said to me . . ." "I could have kicked her face in!" "But she sure is darling! . . ."

I recognized several faces from earlier in the day. Nelga from the dress shop. Heidi, our waitress at Jimmy's Bar. The Swedish blonde twins who had been such a hit until Theola Faith stole the fashion show. But here was a face guaranteed to kill my appetite if anything could. Sheriff

Tom Dougherty sat on a bar stool, nibbling on a drinking straw. I shoved back a quiver of unease along with my hair. The prize might be worth the price.

The buffet table was laden to groaning. I could feel the vibrations in my feet. This was the sort of feed bash with which pioneers must have fortified themselves when there was a forest to be cleared and a log cabin township to be raised before sundown. My palms turned clammy. My body flooded with wave upon wave of wicked wantonness. I was a lioness surveying her kill.

Set out among the down-home delights of baked beans, sweetcorn casserole, macaroni and cheese, and brown-sugar glazed ham, were two great platters of crunchy shells loaded up with spicy dark meat, crispy green lettuce, bright red tomato, and shiny black olives. I merged with the crowd, as safe from prying eyes as any taco thief could wish. Too safe. All around me, disembodied hands loaded up paper plates. Curses! My arms were pinned to my sides by the press of bodies.

Across the buffet from me were the Swedish blondes. Their giggles drifting upward like bubbles blown from a pipe, until . . . a unified gasp. Like a tiny pop. Eyeing each other with identical expressions of bemusement, they said, "Who's she?"

"Yes, don't think we've had the pleasure." A beefy chap in a flannel shirt, fists doubled into boxing gloves, gave me the once over.

I flexed my lips.

One of the twins touched a sculpted nail to her flawless chin. "I feel certain sure I've seen her some place."

"Same here." An unspeakably handsome youth, his mouth carved into a sneer, picked me apart with his eyes. He who had notified me in Jimmy's Bar that I was wearing a price tag. Was I about to pay for being so lavish with makeup and flouncing my hair over my shoulders? The need to mask my hungry eyes had been consuming. Now it didn't take a mirror to confirm that in the eyes of these Puritans I looked a thoroughly bad lot.

*   *   *

"She was in Jimmy's lunchtime gone." A female cattle rustler spoke, thumbs in her belt, salt-and-pepper hair slicked back. She wore leather wrist bands.

"You've got her tagged, Rema!" The flannel shirt man executed a middle weight boxer prance. "She's one of them! One of those crazies staying over on the island." Eyes squeezing from their sockets, he loomed across the table at me. "What's your game, dame?"

The twin on the left wrinkled her nose. "Why are you here spying on us?"

"I . . ."

"Does Mary Faith plan on putting this whole town in her next book?"

Relief at the question restored my voice. "Such a wonderful party!" I gushed. "You can't know how I would love to stay, but I only stopped by to inquire about bowling lessons and—"

Impossible to go on. I was drowned out by a surge of voices. Impossible to continue backing up. The crowd was closing in again, cutting off light and air. Was that buzzing the rush of blood to my head or the mounting fury of the mob? I heard, "Mangés" and "Dangerous weirdos." Followed by "We don't need their sort in Mud Creek."

"What's this, folks? A private party?" Enter Sheriff Tom Dougherty, hoisting up his gun belt. His thatch of grey hair shaken boyishly onto his forehead, the set of his mouth belying the vulnerability of his pouchy cheeks. Here was a man trained to read every twitching muscle and evaluate every flinch. Would he handcuff me before or after reading me my rights? Would he cross to the island and personally inform Ben that his wife was about to become a felon as well as a mother?

What had I wrought in my blind folly? Had I destroyed my love's every hope of becoming a Mangé?

The sheriff silenced the mob with a raised hand. His smile was chummy, but I feared his left eye wasn't narrowed because he had a cold. He was lining me up, for target practice. "Well, young lady! What brings you to the Lucky Strike?"

Hugging my shoulder bag as though it were the arm of a friend, I backed up against the human wall. "As I have explained, sir, I happened to be passing and popped in to inquire about a game of bowling. Finding the tracks shut down, I paused to admire the buffet." I like to think I am not a great liar due to lack of practice. But I thought this one skirted the letter of the truth rather nicely.

"She's lying." The cattle rustler tightened her leather wrist bands.

"Too right!" the twin on the right agreed.

"Not even cute about it." Horrendously handsome young man speaking.

"Now hold your horses!" grumbled the sheriff. "Sounds to me the young lady may be speaking nothing but the blamed truth."

What a lovely man. Had I not been in such a hurry to leave, I would have been tempted to kiss him. "Thank you so much!" I tried a sidestep. "Now, if you will excuse me—"

"Not so fast, honey!" A curvaceous woman in a leopard skin frock reeled me in by my bag strap. Her eyes worked the crowd. "Hey, you bunch of softies, get yourselves a good look at that face. She look the sort to care a hang about bowling? Not her. Doesn't have the class! She came skunking in here up to no good, or my name's not Bertha May Johnston."

A dark and deadly hum of bees swarming. To think I had felt cheated in leaving Massachusetts—the seat of witch burnings and other Puritan terrors. I could feel the hot collective breath of my accusers. Their eyes branded a G for Gate-crasher on my forehead. A dubious look had crept into Sheriff Dougherty's eyes. Was he going over to the enemy? Would anything be served by throwing myself at his feet?

"Book her for unlawful entry!" The flannel shirt chap plopped a meaty hand on the sheriff's shoulder. "And hold her, old gun, until the rest of those Mangé cranks leave the island."

A rumble of approval.

"You can't do this to me!" Something (perhaps the

baby pressing on a nerve) stiffened my spine. "I'm a guest in your country." Mustn't give them time to say they hadn't invited me. Better to rush in with the best of all defence pleas. "And I'm *pregnant!*" Whatever their response I would not break down. I look about as captivating as a crocodile with a toothache when I cry.

Had mention of my delicate condition softened hearts? The only sound in the Lucky Strike was the whirl of the electric fans. Then, a voice, sweet as caramelized sugar, dripped stickily into the void. And cool fingers handcuffed my wrist. Who she was I couldn't tell. She was standing behind me. The crowd was agape.

"Dreadfully naughty of me, darling, to have kept you waiting, but punctuality is death to the grand entrance! And I see the natives have been friendly. Thought you might find this place amusing when I suggested meeting here."

The name Theola Faith burst upon the air, with the fizzy-dizzy rush of champagne bubbles. Monster Mommy was among us.

"And now if you will excuse us . . ." Gripping the back of my dress, she propelled me a couple of steps backward. A sideways peek revealed the silver blonde hair brushing the gamine cheeks, the panda bear eyes and gee-whizz smile.

"Hate to forego the rest of the rusticities but I have a darling bottle of Chateau Vin Rose back at my place that's about popping its cork in anticipation of meeting this sweet young thing!"

I contributed a gasp to the conversation. The question weighing heavy at that moment was, Am I being rescued or taken prisoner? Why was Theola Faith involving herself with a total stranger? Why did the townspeople make no effort to retrieve their prey?

Sheriff Dougherty ambled around, grey hair flopping on his forehead, hand smoothing a crease or a crumb from his jacket. "Hoped you'd spend the evening along of us, Theola. Good as said you would when I mentioned the banquet."

"That was last week, you old Tom fool!" She pinched

his podgy cheek, gold bracelets sliding up the arm of her silky white suit. "You went and caught me at a weak moment. I was feeling the need to be bored."

"Hey!" the woman in leopard skin snapped. "You count yourself lucky, Theola, you're still welcome at Mud Creek functions."

A gurgle of laughter. "You can take the girl out of Mud Creek, but you can't take Mud Creek out of the girl, eh? Not so, Bertha, but because you were always kinda nice to me when we were kids, I'll do you the favour of letting you in on a fashion secret. Leopard skin is dead. And, by the by, darling—makes you look like a motor home with rust spots." The star blew a kiss past my ear. "Love you all, darlings!"

The sheriff's face, droopy with disappointment, swam before my eyes, as I was turned face about and marched past the ball racks and pay desk to the exit door. Mustn't look back. Voices surged after us, threatening to draw us back into their flood.

My head was a jug of martinis being vigorously shaken, but outside on the pavement I revived with each breath of freedom's sultry air. Very interesting the discovery that Theola Faith had grown up in Mud Creek. And some day I would be dying to know why she had removed me from the clutches of the bowlers. But now, all I wanted in the world was to return to the island and fall into Ben's arms.

Shifting my bag strap, I shoved back my hair and extended a hand. "Thank you, Miss Faith. You have been most kind. I do hope we meet again and you will forgive my running along. I have a boat to catch."

"Oh, pooh!" She held onto my hand. "That's not kind, darling! Yes, I stole you from those dreary people in there, mainly to be ornery. But surely I am entitled to the reward of your company!"

"If I were not so pressed for time . . ."

She shifted her hand to my elbow and walked me forward. "Have no fear that I expect an explanation as to why those good souls wanted to tar and feather you. These days I believe no one's life should be an open book. Although I do confess to a teaspoon of curiosity as to why my darling daughter chose to get mixed up with the mad Mangés."

"She met an editor who had a connection with the group." My voice hurried to keep up with my legs.

Theola Faith gave a southern belle laugh. "What a delightful conversationalist you are! I do insist you accompany me to the suite of rooms Jimmy graciously put at my disposal. We'll have ourselves some wine and girly chit-chat."

I could not make head nor tail of my garbled response. Something about abstaining from alcoholic libations and my husband being a sublime human being—in no way responsible for my foibles.

"Doesn't he sound adorable! But, then, only a villain would deny his wife the pleasure of showing proper appreciation to a friend in need."

Somewhere in the midst of this conversation I had turned into one of those pull toys being dragged along by a child who refuses to heed the parental order to halt. I had no business consorting with the legendary Theola Faith. I was her daughter's house guest, added to which Mary was clearly bent on liking me. And Ben certainly had every right to expect me not to make waves that might sink his chances with the Mangés.

What was wrong with me? Why didn't I bid Theola Faith good night and strike out for the mud track leading to the river? Despite myself, was I mesmerized by her fame or rather infamy? Or did this have to do with my mother—the fact that the two women had crossed paths long ago? Ridiculous to expect a film star to remember one of several dancers from one night club scene in *Melancholy Mansion*. But in putting questions to Theola Faith, I might get to remember my mother.

We had reached the alley running alongside Jimmy's Bar. Would extending my absense from the island by one half-hour stamp me forever as an unfit wife? We were almost at the rusted fire escape steps leading to a black-and-red striped door and I was experiencing that same sense of detached reality I had known in my dream of returning to the flat in St. John's Wood, when something brushed against my leg—that cat I had noticed nosing around the dustbins on my morning excursion into Mud Creek. He had a Charlie Chaplin moustache and a jaunty swagger. His resemblance to the departed Mr. Grogg was extraordinary. Automatically I made nice noises but the cat brushed past me to sit meowing up at Theola Faith like an autograph hungry fan. She picked him up as though he were a fur stole she had dropped and draped him over her arm.

"Very well." She turned away from the fire escape steps. "If Mohammed won't come to the mountain . . ."

I had no idea what she was talking about. Was she completely mad? She was walking briskly away from me.

"Excuse me . . ." I hung back for a lone car whose driver must have been very short—if there was a driver. The feeling that this wasn't happening, at least not to me, was back full force. Light-headed with hunger, that was my trouble!

Theola Faith smoothed a hand over the cat still dangling in dutiful silence, as she moved between the trees leading to the river. "You seemed less than elated, Ellie Haskell, by the idea of going to Jimmy's apartment and I'm not the least offended." A sideways smile shiny bright as nail polish. "Darling, had I but a garbage bag big enough I would shove in every beer poster, every stick of utility furniture, and shove it out the door. No, we will have a far more chummy time if I return with you to Mendenhall."

Her calling me by name when I knew I hadn't informed her on that point, leaped out at me, fogging the rest until the very last word.

"Oh, but you can't!" I clutched at her arm, drawing a hiss from the cat. Across the gravel stretch we faced each other like two cats ourselves. She silver sleek, I all atwitch. "You must not set foot in that house!"

"Really? Unwelcome in my own home!" Her smile stretched thin. "Are all the Mangés down with food poisoning or has someone spilled red wine on my finest lace tablecloth?"

"No . . ."

"Good. Shall we make haste then? I dislike being on the river after dusk; a throwback to that final scene in *Melancholy Mansion* when the boat blew up. I ended up with as many mosquito bites as we did takes."

I was running to keep up with her. "I didn't mean the house. I meant to say that you mustn't set foot in my boat—your boat that is! When I rowed over, I noticed a slow leak, and I'm really afraid that it isn't up to taking a second person. And I'm gaining weight all the time. All things considered I'm beginning to think it would be much better if I came back with you to the apartment. I really would love to see those beer posters—"

"Tut tut, darling. All these fibs you're telling! You are scared spitless the fur will fly"—she rubbed the cat's head—"when darling Mary sees me walk in."

"I . . ."

"You British, and your morbid dislike of scenes! What you don't know, Ellie Haskell, is that I phoned Mary this morning and we had quite a pleasant mother/daughter chat."

I suppose all telephone calls lose something in the translation but I had been in the room during that rancorous exchange and "pleasant" wasn't the word that sprang to mind when I thought of it. We were now at the dock. Hope of a reprieve flared when Theola Faith kicked the row boat disparagingly with her tiny foot, then died completely when she took a couple of strides to where a snazzy little speed boat bobbed invitingly in the mottled shade of a weeping willow.

"I had her delivered this afternoon." Theola Faith gripped my elbow. Her jasmine perfume brushed my face. "Please be my first guest."

She was right. I do hate to make scenes, especially with a cat watching. There was something decidedly witchy about this one. He meowed plaintively when put down on the ground and told to shush off home. The moment we stepped aboard he did likewise, refusing to abandon ship even when the motor roared to life. I got to hold him while Theola Faith steered, but he made it plain I was second best. Interesting, considering it turned out he wasn't her cat but Jimmy's. I focused on trying to keep my hair from wrapping around my face—no-handed, because I was afraid to relax my hold on our furry friend. Anything to keep from picturing the curtain rising on Theola Faith's grand entrance. What if Mary jumped from a window or—almost as bad—jumped her mother? Mother/daughter fireworks were bound to ensue. Valicia X would be outraged. Mangéism could not flourish in such an environment. Ben would make every noble attempt not to blame me, but inevitably he would wonder if I had planned the disaster to punish him for the imagined affair. I would feel morally obliged to offer him a quickie American divorce. Probably there were reduced rates for tourists . . .

"A lovely night." Hands light on the wheel, Theola Faith tilted her face to the sky. The setting sun certainly was magnificent; we don't have one like it in England. A jewelled crimson sphere seeming to be painted on what looked to be a sky made of shot silk, in shades of purple, rose, and gold.

"Beautiful," I said.

"Almost there, Ellie, sweetie."

Again, unease. How did she know my name? Perhaps, like the Mangés, her spies were everywhere in the persons of Pepys and Jeffries. A breeze, chill with spray, crept down my arms. The island loomed before us. The engine was turned off; we were leaving the boat. A weight lifted from me when the cat shot down my front onto the dock, but my heart grew heavy with each step up the rocky incline. Never had the turreted mansion looked more like a monstrous living creature, sprouting misshapen heads and gloating window eyes.

"Home sweet home!" Theola Faith mounted the last sooty red step and, turning the massive door handle with both hands, entered the gloomy hall with the cat and me at her heels. My heart thundered. I was braced for confrontation. At the very least Pepys and Jeffries would descend on us and succeed in cowing me into confessing my shameful encounter with the bowlers of Mud Creek. At worst Mary would appear at the top of the stairs, clasp a hand to her breast, and swoon to her death.

As it happened no one was about, not Mary, nor any of the Mangé contingent. Was Solange holed up with Comte Vincent in their room as a result of the pigeon fiasco? Was Henderson Brown in his room fretting? Was Ernestine having an early night? Whatever, Theola Faith and I were greeted by the sort of silence you usually only encounter in houses that have been abandoned for donkey's years.

She flashed me her gamine smile and entered the Red Room. "How about a drink to brace ourselves for the onslaught of my daughter's affection?"

"Perhaps a bitter lemon or ginger ale." I laid my bag on a table and followed her gaze to the portrait of the Cat Cadaver over the fireplace. A gasp. Mine not hers. A knife handle protruded from the painted fur. Last night graffiti on the bath, now this. But neither live Kitty or Theola turned a hair.

"Imagine anyone wishing to stage an orgy in this devoutly Victorian atmosphere! Darling, you don't believe any of those wretched things Mary said about me in her book?" She clasped her hands theatrically to her cream silk chest. "I told Monty Monrose—you know, the musical comedy fellow—only morons would believe that at one of our little get-togethers we had him act the butler, carrying a sweet little silver tray and wearing only a bow tie."

The thought of Pepys in such a guise was too horrible. Turning my back on the Cat Cadaver, I followed her toward the drinks table, murmuring, "I do hope nobody untoward turned up at the door."

"Only the TV evangelist from around the corner." She rattled the tongs in the ice bucket and gurgled, "Whoops! I mean, wouldn't that have been too garish for words if true? As I told that reporter from *Newsweek*, I do have to keep reminding myself that Mary is writing in the fantasy genre. And she did change the names of people like Monty to protect the innocent. Lovely not having to share the limelight with anyone as I stand up to my neck in manure." Glass clinked against glass as she reached for a bottle. "Do tell, Ellie Haskell, have you read my girly's masterpiece?"

"I . . . have skimmed a few pages." Did I hear footsteps out in the hall? Palms sweaty, I backed toward one of the maroon armchairs, braced for Mary to burst in upon us.

"I picture my poppet putting a copy by every bed at Mendenhall. Next to the Gideon Bibles." Theola Faith's silvery hair swung against her cheeks in crescent moons. "Are the mad Mangés all talking about me and my wicked ways?"

The door did not come crashing open against the wall. And whatever those sounds in the hall were, they had died away. For this infinitesimal moment we were safe from Mary. Easing down onto the chair, I realized I had been very slow on the uptake. Theola Faith had stolen me from the bowlers of Mud Creek to pump me for information.

"The Mangés are a closed-mouthed lot," I said repressively.

"How dreary. I do hope Pepys and Jeffries have not gone over to the enemy. I have always harboured the suspicion that those two could be bought for higher wages."

At one time I might have disagreed, but remembering the two of them huddled with Mary in the hall this afternoon . . . Unwarily I glanced at the coffee table where lay, as conspicuous as a man's unzipped fly at a cocktail party, the familiar red and black dust jacket. *Monster Mommy.*

"Comfortable?" Theola Faith crossed her silken legs.

"Yes, thank you." I could not drag my eyes from that book. Theola Faith had certainly not returned to Mud Creek for her fortieth high school reunion. She was here in this house for confrontation. But what form would it take? Was she content merely to embarrass her daughter Mary by her presence? Or was she after a more violent attack?

A chill draft crept along the floor and up my skirt. Suddenly my mind panned out to become a movie screen. Opening scene: Theola Faith plotting to destroy her daughter's credibility. At dead of night she crosses the river and enters Mendenhall. Her house. What could be simpler than to lift two of the swashbuckler knives from the dining room wall and . . . gulp, make mincemeat of two of the guests? The bodies of Jim Grogg and Divonne get dropped down the well, the knives get slipped into the pocket of a jacket belonging to Mary . . . What sweet revenge! "Why Sheriff, darling! I kept trying to tell everyone that my daughter is completely whacko, and if a double murder doesn't prove it, what will? But please don't blame her upbringing, the poor poppet fell under the sway of that cult of chefs."

I almost bounced off my chair when the cat (I'd quite forgotten him) brushed against my leg and my hostess handed me a tall glass in which a cherry bobbed merrily.

Please God, Jim Grogg and Divonne were not bobbing down the well. Ellie, use your head! How could Theola have transported them without help? Pepys' legs barely supported him. As for Jeffries . . . I pushed away the image of her tossing a corpse over each shoulder and looked up at the portrait of the Cat Cadaver. Had Mary panicked on finding the knife . . . ?

I sipped the fizzy amber liquid, the condensation on the glass making my hand wet. "This is delicious."

"A concoction of ginger ale, cranberry juice, a squeeze of lemon and crushed ice. My favourite toddy when pregnant with my one and only." Theola Faith had seated herself on the piano stool, tinkling away with one hand; in the other holding a full-to-the-brim glass of whisky. The cat was stalking the back of the sofa and I asked if she was very attached to him. Anything to get off the subject of Mary, although I was beginning to wish she would come and get the whole damn business over and done.

Theola Faith drained half her glass. "Cats have always been my favourite people. Can always shut them away when they get underfoot or fluff 'em up on a satin pillow when the scene is set for homespun simplicity."

"Indeed." Setting my glass down, I pined for Tobias. He'd have bitten off the hand that attempted to turn him into a pajama bag disguised as a stuffed toy. Apparently our feline Charlie Chaplin was not smitten with the idea. When Theola Faith got up to refill her glass, he hightailed it over to the door. The sound of his scratching was the more eloquent because he made no meow.

"Sorry. To oblige would be to set the cat among the pigeons."

She had a point, but the notion that we were both her prisoners settled on me like an outfit of wet clothes. The house was eerily silent, like the calm before a tempest.

"Sweet cat, would you leave your Theola all alone to entertain our friend?" Bending over me, Theola splashed ginger ale into my glass and dropped in a long stemmed cherry. The booze on her breath would have made a trifle. "Listen to him! He reminds me of when I was expecting Mary . . . and felt life for the first time." She straightened up, the bottle hanging loose at her side. "By the way, have you reached that stage yet?" It was her first—and only—reference to my pregnancy.

"No."

"Darling, it was like soft paws on a door, asking to be let out."

I felt a surge of sympathy and at that unguarded moment—when I was thinking of Mary as an innocent, harmless rosebud-lipped baby—the door opened, sending the cat skittering across the floor. I think I closed my eyes; I know I slopped my drink.

Pepys stood before us, looking as always like a body that had been kept in freezer storage for a thousand years. But he wasn't completely cold-blooded. A flush tinged his cheeks as he looked toward Theola Faith and I noticed a tremor to his bandy legs.

Her eyes narrowed. "Ah, there you are, Pipsqueak!"

"Pepys, ma'am." If he'd had a hair on his head he would have touched his forelock.

"Whatever!" Free hand moving like a thirties' flapper, Theola reseated herself at the piano. "If you dare to say this is an unexpected pleasure I will toss you out on your ear. Now read my lips. Find my daughter and bring her here."

"But Miss Faith—" A skeletal rattle as he risked a couple of steps forward. "I don't see as I can . . ."

Her fingers plunged upon the keys bringing forth musical thunder, and the cat leaped onto my lap. For a moment I feared Pepys would do likewise. "No buts! Out, I say, out! Or I will make you pay in spades"—she rattled her glass—"for draining the good Scotch from the bottles and replacing it with generic."

"Jeffries made me!" He backed into the half open door, smacked his head sharply, and was gone.

Minus his white marble presence, the room seemed redder and stuffier than ever. Silence weighed heavily on me, along with the cat. And then Theola Faith began to play a perky tune, one which I recognized:

"Oh, she do make a loverly corpse she do
Her face the sweetest shade of blue
Dressed up in her Sunday best
She will soon be laid to rest
Alongside husbands one through four
Who could ask for any more?"

The piano tinkled away to nothing.

"That's from *Melancholy Mansion*," Theola Faith said.

I sipped my drink and a chill coursed through me. So that's how I knew the song . . . from hearing my mother sing snatches of it. Setting my glass down, I said, "You knew my mother."

Eyes on the door, Theola Faith finished her drink. "Darling, now you sound like every other groupie." Her smile had a china doll quality and her hair a nylon sheen. Hard to believe forty years had passed since Theola swayed the hearts of millions in her debut film. "Forgive me, sweetie! I see you are being quite sincere. Remind me about your mother. I shouldn't be thought insensitive because I don't remember every chance encounter at a small-town country club or with some teller at a bank!"

The brush of the cat's tail was like the touch of a friendly hand. "My mother has been dead for years. I'm sure you wouldn't recognize the name. She was one of the dancers in the night club scene in *Melancholy Mansion*. Lots of hair, clear pale skin."

"American?" Her eyes were closed.

"English. She and my father came over here to try their professional luck, but she only landed that one small job and they weren't away more than a few weeks."

"The water nymph!"

Perfect description. Theola Faith might or might not be a monster, but she was a witch. She made another trip to the drinks table. "Those dancers all fed intravenously and I'm sure rushed to confession if ever they used bad words like ice cream."

I rearranged my feet. "Was she special? I mean, did she stand out among the other dancers?"

"She stood out all right. Was the worst of the lot. She had a kink in her front kick and a wobble in her jetté. Seems to me there was talk about dumping her but . . . yes, that's right—Billy Anderson, who played the knife-happy schoolboy, suggested keeping her on for comic relief."

I buried my face in Charlie Chaplin's fur. Small wonder Mother had given me the choice of seeing *Bambi* or *Melancholy Mansion*. She, who lived to suffer for her art, must have died a thousand deaths when asked to dance for laughs. But what choice did she have, after financing the venture to America by hocking the family silver? As for me, I had been so angry with both parents for abandoning me to Great Uncle Merlin that I had responded with a child's ultimate weapon—indifference. I had asked virtually no questions about that fateful visit to America.

Miss Faith raised a bottle of ginger ale; I shook my head. She swirled her drink so that the ice cubes jangled in her glass. Another glance toward the door and a shrug caused her drink to tilt sideways, no doubt making splash marks on the cream suit. "Seems to me . . ." Her voice attempted to walk a straight line—one tiny word wobble and over she would go into slurred speech (the wait for Mary was taking its toll on her, too), "One day . . . between takes . . . talked to the water nymph. Told me she had a daughter."

"What a memory!"

"Sweetie, my stock in trade."

"Any mention of my weight problem?"

"Don't think . . . she ever said . . . word about your size. Plied me with the usual mother mush. You were the most marvelous, spunkiest . . ." Theola Faith was weaving her way across the room. ". . . best kid in the world."

A warmth eased into me that had nothing to do with holding the cat. But was Theola Faith making this up? Was her aim to keep me talking? Was she lonely? Fleetingly, I thought of the terrible stories Mary had told of her mother.

She half drained her glass, swayed, then recovered to stand ramrod straight. "Can see your mother. Jeffries was there—pinning tucks in my costume. One of them stuck me. Remember . . . last straw. All that sand-*stand*ing around! Such a frigging waste of time, and here was this woman who was being kept on . . . to prove that Hollywood does have a heart. Like hell she needed my pity. She had a husband whose name she could remember. She had a daughter."

"So did you," I tried to stand up but the cat wouldn't let me.

The panda eyes found me. "Mary!" She cleared her throat with the name. "Darling, my precious daughter loathed me way back then. And for what? Some small neglects that couldn't be helped? Some tiny discomforts? I had my work, my fame, my life as a sexually active woman."

Desperately searching for something to say, I followed her eyes to the door and in fear and trembling, watched it nudge open. The cat leaped to investigate and I too was on my feet, about to make my exit speech when . . . another false alarm.

Jeffries came bopping in, her face screwed up so that it was all mouth under the white cap. "No flying at me, Missie Theola, ain't none of this my fault, or Pepys' for that matter—though you've driven him to bed with a migraine." Taking no account of me she scooted, like a walking feather duster, to an inch or two of her employer, hands on her hips, tiny chin in the air. "Even that French Count of Monte Cristo we have here couldn't produce Miss Mary Faith out of no hat, because she ain't on the premises. She informed me this afternoon that she'd had a word with the Reverend Enoch Gibbons a couple of days back and he'd invited her over for a meal of fasting and abstinence this evening. He wants to interview her for his church paper. Modern Day Martyr—that sort of snappy headline."

Gripping the back of a chair as if it were a walker, Theola Faith worked her way round to the front. And fell into the seat. "You're all in league with her." Speaking in a drone, the limpid eyes which had thrilled millions looked straight ahead. "But she can't escape me forever. All Pastor Enoch's prayers won't keep her from me." Her lip curled. "Wouldn't he like to know that his wife is residing with me in Jimmy's apartment? I needed someone to do the cleaning . . ."

"Pepys tried to tell you about Miss Mary." Jeffries was doing her Crosspatch prance. "He took her over in the boat earlier. She said His Reverence would bring her back—whenever. How say I go fetch you a nice cup of hot milk, Miss Theola?" The pillar box smile should have warmed the cockles of anyone's heart.

Theola Faith hurled a cushion at her.

Jeffries' gnomish face darkened. "That's it, I quit!" The door smacked shut.

"Now what were we saying?" The china doll smile was back in place. The silvery hair bounced forward. Only the glint of her eyes betrayed her as a woman thwarted of her prey. "Oh yes, your mother. How sweet that I can open the door to the past for you, Ellie Haskell! And all because I was kind to a line dancer. How it all comes back! She told me you had been sent to stay with a wild and wacky uncle in a dungeon of a house by the ocean. Amazing you survived. Amazing you haven't written all about it in a charming little exposé."

"Who would read it? Mother wasn't famous."

Again the china doll smile. Theola Faith said nothing. I thought of the lurid headlines, the Donahue show on abused daughters, the Theola Faith *Monster Mommy* T-shirts, the upcoming paperback, the movie.

My legs had gone to sleep, causing Charlie Cat sufficient offence that he leaped from my lap to a table, and skidded across it on a doily, which he dragged with him under the sofa. Only the tip of his tail provided warning that he was listening to every word. Loyalty to Uncle Merlin forced me to say that he wasn't the ogre of my imagination.

"How disappointing! Mary's visit to her Aunt Guinevere was a scream from beginning to end. The little imp convinced herself on the scantiest of evidence that the sweet old lady hated her."

"Goodness!" How I longed to return to the life of sanity among the Mangés. If only Henderson Brown would come in looking for that paperback book he had been reading earlier, or even Ernestine—eager for a brag session about Bingo. I began to dread that Theola Faith would expect me to sit up with her until Mary returned, and at the same time, I felt under an obligation because of my mother. "Didn't you ever like your daughter?" I heard myself ask.

"Darling!" Miss Faith's smile kept sliding off her face as she struggled to sit upright. The silver hair drooped over one eye. "After I got over the shock of finding I was pregnant—and the lucky father a name to be pulled out of a hat—I decided I might enjoy the Madonna role. I was amused when I felt life. And when she was born, I saw the marvelous possibilities of those adorable mother/daughter outfits. I bought some wonderful hats. I worship hats."

I pressed my hand to my middle. "What went wrong?"

"Mary was born a pain in the tush. Forever crying— worse when I was exhausted from being on the set all day. She'd go to Begita, my maid, sooner than me. Her eyes would look out of that tiny face and I knew she didn't like me. And once she could talk . . ." her hand flopped against the cream silk bosom ". . . all I ever got was *whining*. People speak about mismatched marriages all the time!" The fabled voice lurched from high to drowsy deep. "What of a mismatched mother and daughter? Believe me, darling! I did my best for that kid. I kept out of her way. As I said—cats are easy and pigeons . . . even better. Derby and Joan!" With a swoop of her arm Theola Faith staggered to her feet. "Your typical Hollywood marriage! Derby has had a thing going with a tweety pie named Sabrina for years. That dumb bird Joan turns a blind eye. Amazing, isn't it, that such a gem of sleaze never made the *Peephole Press*." Fingers pinching the hem of her skirt, she locked her wide smile in place. "Always had pigeons. Asked my daddy for a kite for my fourth birthday and he gave me my first pair. Said the sk–sky was now my back yard. Used to think there was no place like Mud Creek." Her voice went into a slow slide and faded out. For a few seconds I thought she was asleep on her feet. But she trailed over to the sofa and draped herself upon it, clutching the edge to keep from sliding to the floor.

I pictured Mary coming in to find Theola collapsed in a drunken stupor, and I found I hated the idea for them as much as for me. I had no wish to feature (even with a name change) in *Monster Mommy II*. I know this sounds silly, but I do have an affinity for cats, and looking at her now, standing over her, I could understand why Theola Faith had been called Kitten Face in her heyday.

"How did you get to be a movie star?" I prodded.

"Darling"—she didn't open her eyes—"where've you been all your life? Don't you read the tabloids? I was discovered on a bar stool at the Lucky Strike. So they say! And it was rumoured that *Melancholy Mansion* was filmed here to indulge one of my whims. Truth was Rick . . ."—half word, half hiccup—". . . Ricky Greenburgh, the director, needed to shoot cheap." She lolled sideways, one leg dangling ungracefully—a shoe pivoting from her stockinged toes. Her thick mink lashes fluttered closed. "Mendenhall had been on the market since . . . the world began. Ricky bought it for a song and, when we were done filming, gave it to me. Not a bad guy, Ricky. He could have lef . . . left a rose on the pillow."

Removing her shoe, I eased her leg onto the sofa. Silver hair cupping her cheeks, she didn't look like a monster. She was still talking softly. "Haven't been down here in years. But like to know Mendenhall is waiting. Pepys and Jeffries come sometimes . . . see to maintenance. Mary didn't stop at throwing the book at me . . . invaded Mendenhall . . . claimed Ricky once said . . . was for her."

Something brushed my leg. Charlie Chaplin Cat. He pounced onto the sofa and macho purring blended with Theola Faith's snores. I was at the door when her drowsy, deep voice startled me. "How is my Mary?"

Not knowing what to say, I was glad she immediately rejoined Charlie in their duet and even more relieved when the door cracked into me and I was looking into the eyes of love.

"Ben!" His hair was rumpled, his collar askew, he was Samson ready to bring the temple crashing down. To me he had never looked more beautiful.

"I'm going to kill you," he snarled, crushing me in his arms. "During our five minute break, I rushed up to our room to check on you and found your note. I almost went crazy thinking of you." Kicking the door shut, he thrust me from him and cupped my face with his hands. "How did you get across the river? I hope you didn't hitch-hike?"

"Nothing that foolish," I reassured him. "I took one of the rowing boats."

"You what?"

"Never mind, all's well that ends well . . ." I trailed off lamely, my eyes now looking toward the sofa.

"Yes, Theola Faith!" Ben lowered his voice a notch. "Jeffries collared me with the information that you were in here with Monster Mommy."

"There's quite a simple explanation." Taking a deep breath I set to telling my tale. The hard part was confessing the truth about gate crashing the bowling banquet, but I couldn't have lived through the rest of our marriage keeping that kind of hideous secret.

When I had ended, my love worked a hand over his face. "My God, Ellie, if I had known what you were up to, I would have asked Valicia X to bend the rule about candidates not being allowed to leave the island so I could go in search of you."

"And what would you have done if she had refused?"

"My dear"—he kept one eye on Theola Faith—"that's one of those testing questions—such as, would I marry again if anything happened to you?"

"Well, would you?" I pressed my fingers lovingly to his throat.

"Only if the woman had one foot in the grave and one hand on her cheque book. Shush!" He pressed a hand to my mouth. "The important thing now is to get Mommy out of this house before her daughter returns. Jeffries and Pepys are all of a twit. They have their jobs to consider as well as their Mangé loyalties. Believe me, a bloody scene between the Faiths is something they wish to avoid at all costs. They have pleaded with Valicia X. The upshot is that Jeffries and I will take Theola Faith back to Mud Creek in her speedboat, and Pepys will follow with the cabin cruiser."

I picked at a thread on his jacket. "Valicia X must see you as a knight in shining armour."

"Ellie, please! The last thing I desire is to win Mangé points because the woman is susceptible to my dashed devilish charm."

"Hmmmm!"

"Enough of us, my sweet! Pepys and Jeffries await." He crept toward the sofa. "Do you think I should try tossing the star over my shoulder without waking her?"

No chance for me to respond. As he bent over Theola Faith, she rose up like a drowned being from the deep and coiled her arms around his neck. "Ricky my beloved!" Her silvery hair fell away from his face. "You have come back to me. Take me! Take me now to our own private heaven! Make your Kitten Face young again!"

"Oh, cripes!" Ben muttered.

Jeffries gloated from behind me. "Looks like things may work out easier than we hoped."

Out in the hall a door slammed. Damn! As my cousin Freddy would say, never count your chickens until they are in the deep freeze.

14

The dream was as sharp-edged as the last one. The walls of the narrow staircase closed in on me. I heard water flushing somewhere in the house in St. John's Wood. I smelled fish. That oily mettalic smell that lingers after kippers. The Bundys on the third floor were very fond of fish. Old Mrs. Bundy: the grump. Always pounding her broom on the ceiling when Mother pirouetted with a thump! My father, magnanimous in his smoking jacket, would insist, "Ignore her, my dears! Are we not all entitled to our eccentricities?" And so we ignored, until that time when Mother had insisted the pounding sounded different. We had marched downstairs to discover Mr. Bundy stricken with a stroke and Mrs. Bundy in too much of a state to make it down to the pay phone in the entry hall.

My legs were giving out. I didn't have the energy for the rest of the climb. But I had to reach the fifth floor. Somehow it seemed sly not to tell Mother that Theola Faith had descended upon Mendenhall and that Ben & Co. had spirited her off the premises without colliding with Mary. The banging door had been a false alarm, only Pepys coming in from checking the boat's fuel situation . . .

I reached to touch the door of the flat. My laboured breathing was entirely the fault of the stairs. Nothing at all to do with the question I intended to put to Mother. If she and my father had found fame/land/fortune in America, would they . . . would they have remembered to send for me?

No answer to my knock. And small wonder. Noise poured like smoke under the door. My first suspicion was a party. But when I got my ear tuned in, I realized this was the hurly burly of everyday living. The smell of kippers was gone, replaced—Olé—by the aroma of something wild and Mexican. Had Mother given up ballet for the evening? Would I find her playing a cutthroat game of Monopoly with Daddy? Or would she be wearing the rosy chamber pot on her head, the shaggy bathmat tossed across her shoulders, while she stalked the flat doing her impersonation of Aunt Astrid at Ascot?

The door swung inward . . . Oh, no! Surely my eyes deceived me. Our flat had been invaded by another family. A mother wearing a bib apron was chasing around with the Hoover. A father sat, feet on the fender, reading a huge story book to children of assorted sizes, all with round, rosy faces and wearing hand-knitted cardigans.

A red-headed pudgekin pointed at me. "Mummy! Daddy! Is she a ghost?"

"Sorry!" I said, "I once knew some people who lived here." Turning stiffly, I went back downstairs into sleep.

I awoke feeling I had developed curvature of the spine overnight and that a hundred watt torch was being shone relentlessly in my eyes.

"Ellie . . ." That was Ben speaking and the blinding glare was the sun. ". . . are you all right?"

"Why?" I struggled onto one elbow.

"Sweetheart, it's gone noon." He sat down on the bed, causing it to pitch leeward. My insides went into a heaving roll and, gripping his hand, I eased back down.

"Morning sickness back again. As your mother said in her letter, you get a day or so of feeling good just so you can remember what it felt like. Darling, return to your Mangé meetings and let me die . . . I mean lie . . . in peace."

He patted my hand. "This is my lunch break and I intend to spend every minute with you. Would you like me to fetch you up something? How about a nice poached egg?"

"Please!" I begged. "If you love me, don't mention food. Tell me about Theola Faith."

He went to cross his legs, saw me wince, and in slow motion lowered his foot to the floor. "I aided in getting her to the cabin cruiser, but once aboard she became so . . . aggressive with me, insisting that she show me the sights . . ."

"Of Mud Creek?" I had thought I was having trouble keeping his face in focus but I now realized he had been avoiding my eyes.

"Her bedroom, to be specific. Damn it, Ellie! I don't know what I do to bring out the beast in women! Do I have Eligibility Escorts tattooed across my brow?" Standing, he dug his hands in his pockets and glared miserably out the window at the choppy waters around the island.

"Darling, no!" The room felt as though it were being shaken like a mat. Somewhere in the house someone was running the Hoover.

"The result was Jeffries decided I was more hindrance than help. She said she'd take the cabin cruiser across, Pepys would follow in Miss Faith's boat, and I came back ashore. So no Mangé rules were bent. You were dead asleep when I came up." Head down, he paced toward the fireplace. "Sweetheart, there is something I should mention . . ."

"Yes?" Were we finally getting to the climax? The low-down on why he had turned shifty-eyed?

"When we gathered downstairs this morning, the comte and Solange were gone. Their room is empty. Understand-able they would wish to leave without any fanfare; the only question being who took them ashore. Pepys and Jeffries denied doing so, Valicia X was as curious as anyone, and

. . . what did come as something of a shock . . ." He dropped down beside me and gripped my hand, his lips pressed together.

"Yes?" I gripped the headboard but couldn't keep the bed from going around.

"Lois and Henderson had done a bunk too."

The bed stopped with violent suddenness. That left only Bingo and Marjorie Rumpson for Ben to compete against, I thought, and instantly felt ashamed. This Mangé competition was turning me into an animal. "That doesn't make sense. The comte was disqualified for endangering Joan's life, but Lois Brown was still in the running, wasn't she?"

"A prime contender, I would have said."

"Did they leave a note?"

Ben turned my hand over. "Three words scrawled in lipstick on their dressing table mirror. First word *the*. The second looked like *captured* or *captive* and the third was badly smudged. But began with a *b*."

"Blood?"

"Ellie, curb your imagination. There has to be a simple explanation."

"No one admitted to taking them ashore either?"

"No." Still his eyes refused to meet mine. An ugly thought crossed my mind. Surely no one—surely not Ben—would have *done* something to eliminate competition for the Mangé plum? No. It was too reprehensible to believe. Yet, people did believe the reprehensible things Mary had written of her mother in *Monster Mommy*. Surely . . .

"Perhaps Bingo is playing a joke—although how he could make two people disappear . . ." I shook my head, turned horribly giddy, and lay still. "The comte might be able to manage it. Sorry darling, I know this is no time for jokes."

Ben worked a hand over his face. "Someone is up to tricks. Jeffries was carrying on about all the knives gone from the dining room wall. And finding one in a most unusual place."

A shudder passed through me. Someone below stairs had pounded on the gong. Time for Ben to leave me. He said he would find Ernestine and have her bring me up a tray, but I told him I would prefer to rest a while longer, and if I felt up to eating, I would go down to the dining room.

Stroking my hair, he said, "How do you feel about the barbecue? Remember, it's at five o'clock."

"I'll try and be there." I lifted a wan hand in farewell. Actually the thought of meat—spilling juices and spitting fat on a grill—had brought on a relapse just when I had begun to think I *might* live.

I escaped into sleep, but Lois and Henderson Brown came dogging after me. She was wearing her corsage, his face radiated gloom. *"I warned you about this fire-and-brimstone house, but you wouldn't listen . . . listen . . . listen."* His voice became a mournful echo. Disembodied hands grabbed at me, spinning me around, and when I next looked I was standing under the pawnbroker chandelier at the bottom of the stairs, down which descended a butler with patent leather hair and penciled moustache; his candle held aloft. *"The guests are all dead of unnatural causes!"* A mournful rush of wind accompanied his words and I saw trailing behind him, each of them garbed in white—their complexions the colour of dill pickles—the Hendersons, Jim Grogg and Divonne, Comte Vincent and Solange.

"Shall we adjourn to the Red Room?" The comte drew two large old style pennies from his sleeve, placed them over his eyes, levitated midway between ceiling and floor, and floated feet first down the hall.

"Wait!" I cried as the rest of them drifted upward. *"I have to know who is responsible for this . . . carnage!"*

"Ma fleur"—Solange pinched my cheek in passing—*"You guess right last night when you theenk inside your head that Madame Theola Faith is more than zee monster. She eez a murderess! She slip into the house—chop chop with the knives and plop plop with our bodies down the well . . ."* One last gauzy flutter of white and the Frenchwoman was gone.

Grabbing the butler's sleeve, I was aghast to discover he was Marjorie Rumpson. *"Time's awasting m'hearty!"* He—she—rammed the flickering candle under my nose. *"I have graves to dig in the herb garden before afternoon tea. Nothing brings on parsley like the right fertilizer."*

"This is utter nonsense!" I cried. *"Theola Faith was too drunk last night to make a decent job of murder, she couldn't have returned at dead of night, unless . . ."*

"That's right, darling! Unless I was acting." Theola Faith became the one holding the candle; her gamine smile as bright as its flame. *"Think about it. Did I really leave the house last night, the moment your gallant husband went fleeing back to the house? Or did I tell Pepys and Jeffries that I had changed my mind about returning to Mud Creek? No sacrifice is too much for a mother . . ."*

"Never!" I cried, *"You can't be such a monster as to attempt to destroy your daughter this way!"* I backed away from the candle, but now her eyes blazed fire—shooting toward me like twin blow torches. No place to hide; I had no choice but to wake up.

I had twisted the poppy spread into a rope and was backed up against the headboard. The room was adazzle with sunlight. But I thought I heard a distant roll of thunder and the very stillness of the dead tree outside my window convinced me that a storm was out there waiting. All that electricity in the air, on an empty stomach to boot, no wonder I was having nightmares. Swinging my legs out of bed, I was relieved to find solid ground underfoot. Perhaps my earlier bout had not been morning sickness after all, but too much ginger ale the night before.

Good heavens! Almost four o'clock! And nothing would be achieved by wallowing in shame. I would have a bath, get dressed and accompany Ben to the barbecue. Instead of focusing on the departed members of our group, I should count myself lucky—in this country of instant divorce—not to be returning home as the ex–Mrs. Bentley T. Haskell. What, I wondered, brazenly baring my shoulder of nightgown and flirting with the mirror, what would the lovely Valicia X be wearing?

Ben was coming up the stairs as I came down.

"Sweetheart, you look radiant!" In his enthusiasm, he almost sent us diving over the banisters.

"You look mighty splendid yourself, Rhett!" I said as he put his hands on my waist (or the vicinity where it had once been) and swung me down in a swirl of skirts and hair onto the bottom step. No one was about in the hall except the pigeons; one perched on the grandmother clock and the other on the frame of Dame Gloom.

"Probably spies, just itching to turn you in for conduct unbefitting a Mangé," I whispered.

Ben held the front door for me. "I certainly don't envy the pair of them if Bingo loses. Coming my love?" He crooked an elbow and we set off in high style down the sooty red steps and along the herringbone path toward a refectory-sized table, spread with a white damask cloth and set out under a canopy of two trees. The remnants of the Mangé contingent—Valicia X, the Hoffmans, and Marjorie Rumpson—stood with tall, frosted glasses at the foot of a rock garden whose plants were all of the breed to have unpronounceable names. Pepys and Jeffries were over by a side table, administering to several silver dishes and what looked like an edible American flag.

"A savoury cheesecake." Ben quickened his step. "I glimpsed Pepys carrying it out. The stripes are pimiento and—"

I missed the rest. I was distracted by a plop of rain on my hand, followed a second later by a low growl of thunder. What a pity if the picnic had to retreat indoors. Dodging a wasp, I collided with Mary Faith. Ben reached to steady her as she clutched a granite bird bath and teetered down a slide of rock into his arms.

"I am sorry." She backed into me.

"My pleasure," Ben assured her.

"You look nice, Mary!" I lied. She wore a beige button-down frock that matched her complexion only too well. Her lipstick was too dark, her earrings too bulgy and those damn wing-tipped glasses really had to go—in the river.

"Ellie, you will be mad with me I know, but I have to do this."

"Do what?" Another dollop of rain, on my nose this time. An added distraction was that the breeze was blowing the voices of the others our way. Bingo was talking about the need for different flavours of ketchup. He believed avocado would be a hit.

"You are joining us for dinner?" Ben graced Mary with a smile which I trusted she would understand was not intended as that of a Mangé on the make.

"Sorry, can't do. That's the point, you see! I'm taking the cabin cruiser over to Mud Creek, to meet with my mother. She sent word with Pepys this afternoon, when he went over to grocery shop, that if I wasn't at her apartment by five P.M. I would regret it."

"But it's already past that time," I protested.

Lifting her chin, her glasses sparked defiance. "Exactly. I'm making a statement that I can't be bullied, but I do have to see her." Her mouth hardened into a smile. "The pleasing thought came to me that she may want a hand-out! After all, I am suddenly quite a catch as a daughter. *Monster Mommy* has made me a multi-millionaire. Think I'll hand her five bucks; you can't tip less these days."

I was swamped with pity for her. "Mary, don't go!"

"A shame to miss the party." To me, Ben's quirky smile was irresistible.

Mary looked at her watch, administered a swift hug while whispering to me, "Best friends forever," and suddenly she was hurrying across the mossy rock to the dock. I lingered, thinking of all the damage a bad mother/daughter relationship brought in its wake.

Ah, but the barbecue beckoned!

"What's the big idea?" Bingo leered at us. "Aiming to be fashionably late?"

"Now then, dear!" Ernestine sounded like Kanga admonishing baby Roo. "Mr. Haskell probably lost track of time boning up for a calorie quiz."

Marjorie Rumpson snorted through the veil of her bee-keeper's hat. And, shucky darn, here came Valicia X, a wide, shiny black belt nipping in the waist of her flame-coloured frock, to hand span size. Ha! I had thought that fashion went out with the Civil War.

"How are you doing?" she asked as though I were a cheese set out to ripen, then before I could uncork my lips, she tugged Ben, in a flutter of caped sleeves, toward the table. "Mr. Haskell, I do want your opinion on Jeffries' Wineberry Whip and Artful Artichokes."

No reason for me to feel ignored. Ernestine smiled pityingly my way and Pepys appeared at my elbow, proffering a plate of crepewiches—as he identified the mini-layered slices. I was debating whether I could get away with taking more than six, when Jeffries appeared with some delicious smelling crabby things.

"Drinks are help yourself."

"Thank you." Munching contentedly away, I caught another rain drop on the chin. Was it considered bad form in this country to permit weather to disrupt social functions? Would we be expected to smile gamely through the rain if a real downpour set in? Gazing out at the river I indulged in a fantasy: Ben and I alone on this island, sharing magical adventures out of reach of our own time. He the smuggler chieftain, face masked by moonlight, and I his lady, stolen from a manor house on the Cornish cliffs. On late afternoons such as this, we would take our trusty rowing boat and I would sit listening to the companionable dip and roll of the oars, trailing my hand in foam, white and soft as finest French lace. At the setting of the sun, we would turn back to Mendenhall, rising up like the figurehead of a mighty pirate ship. . . .

The fantasy smashed to pieces. A blazing fireball pierced the sky. My immediate reaction was . . . fireworks. This was, after all, the Fourth of July. But surely the flash was too big, too close, and accompanied by a blast that could have nothing to do with festivity.

Near the boat house a bonfire blazed on the water.

"Oh, my God!" Ben cried. "The cabin cruiser has blown up!"

15

Stumbling over bolders, cracking elbows with each other every third step we headed for the shoreline. Anyone watching must have thought we had been marooned on the island for twenty years and finally someone had cried, "Ship on the horizon!" Marjorie Rumpson forged ahead. Ernestine skidded into a sitdown, but Bingo took her in his stride—puffing over her legs with inches to spare. Valicia X made excellent speed, her high heels never sinking in the sandy sludge as we neared the water's edge. Ben grabbed me as I twisted around to look back the way we had come. Was I missing two people? Ah, here came Pepys and Jeffries! She had him by the elbow, either to hold him up or prevent a vulgar display of haste. Tears stung my eyes, as much from the acrid smell which hung over the island as from shock. I stared at the place where fire still licked the water. All that remained afloat of the cabin cruiser was some kindling.

"Ben! Is there the smallest hope?" Numbly I watched as he tossed aside his jacket, kicked off his shoes, and raced through a sudden blur of rain toward the river's edge, loosening his tie as he went. Marjorie Rumpson beat him into the water. Unnoticed by me, she had stripped down to her Maidenform and bloomers, her beekeeper's hat forgotten on her head—unless it was intended to do duty as a flotation device.

"Stand back m'lad, this is a job for a woman!" Her mighty fin kick sent an avalanche of spray Ben's way; he went over on his back and she rose up pale and gleaming as a porpoise, then opened her mouth as if to breathe in the entire sky and vanished into the depths. Ben followed suit, with the grace of . . . a martyr being dropped into boiling oil by his heels. My brave darling, he hates having his face under water even to have his hair washed.

Every few moments a head would bob to the surface and I would stop breathing. Please let this one be Mary! And when it wasn't, my heart would take a dive along with the rescuers. Hopelessness settled on me, as damp and chill as my rain-spattered clothes. Valicia X was the only person whose hair was not being blown by the wind. Her French twist remained as smooth as her voice. "Surely the explosion was witnessed from Mud Creek. They must have some sort of primitive rescue organization!"

"What if they thought we were just going all-out with the fireworks?" I suggested miserably, watching the increasingly turbulent water.

Nobody responded directly. Ernestine's stars-and-stripes scarf kept flicking her in the mouth. "You all know what this means if Mary is indeed . . . at rest. I don't have to spell it out, do I, in front of Bingo?"

"M-U-R-D-E-R." His jungle print shirt and khaki shorts turned the fat boy into a big game hunter. "You're quite right, Mom, for once. Even people with average I.Q.'s could see this is no accident." His spectacles could not conceal that he was pop-eyed with excitement. And could that be for the best of all reasons! Was the nightmare about to have a happy ending after all? Hands clenched, I jumped up and down, almost knocking Valicia X over. Marjorie Rumpson was plowing to shore, a gull skimming above her wake as she towed in . . . oh, no! Not Mary but Ben. Understand, I was pleased to have him restored to dry land, strongly denying that he had at any time, for so much as a second, lost consciousness. But the realization that Mary Faith would appear to be no more was a bitter pill to swallow.

We stood there in the gloaming, Marjorie pulling on her frock, Ben wringing out his trouser legs. Pepys removed his black tie, and handed it to Jeffries, who, standing on tiptoe, tied it around his arm. "Ain't it always the same, a death in the household and you're never prepared." Her smirk reminded me of Judy bashing Punch over the head.

"Perhaps she isn't dead," I heard myself say. "Couldn't she have changed her mind about visiting her mother and returned to the house?"

"Impossible," said Valicia firmly. "To reach either door to the house she would have had to pass near the barbecue area. We would have seen her."

Eyes burning in skull sockets, Pepys smacked his lips. "I'm the one to blame!"

"You blew up the boat?" Ernestine grabbed up Bingo.

"I ain't no vandal, ma'am! What I meant . . ."

Jeffries shut her cohort up with a well-placed elbow. "What you meant to say, you old gizzard, is you spilled the beans to Miss Theola Faith last night. Going up the fire escape stairs to her apartment, you said there was a barbecue planned for five o'clock this evening. I heard you. And this afternoon she tells you to give Miss Mary the message about coming over."

Yes, how considerate of Monster Mommy to pick a time when Mary would almost certainly make the crossing unaccompanied because everyone else was at the party.

"Don't you be speaking for me!" Pepys wagged a moon-white finger at Jeffries. "I didn't violate the Mangé code speaking of the barbecue, and I ain't ready to toss the boss lady to the wolves. Not yet. What I say is we should've reasoned with Miss Mary. Tied her up and stuck a gag in her mouth. Thought about it when I saw her leaving,

but was afraid the rain would start in and the salad'd
be soup."

Arms folded, Jeffries flashed him a congratulatory smile.
"So she's gone and the meal's a bust anyway. What a
Fourth of July. Enough to turn you unpatriotic."

Valicia X crossed in front of Ben and me, pausing a
moment to touch his arm, and trod a few steps closer to the
river. Her flame-coloured frock ruffled about her legs. High
heels resisting the mud, she cupped a hand to her Grecian
brow. "No sign of activity across the water. The inhabitants
of Mud Creek must all be in the local bar celebrating our
having blown ourselves up with a firecracker. That the
Mangé Society should be linked to anything this unsavoury
is beyond belief."

"Let's look on the bright side!" Ernestine winked and
thumbed toward Bingo. "The boat may have blown up by
accident."

Marjorie, still shaking herself like a dog coming out of
the water, beamed. "Absolutely!"

"Squaws speak with stupid tongues." Bingo folded his
meaty arms. "Wigwam of the Water sabotaged."

Hair matted to her cheeks, his mother wiped a spatter
of rain off her nose. "Honey, must I tell you again? Murder
is no joke."

"Let's not forget 'innocent until proven guilty'!" I pressed
my hands to my middle. Not quite the same as covering the
baby's ears, but the best I could do. "No mother in her
right mind . . ."

Ben put an arm around me; Jeffries flashed a smirk that
lit up her gnome features. "You're right. Every member of
the jury will have read *Monster Mommy*. She'll get off with
insanity."

"We must notify the police." Valicia's eyes singled out
Ben. Rain had moisturized her face to pearly perfection.
How could he do less for his Lady Mangé than take a boat
out into the stormy waters? I didn't want him to go; when
he shifted his arm, I felt like a tree trying to stand without
roots. The sky hung low as though someone had emptied a

Hoover bag up there. A fragment of the motor boat still blazed on the grey waters. The wind not only snatched at our clothes, it lifted Ben's voice, carried it off—so that an echo did the talking.

"Look!" He directed his free hand toward a motor boat zooming our way amidst the lashing of spray. "Isn't that the Coast Guard?"

A unanimous "Maybe!" And in time of need, a boat is a boat for a' that. We made a shrieking rush to shore. Pepys hopped up and down like a rusty pogo stick. Jeffries leaped about doing scissor kicks cheerleader style, and Marjorie Rumpson, her beekeeper's hat sadly the worse for her dip, grabbed up a fallen branch to wave wildly over her head. The boat cut a circle in the water and knifed toward us.

Time for Valicia X to slip the mantle of Mangé authority around her elegant shoulders, her profile offering the stern beauty of a ship's figurehead. "We don't want to overwhelm the man. If you will all return to the house, I'll talk to him alone. Unless"—she extended a wan hand to Ben—"you would stay, Mr. Haskell."

Surely I was woman enough to sacrifice my needs in the public interest. The Coast Guardsman threw an authoritive leg over the side of the boat.

Ben's daring amazed, even allowing for his being chilled to the bone. "Ms. X, might not Pepys be of more use to you? He knows—*knew* the cabin cruiser intimately. And I should see my wife up to the house." A smile aimed to charm. "We don't want the baby catching a cold."

"Whatever your priorities, Mr. Haskell." The onset of sheeting rain masked the beautiful face.

Pepys tottered around Ben. "My math ain't great, but I make that ten points knocked off your score, Sir Gallyhad!" Bronchial with laughter, he joined Ms. X along with the Coast Guard. The Hoffmans, Miss Rumpson, and Jeffries hurried for the house, looking very much like a line of clothes being buffeted by the wind.

Ben attempted to follow suit, but I resisted.

"Ellie, where you going?"

"Only these few steps to the boat house."

"Why?"

"Because I keep hoping for a miracle, that's why." I fumbled with the door latch. "Considering her reason for taking the boat, isn't it likely Mary would have dragged her feet? What if she came in here for bug spray or a favourite cardigan—and passed out when the explosion came?"

"Sweetheart . . ." Ben nudged me ahead of him into the boxy space with its rowing boats and canoes, fishing equipment, shelves of paint and varnished smell . . . but no Mary.

I dropped down on the garden seat, felt it teeter, and gripped the mock stone with my hands. "The madness of hope!"

Gently he touched my face. "Ellie, she won't have suffered."

"How do you know?" I flared. "Have you ever been blown up? Oh, I'm sorry. But her life was so wretched!"

"What I find hard to credit"—he scrunched his hair, sending trickles of rain down his forehead—"is how any woman could so brutally kill her own daughter."

I stood up. "Which is your convoluted way of saying you believe Theola Faith . . ." The words were too awful to say.

"Sweetheart, what else is there to think? Even Pepys and Jeffries, who have been with her for years think so."

"Oh, them!" Twisting my hair into a rope, I wrung it out like a towel. "They'll want her six feet under so they can start collecting their pensions." The steady drip drip of water on my leg was louder than the rain outside. "Even allowing for the barbecue, Theola Faith still ran the risk of bumping off extras. And wouldn't she have to be some sort of bomb expert? Not to sound sexist, darling, but we women are usually better at blowing things up accidentally—blenders and washing machines."

Ben moved to the door and back. "Sweetheart, she probably read up on it in one of those Do It Yourself manuals."

Or recalled how it was done in *Melancholy Mansion*. I could see Pepys lying on the window ledge, hear him telling me about the final scene in the film. But he hadn't told me whether Theola Faith's character had survived.

"So when did she plant this explosive? Did she ride over in her speed boat while Pepys and Jeffries were setting up the picnic table?" Why was I fighting him? This was Monster Mommy we were talking about, not the Flying Nun.

"Sweetheart, you'll never make a murderer. You don't have the nerve. Who knows, maybe she did the job last night on the return trip to Mud Creek or came back sometime today. The woman is an actress—a mistress of disguise. If someone claims to have seen a vagrant entering the cabin cruiser, that only helps her."

I almost sat back down on the garden bench, but decided I needed all the height at my disposal. Why did I feel compelled to fight for Theola Faith? Was I so provincial in my outlook that I thought it rude to suspect someone of murder after spending an evening with her? "Ben, why would she choose to do the deed here? Nowhere else in the world would she be more visible. Theola Faith grew up in Mud Creek."

"So she's hoping for some kind of hometown loyalty."

"Perhaps," I conceded. "I haven't passed any shop windows displaying *Monster Mommy*, and the sheriff said it was banned from the bookmobile."

"Something else." Ben was walking in circles that kept getting smaller until I thought he would collide with himself. "From the sound of her, Theola Faith is the classic example of small town girl who makes the big time, then looks back on the people she left behind as yokels who eat turnips with their knives, think chateaubriand is a castle in France, and count on their fingers and toes. She will be banking on the police being unable to remember the Miranda warning."

I didn't answer. I could hear Theola Faith, just before we left the Lucky Strike, calling Sheriff Dougherty an "old Tom fool." I remembered too the feeling that he was perhaps a little sweet on her. Which, under the circumstances, wasn't to be sneezed at.

"God bless you!" Ben said.

"What?" I blinked.

A tender smile. "See how American I'm becoming. People over here say that—God bless, when someone sneezes."

"So?"

"So you sneezed."

"No, I didn't . . . I thought the word."

"Well somebody sneezed," Ben said reasonably. "And I don't think it was me. We have already agreed there is no one else here . . ."

"Marvelous!" I snapped. "If it isn't bad enough that our child will be born to parents who have been mixed up in murder, now my mind is going!"

Ben drew me to him.

"I wish I could make you understand," I said.

"I do, Ellie." He kissed my cheek. "Mary's death is a tragedy, but that the poor unhappy girl should be murdered by her own mother is unbearable." His face was flushed, turning his eyes a more jeweled green; they held me closer than his hands, enclosing us in a magic circle. Here, no matter what happened to the rest of the world—we were safe. Was I shallow, or a sex maniac because I realized I needed him? All I wanted was to go back to Mendenhall and our silver lurex bedroom. Aunt Astrid believes that lovemaking is for procreation and the warding off of pneumonia.

"Think too, sweetheart, if this is indeed murder and Theola Faith is not the one, the lid is lifted on some ghastly possibilities."

He was right. Pushing up my sleeves, I took a layer of skin with them. Curses! The mood was ruined. The warning scrawled on the bath . . . the missing knives . . . Where—if anywhere—did they fit into the picture? No pun intended concerning the knife stuck in the Cat Cadaver. Time to return to the real world. As Ben and I walked in the rain up the rocky incline to the house, the feeling came slyly as we neared the steps, and clung with the same damp persistence as my clothes . . . something had been different in the boat house. Something missing.

The elements heightened the mood macabre. Rain chattered against the windows. The wind was a third-rate opera singer practicing scales. We were gathered in the Red Room with its velvet cushioned bay, wax flowers and grand piano. Human mannequins arranged *en tableau*. Pepys and Jeffries at the tea trolley, the rest of us, cups poised on our laps, elbows crooked, chins lifted. Every so often someone would risk a smile, then snatch it back. Let none be cheerful nor talk above a whisper. To steal a phrase from Aunt Astrid, we were witnesses to life's most honoured tradition: death.

The mantel clock didn't tick; it picked away at every second, a fingernail anxious to draw blood. Above it hung the Cat Cadaver. More sinister then ever with that gaping wound in its painted fur. Someone stifled a yawn. Someone let an impatient breath escape them. Should I raise my hand if I needed to go to the bathroom? How soon before Sheriff Tom Dougherty rescued us from ourselves? From each other? From leg cramps?

"Who'll get the money from her book now she's dead?"

Bingo had broken the curse. We were free to speak, to flex our muscles, remove our seat belts, even walk about the room if we so desired.

"Bingo, honey! What a question!" Ernestine Hoffman did her darndest to sound cross; but per usual bubbled over with pride that her boy had asked the Sixty-Four Thousand Dollar question. Her scarlet trouser suit against the burgundy chair was enough to strike terror in the heart of any interior designer. Even a retired one, such as myself.

Child Prodigy stopped cramming cookies into his mouth. "What am I supposed to do, cry buckets because some old lady, over forty and looks like fifty, is dead? I hate hypocrisy." He swelled with importance. No small thanks to the cookies.

"Now, Bingo!" Ernestine's eyes said *"Doesn't he have a wonderful handle on life?"* She feathered her Friar Tuck hair. So as to look nice for the police, I suppose. "We sure do respect your honesty—"

"I don't."

"Ellie!" Ben chided.

He was right. Wives of Mangé candidates should be seen and not heard. I remembered myself at Bingo's age— that time my cousin Vanessa got lost at the zoo and how I had stuffed myself with custard creams to crowd out the fear and guilt because earlier in the day I'd said I hoped the lions would eat her. Subsiding into my chair, I apologized. Bingo smirked. I doubted I would be getting a Christmas card from Ernestine.

"We're all feeling the strain." Valicia X crossed the room to administer a consoling pat on Ben's arm. He had changed into a black velvet smoking jacket. I had discovered it at a flea market and hadn't really expected him to wear it in public. But how well it became him and this Victorian room. I had changed into dry clothes and still looked like a Before picture in a fashion make-over. Ms. X wore the same flame frock. Nary a mud splatter or a crease. She had freed her hair from its French twist so that it framed her face in waves of sun-ripened apricot.

Small wonder Pepys scuttled his bandy legs when she asked him to pour more tea. Jeffries, bless her, was made of sterner stuff. Giving the frilled brim of her cap a twitch, she stared into space. Was she concerned for Theola Faith? Or did her affection run from pay cheque to pay cheque? Did Pepys mourn the loss of the cabin cruiser more than Mary? Would my American pantyhose provide the emotional and moral support promised on the package?

Ms. X shone her golden smile on Marjorie Rumpson, who sat like a dear old doggie let inside after hours chained up in the rain.

"Bless you m'dear. I'm bloody miserable." She laid down the paperback book she had been reading—or pretending to read. The *Captive Bride* lay cheek to jowl with

Monster Mommy on the coffee table. Face ashen, Marjorie accepted the white hanky Ben whipped from his pocket with a flourish reminiscent of the comte and Solange . . . and our other missing persons. "I never did think when Mary Faith popped up in that coffin downstairs and we said our first how-do-you-do's, that she would be gone so soon, sunk to the bottom of the river."

"There, there!" I sat next to her and held her paw.

"Not usually such a baby! But after almost losing Mummy, I'm not up to another blow!" She disappeared under the white hanky.

"Honey, you've sure had it hard!" Ernestine's voice was thick with sympathy. "Now don't you go thinking I'm one to interfere, but I do worry about what the strain of competing to be a Mangé may do to you. Especially when you're up against such tremendous competition . . ." Her eyes were fixed on her boy.

"Madame"—Ben spoke with the icy hauteur conferred by black velvet and braided cuffs—"shall we agree Ms. X is the best judge of who is—or who is not—up to the business of becoming a Mangé?"

The inimitable Valicia. A woman who could simper without looking stupid. Ernestine looked stupid with shock. "Bingo honey, did you hear this male play bunny call your mother a madam?" She rose slowly to face Ben. "Do you enjoy being called a hired hand?" Her tongue curled around the words, making them sound incredibly lascivious ". . . Mr. Eligibility Escort?"

"Foul!" Marjorie Rumpson shot to her feet.

Silence fell, like a tablecloth over a birdcage. Bingo froze with a cookie half in his mouth. Pepys tilted the teapot over my cup but nothing came out. Valicia X, far from cracking the whip of authority, stood gazing at Ben, her beautiful eyes brimming with distress. He was gazing at me, his eyes brimming with accusation. I shrank in my chair as if it were the dock. How could he think I would discuss his former career with anyone in this house? Setting his feelings aside, the day I rented him from Eligibility was sacred to my memory. One wondered what was sacrosanct to Ernestine Hoffman.

To what lengths would she go in the name of Mother-hood? She strove to remain staunchly upright, but her knees buckled and her mouth twitched. I pictured a paddlewheel going around inside her head, desperately trying to churn up some—*any*—excuse. She knew she had just dimmed her chances of ever being mother to a Mangé. Should I strike while her face was hot and suggest that the ghost Bingo claimed to see on our first night here may have been his very own mother, spiriting a look at the candidates' files?

She who hesitates . . . Ernestine was babbling an excuse in which PMS figured strongly.

"Is she talking about post mortem shock?" Pepys quavered.

Silence stretched to breaking point. Then Jeffries let rip a scream, almost taking the ceiling off, and the door flung open wide. Sheriff Tom Dougherty filled the entrance, gun at the ready, eyes smoking. "Heavens to Betsy, what's going on here?"

I really must get busy with my postcards and send one off to Dorcas and Jonas saying, Having a wonderful time. Wish you were here.

Amazing how a police inquiry can bring people together! Even Pepys and Jeffries managed to look as though they had been serving our little clan for years, and loving every minute of it. Sheriff Tom asked all the anticipated questions—names, addresses, whereabouts at the time of the explosion. I expected him to probe into my encounter with Theola Faith. I wanted to know if he had spoken with her and if so how she was, but he doubled back to the Mangé Society.

"A secret cooking society!" Patting his broad tum, he smiled guilelessly. "Now that sounds mighty interesting."

"We think so," Valicia X responded curtly. She had not taken kindly to his insistence on having her last name, or the way his pouchy cheeks had filled with a smile when she handed it over on a folded piece of paper.

Jeffries, throwing servility to the winds, perched on the sofa arm. "For your info, we're an ancient and venerable institution. And woe to those who meddle with us. Last year we wrote a very strong letter to *Gluttonfest Magazine* denouncing their continued use of the glacé cherry."

Bingo sat Buddha-style on the heartrug. His derisive smirk didn't reach his eyes.

Pepys pulled out his pocket watch, shook it, held it to his ear and cackled, "Time for my break." Hobbling to the window bay he laid himself out, hands folded on his chest. His bald head shone like an Edam cheese; from where I sat I could see his lids cracked open to yellow slits.

Ah, timing! He was about to be upstaged. The air was rent with the rush of wings and a pigeon slam-dunked atop the urn on the mantelpiece, the one positioned under the portrait of the Cat Cadaver. Head cocked, beady eye intent, the bird urged the sheriff to proceed.

"Howdy doodee, big fella! Now haven't I always said Mendenhall's a charmer! Can't say as how I blame Miss Mary Faith for staking her claim." Brushing against a whatnot table Sheriff Tom caught it before it went over. "Imagine you were happy as catfish on Christmas Day when she offered this place for your meeting?"

"We were pleased." Valicia X resettled in her chair and crossed her golden legs.

"Sure couldn't find many a place more isolated."

"You're darn tootin'." Jeffries winked.

Sheriff Tom moved up closer to her. "You think Mary Faith was showing appreciation to you and Mr. Pepys for your years of faithful service to her ma?"

Jeffries' jeer sent the pigeon sailing up in the air to land on a crimson lampshade. "You put that thought right back in your pocket, mister. Ms. Mary never did nothing to suit no one but herself. She met one of our members at some cocktail party and jumped three foot in the air at the chance of filling the house with people. Wanted to look like she had friends."

I couldn't look at her. I couldn't look at Ben. I was afraid I might start crying. Poor Mary! What misfortunes having a bad mother had brought her!

The sheriff's eyes roved the room. "Word around town was as how there were more of you."

"Six of our number have departed," supplied Marjorie Rumpson.

"Not including Mary Faith." That was Bingo.

"Sheriff Dougherty," Ernestine said, clutching her beads, "I ask your kind permission to remove my boy. You see how pale he looks!"

Valicia X rose from her chair. Face flushed a dusky rose, hair frothing about her shoulders, she stood with arms folded, fingers tapping. "Bingo Hoffman—like the rest of us—is hungry. Sheriff, you do understand the explosion occurred just as we were about to dine?"

A heavy sigh. "This is a small town, ma'am. We do our thinking slow, but we get there."

No one took the Mangé boss lady down a peg in the presence of Bentley T. Haskell. His black brows became one long slash mark; however, he did remain sufficiently in command of himself to press my shoulder. "Sir, surely the person to be put under the microscope is the victim's mother."

"Now which one are you—the boy wonder or the one who makes love potions?" The sheriff's smile was cozy, but he didn't give Ben a chance to answer. "I may be a bit of a backwoodsman but, cross my heart, I know enough to talk alleged victim till we've finished dragging the river and come up with a body."

Thank God I wasn't facing the window. Gripping the arms of my chair, I said, "Sheriff Dougherty, does Theola Faith know?"

He cleared his throat. "Went round to her place and Laverne Gibbons came to the door—said Ms. Faith was in bed, not well. Won't harm to wait until there is something to tell."

"Tell!" Ernestine grabbed Bingo's plump hand and hauled him over to be rocked in her arms. "That monster doesn't need to be told! For crying out loud, she *knows* her daughter's dead! Mary Faith was living in terror. She said so on TV! And again to Ellie, here, and me yesterday. What more do you need—a signed confession?"

Pepys, still lying flat out on the window seat, croaked a "Hear! Hear!"

"How can you?" I marched over to him, strongly tempted to draw the curtains shut.

"Ain't easy!" Jeffries hopped up and down. "He ain't saying Miss Theola hasn't treated him and me decent—when she's sober. But our first loyalty is to the Mangé Society. Or would it suit you better, Ms. Goody Gum Drops, to have our dandy sheriff here suspect one of us?"

"Why not?" I heard someone cry, and that someone was me. "We all had opportunity, and there have been some very strange goings-on here."

All my gothic fantasies fulfilled. Trapped in a gloomy bedchamber, while wind and rain hurled themselves against the window panes; and the black-browed stranger hurled insults upon my head.

"My God, Ellie!" Ben threw himself back on the bed and beat his forehead with his clenched fists. "Admit to temporary insanity, and I may be able to understand."

He had been this way for hours. I kept expecting him to wind down, but he was like a hurdy-gurdy going round and round—*dum-de-dum-dum*—so that even when he paused for breath the sound went on inside my head.

"For the hundredth time"—I rocked back and forth in a chair that wasn't a rocker—"I was in full possession of my faculties when I pointed out to the sheriff that he might not be looking at an open-and-shut case."

"I'm not surprised to see you left the meal Jeffries brought up untouched," he said nastily.

My hand went to my throat. "You think the ragout may have been poisoned?"

"Good grief, no! I'm talking about *guilt*, Ellie."

"Thank you. I was beginning to lose the thread of this conversation. At the risk of one of us repeating ourselves, I will state, for the record, I am not sorry for suggesting that anyone of the Mangé contingent could have blown up the boat. The sheriff isn't a fool! And the only person I pointed the finger at directly was myself. Remember! I stressed that I had been behaving strangely! Rowing over to Mud Creek! Having my hair done in a wild new style! Did I not own up to the grotesque cravings which led me to gate crash the bowling banquet?"

Ben rammed a pillow between him and the headboard. "I suppose I should be grateful, Ellie!"

"Think nothing of it. Lucky you're not handy. How could I convince anyone that you'd blow up a boat, when I know you need an electrician to replace light bulbs?"

"All your charming forthrightness accomplished was to force everyone else to come out with some reason why they too might be guilty. Rather than look like a member of the Theola Faith lynching party."

I stopped rocking and ground my chair round to face him. Tears stung my eyes. "Ben, I was *proud* of Miss Rumpson when she volunteered the information that she had always lived by water and knows boats. Such a love! She certainly went beyond the call of duty in reminding me that she had mentioned her conviction that putting a person to sleep can be a noble and loving act."

"The sheriff must have thought us all a bunch of loonies. Especially when Bingo suggested, straight-faced, that Mary may have discovered that he is really a short man of forty-five. Providing a motive for him or his mother. And then we had Valicia X hinting that she, Pepys and Jeffries, might—singly or together—have done away with Mary Faith because she knew about the medicine cabinet mirror and could have used it to spy on the Mangé Meetings."

He had forgotten I was pregnant. He had forgotten I was his wife, his friend. I started to stand but thought better of the idea. "I know you feel I shouldn't have mentioned the missing knives, because that led to Ernestine mentioning that the comte used minor explosions as part of his act, which led to the sheriff asking if we thought any of the departed candidates might have blown up the boat as an act of vengeance against the Mangés. But Ben, that's what we are looking for—a motive that has nothing to do with Theola."

"Ellie, you raised suspicions that are outrageous."

"You seemed concerned about the missing Browns and the missing knives this morning."

He picked up a pillow and tossed it down. "Naturally I worry about any irregularities in any situation involving you, my pregnant wife. I overreacted. But remember Henderson Brown was unhappy here. Is it so unlikely his dutiful wife would agree to go home?"

"Without a word of good-bye?"

"She'd be embarrassed. As for the knives, someone simply played a joke and is afraid to own up. Especially after *your* hatchet job."

The man had gone too far. I would never darken his bed again. I would never speak to him again . . . after I'd had my say. Crossing to the bed, I grabbed the pillow and dragged off the bedspread before backing toward the window. "Don't come near me! You've made your choice! The Mangé Society comes before all else, your wife, your child— before honour itself!"

"What!" he shouted. "You think my attitude is one of anything goes so long as I don't blow my chances of becoming a Mangé! Well, you're wrong!" Thump on the bedpost. "I object to my wife sticking her nose into the bloody middle of a murder investigation!"

"You landed me full square in the middle of one! I never

wanted to come to America. Remember!" I smacked into a chair and kicked it sideways. "What chance does Theola Faith have if everyone wants to add an epilogue to *Monster Mommy* in order that it may end with a bang? I wish I could make you understand, but how can I when possibly I wouldn't feel this way if I weren't carrying our child."

The rain had changed, grown softer . . . "Ellie!" His hand touched my arm, but I couldn't see him for my tears.

"I have to fight for her. Theola Faith may be a drunk, she may have done all sorts of monstrous things, but she didn't do this. Last night, just before she left she said, 'Tell me, how is Mary?' And I heard something that sounded like love in her voice."

He didn't answer because we heard a scream. And this one sounded different from Jeffries' primal kind. At such a time, what did it matter that our marriage was breaking to bits like Mary's boat? I spurned Ben's suggestion that I cower in the room while he sashayed forth to investigate. The days when I thought pregnancy entitled me a nine-month free membership to a leisure club were long gone.

We came out into the hall to see Ernestine rushing in our direction, one hand gripping the skirt of her maize-coloured jersey gown, the other clutching a long, ugly knife which looked chillingly like one of those missing from the wall downstairs.

"Bingo, Mommy's coming! Oh, God! You sure know how to drive a mother crazy with worry!" Her face was grey with fright. She slammed open the bathroom door, swept along by her maternal dread. Ben and I were about to follow her . . . when we saw Valicia X, Pepys and Jeffries crowding into one of the rooms across from the bathroom.

It was Marjorie Rumpson's room. Over Jeffries' shoulder, I could see the open window, the drenched curtains blowing inward, a damp spot on the floor where the rain had driven in. Lightning cracked overhead; thunder drowned my cry of horror.

"Marjorie!" I cried again. So great was my terror that in taking up Theola Faith's cause I had driven this loveable woman to the edge of the window sill, that I elbowed Valicia X aside without a thought for Ben's feelings. Perhaps Marjorie had truly believed herself suspected and was afraid of the effect of her arrest on her ancient mother? Never, I vowed, would I cause my child a moment's unease. As I raced ahead of Ben, I could see Marjorie lying on the ground, a stray leaf blowing across her face. Would she have suffered, would there be a lot of blood? Would I ever forgive myself?

I almost fainted when Pepys stepped aside and I saw her—ashen faced and all of a tremble in her blue-and-white striped pajamas. But alive! Valicia X, a vision in nylon and lace, and Jeffries, her head knobby with curlers, was holding onto her, as Marjorie pointed a trembling finger and croaked, "Someone's under my bed!"

16

Outside, the wind was still hamming it up, shrieking louder than a soul in torment, while the rain chattered like teeth. Inside, it was as though someone were moving a torch about, but one which shed beams of darkness rather than light. Shivering under my eiderdown, my leg touched something that felt like . . . a man's leg and . . . strangely, my heart slowed. In that half world between waking and sleeping I knew that Mr. Nightmare, determined not to let me slip from his clutches, had come dogging after me, swirling his black cloak about him. But I knew he couldn't stay long. Daylight would come and burn him to dust and anyway it didn't matter. I was safe because my mother had come in. The loveliest, warmest feeling swept over me. But the next moment I was angry. Why wouldn't she move away from the door? Why keep standing there so dark and still? Why couldn't I see her face?

"I do hope I'm not keeping you from something important." My voice sounded fed up and used up and dreadfully old— at least thirty. *"Be my guest, Mum! Do some leg lifts while you're here! I don't want you to get flabby and out of shape*

because of me. I love it when people say, 'Isn't your mother skinny? How did you get to be such a chub?' But never mind my petty grumbles, I have to tell you about my awful dream. I was grown up and married to this horribly handsome man, the sort forever raising a dark sardonic eyebrow. We were staying with the queerest group of people at a place called Mendenhall. Then came a murder, which wasn't nearly as much fun as it might have been because some people wanted me to mind my own business. At dead of night, there came this blood-curdling scream. Out on the landing was a woman with a knife—grabbed up for protection. So she said! We all raced into this lady's room. She was large and shaggy. Exactly what I always wanted in a grandma. And she was absolutely terrified, because she thought there was a man under her bed; and almost as frightened that perhaps there wasn't—after she had raised the alarm. Then, who should crawl out from under, but a fat child genius named Bongo . . . No, Bingo! With some gussied-up story about having gone downstairs and almost walked into—or through—a ghost whom he claimed to have seen once before. Seeing Miss Rumpson's door open, he claimed to have dodged inside for safety. But, Mother, there was something shifty about the way he looked everyone straight in the eye. Oh, I don't mean he was lying about seeing the ghost! The fatty was as white as . . . one. But he was holding something back. I don't believe he had left his room to get a drink—any more than his mother believed Miss Rumpson had left hers to go to the bathroom. Mother!" I tried to keep the frown out of my voice, "The courtesy of a reply would be appreciated. What must I do to pique your interest? Tell me what you think of the inflatable boat being missing, that's what I noticed—without realizing—was different about the boat house. And what of Pepys' and Jeffries' contradictory behaviour? I thought Pepys was starry-eyed about Theola Faith and Jeffries displayed signs of a surly affection last night, but they threw her to the Sheriff . . ."

She didn't answer . . . because she wasn't there. The person I had been addressing was a black silk dressing gown hanging on the door. Morning had broken into the room and driven the shadows under the wardrobe and up the chimney, where they would hide until night came again. I knew who I was and where I was and that this was the first day of the rest of my marriage!

"Good morning, Ellie." Ben sat up.

"Good morning, Mr. Haskell." If I were to be addressed as the chambermaid who had warmed the master's bed in person, rather than with the customary hot brick, I would respond in kind.

"Sweetheart," he stumbled out of bed, shaking his head. "What's that old saying—never let the sun rise on your wrath?"

"Some such twaddle."

He was yanking at his pajama top, forgetting this one didn't fasten with snaps. Buttons flew, one nearly getting me in the eye.

"Nice try," I said.

"Ellie!" Thumping his bare chest. Probably expecting me to crawl the length of the bed, grab his hand and smother it with remorseful kisses. "I still believe you were wrong last night, but I am prepared to believe that you acted more out of a misguided sense of . . . chivalry, than . . ."

"Downright viciousness?"

"I was going to say folly."

"Thank you kindly." With what pleasure I watched, as he threw back the lid of the white suitcase and began tossing through everything. Wifely intuition told me he was looking for his silver-grey shirt. But why should I tell him it was in the blue case? "Ben," I said, "I did a lot of thinking while I was asleep, the result being I am exhausted; so with your kind permission I will stay in bed this morning."

Had I pushed a panic button! His eyes turned neon green and the creases in his face rivaled the ones in the shirt he was clutching. "What's the matter?" He grabbed my hand and for a moment I thought he was going to dot it with kisses, but—curses, he was taking my pulse. "You said that wasn't morning sickness yesterday. Is it something new? Are you in pain?"

"The baby is fine," I informed the wall. "But I relish a lie in with a good book." My eyes avoided the copy of *Monster Mommy* on the bedside table.

"Ellie"—he stood over me like Dr. Haskell making rounds—"you can't hole up here forever."

"One morning—well, make that two—does not a lifetime make. I have not forgotten tonight's grand finale. Ms. X mentioned a formal dinner; I imagine that afterward— while we all sit around sipping our brandy and smoking our cigars—an announcement will be made as to who is to be the Chosen One."

"My dear, I am not at liberty to discuss . . ."

"Perish the thought!" I sank back against the pillows, all the life gone out of me. Neither of us would ever know for sure if I were to blame, should his name not be proclaimed to a fanfare of trumpets. Upon entering this house, I had been aware I must comport myself as a consort fit for a Mangé. And I had done nothing but blunder and bloop.

Last night had been easier on the ego. Last night, I had known right from wrong. *I* had been right. *Ben* had been wrong. Now all I knew was that I didn't want anyone bringing me breakfast in bed.

"You run along to your meeting!" I turned my cheek so that his kiss slid off my face. "Don't worry about me. I'll putter downstairs when the coast is cl—" Memory of the Coast Guard bubbled to the surface of my mind. Was that gruesome business of dragging the river finished? How soon before the sheriff brought us word of Mary's awful fate? Would we be permitted to leave here tonight or tomorrow morning? Mary Faith . . . everything came back to her.

One last, lingering glance and Ben was gone. I was alone in a room in which I did not feel alone. I didn't like the way the furniture was looking at me. What I wouldn't give for the warm comfort of Tobias! Even a pigeon would do. Too restless to sleep, too depressed to get up, I fluffed my pillow—with the result that the handful of feathers sank into one corner. And there went my hand—reaching out for *Monster Mommy*. Was I punishing myself or trying to get Mary to talk to me—one more time? Turning to the last page, I read:

> *And so, Mommy, I leave you standing in the dark shadow of the Mountain of Misdeeds, while I walk towards the Valley of the Sun. Believe that I don't hate you. No longer do I wake in the middle of the night to that*

ache of emptyness because you never once baked chocolate chip cookies. The woman I have become made friends with anger and its sidekick, pity. While you remain entrenched in the quagmire of excuses, we cannot meet again, but should the day come when you dig deep within your soul and find there the words Baby, forgive me!, *my door and my arms will be flung wide to receive you.*

Crumbs! All the pitfalls of motherhood. But I will bake my fingers to a crisp. I will serve fresh squeezed milk at every meal, I will never let my child see me without makeup, with my hair a mess, with my toenails unvarnished. I will never enter the nursery without knocking. . . . And will die of exhaustion if I try to keep this pace.

Tossing *Monster Mommy* down, I reached for *Parenting for Pleasure.* Chapter Seven, if I remembered rightly, focused on perils of Trying to be Mighty Mum. As I must stop fixating on Mary. My being churned up was not good for the baby. Poor sweet must think it was living in a whirlpool. Oh, crumbs! There I went again. Hoping to distract myself from the fearsome image of a Child Raised Wrong, I began singing a lullaby. I have a terrrible voice, but so did my mother—and I always loved that one about the daddy longlegs who got drunk on dandelion wine. If only I could remember the words . . . but Mother had made them up as she went along; she dancing the part of the hero, while my father penguined back and forth as the outraged waiter, wielding an invisible ladle . . .

Some folded sheets of paper fell from *Parenting for Pleasure.* What had we here? Ah, yes! Primrose Tramwell's letter. The one I had received on the day Ben heard from the Mangés, the same day she and Hyacinth made their surprise visit to break the news about the Black Cloud. Now I could hardly remember what the mystic Chantal had said . . . some vague spiel about finding the answer within myself. Did I owe my present feeling of powerlessness to some superstitious nonsense that last night's tragedy was predestined? *A house surrounded by water*—how well that described both Merlin's Court and Mendenhall along with hundreds of others! As for the words *fire and brimstone* and *swathed in shadow,* I thought of the clothes in Nelga's Fashions. One size fits all. Dear Primrose and Hyacinth! Having already resorted to the smelling salts bottle on account of my pregnancy, they had panicked when Chantal had trotted out her vision and I, craving to be pampered, had clutched terror to my bosom and cried *woe is me!* But no more. The Black Cloud didn't blow up the cabin cruiser and I was neither helpless nor hopeless, although not so brave, I must admit, that I wouldn't have welcomed a swig of the herbal remedy Primrose enclosed: balm, horehound, pennyroyal, and cicely steeped in good ale in the midday sun.

Tossing off the bedclothes, I set my feet firmly on the floor—and my chosen path. Something was horribly amiss in this house, and I knew what it was. Believe me, I didn't relish the idea of being a snoop or a squealer, but I must at least try to find the missing knives. Even if they had been taken for a joke—provoked by shades of *Melancholy Mansion*—the matter should be cleared up. As for the ghastly possibility that our departed members might be more reverently named . . . the late lamented—I would think only . . . of the truth setting us all free. Save, that is, for the murderer of Mary Faith.

Hurrying my dressing gown over my head, I glimpsed myself in the dressing table mirror. Why does worry always settle around my middle? Was this my punishment for not eating dinner last night? Another five pounds. Heaven help me, in my green velvet with the lace collar I resembled a Victorian matron wearing a bustle the wrong way round. When I got home—should that glad day ever come—I would inform Dr. Melrose I was seeking a second opinion as to my due date.

"Courage!" Alas, the face in the mirror wouldn't look me in the eye.

Repairing to the bathroom, pink sponge bag in hand, I met no one *en route.* Once there, however, I wasn't tempted to linger. The warm sudsy water could not wash away the memory of those words scrawled on the tile: THIS HOUSE IS

GOING TO GET YOU. And afterwards, brushing out my hair and plaiting it into a twist, I had no desire to snoop in the medicine chest. Too small to be the knives' hideaway, anyhow.

Time, Ellie! Dressed in one of my new maternity outfits—grey slacks and a smock appliquéd with the word BABY and a downward pointing arrow (making me afraid to bend over)—I hesitated on the threshold of my room. Should I go back and remake the bed? No, I would get on with the job at hand. Creeping over to the banisters, I peered down into the sunlit well. All quiet on the hall front. No suspicious shadows. Death had changed nothing. The final Mangé Meeting would be in session, but I couldn't be certain that Pepys and Jeffries would be in attendance. As for Ernestine, I hoped she was making a morning of breakfast, but I would certainly knock before entering her room.

Searching the whole house being out of the question, I had to hope that whoever had taken the knives had hidden them in his or her bedroom. Were I the culprit, I would immediately think of the loose floorboard in my room. No, that was at Merlin's Court, not here. But wait a minute . . . surely I had crossed a room in this house and heard that same tell-tale creak?

Midway down the hallway I stopped in my tracks as if yanked tight on a rein. But not because of a piece of memory shaken loose. What caused the slam-banging of my heart was Marjorie Rumpson's door—open, just a crack. I was certain it had been closed earlier when I returned to my bedroom to dress.

Surely only the direst need would have taken Marjorie from the meeting! I was amazed she had been allowed to leave, unless . . . I tiptoed forward . . . she had been found to be ineligible to— A gasp escaped me. My blasted elbow had caught the door, causing it to slide inward, almost knocking Ernestine Hoffman off her feet. She had the drawer of the bedside table open and was holding a gleaming bouquet of swashbuckler knives.

"Well, what do you know!" Far from attempting to commit *hara-kiri*, the prodigy's mother seethed with righteous indignation. "That nice old gal! Who would have thought it!"

"Are you saying that Miss Rumpson is the knave . . . *knive* person?" Backing away from the glittering blades, I closed the door. "And that you only came here to snoop?"

"You surely don't think I'm trying to shift the evidence to her drawer!" Impossible. Ernestine's pudding-basin hair and pajama-striped frock all testified to her respectability. On the dressing table lay Marjorie's black hat with the big bow, which she had worn on first arriving at Mendenhall after dauntlessly navigating the river in her undies. On the bedside table in question, lay a paperback copy of *The Captured Bride* and a loose-leaf notebook, hand titled, *My Five Hundred Favourite Love Potions*. Mary wasn't the only author in the house.

"I don't know what to believe." Ernestine had been carrying a knife last night, but she might have found it in the Red Room perhaps if it were the one used against the Cat Cadaver . . . which may or may not have been the same used to stab the Comte Vincent's prized recipe to his pillow. Wearily, I leaned against the door. That was rust on the smallest of the three blades, wasn't it? No maniac in his right mind would put away used weapons without first giving a quick wipe with tissue or shirt tail. Would he— she? My mind was screaming at me to stop. Don't think about the missing Groggs, the absent Browns or the de-camped comte and comtesse. Just put one word in front of another. I intended to ask Ernestine if she'd had reason to be suspicious of Marjorie in particular or if she'd been in the process of searching other rooms, but came out with something quite different.

"You've done this sort of thing before, haven't you?"

"What are you saying?"

"Oh, I don't mean the knives," I reassured her. "I'm sure if you'd done anything other than find them, you'd have had the sense to use gloves or wrap them in something."

"Fingerprints!" Her voice hit a high note and the knives clattered to the bed. "I never thought, I . . ."

"Why would you? It's not as though you came here hoping to prove—or *disprove*—that Marjorie Rumpson is a

criminal. All you wanted was to find something—*anything*—
that would knock her out of the running as a Mangé."

"You've sure got your nerve!" Ernestine was back in
gear. "And I thought I was doing you a favour checking out
your crazy accusations that there's been more going on here
than Mary Faith being blown to smithereens! For your information, young lady, I have had my suspicions of Miss
Rumpson since last night when she tried to make me believe *she* had solved the Browns' disappearance. Said she
had been reading that book"—she pointed to *The Captured
Bride*—"and that she'd seen Henderson Brown with it. Some
goofy tale about a man who kidnapped his own wife—"

"Yes!" I had trouble keeping my feet on the ground. I
was buoyant with elation. "I'm sure that's it! Henderson
playing the cryptic! *He* wrote the title on the mirror. The
smudged B word was *Bride*! I suspect he tossed Lois over
his shoulder and raced away with her into the night, probably
in the *Nell Gwynn*."

"What—?"

"And Lois would consider the Mangé world well lost
for love. She was pining for romance from her meat-and-
potatoes lover."

"Make up your fairy stories." Ernestine's plump face
looked so like her son's. "My Frank always tells me I
have an overdeveloped sense of responsibility because I
went into puberty early."

"Oh, quite!" I heard myself say. "Your zealousness as
Bingo's Mum took you snooping the other day into my
bedroom. Solange saw you coming out. Some things were
moved . . . a paperback book. And a bag had been zipped
up. A bag that contained a letter from my mother-in-law."

"So?" She dropped down on the bed and popped right
back up—pricked either by conscience or one of the knives.

"That's how you knew that Ben had worked for Eligibility Escorts. From reading his mother's letter. Somehow I
didn't think that Bingo would have blabbed even had that
information come out at a meeting."

"No, he never would!" Ernestine's face had turned the
porridgy grey of the wallpaper. "And you'd better not

mention your ugly suspicions to my little boy. You can't prove them."

"You're right. I'm only guessing that you started checking up on the competition your very first night here—and that you only pretended to get locked in the bathroom when you and Solange went in search of the Screamer. No one else has complained of that door sticking. It hasn't for me."

"None of this," Ernestine wet her lips, "alters the fact that Marjorie Rumpson hid these knives in that drawer."

I shook my head. "I don't think she did. I think your Bingo put them there."

The words just spilled out. Afterwards, I thought about Chantal and psychic jargon such as transference and channeling. Only fleetingly, mind. Anything of that sort was stuff and nonsense. My subconscious might be kicking in, but not the supernatural.

"I expect he hid them first in his bedroom—who knows?—perhaps under a loose floorboard. And when things hotted up last night, he decided to find somewhere safer." No need to mention that he had tried to move his horde of food goodies to safer—higher—ground in the bird's nest. "In his place I'd probably have tried to return them to the dining room—stick them in a drawer or tuck them behind the curtains—some place where the incident would be waved aside as trivial. My guess is Bingo *did* head downstairs last night and that he saw someone. A ghost perhaps."

"Another prankster?" Furious smile.

"I don't know," I conceded. "Maybe he took fright at a shadow. Or did he make her up? On our first night here, when Jeffries roused the house with her primal scream, I came upon Bingo in the hallway and he was carrying a towel."

"He's a very clean child!"

"He's a very *bright* child. By telling me he had just seen the ghost of The Lady in the Portrait, he kept me from wondering why he was having a bath at midnight."

"Make up your mind! Did Bingo have something up his sleeve or inside the towel?" Ernestine was pumping herself up with sarcasm. I could feel myself deflating. I hated this. I didn't think her an evil woman. She just had an overactive need to succeed through her boy. Sort of like an overactive thyroid.

"My guess is he'd stuck the comte's recipe to the pillow and wanted to listen in to the fun or even pull another stunt." Anxious to get done, I said, "Returning to last night, Bingo backed off from going downstairs because the coast wasn't clear— He saw or heard someone. Would a glimpse of—say Pepys or Jeffries—have deterred him had his errand been something as innocuous as stealing a cookie? As things were, he must have thought luck was giving him a second chance when he spied Marjorie Rumpson's open door. What could have been simpler than to slip inside, open the bedside table drawer? Then the horror of seeing the bathroom door directly opposite open. No time to do more than crawl under the bed. No wonder he had a coughing fit."

"Hard to believe"—Ernestine gripped the bedpost so hard her knuckles were white—"that I liked you. We had fun that first evening, us and the Frenchwoman, almost like a slumber party. You know, I almost forgot that I was here for Bingo. Didn't I help with smuggling in Miss Rumpson? I thought, why can't life be like this more often—me giving myself a good time. But by morning, I'd my head back on. I could sure see Bingo wouldn't be getting a fair shot. There was Ms. X lapping up your husband with her eyes, the comte up to his tricks, and Mrs. Brown and Miss Rumpson ready to cry sex discrimination! How about this to make your day: I actually thought God was punishing me for searching your room and the others when Bingo went missing!"

"But this morning you remembered you hadn't got around to checking out Miss Rumpson?"

"Okay! I thought—*finally* I find something I can use." Ernestine sank onto the bed, gripping the post as if she were riding a merry-go-round horse. She looked dizzy. She believed my accusations of Bingo. Maternal instinct. Not feeling so great myself, I sat down next to her. After a minute she continued, "I never thought Miss Rumpson had used the knives for anything wicked. I don't know what I thought—just that she was a bit off-the-beam, I suppose."

"Ernestine, Bingo isn't a homicidal maniac. He reminds me of myself at that age. I was the token fat kid in the class. I would have raided the fridge at dead of night if staying at the Vatican. And I can imagine pulling such stunts as writing scary messages on bathroom walls and pinching the knives to strike terror in the hearts of all, and having everything go hopelessly awry when murder intrudes."

She ground out a laugh. "Thanks for not suspecting my boy of dismembering our missing members and burying them in the cellar."

"But you believe . . . the rest?"

"That's a mother for you." Cheeks pinking with pride. "Easiest thing in the world to believe the very best of our kids, and the very worst. What I have to do now is figure out why the little monster took them."

She remained on the bed when I got up. Was she hoping Marjorie Rumpson would come up and she'd be forced to confess? Turning back from the door, I held out my hand. "Let me have those things. Don't worry. With the meeting in progress, returning them to the dining room should be a snap."

"No, really! I couldn't let you!" A martyr positioning herself on the stake, Ernestine moved to plump down on the knives, but I was too quick for her. Little did she know that under my righteous exterior lurked a fellow snooper. My parents had raised a meddler. Uncle Merlin had said so on that first visit, when I had told him he should attend church, get married, and leave me some money in his will.

I knew I had no business returning those knives. Would God have invented policemen if he wanted people like me interfering? Creeping down the stairs, hand clutching my smock, I hoped that should anyone see me they would fail to realize I wasn't far enough along for the baby to be jabbing out an elbow. Was there a plea of prenatal insanity in this land of lawsuits? I could see all this was becoming a sickness with me. I couldn't go on believing *everyone* innocent. Although, surely, Bingo had been punished enough for behaving like a child for once. Those moments under Marjorie Rumpson's bed could not have been fun. As for Marjorie, I couldn't expect Sheriff Dougherty to accept, without question, that she had been framed. Unlike me, he had not the benefit of several days' acquaintance with her.

Light, breaking through the stained glass door panel, made a mosaic on the ceiling; otherwise the mahogany hall was as dark and stuffy as a sealed up church. The closed doors had the look of confessionals. Had Theola Faith confessed yet? The sour puss face of the blackened grandmother clock said ten thirty. How long before the sheriff brought news? Or was he here already? Hands shaking, I plunged into the dining room. Back out again ten seconds later and pounds thinner, having delivered the knives to the closest drawer. I'd buffed them off and done the final handling with the front of my smock, but after taking only a couple of steps I came to a dithering halt. What about my fingerprints on the sideboard? Could I explain them away by saying I must have touched the drawer when helping myself to breakfast? There had been some very handsome croissants and rhubarb buns between the coffee pot and fruit bowl.

"God, according to the Book of Enoch, is gonna punish you, Miss Interference." The voice popped up behind me.

"Pepys!" Was that silly squeak *me*? Or a canary being trodden on by a cat? I backed toward the staircase wall. "You really shouldn't speak of God that way as though he's some sort of bogey man. And you shouldn't scare me like that. You might give me triplets!"

"Good!" His bald head shone smooth as marble. His eyes were chipped ice as he let loose a laugh, convincing me a neon sign flashed the word *knives* from my forehead. Naturally I didn't expect to be in high favour after last night. And I couldn't blame Pepys for favouring his own skin over that of his employer. My mental babbling was cut short by the bell. The door bell.

"Tarnation! Here comes the sheriff dropping by uninvited. Man should read Ann Landers on that subject!" Pepys' eyes let me go. Off he shuffled down the centre of the hall, leaving me feeling small and feathery and chewed. I couldn't tell if that was the sheriff's head behind the glass, although the set of the shoulders looked decidedly official. Could I make it up the stairs before he entered? No, I couldn't. But neither could I face the law until I had taken something to settle my conscience. Should I make a dive back into the dining room or—my heart was trying to break through my ribs—take the lift?

Pepys is about to admit the caller; he turns and looks my way as I open the outer wooden door and shove back the accordian-pleated brass one. I feel cornered again, which is stupid. My finger is on the button; I am lurching upward. The concrete walls, seen through the fenced sides of the lift cage, don't exactly flash past. There being no ceiling, I do feel rather as though I'm a skier in a chair lift. But how long can it take to go up one floor? That depends I suppose on whether or not . . . you come to a full stop. I heard a faint wheezing sound as though the contraption were out of breath. And then nothing. Sorry, I'm exaggerating—something *did* happen. The overhead light went out.

This is not a good time for panic. Panic is only fun when you get to share it with someone. If Ben were only here, we could turn this into a romantic interlude—pretend we were a couple of Victorian chimney sweeps. Scratch that! He would be dead by now from claustrophobia. This was much better, I could think of myself, feel free to fall luxuriously apart. But should I? Pause, Ellie. You can re-deem yourself in the eyes of all who resented your theory: Theola Faith did not kill her daughter, ergo someone else is guilty. Here is your chance to prove yourself fit to be a Mangé wife. Come through this crisis with flying colours and you may one day rise to some influential position in the Auxiliary. Groping left, I found the buttons and punched away. Does a passenger on a high-jacked plane care whether he is going to London or Istanbul?

The lift budged neither up nor down. Sweat broke like morning dew on my forehead. I no longer cared to be the sort of wife who held up well under tough conditions—like the pantyhose in the advert that could have danced all night. I began jumping up and down in what probably looked like a crazy dance; luckily I couldn't see myself. Halfway into a leap there came a dreadful thought. What if the lift had stalled because a cable had snagged on a roller, and what if all this vibrating caused the cable to slip, sending the cage smacking down through the shaft, straight through the cellar floor to the rocks on which Mendenhall was built? I knew nothing about the mechanics of lifts, but nothing is more convincing than an imagination fueled by terror. Moments dragged by before I dredged up a more comforting possibility. There might be nothing wrong with the lift at all. What if Pepys had left Sheriff Dougherty on the step and nipped after me? What if he had done something—opened the outer door for instance—to stop the lift in its tracks? How long would the crazy man keep me imprisoned here? How long before he thought I had learned my lesson?

A shadow moved—my arm, as it turned out. Would screaming be in my own best interests? I yelled until my ears rang. No answer. Paranoia set in. A conspiracy was afoot below. Sheriff Dougherty had persuaded the household, including Ben, that I was a threat to the happy solving of the Mary Faith case. Best that I was to be put out of everyone's misery for a while.

The Black Cloud had descended. I found myself huddled on the floor of my cage. Time was a circle always bringing me back to right now. Never had I felt more alone.

And then something magical happened. I remembered the baby was with me, and that if I didn't mind being stuck here, my friend might have other ideas. Hard on the heels of that insight came something else, a wild craving—similar to that which had caused me to pirate a rowing boat and head over to Mud Creek. This time I didn't want tacos— indeed, the very idea of spicy hot food revolted me. No, I wanted—*needed*—plain ordinary toast with an inch of butter accompanied by a steaming, soothing cup of that herbal brew described in Primrose Tramwell's letter. Balm, horehound, pennyroyal . . . I could almost taste them, although I never had. Sound good, baby? And to think there's an herb garden outside and we're in here! 'Tis enough to make you start climbing the walls!

The silence spoke loud and clear. "Finally, Mum, you are making sense."

I was on my feet in a trice. "Yes, my dear! I imagine your average athletic mother could climb that checkerboard iron siding. But this is me. I never met a gym teacher I didn't hate, or one that could get me to climb an inch of the rope without using an electric cattle prod. And think, even if we do this brave thing I don't know how far we are below the second floor. Or if I could manage to get out."

Stuff and nonsense. The Craving was in control. I was already hanging on to that railing like a monkey in a black-out at the zoo. I would have toast or die in the attempt. Common sense told me this part wasn't dangerous. No more difficult than climbing a ladder—with very narrow rungs. I went up a slow hand hold at a time. The dark became a blessing; I couldn't look down. If I was the least bit dizzy it was with excitement at the hope of getting us out of here, until—suddenly I had gone as far as I could go. Either the grating swayed or I did . . . a feeling similar to being on the deck of a ship and leaning too far over the rail. My hand made a desperate grab upward and grasped a door lever. Freedom.

Not yet. The door wouldn't open. Curses! Outwitted by a safety feature. I tried to be happy for all those people who had been saved from plunging down the shaft when they thought they had dodged into the bathroom; but it was a bleak moment. At least when people conquer mountains they get to stick a flag on top. Drearily I took my first step back down and a light went on inside the lift. And there it was, that glorious rusty hum! "Baby, we're moving!"

Wrong. It was the floor that travelled. The wrong way. Down it went, leaving me a prisoner perched on the wrong side of freedom's fence. Ellie, if you ever want to see Ben again, so you can kill him for bringing you to the good old U.S.A.—Don't look! Don't think! And whatever you do, don't scream! The least tremor and you'll go hanggliding for the first time. But it was no good, my lids were fixed, my eyes frozen in horror. My arms were giving way. The urge to jump, to make this quick, was tugging at me . . . The floor had stopped well below the bottom of my grill, but what was this . . . ? Oh, miracle! It had remembered me, it was coming back to the rescue. Ready, set—just step down as though you are getting onto an escalator. That's it and now—the great moment. Only when the door opened did I wonder who would be waiting for me on the other side.

17

"Sweetheart." Ben's voice enclosed me, holding me safe. "How do you feel?"

"Wonderful." I felt not only free of the lift, but of so much that had gone before. When the doors had opened and he lifted me out, every member of the household had crowded around. And the most worried of all was Pepys.

"My fault, I done it."

Too shaken to feel animosity, I thought the skeletal Mangé was confessing to having deliberately, and with malice aforethought, set the trap, but no—he was explaining that he had failed to fuel the generator.

"You've had a lot on your mind." Forgetting he was Pepys and not Jonas, I patted his head, before sagging back against Ben.

"Too blooming horrible for words! She could have lost the baby!" That was Marjorie Rumpson.

"She'll be all right, won't she, Mum?" Bingo stood close to his mother, clutching a bag of potato crisps.

"Sure, hon!" She didn't look convinced.

"She should be off her feet." That was Jeffries.

"Should I boil water—for tea, I mean?" Was that Valicia X speaking? Looking more beautiful than ever because she was misty-eyed.

"How was I to know she was having a baby?" Pepys definitely looked in worse shape than I. "Thought she was buxom. She did say something about me scaring her into having triplets, but thought was an expression. Same as having kittens."

Suddenly I was floating on air. My husband had swept me up in his manly arms. When we entered the bedroom, Jeffries was already smoothing back the bedclothes; Pepys skedaddled past to close the curtains while the rest milled around doing nothing, but looking as though they couldn't do enough. As Ben eased me back against the pillows, fear did return like a familiar friend. Was Pepys lying about the generator? Or, I remembered Ernestine was upstairs when I got into the lift. Perhaps she heard it coming and managed somehow to jamb it.

"A baby!" Bingo approached the bed as if it were a board room table. "A member of the most unproductive segment of society and yet . . . kinda neat."

"Nicer even than a puppy." Marjorie Rumpson put a stout arm around him.

"I'm jealous!" Valicia's bountiful smile divided itself between Ben, seated on the side of the bed, and me. "Waiting for new life to begin. I can't think of anything more incredible."

"Yes!" The word went up as a collective sigh. And I got the strangest feeling that right here and now this was everyone's baby. Searching the circle of faces I felt cocooned in warmth, and certainty surged through me. What had happened in the lift was an accident. I was no longer on the Most Hated list. How sad that Mary Faith's death had brought us together like this—almost as a family. There *couldn't* be a murderer in this room . . .

"Darling . . . " I asked Ben when we were alone. "Did the sheriff come with news? I sensed that the others were holding something back."

He straightened the tray on my lap and tweaked the

rose in its jam jar vase. "Ellie, I want you to finish that last piece of toast and drink your herbal brew."

"Yes dear!" How could I refuse? Valicia X, Pepys, and Jeffries had all offered to fetch me whatever I wanted, but Ben had fought for a man's inalienable right to cook for his wife when she was having the vapours. In the manner of a priest regretfully renouncing celibacy for a higher calling, he had informed Ms. X that he wished to be released from his sacred commitment not to engage in any and all cookery practices prior to his assigned role in the Inaugural Dinner. Even more amazing, Bingo had seconded the motion, with the result that here I was fifteen minutes later, the cravings that had attacked me in the lift assuaged. A pity the same could not be said of my curiosity.

"About the sheriff . . . ?" I gazed hopefully into my love's brooding eyes.

"Yes, I blame him for your not being found sooner. I don't suppose he gave Pepys a spare moment to think about the generator, but doesn't do to dwell." Turning my cup around so I wouldn't have to expend energy reaching for the handle, Ben settled himself more comfortably on the edge of the bed and drew a paper from his pocket—Primose Tramwell's letter, as it turned out. "Sweetheart, I have to be honest with you; I made some substitutions with this recipe. The herb garden was out of several ingredients and I used apple cider instead of ale because there was some in the refrigerator. Although there are two schools of thought on the matter, I believe it preferable for a woman in your condition. As for sun brewing, you understand there wasn't time; however, I am convinced that by warming the sides of the coddle cup with a match—"

"Ben!" I gripped the tray. "Has the sheriff arrested Theola Faith?"

His face was grim.

"Yes."

"Well . . . that's that then."

"Sweetheart . . ."

"I'm relieved really."

Removing the tray to the bedside table he stroked my

hair. "You don't have to pretend. This morning during the meeting my mind wasn't on the subject at hand: whether or not scrambled kidneys should be served with a slotted spoon. I was thinking about how I had let this business come between us, and I remembered Chapter Seven of *Mommy, There's a Strange Man in the House.*"

"Oh, yes, exercises an expectant father can do to build up his parenting muscles. You're supposed to imagine that you're the one carrying the baby."

"That's it! Ellie, suddenly I was *you* for a split second; I knew why you wanted the bad guy to be anyone other than Theola Faith."

"Thank you." The words came out in a sigh in which sadness and joy were all mixed up together. Pressing tight against him, I breathed in the wonderful safe herbal smell of him; my fingers moved through the crisp silk of his hair, then found the beat of his heart under his shirt. What riches! We were alive, the three of us! "Ben, did they find Mary's body?"

"Not yet."

"Then how"—I drew away from him—"how can they be sure she's dead? What if she were thrown overboard by the force of the explosion and was swept downriver? What if she is still alive? She could have been washed up on a beaver dam or—"

"Ellie—"

"I know."

"Pepys fetched all of us—other than Ernestine and yourself—into the Red Room to hear what the sheriff had to say. An alarm clock used as a crude timing device has been recovered and Laverne Gibbons who is living-in as Mary Faith's housekeeper had refused to discuss what she knew of Miss Faith's whereabouts yesterday until she consulted an attorney.

"What did Miss Faith have to say for herself?"

"A lot of bravado, according to the Sheriff."

"Well how does Miss Manners say one should act when accused of murder?" I'll confess I sounded a little tart.

"Ellie, he's not trying to railroad her. You should have seen him, the poor chap looked grey. Mud Creek can't be a river bed of crime! Don't suppose he does have the Miranda warning memorized. He said several times that, whilst Theola Faith had been arrested and charged with the murder of her daughter, she gets a preliminary hearing before being bound over for trial."

"Where is she now?"

"At the police station until bond is set, which should be tomorrow by the sound of it."

"Well." I sat up and shook back my hair. "I can't lie here glooming. Shouldn't you be downstairs getting revved up for the final lap of the competition—the Dinner?"

"I suppose so." He stood.

"You don't sound too excited. Nervous?"

"When I think of what the shock of being stuck in that lift could have done to you and the baby, I realize that as long as you're all right, I'm a winner."

I smiled up at him. "We love you, Daddy."

"And nothing hurts?"

"Of course not." No point in mentioning the stitch in my back. I knew how I'd got that—from leaning against the door knob in Marjorie Rumpson's room when talking Ernestine into handing over those awful knives. But to please Ben I agreed to stay put and rest for a while.

When he left the quiet felt good, as though I were snuggling down inside the comfort of Ben's love. Sleep drifted close then ebbed away—the tide playing catch-me-if-you-can games with childish feet planted in the sand . . . the ticklish delight of gooey silt oozing up between the toes. I'd had some lovely hours on the beach during my first visit to Merlin's Court. My time there hadn't been one horror-packed moment after another as with Mary's visit to her gruesome Great Aunt Guinevere.

And suddenly the quiet turned into waiting. For what, I had no idea; but I knew—from the way the shadows stood to attention and the furniture shrank against the walls—that the room felt it too. The curtains being closed didn't help. I had this crazy feeling that outside the window a flock of questions and answers was whirling about in a storm of feathers. I could hear the beat of their wings, the chipping of their beaks on the glass. Was this the result of drinking that herbal bev? Primrose Tramwell had stressed the calmative effects but had said nothing of ensuing flights of fantasy and Ben had, from the sound of it, reduced whatever potency there was. . . .

"Look," I told the window, "the important questions have been answered. Theola Faith murdered her obnoxious child to put an end to all that horrid publicity. And I am not the least bit worried about our departed candidates. The Groggs and Le Trompes were told to leave, and the Browns opted for romance over gourmet meals. How they got off the island only constitutes a mystery because I don't know the answer."

Who . . . what was that knocking?

"Ellie?" Ernestine pushed open the door. "How are you feeling?"

"Glad to see you." The pumpkin trouser suit turned her back into the woman I had met and liked on our first evening here, not the one I had caught snooping in Miss Rumpson's room that morning.

"I won't stay above a moment, but wanted to tell you I talked to Bingo a short while ago. You were right, he did take the knives and hid them first under the floorboard in his room—and again last night in Marjorie's room. That last was panic, he sure never wanted her blamed; he was going to move them later."

Her face had a naked vulnerability. "He wanted to create a scare. He wanted me to decide this was no place for him and get him out of here. You won't believe it, Ellie, but Bingo doesn't want to be a Mangé. He says he wants to be a kid. What I don't understand is why he couldn't come straight out and tell me. His dad and I only want what's best for him."

"I'm sure." I thought about Bingo trying to move his treasure trove of snack foods to the bird's nest for greater safety; had he hoped the knives would be found—before murder entered the picture?

"Bingo's with Ms. X now, telling her he wants to drop out as a candidate, which means"—she put her glasses back on—"the battle's on between your husband and Marjorie Rumpson."

Rubbing my back where it still ached, I swallowed hard on this piece of news, when there came another knock on the door and in came Jeffries and Pepys. Her cap was askew and her bunchy curls lopsided. She was wheeling a television. He was carrying a small cardboard box atop a large plastic one.

"Visiting hours ain't over, I hope!" She executed a swivel and a run around Ernestine. "Baldie and me decided as how you might like to watch a film on the VCR."

"How kind! But really you mustn't pamper me."

No answer. They were busy plugging in and setting up. Seconds later the TV was angled toward me and I was sitting up straight. No slumping shoulders! I would have preferred to take a nap. But this was a wonderful treat.

"There!" Pepys tottered over and placed the remote control in my hand. "Press the red button, that's all!"

"Thank you."

I didn't get to say any more because Jeffries' face squeezed into a frown, and she was across the room, flinging open the window. And in hopped a pigeon. So I hadn't been fantasizing! I *had* heard that fluttering and pecking at the glass.

"Sometimes he's like the rest of us, forgets his place and refuses to come by the tradesmen's entrance." Jeffries scooped him up. "I'll get him out of here."

"Please," I said, "Leave him! We can watch the movie together."

At the press of the red button . . . A surge of surflike music holding under currents of tidal terror. A swirl of mist, twitches away in moments—in the manner of a magician's hanky—to reveal a full moon, hovering above a house of finest Gothic Horror design, rising up out of a dark body of water. A crashing of cymbals, the front door lunges open, and the viewer is swept into a wainscotted hall of magnificent gloom. All in glorious black and white.

My breath caught when the imperious butler, complete with patent leather hair and penciled moustache, descended the stairs, a candle held aloft.

"Ladies and Gentlemen," he intoned, his voice dripping gore, "I regret to be the bearer of inclement tidings . . ."

Melancholy Mansion! The feeling was most peculiar. To be here in this bedroom while at the same time downstairs in the Red Room with Theola Faith as she comes upon the bespectacled schoolboy busily finger painting.

"Gerald, sweetie! Have you been playing pirates again?"

A boyish pout. "How'd you know?"

Bubbly soft curls, dimpled cheeks—she really is enchanting. "Gerry, you are the most exasperating child! For mercy's sake, you've dripped blood all over this nice clean rug! You can't keep knifing people to the wall like you're posting them on a bulletin board. Soon there won't be any room for pictures."

"You don't want me to have any fun."

"What a tall story! You know I don't want to come on like the heavy-handed stepmother, but you've got to stop this acting out—we're not going to have any friends left at this rate. And all because your darling daddy cut you and me out of his will."

"You got any better ideas?" A boyish grin.

Coming up behind him, she popped a kiss on his head. "I think it's time we go pay a visit to that nightclub where I used to work. Used to be a bouncer there name of Joe who may have some interesting ideas on how we can torch the boat."

I felt sick, but I had to keep watching. Here was the nightclub scene I had waited all my life to see. A room thick with tables and smoke and fleshy-faced people in flashy clothes. The music got louder and fuller; it drew me towards a round, rotating stage, where on was a chorus line of high kicking lovelies with plumes in their hair. The young woman third from the end on the right—her leg going the wrong way in an arabesque and her arms doing a Swan Lake float—was my mother.

I couldn't believe that I was seeing her again. I wanted her to look at me. I wanted to tell her that being out of step could be wonderful, but she had gone around. And I didn't know how to stop the damn video and I . . . had felt something move inside myself. I heard myself cry, "Mother, the baby moved! I'm sure of it, even though it wasn't what I expected at all. So delicate, so sweet. More of a flitter than a flutter, like a butterfly imprisoned in my hand."

She hadn't come around again, but something else had—the memory of what someone had said. Which meant I had to be wrong . . . unless Chantal the soothsayer had been right all along! Sitting bolt upright, I was staring at that video stage and my mother finally looked straight at me, before the scene switched. And the truth came crashing down on me in a frenzy of orchestral music, while wind and rain beat against the walls of Melancholy Mansion. For a moment, excitement was like helium filling my bones, I could have floated to the ceiling; but quickly I sobered. This wasn't some crossword puzzle. I must think what was best to do.

Lying back, my mind was like the film, moving from scene to scene and back again and it was getting to the point where I couldn't make head nor tail of either when the pigeon strode onto the television set. He fixed his beady eye on me, I fixed mine on that small cylinder attached to his leg. A homing pigeon! And if his home is where the heart is . . . Suddenly I was fully fifty percent convinced that my best cause of action was to send a message to Theola Faith. Bother! I could hardly expect our feathered friend to track her down at the police station. Oh, well! I would have to hope for the best—that Laverne or Jimmy from the bar would spot his arrival, check his leg for mail, and deliver it to the proper party. Because of the uncertainties involved, I must write something whose hidden meaning Theola Faith alone would understand. Finding pen and paper, I wondered if I was being too cryptic, but I couldn't think of anything else that said it all. And, as she had said, her memory was her stock in trade.

Chasing a pigeon around a room is excellent exercise for the pregnant woman. I forgot my backache the moment I cracked my knee into the dressing table and scraped my shin on a drawer handle. At last! My hands closed on his bulgy feathery form. Into the cylinder with the message and it's over to the window with him. Over and out.

"Good-bye!" I called. "I'd feel a lot better if you were wearing a St. Christopher medal, but my chances of achieving a result can't be any worse than if I were to cork up a bottle and toss it into the river."

Drawing in my head I rammed down the sash. Yes, I was a little emotional but what had almost knocked me off my feet was the heat. My arms were broiled medium rare from those few moments of exposure and the hair close to my forehead had singed into a frizz. The bedroom was suddenly stifling. Could that waiting feeling I had experienced earlier have been due to a buildup of atmospheric pressure—the meteorological, not the human kind? Were we in for another storm?

The English preoccupation with the weather! We like murder, too, between the pages of a book or on the stage, but I wouldn't think about any of that now. The dinner hour would soon be at hand. Would my red top look a little too optimistic of Ben's chances? Perhaps the black dress . . . No, mustn't appear to be anticipating the worst.

The dining room positively beamed with festivity. A table set with purest white linen and china and glass completely free of those embarrassing dishwasher spots. Cutlery laid out with geometric precision, subdued lighting softening the heavy featured furniture. And that sense of refuge, brought into play by the dun-coloured curtains hanging open to reveal dark clouds herding across the sky. The six deadly knives gleamed again on the wall. As for the assemblage—every hair, every smile in place—we graced the thronelike chairs around that tribunal table and waited for Valicia X to call the fateful dinner to order.

Lovely as an air conditioned summer's day, she clinked a spoon against her wine glass and rose to her feet. "Ladies and gentlemen, fellow Mangés!" Her smile reached to include Pepys and Jeffries positioned at the sideboard, guarding the chafing dishes and soup tureens. Two vacant place settings indicated they would soon join us. "We are regrettably depleted in number. Three of our candidates are gone from this house and Mr. Hoffman this afternoon informed me of his decision to withdraw."

Bingo and Ernestine, wearing mother-and-son navy blue ensembles, beamed back smiles. Hers was a little too bright not to conceal some regret.

Valicia slid a thin gold bangle higher up her arm. "And so, only two candidates remain tonight competing in the final segment of the admission process. Let us salute Miss Marjorie Rumpson and Mr. Bentley Haskell with some well-deserved applause."

Staunch clapping from Ernestine, polite stuff from the rest, while the candidates sat royally across from each other. Ben was magnificent in basic black, Marjorie splendid in a plumed evening hat. Its electric blue matched her satin gown, which, with its front planted with seed pearls, could only have come from a rummage sale at Buckingham Palace.

"The scores accumulated over the last few days," Valicia X was saying, "have been tallied and we have an interesting situation." I couldn't look at Ben. I couldn't breathe. The entire room stopped breathing.

"A tie. Which means that this"—she gestured with an impeccably manicured hand to indicate the silver condiment set and other accoutrements of feasting—"the hands-on portion of the program, will decide who of these two fine people is to be the next . . ." For a moment I thought she would slip up and say the next Mr. or Ms. America ". . . the next Mangé."

Someone let out a long shaky breath and two candles went out. Jeffries stepped forward and flagged Pepys to follow. "Call me a butinsky, but if we don't get the show

on the road and the food on the table, Most Honoured
Leader, the hot will be cold and the cold hot. For Mrs.
Haskell and Mrs. Hoffman who don't have the inside scoop,
here's how we work the cookery comp. Knowing that
gourmet is kiddy play to any of the candidates. In other
words *Boring* for all of us. So we pulled a fast one. We
instructed the candidates to prepare a dinner using *only*
Convenience Foods."

A gasp from Ernestine. I remembered Ben's fear that if
he should in the midst of nerves slip up and use the
dreaded C word, he would instantly be damned.

Tenderly stroking a soup ladle, Pepys explained that
had all the candidates stuck it out to the end, each would
have been assigned one course to prepare. "But seeing as
how we wasn't left with enough chefs to go round, Miss
Rumpson and Mr. Haskell divvied up the meal between
them."

"Using the scientific selection process of drawing numbers from a hat." Jeffries flounced her curls. "Mr. Haskell,
if I do remember correct, picked numbers two, three, four
and seven—meaning he got to prepare soup, salad, bread,
and entree."

"Whilst I got the jolly old appetizer, fish course, vegetable and the pud. I mean," Miss Rumpson cleared her
throat and barked, "dessert."

"And now," Valicia X resumed her seat, "let the games
begin!"

With the speed of Greek runners bringing word that
Hercules was on steroids, Pepys and Jeffries went into
action. Wine was expertly aimed into our glasses, a platter
of rolls took centre stage, and small glass dishes brimming
with fruit, and rimmed with sugar appeared at each place.
Panting, P and J dropped into their seats and assumed the
ready positions with their spoons.

So instructed by Ms. X, Marjorie Rumpson named her
contribution as a Gingered Fruit Compote with a marmalade base. Oh, my aching back! With feelings of greatest
trepidation, avoiding Ben's eyes, I took a minute sip. My
darkest fears confirmed. Delicious.

Heart pounding, I saw my empty dish whisked away and a salad appear. A stunning mix of endive, broccoli and red onion rings, accented with sesame seeds and crumbled bacon, the colours polished to vibrance with a thin coating of Belgian dressing. Ben stressed the use of frozen broccoli, while keeping an eye on the Herbed Crescents coming around. Hard to believe that my love had cracked open a cardboard tube to produce these little wonders. The only egg cracked had been used for glazing.

"Blooming wonderful!" The magnanimous Miss Rumpson was immediately abashed. "Shouldn't have spoken up, I know—but when you love this work and get to witness creativity of this calibre, it knocks you back."

Ernestine and Bingo raised sceptical eyebrows at me, but I didn't believe for a minute that Marjorie was trying to win points as Miss Congeniality. She was a dear. As for Ben, it bothered me that he looked so cool. I would have preferred him on the edge of his seat, choking on his collar. I don't like smugness in my husbands. Pride cometh before a fallen soufflé . . . And here cometh the soup—rich with cream and fragrant with tomatoes and sherry. Mr. Campbell could be proud. Several belt notches later—the Salmon (fresh from a tin) with Cucumber Sauce. Score more points for Marjorie.

Would this meal out-last my pregnancy?

Roast Beef Marinara, basted with candlelight. Bentley T. Haskell forges ahead.

Artful Artichokes—Marjorie Rumpson is neck and neck with him coming down the straight. I can read indecision in the Mangés' eyes.

Tension mounts as we face the final curtain. Dessert. Pepys totters away to fetch it from the kitchen, while Jeffries makes the rounds with the coffee pot. No one speaks. No one looks at anyone. We could be an advert for antacid tablets. Out the corner of my eye I see an amber glow beyond the window . . . must be a reflection of the candlelight. I wish I could kick off my shoes, but my feet had gained several pounds. The door creaked open. In came

Pepys, a tin foil pan balanced on one hand . . . his expression one of . . . pity.

"Miss Rumpson's Frozen Daiquiri Pie." His skeletal hands shielded it. "Only it ain't froze."

"Couldn't pour it out and have milkshakes?" Desperately I signaled Ben with my eyes, but he wasn't taking messages. Marjorie's homely face was dissolving, caving in, as if it too were underdone. Unbearable—that it should come to this, for the woman who had flown the unfriendly skies, swum the raging river and survived a schoolboy's lethal plot and a mother's infernal machinations!

A scream ripped through the room. But Jeffries quickly got a grip on herself and snatched the pie away from Pepys. "You saying there's been foul play?"

Valicia X was staring at Ben, who was sipping water, as though seeing him for the first time. "Someone sabotaged the pie."

Bingo shifted uneasily in his seat, his face red, his glasses sweaty; his mother's eyes were squeezed shut, her hands locked in prayer.

"I don't believe anybody did any such thing." I was on my feet, my voice raised in futile hope of deadening the sound of Marjorie's tears plopping on the table. "There has to be some explanation, other than ambition or spite. Perhaps the freezer didn't kick back on after the generator went out."

"That's not it." Marjorie lifted her head and made a noble attempt at steadying her features. "Nothing nor nobody's bloomin' fault but my own. I'm not used to those side-by-side freezer refrigerator jobies and I was all right to left when I opened that door and shoved in the pie, but you know how it is—you see things without noticing them. There was a bowl of fruit on that same shelf and some jars—of pickles and jam. So you see m'hearties," mighty sniff, "this old gal's got no one to blame but herself."

"Miss Rumpson, I am sorry." Valicia sounded crisp, but her lovely eyes had the shine of tears. "And Ben . . . Mr. Haskell, I never suspected for a moment that you . . . but none of that matters, does it. The important thing is that the Contest is over. And in accordance with paragraph E, Section Two Nine Seven of the Mangé Code, I am authorized to forego discussion with my fellows . . ." Pepys and Jeffries, having reverently covered the pie with a cloth, each creaked a bow. ". . . And name you, Mr. Bentley T. Haskell, our new member."

Amazing, but at that heart-searing moment, I wasn't looking at my husband, but at the window. Outside I could see a gathering of yellow lights and shadow people. What tricks our reflections play . . . And our minds too. For surely Ben couldn't be saying what I heard him saying— that he was, with regret aforethought, refusing membership in the Mangé Society?

"You can't be serious!" Ms. X cried.

"He's out of his gourd." Pepys and Jeffries spoke as one.

"Ben . . ." I whispered.

He didn't look at me. The table divided us but I knew he was drawing me to him, holding me tight with his mind, because it took both of us for him to get through this. Rising, he spoke to a space just below the iron chandelier. "Honoured Mangés, I ask to be disqualified on the grounds that I have on several occasions fallen short of the standards set for candidates. You will remember," he now addressed Ms. X, "that I requested permission to leave the island on one occasion."

"Yes." Her face was bathed in candlelight and womanly vulnerability. "And I . . . persuaded my fellows that the request was justified, in the light of the abrupt departure of Lois Brown and her husband.

"I also broke the rule that precludes any cookery other than participation in this meal, when I made toast and herb tea for my wife this afternoon."

"What is this?" Jeffries scooted forward. "You joined the Reverend Enoch's church? We told you to feed her" —fingers rapping on my head—"whatever her little heart desired. Ain't we humans first, Mangés second?"

Ben cleared his throat. "I'm respectfully submitting that you have treated me with great sensitivity, which makes my lapse the graver. This afternoon I let slip, to my wife, that deviled kidney came under discussion during this morning's session."

Valicia X gasped.

I remembered . . .

Jeffries opened her mouth, but thought better of wasting time on a scream. Instead, she assisted Pepys as he tottered into a chair, muttering, "God save us from honest fools."

The faces around the table blurred into one, except for the one that counted. Valicia X managed a valiant smile as she lifted her wine glass. "Congratulations, Miss Rumpson! In the Mangé scheme of things, what's a failed pie?"

We adjourned to the Red Room. All that sweltering crimson and stifling maroon! All those doilies. And people, people everywhere and not a drop of conversation. Only way to ensure not saying the wrong thing. Awkward, exhausting, but bearable if only I could get to Ben. We had left the dining room separately, without exchanging a word, like undercover agents waiting for the rendezvous. He was trapped on one side of the room and I the other, until a gap opened up between Bingo and an overstuffed chair and I slipped past him and Ernestine talking to Jeffries and with only a couple of yards of carpet to go I had to fight the urge to rush into his arms.

I was breathless when I reached him. "You were wonderful." I gazed up into his eyes.

He pressed a finger to his lips, but only a potted palm was within listening distance.

"You needn't have turned yourself in." Clinging to his hand, the ache in my back, the crick in my neck, the fact that I hadn't started packing for our departure tomorrow— none of that mattered. "You let your dream of becoming a Mangé go, because you knew Marjorie needed it more than you did."

He looked away from me, fingers on his tie.

"Well, she doesn't get to be a father."

"You did a shining thing."

He grinned. "Aw shucks, Miss Ellie!"

I wanted to lead him from that room and up the stairs to our boudoir with the silver lurex wallpaper. I wanted to tell him about the baby moving and what I had written to Theola Faith. I wanted to unpeel his tie and unbutton his shirt, and bestow upon him the shiny medal of my love. But that would look like running away. A particularly bad idea when it was the truth. I did feel trapped by the silence, by whatever was outside.

"What's going on?"

Ben edged us toward the others who were pressed close to the window. Kneeling on the seat, Bingo provided some running commentary; Pepys and Jeffries yanked on the curtains as if ready to shin up them at any moment.

"I don't know!" I said. But there had come a sickening thud of memory. Those flickers of amber light and the people-sized shadows I'd seen from the dining room . . . The patch of island we could see through the parted drapery was thick as a jungle with men and women holding lanterns. The Mud Creek armada. Their faces shone pale as moons in the drizzling rain and as we pressed close to the window they began to chant. Some of the words they hurled were lost to the wind, but others made their mark, hitting the window, stinging our ears.

"Hippies!"

"Yuppies!"

"How can we be both?" Marjorie fumed.

Pepys made a gargling sound. "Don't know about that. Jeffries is a hip. I'm a yup."

Ernestine was trying to drag Bingo off the window seat when the next epithet caught us all between the eyes. "Witches!"

Merciful heavens! I had eschewed Salem, Massachusetts, for this!

Valicia X grabbed hold of Ben's sleeve, and I didn't begrudge her the liberty. Miss Rumpson looked ready to leap into Pepys' arms—or was it the other way round? Never mind. Valicia brought up a very valid point.

"I suppose we should check to see all doors and windows are secured."

"Right!" We all said it at once, scattered a few inches, then knotted back up again, in a babbling attempt at keeping from rushing to the same exit, leaving the rest offering free admittance to the enemy.

"I'll take the front door!" Ben was halfway across the hall. But too late, too late! A shuddering crash of wood flung against wall and hundreds of booted, spurred feet pounding the flagstones. The clank of armour, the swipe of swords. All right, so this wasn't Cromwell's army invading Mendenhall! But the imagination has a way of providing sound effects.

The Red Room door banged inward. A hand thrust Ben into a table. It toppled sideways and he was sitting on what now amounted to a foot stool. The mob swarmed forward; the room threatened to split at the seams. At first it had only one face, but then it began to divide up like pieces of cake and I saw people I recognized, Nelga from the dress shop, Barbara and Great Grandma from the Scissor Cut, the lovely Swedish twins, and several people from the bowling banquet—the unspeakably handsome youth, the man in the plaid shirt. None of this was good for a woman in my condition. I'd spotted Laverne and there was the ogress—Jimmy from the bar. But it was the face of the mob leader that struck the most unwelcome chill. The Diethelogian minister. The Reverend Enoch. The room grew dark with the press of humanity.

"Why this is neighbourly!" Valicia's voice floated above the sea of heads. My hope was that if I couldn't see her, no one else could. The reverend, to name one, was quite likely to take her beauty as a personal attack on his religious convictions.

"Silence, woman!" Yes, that was him.

"Now, just one moment!" That was Ben.

"We want the witch!" a thin voice piped up.

A deeper one told it to "Hush up!"

"Mud Creek has never been a town without sin!" ranted the reverend, "but, praise His name, there were no Mangé mumble. But with your coming, evil has spread its wings and unleased its talons. We have in our midst a young wife who fell from the ways of righteousness by taking up the life of a beauty operator. Do we pray that she be smote down?" Rhetorical pause. "All in the Lord's good time. It is not His plan that her husband succumb to the wiles of a Jezebel at The Mud Creek Savings and Loan. Such evil has come fast on the heels of the invasion of this cursed house. My own wife has fled the sanctity of our matrimonial bed. We have witnessed the decadent revelry of a bowling banquet, at which a female member of this foul society put in an appearance and when spoken to, responded in an alien tongue. We hear tell of a witch who casts love spells—"

A squeak from somewhere in the room. That could only be Marjorie Rumpson.

"And what is the culmination of all this?" The reverend's voice rose to a shuddering swell, like organ music. "Murderrr!"

"Shut your fat face!" There was a thwacking sound, as if someone had hit the reverend over the head with a handbag. The new voice went on. "Who damn well asked you to lead the posse? I near as hell knocked you overboard when you climbed in the boat, but naw, when it came to it, I wasn't 'bout to give you the chance to try and walk on water."

Someone shouted: "Get on with it, Jimmy!"

The Ogress from the bar . . . the woman who had lent Theola Faith the flat. "Give me a minute to work up some spit," Jimmy growled. "And someone get Enoch out of here before Laverne comes apart."

I could make out Jimmy's profile as she worked her way to the front of the mob. "Lookee here, you Mangé slobs, what you sees is the Mud Creek Moms along of some token fellers. Before we kicked our boats into the water, me and the gang mosied on down to Sheriff Tom's home away from home and set Theola Faith loose. Would a woman, who grew up here—played ball and swapped valentine cards with some of us—murder her own daughter? Like hell we'll believe she's guilty when there's the likes of you people just crying out to be suspects. . . ."

"All righty, hold it right there!" The voice blasted the room, scattering the lynching party like a bunch . . . of pigeons shot to feathers. Instant pathway to the door, where stood Sheriff Tom Dougherty, his gun looking everyone straight in the eye. "Guess I didn't rate an invitation to the party!"

"Sometimes," Laverne stepped bravely forward, "we have to remind ourselves as how the law is a good servant, but a poor master."

A thin man with spectacles zapped a pencil from behind his ear, a notepad from his pocket and said, "Ron Horbett, *The Biweekly Byword.* May I quote you, ma'am?"

"Quote *me*," responded Sheriff Tom dolefully. "I'm arresting anyone who doesn't back up, sit down and shut up. I've brought someone along with me who'd appreciate a word with you all."

"Who?" The word got squashed along with arms, legs and noses as people attempted to comply with the sheriff's orders. Perhaps they were only playing for time, but suddenly the room had become a sit-in. Our Mangé group took over a section of hearthrug as though it were an embassy. Ben's arm had just slipped around me when Sheriff Tom stepped to one side and she came through the door.

Mary Faith! Looking for all the world like a secretary arriving to take dictation. Brown hair, brown linen suit, the wing-tipped glasses set squarely on her nose. This was no ghost risen from a watery grave.

"Hoax!" The word went up in a roar.

"My God," Ben whispered, "she set the whole thing up, contrived her own death to incriminate her mother. Will authors stop at nothing to sell books?"

"Hello, my darlings!" She gave a devilish smile, but her voice . . . It didn't fit Mary, any more . . . than her hair, which she was peeling off to reveal . . . a shiny platinum bob underneath. Now it was away with the glasses, off with the brown jacket, the skirt unsnapped and tossed aside. A repeat performance of her strip tease at Jimmy's Bar.

Theola Faith.

And suddenly I knew.

Sheriff Tom pushed a stool toward her and gracefully, seductively, she perched on it as though this were a night club and she was beginning her act. "Darlings, I know you must all think me dreadfully wicked and I do wish I could honestly say I am riddled with remorse, but I'm not. What greater challenge to an actress than to create a character that people—publishers, media, fans—all believed to be real. Two characters really, because there is no Theola Faith —Mother. Never wanted to be one the way so many women do, but the strange thing was . . ." She looked directly at me. ". . . I grew fond of her . . . Mary and I found that murdering the only child I never had was much more difficult than I had thought."

"Why did you do it—make her up, write the book . . ." Nelga from the dress shop stammered.

Drawing her feet up on the rung of the stool, Theola Faith smiled at her. "Money was the original inducement. Darlings, I did think about simply writing my memoirs. But I quickly saw I had to be kidding. This will shock most of you, but much of the time I have led a deadly dull life. I have never never tried to save a species of wild animal from extinction or tried to stop a war single handed. Oh, I've had my share of love affairs. I've been rude to people at dinner parties. But you think people are going to pay twenty-one ninety-five for that? Sure I realized that one excellent possibility . . . would be to write about all my dearest friends and strip them naked in public. But, sweeties, that wasn't my literary style. Oh, the burning resentment every time I went into a book store and saw yet another bestseller by someone whose only credential was the mother or father she—or he—was feeding into a manure mixer. I was being denied infamy because I was childless . . . And then it hit me how many of these books were ghost written—"

The Reverend Enoch beat his breast. "Lord, this woman has committed the deadly sin of fraud!"

"So," Theola Faith said serenely, "does everyone who writes fiction."

Sheriff Dougherty shook his head. "Beats me how you thought you could get away with it."

"Darling," she tucked a sweep of platinum hair behind her ear, "living on the edge made a pleasant change after being retired from the world with only my house plants to care desperately whether I got up in the morning. The most minimal check would have revealed that Mary sprang full grown, but I counted on the public's insatiable desire for the truth, to blind them to the truth."

"Did you plan for to get rid of her right from the start?" That was great-grandma from the Scissor Cut.

"Mary, Mary quite pathetic had to die. She was a part I played in a script I wrote. Every play has its conclusion but what a challenge the last act! I saw myself in the witness box, wearing a marvelous hat—so few parts call for hats this days. Motherhood On Trial. If I got off, no one need know the truth. If things went awry, I would come clean and write my memoirs while doing time for perjury! Such fun planning the murder. As there could be no body, I had to stage her death—in full view of an audience. I always knew this house would be perfect for my purpose. I could have asked my few cronies from the old days, and my former maid Begita for help. They had been such sweets already—begging to be allowed in the book. Graza Lambino graciously offered to put all her deceased husbands at my disposal. But one doesn't like to impose. So when Pepys and Jeffries asked if I would agree to Mendenhall being put at the disposal of their cookery club for a weekend, I was delighted to oblige. Very selfish of me to involve them." The panda bear eyes turned wistful as a child's. "I see that now . . ."

Pepys opened his mouth, but Jeffries tapped him on the head and it snapped shut. "Him and me, never did nothing to betray our Mangé oath; we knew you didn't want no one here blamed." Her eyes forced me to lower mine.

"So tell us, Theola, how did you manage the murder?" came Nelga's neutral voice.

Miss Faith shifted on her stool. "I was delighted when I heard there would be a Fourth of July barbecue. I would have my audience. And everything went without a hitch. My one hangnail was the weather, but the storm held off and in the end proved an ally. I returned from Mud Creek in the boat with Pepys. I made my appearance as Mary when the barbecue was about to begin and announced that once and for all I was going to have it out with my mother. Once on the boat, I went up to the flying bridge, cut the wires to the engine compartment fan exhaust, attached the engine ignition with insulated wires to the hands of the alarm clock which was set to go off in five minutes, and poured gasoline into the engine compartment. This lady's a river rat, remember? I got off the boat—"

"Where did you hide?" Valica X asked.

"In the boat house, under a prop garden seat used in *Melancholy Mansion*. Then when everyone had returned to the house, I slipped in and hid out in the cellar. If anyone had come down, I would have gotten into the coffin. But no one did. And when I thought the coast was clear in the early A.M. I left the house . . ."

"Dressed as the ghost of the Woman In The Portrait?" Bingo panted. "I saw you twice—"

"The first time—the night you Mangés arrived—was for practice and fun." Theola Faith smiled sadly at him. "I knew Laverne would buy me time on the fatal night, until my return to Mud Creek. She told Tom I wasn't to be woken until morning when he came knocking with the bad news and he," she tossed the sheriff a smile stiff with bravado, "as I counted upon, he was too much the gentleman to insist."

"How did you get back across?" someone demanded.

"In one of the inflatable orange boats Irv sells at the gas station. I noticed one in the boat house when I was casing it out, but that one disappeared, so I bought my own."

Silence.

"Well?" Theola Faith prodded, "what happens now?

Do I get green stamps for not letting the Mangés burn for my murder?"

Voices climbing over and under each other, heads nodding, chins wagging. Everyone looked at Sheriff Tom as though he were Moses and could lead the way out of the desert.

Sliding his gun back into its holster, he said slowly, "Theola, you always were a gal for exaggerating. Likely one of those big city cops would see things different, but here in Mud Creek never has been a crime for a taxpayer to blow up her own boat. And no one here can say they saw Mary go aboard. Because there was no Mary. Seems to me, if we could all agree to keep our mouths shut . . ."

"The secret's safe." I smiled across at Ben. "This town protects its own and the Mangé Code produces men and women trained to keep mum." What's the harm if *Monster Mommy* continues to sell millions of copies, year after year?

"But if you would like us to take an oath," suggested Bingo, "we will slice out our tongues for luncheon meat, if we should ever reveal to a living soul . . ."

Theola Faith winked at me.

Epilogue

The dream picked up where it had left off. I was in the hall at Merlin's Court, searching for Child Ellie who had rudely bunked off as soon as I tried to tell her I was going to have a baby. The fox heads grinned from the walls and the twin suits of armour exchanged nervous glances when I brushed aside a giant cobweb and started up the stairs.

"Ellie!" Her voice crept up behind me, like a touch on the shoulder.

"Mother! What are you doing here?"

"Why, darling! I thought you would be pleased to see me." Hand on the banister post, she did a couple of knee bends. Sinking down on the bottom step in a swirl of gauzy grey she patted for me to join her. "I do confess to a certain curiosity about the Theola Faith affair."

"She remembered you," I said.

"But, naturally!" Mother turned her water nymph face away from me. "That segment in *Monster Mommy* about Mary visiting Aunt Guinevere was a remake of your first visit here."

"True. I figured that out when Theola Faith told me.

Mother, I never guessed you felt guilty about dumping me on Uncle Merlin, to the point where you would talk of it to a virtual stranger."

"Darling, I do love seeing you. But I can't devote all eternity to the visit. One only gets so much time off for good behaviour. What did you say in the message you sent by pigeon?"

"Three words. *The baby moved.* The psychic Chantal had told the Misses Tramwell that I would find the answer within myself, and when I felt that flicker . . . of butterfly wings, I . . . just knew that Theola Faith had never had a child. She had likened the quickening experience to a cat pawing a door. And she told me later, before Ben and I left Mendenhall, that she had been swept away by what she considered her acting triumph. I think she minded not having been a mother . . ."

"Speaking of objects d'amore"—Mother shook out a sleeve—"Ben certainly exercised maturity in relinquishing his Mangé ambitions."

"Oh, but didn't you know?" Sitting down on the stair directly above her, I tried to rub away the ache in my back. "My darling was admitted to membership after all. Rather in the manner of the comte pulling a rabbit out of a hat, Ben, at the final hour, produced the Tramwells' herbal tea recipe from his pocket and in tremulous accents declared himself convinced that it was in truth the centuries' lost Queen's Jaffy, invented by the monks of Cloisters, and served to such as Anne Boleyn to ensure a walk to the block with head held high."

"My congratulations to Ben." Mother raised her arms and the gauzy sleeves fluttered into wings. "Darling, this can only be a flying visit."

The pain in my back took a huge bite out of my spine as I stood up. "Don't you want to hear about the missing candidates? The man who delivered drinking water to Mendenhall each day at the crack of dawn revealed that Jim Grogg and the vampiric Divonne, and later the comte and Solange had paid him handsomely to ferry them away from the island rather than face ignominious farewells from the Mangés. By the way, Mother, there is an interesting post-script concerning Mud Creek. Theola Faith has decided to purchase Old Josiah Mendenhall's abandoned brewery and turn it into a bottling plant for the world's finest Adam's Ale. Watch out Perrier!"

"I love it!" Mother's lips curved in a dreamy smile. "I do hope the long arm of the law does not reach out for her to spoil everything, although I rather suspect that if the sheriff is patient . . ."

"You're such a romantic!" I said. "You should be pleased about the Browns. Marjorie Rumpson was correct in her suspicions. Henderson, driven to desperation, read his wife's copy of *The Captive Bride*, and was hit by the blinding realization that to save Lois from the Mangés, he must sweep her off her feet. In the middle of the night. Any screams would be blamed on Jeffries. It was he who purloined the inflatable *Nell Gwynn* . . . Mother! Where are you going? Anyone would think you had a train to catch!"

Remembering how she had died, I could have bitten off my tongue, but she laughed and slid her silken arms around me. "Darling, I don't know why you bother with me! I wasn't the best mother in the world."

"You were the best mother *I* ever had." I could feel her slipping through my fingers. "Don't go!"

"Hush!" Her voice was a soft breeze blowing around me. "I'm not the one you came for. And Child Ellie isn't hiding from Uncle Merlin. She's hiding from you, because—to be blunt, darling, you did turn a little self-righteous after you lost all that weight." The air became still. And when I turned around, the child, wearing the blue-and-gold striped blazer and bows like giant moths in her hair, was sitting halfway up the stairs.

"Hello," I said. "How about splitting an ice-cream sun-dae? And Mother, if you are listening, I want you to know I have decided to name the baby after you. I'm certain I am going to have a girl and . . ."

"Darling," her voice floated high above me, "you know I always detested my name. How about Abigail? Now there's a name with an arabesque to it! And Grantham is a name fit for any boy. Such resonance! Ellie, don't wrinkle your nose at Mother. I always strove not to be an interfering parent, but surely death confers some privileges. . . ."

I awoke to find myself lying on the sofa in the sitting room. A fire crackled in the hearth and painted rosy shadows on the wall where hung the portrait of Abigail, Uncle Merlin's mother. Not the Cat Cadaver. This was not the Red Room. The curtains and sofas were ivory damask. The style Queen Anne not Victorian. On either side of the mantel clock stood Chinese yellow vases and the carpet was of a bird-of-paradise design in shades of turquoise and rose. I was alone with my cat Tobias and concern was spread all over his furry face. Had I cried out in my sleep?

Sitting up was a major accomplishment. I was as unwieldly as the inflatable orange boat; for the last month I had been afraid to go anywhere near a pin in case I popped. I watched uneasily as Tobias prowled toward the mound of green-and-gold foil packages I had wrapped before succumbing to an afternoon snooze. We were barely into December, but with the baby due in a month, I was making an effort to be beforehand with as many responsibilities as possible. Several naked boxes, rolls of paper and an assortment of scissors testified to a job half done. The clock chimed five. A dark crack of sky showed above the snow crusted window panes. Reindeer weather. Ben, unlike the Tramwell sisters' late papa, continued to go gadding off to work, but he planned on being home early this evening, leaving Freddy to oversee Abigail's. A husband in a hundred! He had already iced the Christmas cake and lined the pantry shelves with enough pots of mincemeat and brandied oranges to stave off a famine. Must he come home to wrap presents too? Did we want a repeat of last year when Jonas received the handbag intended for Dorcas and she men's underwear?

I tried to remove a ball of red twine from Tobias but he was fleeter of paw than I. Peering out from a wrapping paper tent, he was having a great time fighting for the mastery, until I cheated by squealing.

"Sorry, didn't mean to scare you." Cautiously I leaned back against the cushions. "Just a twinge of backache. Remember now . . . came and went during my dream." Why was that wretched clock staring at me that way? Why the smirk on its stupid face? With every *tsk! tsk! tsk!* I grew more aware that Jonas was off on his daily constitutional and Dorcas not yet returned from the village school. A heavy wheezing from somewhere outside the room had me gripping the sofa arm. Must be the wind, I told myself, until I remembered. Mrs. Malloy, Faithful Household Helper, hadn't left at four-thirty as she usually did. She was putting in extra time giving the nursery the once over, including a shove round with the Hoover. I really should head for the kitchen and fix her a cup of hot cocoa for the road. Dorcas and Jonas would welcome some too. . . .

Fifteen minutes later I hadn't budged an inch. But I had rearranged my thinking on certain man/woman relationships. The sitting room door swung open and there stood the dark browed villain of the piece. He who had gotten me with child while retaining his own sylphlike figure. Damn his eyes. His raven hair was frosted at the temples and he was shaking off his coat and stomping his snowy shoes on the good carpet.

"Sweetheart, I got the most incredible inspiration this afternoon for an addition to my repertoire of gourmet baby foods. How does Codled Codfish *avec* Cornflour Custard grab you?"

"Lipsmacking." I mopped up my brow with the back of my hand.

"Ellie, I believe there's a Kiddie Kookery Book inside me trying to get out; can't leave *Monster Mommy* languishing on the bestseller list without any competition." He tossed his coat on a nice clean chair. "Want to tell hubby what you've been up to all day?"

"Back . . . hurts."

"Poor baby!" He bent to land a kiss on my head, and I shrank away as though from Bluebeard's son and heir.

"Ben, there's no way to break this gently. I'm in labour."

"No!" Hands clenched to his chest, he backed away from me, stomping on a couple of rolls of wrapping paper, and missing Tobias' tail by inches in the process. "You can't be. It's way too early." Grabbing the copy of *Special Delivery* off a table he thumbed wildly through it. The sparks from his eyes almost set the pages alight; within seconds he dropped the book as if it were, indeed, red hot. "How close together. . . ?"

"Every four minutes."

"Oh, my God!" He fell to his knees, eyes raised to the ceiling. "Have you forgotten . . ." I wasn't sure if he was talking to me or the Almighty. ". . . I took the car apart in readyness for the Big Event. It's in more pieces than a jigsaw puzzle. Freddy drove me to work and brought me home."

"Then he's done more than his share . . . can't ask him to take me to the hospital on his motorbike."

"He's already turned tail lights about and roared back to Abigail's."

"That's nice," I soothed. "I now have a handle on these contractions (pain is a four letter word). Probably a false alarm. Have you ever known me be early for anything? I was late for our wedding, remember?"

"Ellie!" Ben was racing toward me on his knees. "All the books say that it is undeniably the real thing whenever one thinks it is false labour." He gripped my hands as the pai . . . contraction swamped me. "Think Lamaze, my sweet!" He panted encouragement, while I relived the experience of inflating the *Nell Gwynn*. Our man of action was back on his feet once again. "You're doing splendidly, my sweet, for a beginner. Hold tight while I dash out to the hall and phone for an ambulance . . ."

Panic clamped its prongs into me. The phone had been out of order all afternoon. Not an unusual occurrence— probably some rodent snacking on the wires; I tried to stand up, but couldn't find my feet. Ben was at the door when it cracked inward. Enter Jonas in his World War I bomber's jacket and fisherman's cap and Dorcas in her egg yellow jogging suit. They were lugging a Christmas tree between them. Here I went again, spoiling everyone's fun.

Upon hearing the medical bulletin, Jonas' face turned grey as his moustache which, incidentally, was going like an electric toothbrush. Dorcas cried, "Good show!" but mercifully did not clap me on the back. "Everyone on their marks. Remember the team's the thing!" An earsplitting shrill of the whistle strung around D's neck brought Mrs. Malloy on the scene. She wore the fur coat which looked as though it had been washed in hot water instead of cold, and smelled strongly of her favourite perfume, Booth's Dry Gin.

"Mrs. H," eyes snapping under neon painted lids, "I've told you dunno-many times—I don't do outside windows, I don't do drains and I don't do confinements. But what I will do is have my gentleman friend, what's just come to pick me up in his late model Ford, nip over with me to the Vicarage. Reverend's got a nice young doctor staying with him, so I've heard from Mrs. Wood who does over there. Ain't no good crying for Dr. Melrose because word is he's down with tonsillitis. Now let's not go having that baby before I get him back here with the stand-in, Mrs. H, or I'll look a right fool . . ."

Ben and Jonas exchanged glances of male outrage, while Dorcas gave another inadvertent blast of the whistle.

"Please!" I cried. "Everyone calm down! Isn't this supposed to be My Moment? All I ask is to be able to sit back and enjoy my contractions while a dear one holds my hand and tells me stories about women delivering in rice paddies . . ."

*   *   *

The doctor didn't look old enough to shave. His name was Smith, which immediately made me suspect him of working under an alias. Certainly he nipped in and out of the room rather a lot. I pictured him having quickie cribs of his *Beginner's Manual*. But he was very pleasant. He admired the pheasant wallpaper, the four poster bed and said that the log fire added a delightful Victorian touch; whereupon Ben, pacing by the door, said we were great believers in twentieth-century health care.

Doctor Smith clearly regarded husbands as a modern inconvenience but he told me with great kindness to feel free to scream all I wished.

"Thank you, Doctor." Pause to pant. "But we have neighbours on both sides within half a mile." Besides which I didn't feel I could add to the noise taking place outside the room. Footsteps pounded up and down the stairs. The telephone kept ringing and once I thought I heard the front door bell. Seconds later a rapping came at the door. Ben opened up and Dorcas informed him the Misses Hyacynth and Primrose Tramwell were below stairs, having brought tidings of vital importance from the clairvoyant Chantal.

"Tell the ladies my wife is not presently receiving visitors." Ben's voice was muffled by his mask. "Coming, sweetheart!" Barely had he stumbled back to the bed when our daughter was born. All I wanted was to hold her. I never thought to ask if she had a nice figure, but I did wonder, in passing, why I didn't feel noticeably thinner . . .

"Abigail!" I clung to Ben's hand, glorying in that newborn cry . . . the glimpse of an exquisitely wrinkled face and spiky black hair. "Mother picked the name. I hope you don't mind."

"Whatever you want, my love."

Starry-eyed we gazed upon Dr. Smith, who held our five-pound, two-ounce miracle in his noble hands. He was in the process of congratulating us, when I pressed a hand to my damp brow and rudely interrupted him.

"Doctor, I know I am a novice at all this, but I have the strangest feeling . . ."

"Nerves, Mrs. Haskell!" But suddenly it was the man of medicine who was all of a twitch. He bundled the baby into Ben's arms and . . . five seconds later her brother was born. No wonder I had gained so much weight. I'd been eating for three! But Dr. Melrose couldn't say I had been twice the work, because he had never suggested I was expecting twins! Not bad for a beginner, I thought smugly even as tears stung my eyes. Mother had known, I was sure.

"Did she pick a name for him too?" Ben asked gently.

"Grantham," I whispered.

Hours later I woke to find Dr. Smith gone, the cradle rocking gently in the firelight and Ben reading beside me. The door was open a crack and I glimpsed the prideful faces of Dorcas and Jonas and the Tramwell sisters before they tiptoed away. No need to ask what Chantal had predicted. My happiness was so magical, so fragile that I was afraid to take deep breaths in case it shattered into a thousand multicoloured pieces and vanished into the night. Blast him, Ben chose that moment to press a butterfly kiss on my brow and I began to tremble.

"I'm not up to the job," I cried. "I feel like an apprentice and I've got this deep down certainty that I'll remain this way until my babies are eighty. I'll never get mothering down pat, I'll never get it quite right!"

"No one ever does," my husband said with all the newfound wisdom of fatherhood.

Waves of relief flowed over me. Twisting my hair into a no-nonsense braid, I sat up—ready and eager to begin. "Ben, take my hand while I swear to be the best imperfect mother I can be. And one thing you to have to promise me: no more How To manuals."

Squeezing my fingers, he hedged. "We won't need this one again." Handsome as fathers come, in his velvet smoking jacket, he strode over to the fireplace and tossed *Pregnancy for Beginners* into the flames. As for me . . . as soon as I had fed the children and got them to bed I would write to Theola Faith and ask if we could visit her one day soon. Abby and Tam must meet the fascinating woman who had known their grandmother and discover that very special community, Mud Creek.

Lesson one, my darlings, never judge a town by its name. Or a book by its cover.

DOROTHY CANNELL is the author of *The Thin Woman, Down the Garden Path* and *The Widows Club* which was nominated for an Anthony Award for Best Novel of the Year. She was born in England and currently resides in Peoria, Illinois. She is hard at work on her next Ellie Haskell novel, *Femmes Fatal*.